# SHAKING
# TENT

Based on true events

By Anne Michael

All images referenced in this story are cited with websites and copyright, or created by the author. Photographs of actual places are used to enhance the reader's understanding of a culture, a belief, or the terrain. A few references of places are not correctly geographically located such as the hoodoo mounds, being relocated in the story to emphasize cultural beliefs. Any change in geographic reality is not meant to single out any locale or inhabitants in any derogatory manner or to mislead the reader. There is no medical tower named Obigon Sakawa Cancer Tower at the Cancer Center of the Americas in Chicago. Any likeness to a person living or deceased is purely coincidental and not intended to judge anyone, anything, or anyplace. Characters, organizations and events portrayed in this novel are fictionalized, created by the author, or are based on true events primarily referenced in official documents, the TRC and the I.R.S.S.A. which are in the public domain and "offered in its entirety without copyright infringement."

The terms used for the First Nations people in Canada, have long been a subject of great controversy. In describing these people—this culture, great effort was taken to be considerate of what has been determined correct in 2017 at date of publication. The reference for the usage "First Nations" in this book is taken from the following website on the cultural changes of the Native decent from "Indian" to "First Nations people" *in Canada*, and not *of Canada*. For greater understanding of this name progression and to understand the political transition, please refer to one of many websites : www3.brandonu.ca/cjns/25.2/cjnsv25no2_pg609-626.pdf.

The publisher and author are not responsible for websites (or their content) that are not owned by either party.

Anne Michael is available for a wide variety of topics for speaking events. To find out more, contact her at pushpinned@aol.com and reference *Shaking Tent* in the subject line.

Library of Congress Catalogue entry
Printed in the United States of America

"A nation that kills its own children has no future."
*Pope John Paul II*

"Earth will not continue to offer its harvest, except with faithful stewardship. We cannot say we love the land and then take steps to destroy it for use by future generations."
*Pope John Paul II September 17, 1987*

"Most of the evil in this world is done by people with good intentions."
*T.S. Eliot*

*Tomorrow is promised to no one*

## Top Reviews:

**Steve B. Crowgey, Atlanta GA**- *"This book caught me by surprise and totally took me to another country and 100 years in the past. Shaking Tent is the most beautiful story I have ever read. It is such a perfect melding of so many different topics, many of which I have never even heard about before reading this book. Anne has created the most significant story I have ever read blending mysticism, aboriginal culture, Canadian history, environmental consciousness, and family love into a single tory. This book is the ultimate work of art, in literature and I was totally engrossed in it. Anne is my new favorite author and she has opened my eyes to many injustices that all people who care about a better world need to learn more about. I instantly went online to search for all of Anne's works of art,* **www.annemichaelart.com**. *Please give us more stories like this.*

**Scott Kendrick, Charlotte NC**- *"Excellent book. This book incorporates a diverse cast of characters that the author brings together in a fantastic story. Native American history and their connection to the spirit world and after life combined with real environmental concerns of the oils sands in Canada cause a roller coaster of events and emotions. The legal aspects of this book with Indian law, The Catholic Church, combined with American law, is both fascinating and intriguing. I think this book appeals to a wide range of readers. Highly recommended!"*

**George Barr, Denver NC**- *"Terrifyingly sad and tearfully happy! Dark and light are juxtaposed throughout with lovely character development. Both terrifyingly sad and tearfully happy at the same time. Thanks, Anne!"*

**Abby Appelt, Rhoatán Island, Caribbean**- *"A must read! This was such an interesting book, with many complicated story lines woven in, but was written well. It was easy to keep up with. By the time I was a quarter of the way through the book I was hooked and could not put it down. I must read. Timely, relevant and captivating."*

# SHAKING TENT

# CHARACTERS

Obigon Sakawa Sr.

Snowbird Sakawa

Kinoo Kiyasew

Merinda Kiyasew

Maude Weidner

Bexley Hargrove

Amanda
Randolph
"Shinski"

Greg
Randolph

Princess
Natawee

Dan
Jenkins

# THE SPIRITUAL CHARACTERS

 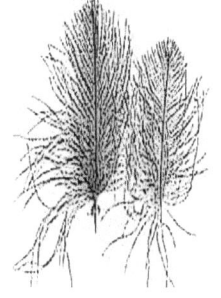 

Wren Feather      Swisher Feather      Little People

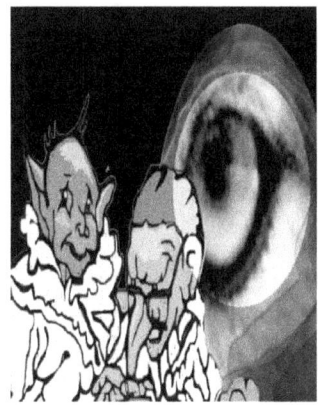 

Fairies                The Hoodoo Mounds

The Shaking Tent          Snowbird's Shaking Tent

# ANNE MICHAEL

## TABLE OF CONTENTS

## TABLE OF CONTENTS *(continue)*

### APPENDIX:

# Prologue

### The Pig Farmer Syndrome

Bex exhaled slowly, counting to herself surpassing the threshold of denial into pure, unadulterated anger after hearing the jury's verdict. She yelled out, "Lord, I'm dying in this place."

She had had it! She whipped her head around to make sure the judge had exited, that the well between the bench and counsel table was clear. She then had had the immense pleasure castigating her client!

She leaned across the table, her eyes just slits now, like knife punctures you make in a sweet potato before popping it into the microwave, and lowered her voice. She deliberately poked her client repeated in the chest, clarifying her disgust with spit flying, and uttered unmercifully, "*YOU* are a filthy lying pig, go wallow in the manure fields where you belong…"

Bex was fuming, the rest of the intended outburst knotting in her gut! She rolled her lips inward, her mouth stretched thin as a whisker of a tiger. She quivered, waiting for that precise moment to pounce, rip its prey to shreds beyond recognition in the next split second to eclipse her pig farmer client from Earth! *Forever*!

*Hell hath no fury like an insufferable, hell-bent woman with a will to vent,* Bex thought as she created a new version of an old adage. Instead, she turned and marched out of the courtroom. The rapid clicking of her high heels reemphasized each deliberate poke on her client's chest that had increased his blood pressure.

He had melded into the fabric of his chair remaining awestruck, horrified and speechless waiting for a courtroom exodus that might secure a safe escape from his dragon lady lawyer. Unconsciously holding his breath, he heaved a laudable sigh hoping entourage and spectators would quickly vanish!

Five minutes prior to Hurricane-Lawyer-Hargrove's unleashed fury, he had ecstatically jumped up having heard his innocent verdict, had extended his hand in admiring gratitude to his lawyer, only to have had it viciously slapped aside. He realized his business practices would be under hawk-eye surveillance to track every gallon of excreted manure henceforth. His euphoria dissipated, his hand stung!

Bex had leaned in close, her nose almost touching his, to delineate one more point before leaving, "You better hope your pigs stay constipated!"

Bexley had marched through the double mahogany doors of Courtroom A into the two story vestibule and slammed her briefcase onto a wooden bench braced against the granite walls, exasperated and seething. The acoustics carried the reverberation alerting the eardrums of every person exiting Cook County Criminal Court Building as they pushed their way through the turnstiles to the freedom of the outdoors.

But Bexley Hargrove had no intention of stalking her client or tracking his farming practices. She had had it! She drove back to her penthouse office, down the way a bit on Michigan Avenue, rode the elevator to the top, tapping her heel with every ascending floor number. When the doors opened, it was like Cruella de Vil parading through the office ignoring her minions. She jerked out a piece of letterhead: Anderson, Hargrove, Jenkins and Associates, crossed through her name at the top and scrawled, I QUIT across the blank sheet with a red Sharpie. She slapped the paper neatly in the middle of her desk and left in the manner in which she had come leaving her co-workers gossiping!

She rode the elevator down to the first floor and exited, glancing back only once toward the building directory on the wall. She snapped her neck around, her sharp chin pointing toward sovereignty and choice and walked out of the building forever! She knew that directory name display by heart; she'd memorized every line. The letters of her name were carefully aligned on top in the penthouse location, for the time being anyway, alongside her partners.

She mumbled, "I'm only an eight-letter entity in this world. It'll be so easy for someone to take me out of the lineup! Hard to get on that top rung! So easy to walk out and be taken out of the lineup! To be plucked out of the folds of the directory, one letter at a time and for trying to the right thing—*for trying to save the planet!*"

*What am I doing? This is so unlike me to quit*, she thought exhaling in grand accord. *But damn this world! We are the consequences of our choices! All of us!*

She knew she'd lost her cool in the courtroom. What's more, she knew if she had had a gun, she would've shoved it up her client's ass and pulled the trigger. What kept her in check? What kept her from completely ruining her career? She chuckled looking down at her Italian heels as she walked to her car, parked in the lower garage under the office building. *Sour grapes! I hate my clients but there are benefits! Oh how I love the smell of expensive leather!*

*If I'd blown the farmer away, I'd be fingerprinted and in jail by now. I don't do state issued flats with rubber heels or orange jumpsuits. That color doesn't flatter my skin coloring*, she admitted as she unlocked her car door and got in.

She knew it wouldn't be as easy as submitting a resignation in the form of those two words she had scrawled, "*I QUIT.*" Hell, she was a partner with ownership and financial stake in the bloom-ass law firm. Determined and pit-bull mad, she had wanted to make a statement—no matter what the cost!

Dan, a law partner—the Jenkins part of the firm, the third one spaced out in that directory case lineup with hers, called that evening. He pensively asked if the storm had passed before venturing to ask how she was doing otherwise.

"I'm pissed, okay? I'm still pretty damn mad at my guilty client, the frigging judge, the legal system, the stupid plaintiff's attorney. Dan, come on, you heard the case argument. How lame can one be? The opposing lawyer, sitting ten feet on the other side of the aisle, is a nut case. Any first year law student could have beaten him today. His clients shouldn't have to pay one darn cent for that shitty performance—pardon the pun."

"Okay. I think that answers my question, Bex. Hey, I saw that resignation letter you slapped down on your desk. It was concise, blatantly poignant and ridiculously childish!"

"Dan, I'm in no mood for any of your malarkey. My resignation was no joke."

"Bex, I'm coming over. You're a wreck and I've never heard such a sewer mouth! This is not like you! I don't like this side of you one bit."

"What—ever. I'm opening a bottle of wine and I intend to drink every bloody drop, so if you want to participate, you'd better get your ass over here in a hurry!"

Dan arrived twenty minutes later. Bex was on her third glass, as best he could determine, lifting the wine bottle to the light noticing less than an ounce left for him.

"Great," Dan said as he finished it. *The last sip of the bottle,* he thought, and tossed it in the trash hearing a hard clink. He looked into the receptacle and saw its brother—a dead soldier boy already buried there. He couldn't be sure when that bottle had been dumped, but in recalculating the consumption, he figured Bex was either well into her third full glass, since she had told him she had just opened the bottle when he called, or finishing up her sixth. He couldn't say for sure, the previous bottle might well be from a previous pity party!

He found an empty glass, filled it with cold, filtered water, straight from the refrigerator door, plopped in two Airborne tablets, and watched it fizz to the top. He handed the concoction to Bex.

"Drink this, Bex."

"Water better've come from the 'frig door, because the faucet spits out c-r-a-p!" Bex retorted, feeling a little woozy.

She took the glass from Dan.

"Oh, yeah right; like this'll make things all better—a glass of foamy, pissy water erupting like a frigging volcano."

"Bex, stop it, you're stressed out and all sassy mouthed. It's not becoming to your profession or gender! Drink it. It'll help your immune system while you grunt, slur and curse! Heck, I don't know what's worse, Hurricane Hargrove the lawyer or this fizzing Vitamin Volcano about to go down your hatch! Together, the two could be Armageddon."

"Dan, I gave that lawyer every opportunity to win their damn case—even outlined it for them, step by step," Bex said rhetorically and whiny. She was in no condition to be ladylike or coherent in her moment of self-glorification in front of Dan.

"They should've won. Heck, it was right for them to win, *God Damn It*; they blew their opportunity to smithereens. I'll admit something, dear ole Dan. But only to you, Danny Boy," Bex said beginning to fade.

"I allowed a *wee lee-tul bit of ev-i-dence* to find its *wee lee-tul way* to that idiot lawyer's *off--ice*. They must live in a pigsty over there if they didn't find that *im-por-tant* packet of pictures, *toxi-col-o-gy* reports, case *pre-ce-dence*. It was even with bullet points and all—taboot! Stupid, they must be over there! They probably got the lame package and didn't look at it. *Prob-a—bly* still sittin' there! Unorganized and *in-e-fficient*! Stupid! It probably got buried all under their crap and such! That's ALL I gotta say, Dan," Bex said with a drawl giving each word a punch and pronouncing legal terms as best she could as if about to come staggering out of her boxing corner again!

"I laid out the case for them and they didn't even use it. I know they received the packet because here's the *lee-tul* green delivery card and somebody's name's on it. See?" Bex muttered in a singsong drunken jingle waving the card in the air.

Dan reached for the card.

"Oh no, not a chance, sonny boy! Don't want ya testifying you saw this lee-tul card up close, this lee-tul ev-i-den-ti-ary morsel. If anything comes of this lee-tul prank, or my fussiness in the courtroom today, I don't want the existence of this card, this a-ccom-mo-dating memento, to be the nail in my or your coffin. It might be taken as an intention to deceive, a malpractice—or trying to educate the stupid lawyer so he could win his poo-py case. I don't want us sued by the lee-tul farmer boy!" Bex said in a mocking fashion!

"*Poopy*, Bex? Just a tad juvenile, don't ya think? You have crap on the brain! If you're so unhappy being such a successful corporate defense lawyer, making a six-figure income, then GEEZ," Dan said facetiously, "whataya want, Bex? Go work in Kenya as a missionary, for God's sake. What's wrong with you? You're a top notch lawyer and very professional, if I discount what I see here tonight! People would die for your career and the money you rake in. Don't throw away your talent or quit the entire profession—or the firm. That's ludicrous."

Dan looked at Bex in her Armani skirt, half-buttoned Diane von Furstenberg blouse and laughed.

"Besides, you'd look ridiculous in Kenya wearing Armani. Do ya even own a pair of jeans? Come on, Bex, consider a vacation to lower your blood pressure," Dan strongly advised.

"Bex, you chose corporate law, and criminal law at that! You knew what that meant. Defending scumbag businesses like your pig farmer client! You're a damn-good corporate lawyer. Our duty is to defend—not judge. It's just the way it is. You get paid beaucoup money for your defensive tactics. We work hard for our money and work long hours. Remember these scumbags pay our bills; they pay for your chic penthouse office, Bex."

"You have an incredible ego. It takes ego, creativity and tough skin to do what we do. Even the guilty ares guaranteed representation," Dan argued.

"We don't have the luxury of pissing off our clients. Especially when we win. We'll be on the street without a firm, without an office, without a job, and certainly no clients if we've lost our reputation. We would have risked everything. Why do that? We're already on top!"

"If you fail to acknowledge that, be an advocate for some worthy cause. Do charity. Volunteer in a soup kitchen. But you'll have to hang up your Armani and your bad-ass heels! You need an attitude adjustment. Did ya have your back cracked this week at the spa?"

"Dan, why don't I love this life? Don't scold me, please. I've had a rough week!"

Dan looked at Bex, sighed, and shrugged his shoulders.

"You should love your life, Bex. Hey, listen, I'm sorry. You know I care about you, Bex. I just hate seeing you like this, getting so fanatical and strung out about a client, then taking it out on the rest of us. Yes, *shitting,* all over everyone and getting all stirred up all over again!"

"Bex, you can't be on both sides of this argument as a defense lawyer in the real world. You have to keep your thoughts to yourself. You're living in some sort of dream word, a fantasy world. We're not in college debate classes anymore where we used to switch sides after thirty minutes and argue the opposite side for fun. I'm not doing that with you on this."

"Dan, I've tried. I've been thinking this way for months! The system is the pits. I hate being a lawyer. I *know* I'm acting like a child. So what? I want to have a little temper tantrum right now, okay? I don't want to sit in the corner of the boxing ring with a bloody nose and have someone wipe the sweat off my brow. I wanted to come out swinging and beat the daylights out of someone today and throw a knockout punch over this dirty rotten society and this screwed-up judicial system!"

"I think you had that grandstand today with your little round of defiance in the courtroom. You're wallowing in your own pity, Bex."

"You came dangerously close to doing something illegal today! And then with this little green card you're waving around right now? That's the stuff that gets lawyers disbarred."

"What? For me trying to help poor victims by ousting the truth, Dan? Insisting on clean, safe drinking water? I can't even be sure my own faucet water is safe! What's this world coming to? We're all victims! I am! You are! Heck, the judge is for God's sake! He still ruled in favor of our client! Don't you see how po-LIT-i-cal and biased all this is?" Bex implored. She sat back and closed her eyes again.

"Hey, my dear, you're overworked. Why don't you take a break? Go on a vacation somewhere. Book a trip. Soak up the sun in a remote island somewhere. Skinny dip in a crystal clear, blue lagoon and sip on banana daiquiris. Get out of Chicago, away from all this for a while."

Dan stepped closer, put his arms around Bex and kissed her.

"Let me stay, tonight, Bex," Dan suggested. "I'll rub your back to make your worries disappear," he whispered, kissing the top of her head as she laid back against the soft couch cushions. He stroked her arms with the back of his fingers.

Bex turned away with her face in the cushions, not wanting their eyes to meet.

"Bex, don't shut me out."

"Dan, please don't. Go home. I'm not feeling it tonight. I'm numb to everything. You're right. I need to get away to think and find myself again. I've got to resurrect that persona of a fierce, unfeeling, competitive, cold lawyer I'm known to be! I'm looking like a whipped puppy dog with a sad face," Bex declared sitting up as straight as she could still holding the glass of diluted Airborne. The sides of her glass, coated with fizz, resembled dirty, polluted foam of receding ocean waves lingering on a wet grey pad that marked the high tide.

"But right now, Dan, I'm feeling more like a lee-tul girl who has lost her Barbie doll," she said slumping back into the couch pillows.

"I'm getting too soft and emotional about victims—that *we*

create, Dan!" Bex sat up straight trying to be aggressive; the last remark stimulating a second wind, but maybe more a whirlwind of nonsensical gibberish. She lifted the glass ignoring its contents and gestured a toast towards the ceiling light fixture and glanced towards Dan with her head bobbing.

"I think my closing remarks, to that pig farmer in the courtroom today, was like the Dragon Lady's warning in the Game of Thrones. Telling all her people she was going to kick ass in the comeback of the century!"

"Calm down, Bex. Chill out!"

"Dan, you know, we've NEVER lost a sin-gul case!" Bex said saluting the air again. "We've argued to-gether in the courtroom like champs. Have ya ever kept count how many vic-tims' lives we've ruined and changed for-e-ver, though? I'm not proud of that part of our, un-bri-dled no-tor-i-e-ty, Dan," she said tilting the glass. With an unstable jerk, she gulped the rest of her immune therapy.

Dan sighed.

"We can't think about that, Bex. Our pig client has to make a living too. He can't harm others, though, by polluting water with his mountain of manure. That's a fact! If his business practice break the law, he'll be brought before a jury of his peers and a judge. We make *our* arguments! The other side makes *theirs*. The jury *listens*, the judge *advises* the jury of rules they are to follow and..." Dan sighed and looked at Bex.

"Bex, we convinced the jury that our client was not totally liable. This was a *reasonable doubt case*. We're just good at what we do. They could not prove *our farmer boy* was totally responsible for killing the half billion fish that bellied up."

"Dan, ya know how Mother Goosey you sound with all your lee-tul riddles as you rat-tle on? To be a lee-tul lying; I mean li-a-ble, is like being a lee-tul pregnant!" She took a breath.

"As Big Alexander the Great-est once said to all his lee-tul people, 'Remember upon the conduct of each, depends the fate of us all,'" Bex sputtered giggling when she spilled a little wine.

"We know our wee lee-tul pig farmer is a b-i-g part of the problem, but we know oth-er pig farmers dump into the wa--ter also! Other in-dus-tries do---too! So where does it end? Do we begin to default to a norm with everyone thinking it is A o-k-ay to pollute day after day, then we all get sick, die of cancer, accustomed to a destructive way of the life we've chosen as a tradeoff?" Bex cried out blinking hard to stay alert.

Both remained quiet for a moment. Then Bex broke the silence again.

"Dan, you know the difference between a bucket of manure and a lawyer?"

"Bex, don't do this…"

"Dan, it's the bu--cket! The BUCKET!"

Bex turned away from Dan, sank back into the couch, sprawled out in exhaustion, and passed out. Dan covered Bex with her favorite faux-mink coverlet, shook his head and walked toward the front door. He had a key to Bex's penthouse condo. Just before he opened the door, he turned to look back at Bex, who was sleeping soundly with her mouth open. He laughed and shook his head when Bex snorted very unladylike just as he reached the door. In a clear voice he said, "Alexa, turn off lights." Dan was standing in the dark. He turned the knob. "Alexa, set the alarm," Dan said. With that command, he had ten seconds to exit. On the other side of the locked door, Dan sighed. *What would Bex do without Alexa—or him?*

# PART I

# Chicago, Ill
# Port Washington, WI
## 2017

**The United States Environmental Protection Agency (EPA)** is an agency of the Federal Government of the United States, created to protect human health and the environment, enacted into operation in 1970 under President Nixon with 10 EPA regions. Its history began with the Resources and Conservation Act of 1959. Its six areas of concern are: 1) Air, 2) Water, 3) Land, 4) Hazardous wastes and 5) Endangered species, 6) Other: controls of insecticide, national policies, federal policies, toxic substances, nuclear wastes, food quality.

Subcategories of the six areas above are a complicated structure of regulatory acts and policies outlined in numerous sections describing implementations to ensure preventative measures, educational initiatives, inventory-tracking methods, elimination systems, protection plans, impact studies and explanations.

**Environmental Canada** is a similar agency of the Government of Canada organized to protect its environment and the 5500 mile border between the United States and Canada. Its three main areas of responsibility are: 1) Weather and Environmental prediction 2) Clean Environment, which develops pollution standards and control of toxic substances, 3) Nature, which is conservation and protection of biological diversity and endangered species.

Other similar concerns outlined in the U.S. agencies are not controlled by the Government of Canada but rather fall under the separate control of the individual Provinces of Canada, which is constantly confusing and at odds in their adjudication of fines, punishment and resolution.

**Note:** The agencies' acts and controls—their *rules,* are no different than any other set of laws. It is an ongoing process to address public concerns affecting mankind and the environment. When aggressors violate the law and harm another entity, it is an *after-the-fact* situation. Laws are enacted to adjudicate when harm is evidenced. They cannot protect *against* being harmed. *Acts* and *Controls* are subject to the interpretive wiles of lawyer tactics, loopholes and the ability for judges to greatly reduce fines. In essence, enforcement of laws is inconsistently administered within regions, districts and provinces. *Precedence* is only a guide, not a conclusion. History repeats itself. Social behavior is hard to change. Laws are made to be broken. Those in power make the rules. *TRUE!*

# 1

## Bexley Hargrove

Bexley Hargrove, *Bex*, as her close friends called her, had pulled her hair out, lost sleep, lost weight and had developed a taste for fine coffee blends while working her way up the corporate ladder. She had finally made law partner in a prestigious firm. She was young and fortunate to have forged an admirable reputation as a successful corporate lawyer so quickly. She loved the attention! She was OCD personality. Her career was her life. Her hobby was memorizing case precedence at night while working out on her stair stepper, catching up on CNN's breaking news on her flat screen television—her only wall art!

She had never married and the closest thing she had to a pet was *Alexa*, a black computer tower, which sat on her kitchen counter. It had been her housekeeper, who had trained it, teaching it to turn things on and off and perform simple tasks.

Bex could get depressed about her lonely life, having never married, if she would ever give herself a moment to think about it. But she never did since it would drain her of every ounce of energy it took to keep her on top of her game.

Bex's life hadn't always been so glamorous or fast-paced. She had been unable to meet expenses, living on a shoe-string budget years before, when she was employed by the State as a rural inspector with DNR (Department of Natural Resources).

Her journalism degree hadn't panned out either, since she had thought she would own the Chicago Tribune by now. She had always being a tad overly optimistic. Tenaciously, she had stayed the course through law school, graduating in three years, and had succeeded in not only becoming a corporate lawyer, but had squeezed her way through that broken glass ceiling to becoming a senior partner in one of Chicago's largest law firms. Her name second in the hierarchy and letterhead.

Working in a high rise office building, there was the perfunctory backup each morning at the elevator with all the suits and professionals standing shoulder to shoulder. The ones nearest its mirror-polished doors could pretend to be staring straight ahead; yet allowing their eyeballs to scan those around them. They could catch an unobvious sneak-peek at each other's clothes, their hair, what might be tucked under their arms without any communication or detection. They could pass the boring, daily wait for the elevator by memorizing the cased-in wall directory of companies that occupied space in the building.

The locked directory box was mounted to the side wall next to the up/down buttons. Bex had waited so long for the elevator doors to open one morning that she had had time to count the little white letters inserted into the black velvet folds on each line inside the case. She was proud to see her name, alongside those of her partners, aligned at the top, directing clients to their penthouse lawfirm. The eight letters of her last name were positioned like little diamonds in a jewelry box.

Every day, while waiting on the ground floor of the Michigan Avenue building, she considered how quickly those letters could be removed from that little jewel box, if she didn't stay ahead of her peers! Starbucks lattes got her going each morning; but the little letters spelling out her name, positioned on that top line, protected from dust and theft or anything else in the outside world, were what kept her blood pumping!

After years of sacrifice, long hours, allowing chiropractors to crack her back, weekly, to relieve stress, Bex had made it.

For a time, she had thought she *had* made the right career decision; she had bought a fancy-schmancy condo overlooking Lake Michigan, had a wardrobe to die for, drove an expensive car—a Lexus RX SUV, which Dan, one of her law partners, never liked. He thought she should be living it up, driving around in a showy Mercedes convertible!

Bex never liked down time, though. She liked her cars to be like the men in her life, dependable! When she needed to be somewhere, or to browse in a favorite shop, she abhorred a car seemingly destined to be *in* the shop, like most high end cars are, rather than parked in front of a boutique *while* she shopped!

Defending big business, she learned bird-dogging loopholes in the law, which proved invaluable in winning verdicts. In fact, she and Dan often joked how they seemed invincible, the *dynamic duo.*

After a quick five years focused on making money and banking a nest egg, Bex was feeling she had made a mistake, though. The glamorous, fast-paced life was taking its toll. Her career had become just a job; it had become an incessant mind game. Her conscience was bothering her—the tough façade, cracking wide open. It was bleeding huge guilt puddles from defending those not worth defending!

She had been climbing up that staircase to a heavenly lifestyle for some time. The bottom rung had been her employment as a rural inspector, trudging through the mud with state-issued boots, which didn't quite fit her image of successful and sassy.

She had always been an advocate for the environment hoping to make a difference in the world and believing in the mantra to stick with a passion and the money would follow. She didn't expect her interests and desires for a finer life to clash so! She clung to the passion of fighting for what was right but finally succumbed and chose money over the environment.

She found herself fighting for the client and not necessarily for what was just and right. she found herself loving the idea of how clever a defense she could maneuver.

Begrudgingly, with a good measure of guilt, she had taken her invaluable inspector experience and jumped ship using her knowledge against the environmental protection system. She saw herself as her own adversary, a Jekyll-and-Hyde in a lucrative corporate law career. But it was slowly chipping away her core belief system.

She had quickly found she'd never make any money being an inspector. After going back to school and graduating with a law degree, she had climbed a few more steps on that stairway to become a top, influential lawyer making good money. She had tasted what money, power and what the two together could do. She enjoyed Armani brand items and Italian leather shoes, expensive handbags, posh briefcases, carrying the latest iPad, iPhone, Fitbit arm bracelets and getting prepared foods delivered to her condo each day by Uber or the Blue Apron!

She enjoyed being successful and having office attendants bring daily Starbucks lattes to her as she sat majestically posed behind her costly, fifteen-grand, *Elisabethian* writing desk of burl wood, a fine specimen of the exclusive Houzz collection, designed by Francesco Molon. The firm had given her the desk when she had become partner.

*Alexa* turned on her favorite television channels, made her annual doctor's appointments, managed her room lighting, and woke her daily with a cheery *Good Morning Bex*. The housekeeper, Evelyn, had even sync'd her clock with the coffee pot. Evelyn cleaned her condo and ironed her sheets! What more could a princess living in the tower of a Lake Michigan Avenue condo desire?

Bex had left the pay scale of that thirty-five-grand salaried inspector job in the dust years ago. It had been so inadequate for her definition of meeting-basic-needs. She had begun to see what society defines as success. With the extra spending money she had pampered herself a tad, *but not too much*. That was the excuse she always gave Dan when he raised his eyebrow at various indulgences.

*Her desk cost half the annual salary she had made when she was employed as a rural inspector!*

Bex had grown used to separating her status in life from the penniless and terminally ill. Her status had begun to transform her; it was threatening to harden her empathy for people. She understood the extraordinary time it took to forge relationships, maintain them and still have time for her career. It was difficult. She had chosen her career. She was beginning to feel petrified—dead. *Impenetrable!*

Bex had sold out for the big bucks and still wasn't happy with her fabulously, successful lifestyle. Or maybe she just needed to choose a different type clientele. She had only herself to blame for that since she was the one deciding what cases she would take—she and Dan, together. The other partners had their niche, were just as successful, but traveled a lot for their clients work. Bex didn't even have to travel!

Bex's last case identified the pork industry to be creating water quality issues for Chicago. Bex realized she was a victim of the very thing for which she was defending her client. She thought through the day's court proceedings and how she might have defended the victim:

*Your Honor, in closing, we implore this court to consider the basic rights of man: to protect and defend him from all harm in this world—the air he breathes, the water he drinks and the land that has always provided...yadda, yadda, yadda.*

She had begun to believe that rhetoric was nothing more than hogwash; she knew then she was becoming a hardened entity, inhumane, without a soul, petrified in more ways than one!

She could not square with her farmer-client's actions. Equally offensive was the other side's incompetency!

Bex, the dragon lady, had won the case but spewed her fiery anger her client. She was angry they had won. Angry he had gotten away with polluting Chicago's water!

# 2

## Damn Loopholes

—‡—

Chicago is the fourth largest pork producer in the United States. Bex figured no matter if that industry is guilty of polluting Chicago waters, *which it is,* no judge would convict such an important revenue-producing industry. It would be the death sentence for that judge and detrimental to Chicago's growth.

"They should've thrown the book at them!" Bex's ego erupted as she shouted at the packers the day she was moving from of her penthouse condo. "If I'd been the attorney for the plaintiff, I could've and would've won for the victims!" Bex mumbled, still reeling with her victorious outcome shaking her head at the packers. The baffled packers nodded, continued in silence, getting out of her way as she paced the floors rehashing the case.

"Your Honor," Bex pretended again to grandstand, "but there are so many businesses polluting the waters that it would be impossible to determine a sufficient quantity to kill a half billion fish and blame my client!" She went on and on.

*One sentence, case won!* Bex thought proudly.

"Did you know a half billion fish—'B' for BILLION— went belly up?" she asked a packer who did not speak English.

The man nodded, accepting her bank check for packing and left.

"Objection!" Bex screamed out as she whirled the vacuum around cleaning up after the movers. "The burden of proof is on the plaintiff!" Bex continued as she cut lengths of tape to seal boxes of breakables she had set aside to pack herself.

"This protest is headed for a class action suit!" Bex continued enunciating each word slowly and distinctly as she jerked off the final piece of tape securing the last box.

Bex had grown accustomed to a simple phrase, "Sue one company at a time and you'll never get anywhere trying to stop the pollution. Sue the entire industry, getting into those deep pockets where it hurts,—that'll get their attention!"

Bex knew, even before she had taken the pig farmer's case, she would have a 99% chance of winning in court. Time after time, she had walked out with another winning verdict. Did anybody ever notice her tactics? Yes, the guilty clients had!

Poor victims! Not enough money to go up against deep pockets, which could keep them in appellate courts bleeding them dry!

*They don't have a chance and don't even know it!*

Bex knew it and she was having a change of heart about her clients—her career. It was no longer a challenge; winning had become as simple as a broiler plate of reasonable-doubt pleas.

It would be more a challenge to *help* these victims, especially when she knew *why* they were losing their cases! It wouldn't be as lucrative representing them. Maybe she would even have to do the old pro-bona thing for a while. But she would be able to sleep at night and maybe secure a place in the afterlife for doing good deeds for the underdog!

# 3

Princess Natawee
Traded for Nine Horses

———

Bex had had to make some painful changes leaving her downtown Chicago penthouse condo. She felt she could no longer afford her current lifestyle since she was no longer employed. She had a tidy nest egg. But that would have to support her during a transition to another career. She had no problem selling her condo on Michigan Avenue, which was the final act of walking *away from it all* to save her sanity. *Hopefully*, she thought, *I've considered all angles to dump this rather posh, lavishly, wonderful lifestyle. I hope I haven't made a mistake.*

She had found an adorable little South Chicago bungalow, which she paid cash for, and the little community was quaint in a simplistic way. If she was looking for a change, she certainly succeeded in that regard. The cozy abode seemed to fit the bill just fine, for now, and the price had been right. But would she be happy in this new lifestyle either? For now, she was not regretting her decision to quit the law firm nor was she sad to be taking a break from Dan.

She didn't think she was a hothead, just definitely strong-willed and stubborn! She tapped her spoon against her coffee cup that next morning, thinking. Suddenly as if someone had cranked her happy box to its sweet spot, she jumped up from her chair like a jack-in-the-box and sprang into action!

She grabbed her cell phone, scrolled through her network of contacts and strategized how to squeak out the slightest interim employment opportunity, *other than law,* to keep herself… still challenged, let's say.

"Hey Andrea, how's the Tribune lately? Ya have anything for a wannabe writer to do while taking some time off?"

"Hey there Bex, wadya say?"

"Taking a sabbatical from the courtroom scene for a while; think it's getting to me. Have some freelance for me?"

"Well, as a matter of fact, yeah, there are some human interest stories you can tackle, if you're game. I'll send you a list. Choose your medicine and email me what you've chosen. We could use some assistance and a fresh outlook on the world. I've always admired your *strategic insight*, your way with words in the courtroom. You say what needs to be said without really saying it, you know? You just smile sweetly and go in for the kill. I've seen you in action."

"Well, I don't know about all that," Bex replied thinking about her recent dragon lady routine! "But thanks. I'll look at your list and get back with you."

There was a little café down the street within walking distance. Bex had spotted it the day she moved in. She found it to be a delightful hideout from the social scene; she would read the *Tribune* and write. *Maybe even buy a pair of jeans and a Chicago Cubs sweatshirt for camouflage!*

As a matter of fact, Bex began to spend most every day at the café, properly named—*Maude's Café,* after its owner. Bex sought privacy at a little corner table pounding away on her laptop. Soon she discovered the café's coffee was a far cry from any gourmet blend she'd been used to, working for the firm. A latte of any kind was absolutely out of the question in this little cafe. Bex had been spoiled with fancy lattes. She had to admit she missed being catered to with daily Starbucks lattes and the fresh, warm donuts served to her purchased from Chicago's finest corner street vendors.

Rather, Bex covertly eavesdropped on the café's customers and swallowed up the delicious conversations at nearby tables; she tried to work their gossip into one of the topics on Andrea's Chicago-Tribune list. She listened like a bottlenose dolphin remaining as quite as a mouse as she strained to hear over her little clicking sound on the keyboard tapping away with her fake fingernails. Others let her be, including the café owner, who was the only one who waved to her leaving each afternoon.

Bex noticed a community bulletin board, which was screwed to a back wall of the café. She had made a point to read daily what was posted there. One particular post, a tattered, old newspaper clipping, remained in its permanent spot day after day. By the look of it, it had been there for years. Once it had been a black and white photo of a dark-skinned woman, seemingly, a Native American Indian, sitting with a Caucasian family. Now, it was simply someone's yellowed memory of a time and a place. The article, while interesting enough to catch her attention, had begun to plague her. *Why was it there; who had posted it?* Bex asked herself. She decided the photo and content merited a little more investigation to be worked into her schedule. Right after her high school reunion, she would jump right on it! It would be her next assignment!

Bex's mind wandered back to the café owner, Maude; Bex had noted a resemblance to this woman in the photo. Maude's whole life in Chicago was a mystery, it seemed to Bex. She didn't know Maude personally, but it was obvious her new little neighborhood didn't have much of a *Native Indian* presence. Maude wore curious attire with a particular necklace; it was donned with strange, bird feathers interwoven in leather braiding that encased a curious little stone. Obviously, it meant a great deal to her; she wore it every day.

After a bit, Bex walked over to the coffee bar, stuffed three dollars into the Mason jar. She poured a cup of Maude's cheap, tolerable coffee, walked back to her corner and began tapping away on her laptop. She waited until a few more customers arrived, then walked back to the bulletin board again. She wanted to read the curious article once, more without raising any eyebrows, jot down the name of the lady in the photo and look for a date on the posted newspaper clipping. She snapped a photograph of the article using her cell phone, slipped into the bathroom, and using the café's free Wi-Fi, she googled the name, *Princess Natawee,* to see what she could find.

The Internet immediately found an article with a picture of the dark-skinned woman with braids sitting with a man and child, just like the photo on the wall. This type family photo was not indicative of normal 1870 family life and the ethnic mix would have been socially unacceptable for the times. Additional comments revealed the woman, the Indian Princess Natawee, was born in 1860, died in 1930—and had been quite the *Chicago socialite.*

Bex decided to check with a friend at the Tribune to see if their archives harbored secrets about this princess! She emailed Andrea with her request and attached the photo of the posted article. Bex was delighted to receive an immediate response from her friend requesting she call her immediately.

"Andrea? Great! You got the photo and the article then! Did you find anything else?"

"Yes, I sure did. I'll send you an email. Lady's got a fascinating background, Bex. Let me know if you need me for anything else. Sounds interesting, my friend! Good talking to ya. Call me and we'll go for a quick bite down at the Billy Goat Tavern near the Tribune Tower."

"Sure, Andrea, hey, thanks for your help! Bye."

Bex quickly walked back to her little spot. She opened her laptop, pulled up the email and began reading it slowly. She whispered the words; she tossed her head side to side teetering on the edge of an orgasm as she read all the juicy details. This was more fascinating than pig poop for sure! Her little whisperings, speed-reading through the email, sounded like a tea kettle whistling in her little back corner nook.

"Quite an impressive string of titles, little lady there! Let's see, Princess Natawee, you were the daughter of the Blackfoot Chief Elder Big Tree, the *Dame Cuther*, and married to a major in the army who was a former fur trader. *DAMN! That's impressive!*"

Andrea had quickly summarized the few articles before sending the email to Bex with enticing excerpts attached as PDFs of the original articles.

*Wow*, Bex thought as she read Andrea's subject line memo—*TRADED FOR NINE HORSES*! Interesting!

"Okay," Bex mused. "This lady is one-hundred, fifty-seven years old. So an interview is out of the question!" she laughed.

"Let's see what else we have here: lived in Chicago, died in 1930. Lived in a huge mansion, wow! Quite a change from the wilderness of her homeland and now she's wearing white gloves and fancy dresses!"

"Wore a corset?"

*Really?*

"'Society women attended socialite's tea then when the ladies left, she...'"

*Wow, this lady is leading a double life,* Bex thought, reading the tasty little tidbits written as community gossip of that day!

"'Madame Cuther put on her moccasins, Indian dress, took an Indian doll outside to a teepee on their mansion's front lawn and danced around like a *savage Indian*.'"

*Nobody dare use 'savage Indian' today in an article!* Bex thought.

"Former Cree, Blackfoot culture, long black braids..."

Bex read on how the doll reminded the princess of the son she had had to give back to her people in her homeland, in Canada, as a prior agreement that traded her for nine horses

AND her first born child.

"The baby boy's name was Moose Jaw," Bex whispered. *Moose Jaw? What a name! You had to give your child back. I'm so sorry, princess,* Bex thought.

"OMG. Neither could you have any future contact with your biological son, Moose Jaw!"

*You poor woman, what a sad story!* Bex thought feeling little prickly chills run up her spine.

*Okay Moose Jaw. Let's see, you would have to be about a hundred, forty-two years old if you were still alive. Not hardly!*

*But what about your son? Where is he? The son of Moose Jaw?* Bex wondered. *Gosh, he would have to be close to one hundred years old. Would he be alive? And how about the mansion? Wonder if it's still standing? It would be well over a hundred years old, too.*

Bex didn't have the stamina to go house hunting again unless her new place didn't work out as planned. And even then this lady's house was over a hundred years old, Ugh!

She had just found her new bungalow and didn't need to be gallivanting around Chicago again looking for another one. It had been a nightmare moving from her penthouse; that move had taken the wind out of her sail. She needed to relax!

Bex decided to turn her attention back to the now, front and center and quit pushing it to the back burner; next on her agenda should be the upcoming high school reunion, not some fantasy. She would attend her high school reunion and catch up with her best friend, Shinski—if she could get a word in edgewise. Shinski could talk the chicken right off the bone!

# 4

## Amanda Shinski Randolph

Amanda Shinski Randolph was quite a character. Nobody ever talked when she talked, they couldn't talk over her and she never stopped talking. The best anyone could hope for was to be her audience. She was loud, whiny, demanding, high-maintenance. Yet, she could be quite funny, charmingly naïve, but seemingly incapable of taking care of herself. She and Bex were like two peas in a pod, though, when it came to aggressiveness. Both possessed pizzazz, both could be sassy and were quite a live wire duo! Bex was a tad more conservative, more realistic and quite capable of taking care of herself; anybody would attest to that!

Shinski did have one up on Bex when it came to designer labels. She had taught Bex quite a bit about high living and luxury and had been shopping with Bex insisting on the purchase of those ridiculously expensive nickel-heel, Italian heels when they didn't fit her own feet. Shinski was definitely the queen bee in the label category; she could spout them off like the ABC's.

Shinski, as Bex called her, was Bex's best friend in high school. She was the social butterfly and would most assuredly be attending the reunion since she had recently married an up-

and-coming, highfalutin executive and would want to show him off. Now that she was married, Bex held the sole honor being dubbed the last single, unmarried classmate.

*What a bummer, I'll be the target of embarrassing gossip!* Bex thought as she crawled into bed that night by herself. *I guess if Shinski goes to the reunion, then I'll go.*

She yawned and never remembered a thing after that.

It was late, or really early in the wee hours when Bex awakened.

"What was that?" she wondered. She had only been asleep for few hours.

*Bam, bam—bam-bam-bam.*

"What the h-e-c-k?" Bex yelled as she slipped from underneath her Martha-Washington quilted bedspread and ran to the window. She didn't see anything at first then she heard a few cars slamming on brakes down the street and some screeching around the corner. She saw the cars speeding after one another, right past her house, like bats swarming from a cave at night!

"That's it," she decided. "I've heard gunfire every night since I've moved in. I don't belong here!" she grumbled.

The little bungalow, intending to be a future rental income property, the place she had just purchased outright and thought she might reside there for a while, was already not working out. All the extra-curricular activity going on outside her house, each night, was intolerable. What had appeared like a quaint, thousand-square-foot house on Honor Street in South Chicago, was turning out to be too close to a hotbed of gang violence!

*I don't want to move again*, she thought climbing under the covers and pulling them up over her head!

She heard angry screaming and sirens in the distance. She hadn't felt the place looked dangerous during the day, but in the short time she had been there, she had begun experiencing chilling night sweats, insomnia and yearned for the security system she had had living in her downtown penthouse condo. There, she had had underground parking, security cameras, and a doorman separating her from *this* sort of crime—oh, how she was regretting having left that. Frustrated with what had been just less than a month's ownership of the bungalow, she knew she would have to make a change, do some scouting around Chicago for another place to live. *It'll still be good rental property. I can't move back home with my parents, not even for a little while—not at forty! But my nest egg is tied up in this place.*

—*⟊*—

Bex was up bright and early the next morning. She was thinking about her hometown, Port Washington, Wisconsin. She was making plans for the hometown reunion and thought she might visit her parents while she was there, as long as the conversation never drifted to her not-having-a-job-or-husband. Maybe in the next two weeks, before the date of the reunion, she might hit the jackpot and finagle all three: another place to live, another career and a fiancé to satisfy her friends and family.

Bex chuckled thinking *Dan didn't count; he was just a friend—at least for now!* She winced. Dan wanted marriage. She couldn't give him what he wanted right now! *Ugh! Too much stress!* She sighed.

Bex phoned her high-school friend, Amanda Shinski—*Amanda Shinski Randolph*, her newly married full name. Shinski answered right away without even saying hello or waiting for Bex to begin speaking. Shinski had seen her friend's name pop up on her caller ID, picked up her cell phone and began talking right away anticipating Bex's question.

"Wouldn't miss it for the world, best friend forever," Shinski blurted out cutting Bex off right from the start.

"You must come up early though, Bex. We can go to the places where we used to hang out. Maybe drive back to Chicago, fly out to Colorado or do the LA scene, or the east coast—New York."

Shinski was coming on a bit too strong.

"Hello to you, too, Shinski! I think I'll be able to make just the reunion," Bex commented. "I'm working on some big things in my life, right now, Shinski. I hope to wind those up before attending the reunion," Bex said trying to sound convincing, pretending to be the big shot she had been—one who juggled a busy life in order to even consider working anyone into her schedule.

"Right, my dear friend. Well, good talking to you. Please do call the moment you get to Port Washington."

Shinski was about to hang up, then hesitated. She began whining and unloading the troubles cascading down on her life.

"Bex, please come. I didn't want to talk about it over the phone. But Greg is being transferred to *Canada*. Something about an oil project up there having environmental issues and public relation sensitivities. If he takes this assignment, he will be in line for major advancement, even CEO eventually, or taking over the Canadian operations. We'll eventually be living in Calgary. Greg's company is going to house us in a luxurious B&B somewhere north of Calgary for a few months, paying all expenses while we build our dream house. But we'll have to live nearer to where the problems are, which has to do with the reason for this early transfer. We'll be living in a place where I cannot even pronounce its name."

Shinski took a breath. "I'd like you to come for an extended stay. Do you think you could get some time off, maybe a month or two?"

"Two months! Wow, that's intense. We'll see, Shinski," Bex replied grinning. She was not at all surprised with such an outlandish request considering the source.

Bex meditated on Shinski's request trying to get a handle on the cost of such a visit. She had had a good-paying job, yes, and had *had* a tidy little nest egg until she delved into purchasing the bungalow. Being unemployed at the moment, she would have to watch her money for the first time in a long while.

A trip, like her friend was highlighting, might cost upwards of ten grand—a price tag she wasn't comfortable spending right then. But maybe Canada would be a good place to clear her head. It was not the islands as Dan had suggested. It was completely in the wrong direction, in fact! Canada! *Canada? No more buying sprees for anything if she was going to take her friend up on her invitation!*

Shinski was still rambling on about this and that. Bex continued mulling over the cost of such a vacation and the distance between Chicago and Alberta. Half listening to Shinski, she opened her laptop and googled *Calgary, Canada.* She gasped—"*1,548 miles! Gee whiz!*" *Don't want to drive that,* she thought.

Bex was not even sure where, in Alberta, her friend was staying. And if her friend couldn't even pronounce it, that wasn't a good sign! It was not going to be a lively vacation!

"What hon? What was that?" Shinski asked.

"Oh nothing; I was just clearing my throat," Bex replied. *Too far, too much money,* Bex had initially determined.

"So, then, it's all set! We'll finalize the trip at the reunion. Greg will pay for everything! All you have to do is carve out some time to come. Truly, Greg will pay for everything, Bex. Everything! He'll treat us like princesses. *Puhhleeezzze?*"

# 5

## Port Washington, WI

11a

12c

*Sauk Creek Bridge, Port Washington, WI, November 2, 1979*

$B$ex drove from South Chicago to Port Washington in two hours. She could've driven it in her sleep considering the number of times she'd made the trip. She crossed the familiar Sauk Creek Bridge and stopped at one of her favorite high-school hangouts and decided to grab a bite at the Newport Shores Marina, right next to the bridge. Oh, how her mouth watered for their fish chowder. *I'll definitely order that.* She hurried inside, ordered the chowder and wolfed down every bite savoring her first hour back in Port Washington. It was late afternoon; she hadn't even told her folks she was coming into town. She opted to keep it that way and cash in on her reservation at the hotel, get a good night's sleep, and attend the picnic the next morning.

12a

The reunion picnic was as expected. Everyone seemed in good spirits, looked pretty much the same as ten years ago except for a few inches around the waistline! Her female classmates had all begun wearing styles that covered their widening butts.

Nobody had asked if she had ever married; in her mind, then, it was a thoroughly delightful afternoon. Everyone had packed up by three o'clock leaving crumbs and hotdog morsels for the winged scavengers, which were holding court beneath the picnic tables for the rest of the afternoon. Seemed the humans opted to spend their afternoon sightseeing, including Bex.

"Bex, I'm so sorry," Shinski apologized as they met in the parking lot headed back to the hotel.

"For what?"

"Well, I guess I was too busy showing Greg off to everyone Else and I neglected you. I'm sorry. We didn't get a chance to catch up on old times. We'll have all the time in the world to do that in Canada. I'm so excited! Did I even introduce you to Greg?"

"Yes, we said hello!" Bex said sarcastically.

"Sit with us at dinner tonight. I'll save you a seat."

"Okay, Shinski. I'm going to do a little sightseeing before then. See you later."

"Okay, see ya," Shinski said.

Shinski hopped into her car. Greg waved to Bex as they left. He had company reports to finish in the hotel room before dinner.

Bex drove down to the Sauk Creek Bridge. She circled around and took a few memorable photo shots of the lighthouse to capture all those high school memories. The town harbor had been a favorite place to hang out when she was seventeen.

*Oooowheee, time flies!*

The older buildings had changed tenants and their façades were adorned with new signage. Some had remained the same. Just down from the town harbor on Main Street was a new café that had moved into the corner building. There were a few other new restaurants. And, of course, the corner vendor was what else? Yes, a *Starbucks* had squeezed in between Haven Diner and Yummy Giro! She couldn't remember what businesses had been there before. *Times change and so does the landscape*, she thought. *Enterprise and growth come in and their pollution changes everything.*

Bex headed across the Sauk Creek Bridge. She slammed on brakes. People stopped and looked her way when they heard her screeching brakes. Then they saw no accident and immediately resumed fishing off both sides of the bridge as if the town rule was, *nobody hurt, everybody's okay, go back to your own business!* Bex could not believe her eyes. She pulled over to the edge, parked and walked briskly back across the bridge toting her camera.

*Look at all these people, s*he thought.

"What's the event, sir?" Bex asked the first person on the

bridge.

"Salmon's com'n," one person replied.

"Oh," Bex exclaimed as she walked through the crowd, across the planks of the bridge deck, headed to the railing to look over.

"What's this slimy, oozing stuff in these red jelly puddles?"

"If you hadn't stepped in them and liquefied the eggs with the soles of your shoes, I was about to scoop them up and put all the 'jelly' in my bucket," one man curtly replied with an irritated look of disgust at the stranger's intrusion.

Bex looked over the edge of the bridge seeing salmon by the thousands fighting their way upstream.

Bex had forgotten. This was the annual salmon spawn event; she had to admit she had never attended the event even though she had grown up in the town.

As she watched, she determined the goal of the local fishermen was to catch salmon, slit their bellies harvesting their eggs, which they would sell to nearby fish processing establishments.

"How much does a bucket of *caviar* go for?" Bex asked another fisherman. "If that's a five-pound bucket and caviar goes for what? Upwards of eighty dollars per two ounces? Geez, you're holding a little over three grand in that bucket and I have about five dollars on the bottom of my shoe!"

Bex looked around at all the buckets and fishermen working lickety-split and doing some fast calculating.

Several men stopped and laughed.

"Caviar? Lady, this *ain't nobody's caviar*! We sell the eggs to local delis and they sell it in quantity to fish houses that process it as industrial fish-bait! Wish it did go for that much! We sell the other fish and the salmon carcasses to nearby restaurants."

"Yum," the fishermen chuckled!

After seeing the process, Bex couldn't imagine anything more disgusting than eating fish out of this creek that could possibly be ordered off a town fish restaurant menu!

Bex took a few photos of the fishermen, their buckets of *faux caviar* and started walking back to the car. She couldn't help noticing a fisherman holding up his catch. He wasn't in a hurry to slice its belly; he just stared at it.

*What a photo opportunity.*

"May I take your picture?" Bex asked as the man turned around to show his face and lift his catch closer to her. Bex's mouth dropped open as her camera fell against her chest just hanging from its safety strap.

"Oh my God," Bex cried out looking to the other fishermen for explanation. "What happened to it?"

"It's a beauty—this one. Seen worse, though," he said.

The head of the fish was a mess. Its mouth was mutated, twisted, and hung in multiple folds outside its body. The mouth lining was folded in rope-like coils, like an umbilical cord during human birth. One side of the coil angled outward ending abruptly like a stump that looked like a bloated person's thumb.

"You want it?" the man asked.

Bex frowned.

"Nope, I think I'll pass, Just a quick picture, though," Bex replied. She was thankful she didn't have a cooler!

"Well, I guess I could cut off its head and sell the rest of its body to a local restaurant for fish chowder," he said and winked at his buddies.

Bex wasn't amused! She turned green and gasped.

The man turned to Bex and laughed, "Is that all ya want, just a few pictures, ma'am? I've thrown away some prettier fish over there!" the man said pointing to the discard pile at the bridge's edge.

"Oh, my God, is this normal up here?"

"Yes ma'am, pretty much. Pull 'em up like this often. I wouldn't want to be those fish! Nobody goes near that pile. Not even dogs or birds."

12e

*Fishermen Crowding Sauk Creek Bridge November 2, 1979*

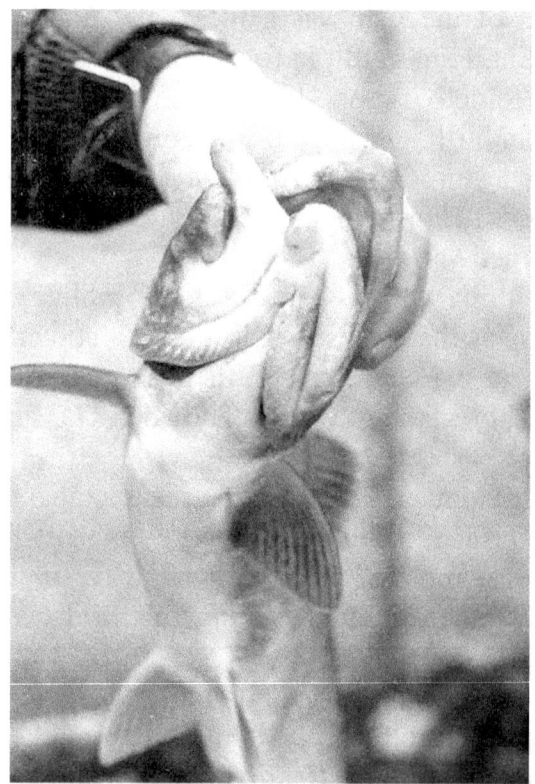

12f

*Photo of Deformed Salmon Caught November 2, 1979,*
*Sauk Creek Bridge, Port Washington, Wisconsin.*
*Photos by Anne Michael, the author.*

*There's bound to be toxic chemicals in these waters,* Bex thought. *If part of the fish is bad, the whole fish has to be bad! The stuff has to be in its very DNA*, she shuttered.

In town, Smith's Fish House and Enoch's Bros Family Fish Market paid by the pound for the fish eggs. The eggs were worth more than the whole body of the fish. So, many of these fish carcasses lay discarded on the bridge and the creek banks.

"Sometimes you get one that doesn't look that bad; I've seen people cut off the bad part and take the rest home to cook. If they stay over there—in that discard pile, they'll eventually get pushed back into the water by someone's foot, if the street washers don't get 'em first. We figure the chemicals from the power plant up-stream makes 'em all like that," the fisherman said pointing in the direction of the power plant.

"Saw a goat floating out beyond the harbor a month ago," he told Bex. "We laugh about it and joke that the power plant is nothing but a chemical plant that produces energy!"

"What a description!" Bex replied.

Bexley had a burning desire to ask one more question.

"When you sell the fish-egg bait, how does anyone really know if the eggs come from a healthy fish or a deformed fish—like those?" Bex asked pointing again to the discard pile.

"How do you know whether the professional fishermen, on the big boats out there in Lake Michigan, are buying good fish bait?" Bex asked pointing randomly out from the city. "How do you know whether fish chowder isn't made from chunks of that kind of polluted, deformed fish? Or whether the fish that people buy from the local markets, aren't polluted down to their DNA?" Bex pointed to the reject pile again.

"Well, I guess you don't. I don't eat much fish myself, ma'am. Not unless it comes from the *deep, deep* blue sea."

"The deep blue lakes and seas are just big bathtubs of diluted chemicals, too" she added thinking about all the brown suds and bubbles that wash ashore at times with dead fish and debris.

She wondered how long it would take for the oceans to

ANNE MICHAEL

become completely contaminated or whether they had already reached that state!

Bex was dumbfounded. She looked at the fish houses lining the street behind her. She thought about all the fish in the lake behind her and how many restaurants there must be along Lake Michigan and everywhere serving fresh catch daily from the waters. She estimated the numbers then shook her head at such a compounding, frustrating thought.

*Will I ever eat fish again? What a bunch of jokesters, those fishermen! Surely they're kidding me about all that!*

She arrived at the hotel just in time to get dressed and meet the other classmates for dinner.

Of course the dinner special offered was none other than the *fresh catch of the day!* She figured that and looked around for the menu. The waiter proudly boasted the fish on tonight's menu was caught locally—fresh daily. He pointed toward the bridge then out toward the harbor.

"Sir, I'd like to see a menu," Bex said.

"Yes, I'll bring one to you. Let me tell you about tonight's specials. We also have bison steaks, moose barbeque and caribou kabobs flown in from Canada for your class reunion. We're proud to offer those as unique entrées tonight too, ma'am."

"Where'd you say the meat was from, sir?" Bex asked.

"Just over the border; bison, moose and caribou are a few of Canada's mainstays—something special on our menu tonight. We do have many nice selections, ma'am. May I again recommend fish if you are looking for something other than red meat. Try our fresh catch of the day? The salmon is a good choice. As I said, the fish is fresh, just caught today as I mentioned."

"Thank you. Give me a few more minutes to look at the menu, please."

The waiter's response did nothing to pacify Bex's concerns. She looked at the salads and ordered a wedge of lettuce with blue cheese and bacon bits. She did not have the heart to ask if the bacon bits were artificial or real. She was actually no longer hungry. The rest of the group eagerly ordered from the catch of the day choices: salmon, trout, perch and walleye. She thought she'd puke thinking about those surface ulcers she had seen on the fish down at the bridge earlier and the milky diseased eyes she'd seen on fish in the discard pile.

Bex quietly ate her salad. She glanced up now and then half expecting someone to barf!

The roll of photographic film, she'd taken earlier, was burning a hole in her camera. She watched in horror as everyone gorged themselves on the special selections; grilled, broiled, blackened fish, and the special, chunky fish chowder.

Bex wondered if any of the fish, used in tonight's chowder special, had had two mouths, bulbous eyes, boils and blisters on their scales. She wondered what parts of the fish the restaurants were allowed to use in making fish chowder and whether the cook had just cut around the bad parts, tossed them like the bruised part of an apple and keeping just the *better* part. She wondered what the regulations were in assessing the health of fish bought from local fishermen—from the likes of the fisherman she had spoken with earlier.

The next morning at breakfast, Bex was sickened with the same scenario. She had decided to grab a bagel and coffee and hit the road after seeing her classmates pigging out on a breakfast of chopped eggs, fresh salmon, bagels, capers, with cream cheese on toast points. They were drinking fresh brewed coffee, eating fresh muffins with salmon croquets, salmon fritters and poached salmon over eggs benedict.

Bexley wheeled around on her Bandolino pumps headed to her room. She ducked behind a hotel column near the restaurant patio and texted Shinski that she was already on the road to Chicago. She sneaked back to her hotel room, packed up, checked out and left the city. She wanted nothing to do with any more seafood specials.

On the drive back to South Chicago, Bex thought about those fish in the discard pile. Surely, they would spoil in the sun, no matter the cold temperature. But somehow those fish had been deformed, not by Mother Nature, but mutated by something, someone or some power plant's toxic levels of chemical-laden discharge.

*It was no different than the pig farmer dumping manure into the water,* Bex thought. She drove by several fish houses on her way home and shrugged as she pressed the pedal to the metal.

Bex thought about fast food places that served fish sandwiches on a bun, grocery stores stocking salmon on their shelves in the canned goods section and fresh fish displayed on ice in the display cases in the seafood section. She had loved fish—until now.

She wondered if anything she ate or drank was really safe. How about the drinking water in Port Washington or anywhere? She already surmised her own water source in Chicago was tainted! The *Flint Michigan* water crisis had been in the news for a couple of years. That area had certainly been a hotbed of complaints blaming the city, threatening lawsuits with innuendos of government corruptness and policy mismanagement. Bex asked herself whether it was better to know if the drinking water was polluted or just go on with life ignorant to what might be killing you while you trusted your government to provide safe water to drink, cook with, and bathe in?

*Scary thought!*

She drove on down the road noticing irrigation apparatuses in the fields along the roadside watering the crops.

*Could that water be toxic to the soil? She already knew about fertilizers from her* career. *But how about the water used to irrigate the crops?* Bex felt she was downstream of everything harmful, bombarding her from all directions!

Bex was well versed in the language of contamination, of toxic levels of harmful chemicals—heavy metals, cadmium, selenium, mercury, arsenic, chlorine, fluoride, feces and all sorts of germs and chemical mixtures that were considered harmful to living things. Some, she knew were actually utilized in a positive way counteracting and killing germs.

Yet, too much sanitizing agents, certainly chlorine and fluoride, were known to cause a tipping point in the opposite direction and become harmful also. Bex knew too well that such a determination of safe levels could be skewed by *human error, human manipulation or acts of God.* It's a tricky business to treat and maintain safe water. Agency standards vary from state to state and country to country. On top of that, Bex had been disgusted when she found out the White House administration was posturing to do away with the entire EPA (Environmental Protection Agency), a government-run program!

The human body is amazing. It can fend off a host of evil things. But once a harmful host gets into the body and begins to mutate healthy cells, it becomes a domino effect. Sooner or later, the body succumbs to some sort of cancer and dies. Bex recalled that from her toxicology classes in college.

Bex had been daydreaming and not paying attention to her gas gauge. She sighed. Her thoughts suddenly turned to her dependency on gas to operate her car. *Another example of tradeoffs*, she thought.

She stopped at the next gas station, bought a banana Popsicle and began pumping the gas into her car! *This Popsicle probably isn't even made from real bananas,* Bex thought.

She had always loved them, though. She didn't want to know what chemicals were in her Popsicle. She threw the wrapper away listing its contents and stood there like a robot filling up her tank with gas. She looked down the road, facing away from the pumps, trying not to inhale the fumes while she sucked on her Popsicle. She eyed the edge of the discarded wrapper sticking out of the trash receptacle; it was messing with her mind.

*Hell, it's just a POPSICLE* for God's sake! She told herself.

# 6

## Dan Jenkins

As soon as Bexley arrived home, she realized she was suffering from serious paranoia! She wanted to call her former law partner, Dan, but she'd been rather cool toward him after the trial when he had tried to be comforting and affectionate.

Bex had known Dan since college when they had been lab partners in toxicology classes. She still thought of him as a dear friend but just didn't have time in her life right now for a serious boyfriend—certainly not marriage.

Those toxicology classes had shown some pretty convincing environmental disaster films. Over the last five years as law partners, the two of them had defended some bizarre cases together resulting in an appreciation what man could do to his environment.

Dan was more the silent type and had always been a good sounding board for Bex. She knew Dan loved her. She just didn't know exactly what her feelings were concerning him. He was a loyal friend, though.

Bex walked around her bungalow for a while debating whether to call him. She picked up her cell phone and dialed his number.

"Hey, Dan, it's Bex. How are you?"

"Bex, what's up? Enjoying unemployment? Found your dream job yet? Have you decided to retire for good? Or are you coming back to the firm?"

"Well, not yet on any of the above. But not discounting anything, either! Do you think we could meet somewhere, Dan? I'd like to talk to you about something. Do you have some time tomorrow?"

"Okay, what about?"

"Well, I need a sounding board. I could always depend on you to shoot the bull with me for hours on all sorts of topics dreaming up hypothetical situations. Dan, I'm freaking out about something."

"That's not a first, Bex. But, okay, I'll bite. You've caught my attention. Whenever you admit to freaking out, it means you're on to something big!"

"I'm obsessing about water. Here, there, it doesn't matter—everywhere! I need to meet with you and tell you about some strange things I saw in Port Washington. I quit my job over all this, yet I can't seem to get away from it! I find myself out here crusading for the very environmental issues I told myself to avoid like the plague! Here I am, out here finding more victims of pollution. I feel like a magnet for mayhem. I'm not getting paid one red cent now, though, and don't even have a client—unless you count me as my own client, representing myself in a case that's only in my mind! And that's ridiculous. I hate this! I'm documenting evidence like a pre-programmed robot—cannot get out of the mode! Don't know why I keep doing it. It's like it's my calling or something—no matter how hard I try to get away from it!"

"I just feel the world is becoming one big cesspool. I don't know what to do about it. Can't put the guilty people or liable corporations behind bars! Can't get the violators to stop polluting! I'm so frustrated and keep thinking everything I put into my mouth is contaminated—even Popsicles!"

"So please meet me tomorrow morning at the Starbucks on

the corner just below your *p-e-n-t-h-o-u-s*-e office," Bex said sarcastically since she no longer worked there. "We can talk about it then."

"Okay, tomorrow morning at seven. I'll have one of your special Starbucks lattes waiting for you, okay?" Dan asked.

"It's a date!" Bex said, cringing over her choice of words.

The next morning Dan had already arrived and was sitting at a sidewalk café table. He was enjoying his cup of coffee to stave off a Chicago morning chill. He had purchased a second Starbucks latte for Bex and a warm donut to surprise her, just like her office subordinates used to serve her first thing each morning when she worked for the firm.

"Say, hey Bex, what, no fashionable Armani skirt and blazer? I like the change! Sort of scruffy-chic. Jeans! But a sweatshirt without the Chicago Cubs across the front? Didn't think that existed in this city! You do know this is downtown Chicago, don't you? Either you support the cubs on all sweatshirts or make big fashion statement snafus! Aren't you concerned about keeping up your image rather than standing out as unemployed and not even a cub fan?" Dan asked, anticipating a particular *denial* response so Bex-like.

"Dan, since when did I ever really care about what other people think?" Bex started in as Dan mimicked her response rocking his head sideways in cadence with every anticipated word.

"I knew you would say that; I was trying to get your goat and mess with your mind a little bit," Dan replied.

"Dan, I only wore those fancy clothes to look like I was important and successful. You know how that goes. People align with those that talk big and look successful. Hey, look at Trump!" Bex said scarfing down a mouthful of the scrumptious treat Dan had given her.

"Okay, Dan. In a nutshell, here's the scoop. There's something polluting the waters in my hometown, Port Washington. And it's not the Lock Ness monster. It's bigger than that; maybe causing some real deformities in the fish up there. I think this could be leading to people getting sick, maybe causing cancer, like the manure in the Chicago water. I'm feeling like an enabler allowing these polluters to go scot-free and contributing to peoples' ill health. Now it's in my hometown!"

Bex took a delicious long, slow swallow of her latte.

"Oh, this is so delicious, Dan! I miss…*this*," Bex lamented.

"Okay. I saw these really wicked-looking fish thrown to the side in a discard pile on the Sauk Creek Bridge in Port Washington. That creek runs into Lake Michigan. And I mean these fish were really disfigured, Dan. With boils, double mouths, cloudy, milky eyes. Whataya think?"

"Dan, those fish were thrown out to rot in the sun. Nobody wanted them. Even the birds rejected them. But they weren't spoiled, yet. People were catching fish by the scads and if they looked bad, the fishermen were randomly deciding whether to cut out the bad part and sell the rest to restaurants!"

"Ugghhh, Bex!" Dan exclaimed, swallowing hard on a soft mush of donut and coffee. "Were they joking?"

"Don't know! Dan, it was gross. It worries me because I went directly from there to a high school reunion dinner where they were serving—guess what? Fresh salmon!"

"Okay. That's repulsive," Dan choked on his reply.

"I took some photographs, thinking they might be handy if it ended up in litigation. I think heavy metal compounds are being discharged into the water by the power plants in a much higher percentage than allowed," Bexley sighed.

"I think the nuclear power facility might be part of the problem because the affected waterway is downstream of that plant. This is getting more personal and offensive since I might well have eaten toxin-laden, polluted fish chowder earlier that day when I first arrived in Port Washington. I don't want to make any comments or lay blame, just yet, if it isn't true!"

"Well, you could always hire an environmental lawyer!" Dan laughed. "I know quite a few!" He laughed again.

# 7

## Afraid of the Water

—◁▷—

With the reunion behind her, Bex delved into her temporary venture with the Tribune with a vengeance. All the next week she worked hard on four human interest stories, finishing up by Friday night. The weekend was hers and she puttered around the bungalow and caught up on some much needed sleep. She hadn't seen Dan all week nor heard from him.

It hadn't been a particularly eventful weekend all around since Bex never left her Southside Chicago bungalow! The big event was another brief round of gunshots that drove the nail in the coffin; she was determined to find another place to live.

*Bye-bye job! Bye-bye bungalow! Bye-Bye nightmares!*

—◁▷—

Bex was the second person to arrive at the café Monday morning. Maude was sitting on her corner stool as usual. She glanced up, smiled at Bex then resumed filing her nails while engrossed in a magazine article.

Bex sighed. *How nice it must be not to have any worries,* she surmised watching Maude file away.

Today, Bex decided she would approach Maude, which she had never done. After fiddling with the lid of the Mason jar and successfully stuffing in three dollars to pay for all-day coffee, Bex spoke up.

"Good morning, Maude."

"Well, Hello Ms. Bexley."

"Oh, I didn't think you knew my name."

"I make it a point to know my customers. Hope you enjoy your coffee today."

Bex nodded and went over to the coffee pot. She laughed. Of course the coffee was not ready. Bex had been the first customer to arrive that morning and she knew Maude's rule, *first one here, you're duty is clear.* It was her way of saying feel free to make the coffee.

Bex glanced back at Maude. She was grinning.

"There are cans of regular and decafe under the counter, dear. Make the first pot, *regular*, please," Maude called out softly.

Bex smiled back and nodded.

Maude remained silent sitting on her barstool. She never looked in Bex's direction again the rest of the day. When Bex left later, Maude said goodbye to her in a soft voice.

—◦|◦—

Bex needed a FOR SALE sign to post in her front yard. She drove to the nearest hardware store, bought a sign and erected it in her front yard!

"*Okay*! Done!" Bex announced stepping back with satisfaction. *Progress!*

Bex spent the rest of the day cruising around in other neighborhoods searching for another place to live. She wanted to sneak away to find Princess Natawee's mansion, but that would have to be a fun outing for another day. She had to find a place for herself, first. And she did.

Bex had driven to the northern side of Chicago, down 26th Street into the Zion district and turned left onto Elisha, just moseying around. Ahead was a huge building. She passed by it seeing it was the Cancer Treatment Center of America, the Chicago center. There were no large buildings in the area except the center. Shiloh, Emmaus, Elisha and 26th Street were its four boundaries. She drove a little ways to Emmaus Avenue and stopped. There in front of her was the most beautiful park setting with a pond, a walking trail and parking all along its banks. There was a fountain in the middle of the pond.

Bex parked her car, walked along the sidewalk and over to the soccer fields. She crossed the street to the main entrance of the cancer center and went inside.

"I'm assuming there's a cafeteria somewhere in this center?" Bex asked softly trying not to startle the receptionist busy reading a book and had not looked up when Bex entered.

"Second floor; coffee's available up there, too," the attendant said while continuously flip-flopping her cupped fingers beckoning Bex to surrender her coffee cup.

"Sorry, dear, food and drink are not allowed in this area, only in designated areas and none allowed from outside the facility."

"Oh," Bex laughed handing over her almost empty, recycled Starbucks paper cup, the one she had rinsed out at home and refilled with home-brewed coffee. The lady promptly tossed it in an under-the-counter receptacle. Obviously it was a well-rehearsed routine.

Bex did just as the lady suggested. She went to the second floor, bought a tall latte and took a seat by the window to look down on the beautiful landscape below. She listened to the conversations around her like she had in Maude's café.

But the conversations were a bit different; yet, all the same. These folks were discussing loved one's medical conflicts and funerals. These people were visitors to the center because they had loved ones there as patients undergoing cancer treatments. Bex was touched, taken aback by their compassion. She finished her coffee and left. She walked toward the exit with tears flowing down her cheeks.

*Why are there cancers in this world? It sneaks into the body and invades every last cell over time.*

Bex was convinced cancer was a man-made abomination.

Bex headed for the front entrance with tears in her eyes. People nodded as they passed her—as if tears were a greeting.

A lady passing Bex patted her shoulder and whispered, "Don't worry, dear, pray. Prayers answer many questions. Just remember there's a bigger force at work out there. This place is about hope, not sorrow!"

The woman smiled and walked away.

Bex hurried back across the street to her car. She felt more energetic. She had a great idea. She felt energized with a new crusade as a spinoff from the Tribune human interest stories— write about people who have loved ones as patients in the cancer center. It was a project worth pursuing.

Just as she was about to pull away from her curb parking spot, she noticed a *FOR RENT* sign in front of an apartment building across the street from the center. She scrambled out of the car and walked quickly toward the building.

*Pretty, tree-lined sidewalks, too*, she whispered. *This is it! I love this place. This is my new home.*

The next morning, Bex walked down Honor Street, where she currently lived, to Maude's café. She was feeling something she had not anticipated. She was all teary-eyed. She was going to have to tell Maude she was moving. She was actually going to miss the mysterious café owner—a person she really did not know well but for whom she had developed a kindred spirit. She had grown to love that little corner café; it had become a second home to Bex in such a short time.

Bex had to find someone to rent her bungalow. She could not afford both places forever! Maybe six months tops! Time would tell whether North Chicago would be any different than South Chicago. Or whether any place was any different than another.

Bex walked into the café. She avoided Maude at first. She felt guilty, as if she was betraying this woman by moving away. *How ridiculous was that?*

Maude noticed Bexley shunning her and walked over to the table.

Bex saw her coming and thought how strange it was for Maude to be initiating contact first, quite possibly getting ready to start a conversation!

"Ms. Hargrove, is something bothering you?"

She paused then asked, "Want to talk?"

So, for the next several hours, Bex talked about her life, career goals and her woes.

Maude sat listening. Then she said, "I'll rent your house until you're satisfied with your new place."

Bex looked at Maude. "Are you looking for a place? Where do you live now?"

"Never mind that, don't worry. I'd like to rent your bungalow if that'll help you."

"But..."

"Done then! I'll give you six month's rent; the same amount you'd pay for your new apartment, I think you said, so you won't be out any money," Maude said.

"Wow, Maude. This is too good to be true."

"We've come to know each other in a short time. I see you every day. You mind your business, I mind mine. You help me, I'll help you," Maude said.

"I don't know what to say. I came this morning with the worrisome task of trying to figure out a way to tell you I was moving. I realized how much I'd miss this café. My new apartment is right across the street from my work, which will be more convenient if I lived there rather than my current bungalow address."

"We're good then. I've read your recent stories in the *Tribune*. They're good. Compassionate. I think this is your calling."

"You've read my stories? I've only written a few," Bex replied.

"Yes. I get the *Tribune* and have read all of them. I know you; I see your heart in what you write. I speak a language of love for all things and you do too. I trust good people who do the same. I see that in you. I'll give you the six-months rent in cash today when you bring a contract back to sign. We'll finish the transaction later then, right?" Maude asked.

Bex nodded and thanked her. As Bex walked home thinking about Maude's offer, she decided to take her up on it. She found a simple rental contract on the Internet, printed it out, completed the blanks and returned to the café.

Maude signed it. She had an envelope already prepared with $7500 cash as discussed. Maude had retrieved it from a backroom metal safe. Bex couldn't believe this was happening so fast. She warned Maude how unsafe it was to keep so much money onsite.

"No problem any longer. It's all gone. You have it!" she laughed.

"I'll bring the key to you on Friday or first of next week," Bex said.

*Now all I have to do is pack up and move out!*

She hugged Maude and left. She knew a notary public who'd sign off on the contract without Maude being present.

*God moves in mysterious ways,* Bex thought.

The rest of the week, Bex threw herself into warp speed organizing and scheduling movers. Having met with the executive director of the cancer center and laid out her project proposal, she was thrilled it had been received with open arms. So with the apartment chosen and rented, her belongings being packed, she also had her first two cancer patient interviews behind her and it appeared things were clicking along as she had hoped.

Friday, Bex drove to the café to give Maude the bungalow key. Maude smiled when Bex entered.

"So we are all set?" Maude asked.

"Absolutely," Bex said giving her a hug, "all signed!"

Maude pulled back a second and beamed! She reached around her neck and took off her favorite necklace. She held it up for a moment then placed it around Bex's neck.

"This is a special gift for you. Consider it a house-warming gift, Ms. Hargrove. It will keep you safe. It's a leather braided necklace with special bird feathers. A precious stone from my homeland is wrapped in the middle. It holds a special meaning, a reminder of a special friend lost a long time ago."

Bex stared at her.

"Thank you," Bex managed with a hint of tears welling up.

# 8

## To Nowheresville

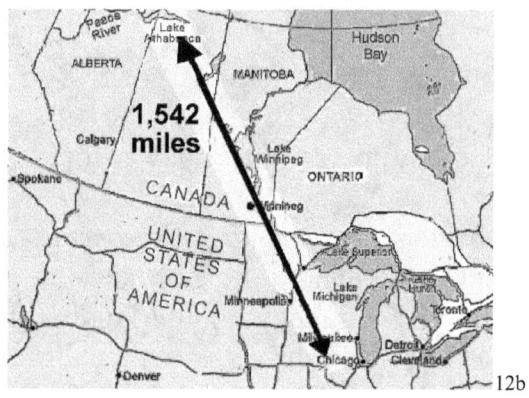

12b

Bex was feeling more confident she could manage her new lifestyle. It was time to connect with Shinski again. It seemed the two friends were reading each other's minds. No sooner had Bex walked into her new apartment than her cell phone rang. It was her friend from Port Washington.

"Hi, Shinski..." Bex said, recognizing her number.

"Bex, where have you been?" Shinski started in like always, cutting Bex off at the pass.

"I've been calling you all day and you haven't answered."

"I'm sorry, Shinski. I've been busy with things and interviewing people in the cancer center."

"Well, I've been trying to contact you, Bex. You have to come to visit now...What? Did you say cancer? Do you have cancer?" Shinski asked, beginning to sob in the middle of her frenzy and spittle.

"Where are you, Shinski? You sound so stressed out!" Bex replied. "No, I don't have cancer. I'm working on a project at a cancer center right across the street from me."

"Oh. Bex! It's terrible. Greg and I have already moved to Canada. We'll eventually move to Calgary. Right now I'm temporarily living in a place called Fort Chipmunk or something like that. It's the pits, Bex. I'm in the middle of nowhere. NO MAN'S LAND in Nowheresville! I can't stand it. It's nothing like I thought it would be. There's nothing here! The closest place to shop is 170 miles from here at a *WAAAAL-MART...*"

Shinski's wailing started high and ended low in a continuous downward drone followed with episodes of sobbing, exaggerated nose blowing and—phone static.

*This is so like her*, Bex thought while listening. *Everything revolves around Shinski! She never considers the problems of others and always has to be the queen bee.*

"And there's N-O-B-O-D-Y here. Less than a thousand people live here, Bex," Shinski cried.

"God, I've thrown larger parties at the country club in Port Washington than the entire population of this place!" she sobbed.

"Shinski, where are you again, exactly?" Bex asked.

"I don't know. You'll have to ask Greg. But he's not here. He's never here! He's in some hellhole down south. Everything there's so dirty and black. When I was there, it smelled like gas and tar. It was suffocating like those fumes that make you sick when you pump gas yourself at a service station; except it's a hundred times worse! The sky's black with smoke, doubly worse because there was a huge fire recently. The food is awful—I don't do fast food! The water tastes funny; everybody drinks bottled water, and I think it's because the water's not safe! I refuse to use my good bubble bath in this dreadful water and it's a pain trying to fill a tub with bottled water especially since it doesn't bubble-up like it should!" Shinski whined.

"I refuse to go to a hair salon up here. As a matter of fact, I don't think there is one up here. How could Greg possibly bring me to a place like this?" Shinski complained.

"Shinski! Okay. I get it. But didn't you say you would be staying in a classy B&B or something like that when we talked last?"

"Ohhhhh, Bex, if you only knew," Shinski moaned.

"I wouldn't exactly call it classy, even though the brochure did."

"Bex, it seems people are angry at everybody where Greg works. They carry protest signs, saying *Go home, Stop killing, Stop polluting!* They want the companies to stop digging the holes down there—Greg says it's the Canadian companies, the Americans, Russians, Chinese... It seems all the big countries are investors. The people hate these oil companies; yet, everyone works for them. They hate this Alberta Oil Sands Project; yet, they desperately need the jobs and the money working there. Everybody's frustrated. Well, so—am—I!"

"Greg likes the company, says he's being groomed for top management and eventually we will live in Calgary—not this place. It's just that the public doesn't like what his company is doing to the environment and I'm not sure what that means for us now or long term."

"What's this project you keep talking about, Shinski?"

Shinski bypassed the question and continued.

"I'm afraid for Greg and not sure what all the fuss is. It's so scary up here. It's too cold and you can't go anywhere because the cars sink in the lake. There are no movie theatres nearby. I can't find a custom baked cake for Greg's upcoming birthday. He's going to be turning forty-five while we're up here! I can't use the computer because the Internet's too new. There are still connection problems and Greg did all that stuff for me, anyway, in the past and I didn't have to worry about using it."

"The Internet, Bex! This is 2017! We're talking about the Internet, for Christ's sake! Hasn't that been around since, gosh, the 1970s? I think my folks have had one in their home since the 90s. I thought Internet was everywhere by now, isn't it? There's limited service in the B&B; doesn't work all the time so it's hard for Greg and I to communicate by computer or phone when he's away. You have to make your call in the bathroom because that's where you get the best cell phone reception!"

"They don't have *Netflix*! Greg said he heard more modern conveniences were coming; but it's not soon enough. I'm in the boonies up here. If I want my hair done, like the way they did it at home, in the States, I have to travel to Fort McMurray. I don't have a car and if I did I don't drive in the snow and ice. I never did in Chicago, Greg always did. I found some gray hairs showing and I can't let Greg see them. Please come, Bex. And when you do, will you bring a box of my hair color, level-7, L'Oréal's Golden Blonde?"

"Shinski, calm down for heaven's sake! I have some things I have to take care of first but I'll try to find a cheap flight. I'll come as soon as I can. I *can* fly there, can't I, Shinski?"

"It depends on when you come, it seems. If you come by plane, yeah, right! Sometimes sea planes come in and out of this place certain times of the year and I've seen a few bigger planes. I know Greg's company jet can land here because I was on it!"

"Since I've been here, the lake's been frozen. They call it the Ice Road. People drive on it. When it thaws, I understand a barge can get here. Who knows! Then the people who live here bring out their canoes! Do you own a canoe, seriously?"

"Don't worry about it. Just talk to Greg. He said he'd pay for everything to get you here *and* while you're here! His company travel agency will arrange everything. I'm so miserable up here. I cry every day, Bex! *Every day*! Did I tell you the cars and huge trucks sink in the lake?"

"Yes, you did, Shinski. Okay, have Greg call me."

Bex hit the end button and completed the call.

*What a week,* Bex thought. *The last few weeks!*

Her best friend had totally lost it. Bex had quit her job, moved out of her penthouse condo, moved into a little bungalow, was moving out of that already into an apartment, didn't have an income and was thinking about taking a vacation to Canada for a month or two that might cost her ten grand if Greg didn't come through paying her expenses and if she decided to go!

But a new friend, Maude, *an angel*, had come along and answered one prayer at least! She had someone to rent her bungalow. One problem had been resolved.

*What on Earth is going on up there? What's Greg thinking would be so great moving from the U.S. to Canada? Guess I'll find out soon enough,* Bex thought.

It was about 10:00 p.m. Chicago time—9:00 p.m. Alberta time when Greg called.

"Bexley, good evening; how are you? Amanda and I enjoyed talking with you at the reunion. I refer to my wife as Amanda, not Shinski. I guess you're the only one who still calls my wife by that name."

"I'm fine Greg. Thanks for asking. I enjoyed meeting you too, even if it was only for just to say hello and sit with you two for a quick dinner. Yes, I know. She'll always be Shinski to me, though."

Bex paused after hearing a little static in the connection.

"Where in Alberta are you and Shinski, I mean Amanda, staying? I was just looking it up and I'm having trouble locating it. I found Calgary. But this Fort Chip something, I need some help locating that one," Bex said.

"We're up in northern Alberta, Bex, in a place called Fort Chipewyan on Lake Athabasca. Actually, at the moment, I'm staying in temporary housing in Fort McMurray, south of where Amanda's staying," Greg replied.

"She's staying in a B&B at the edge of Fort Chipewyan in Alberta in a little place that's quite remote. It is called Fort C—H—I—P—E—W—Y—A—N. You'll have to google it, Bex, on your computer, when we finish this call. Listen, Bexley, Amanda is really miserable up here. It's not at all what I expected for us and certainly not what she expected. I knew I was sugar-coating the place a bit. I just didn't know how much until we arrived. It is pretty bad for any woman, much less a woman like Amanda, who's used to so many modern conveniences, shopping boutiques and country clubs. All I hear about is that there are no dress shops, Gucci bags, no place to get her hair and nails done or go out to lunch with friends. I told her it would be different; but it is really different and certainly not Amanda's thing!"

"Bex, we sold our home in Port Washington and most of our belongings, so we have to stick this out until we can build a house in Calgary. Or until I get transferred somewhere else. I don't see that happening anytime soon. They said it would take about five months to build a house in Calgary. Bex, Amanda won't last that long. I don't want to lose her! Can you come up for a while to help out? I'll pay for all your expenses getting here and while you're here and if you two want to jump back and forth across the border to Chicago or visit other places in Canada together, I'll pay for everything—commercial flights or even fit you two on the company jet, when possible, anytime you want. The B&B isn't so bad; it is rather small and definitely remote. And it's cold up here, so far as we've been here, so you'll have to come prepared for that," Greg said.

"Wow, Greg, this all sounds pretty bad. Is it that bad?"

"Yes, for Amanda. If it weren't for all the politics, employee picket lines, opposition to this oil project, the smell, the food, the awful water and how black it is where I'm staying, I would say Canada's wilderness can be totally awesome and beautiful in places."

"But the beauty isn't where I'm staying and Amanda doesn't like where she's staying, either. It's too remote for her. We haven't seen green grass since I've been here—too much snow. Course, this time of year, it's primarily snow and ice for months, worse than Chicago, though. Where I am, it's nothing but black, deep craters sprinkled with a little semblance of civilization here and there!"

Greg paused a moment.

"Most of the rural areas of Canada can be very backward and lagging in technology. A lot of Canada still is. It's just not like the States, or for that matter, not like anywhere I've ever been. When you go to the touristy areas in Canada, the country is beautiful. But other than those places, I'm not sure how people survive here. It's wild, desolate and even moonlike."

"But to answer your question how we feel about it for us? It's pretty bad. Google the Alberta Oil Sands Project on your computer tonight and let me know what you think next time we talk."

Greg paused.

"I shouldn't be telling you this. Being in the upper ranks of N-GerDon Corporation, my comments should be more filtered, professional and politically sensitive. This isn't at all like me rambling like this. I'm more professional most of the time, but this is becoming emotional for me and creating a problem in my marriage. I love my wife, Bex, and you are her dearest friend, she says. She's not in a good place emotionally right now. She needs you, Bex. I do too."

Greg hesitated.

"So, we would be grateful if you'd come visit us for an extended stay as long as you can afford to take the time."

Bex listened. She could not believe how bad it sounded. Greg *must be in denial,* she thought.

"Sure, Greg, I'll come and do what I can for Amanda. I mean Shinski—I'm sorry. I'm not sure what to call her, now."

"You keep calling her Shinski. That makes her feel good, she says. Makes her feel like she's back in high-school with you! Call her Shinski. I know who you're talking about and nobody else really knows us up here!"

"I've got some free time coming up. I'll take you up on that offer to pay for my flight and expenses, though. I just moved and I'm working on a new venture," Bex said stretching the truth a bit.

"I thought you were a partner in a law firm," Greg commented.

"I'm taking some time off and am starting a new business."

Bex quickly changed the subject.

"I'm grateful for your generosity to help me out on the cost," she added.

"Of course and we wouldn't think of asking this of you if it wasn't an emergency. Okay, I'll book a ticket for you, in your name. Can you come next week? Friday of next week? I'll have the travel agent make all the necessary arrangements; they'll call you. All you have to do is get to the airport. I've gotta run. Bye Bex. And thank you!"

Bex put her cell phone down on the table. She just stared into space. All of a sudden she jumped up.

*Oh My God, Friday of next week? This is Monday. Did he say Friday of next week? Like in eleven days? And stay for a couple months? I've got so much to do. Whew!*

Bex turned the table lamp off and hurried back to her bedroom. She felt so badly for her friend and her husband. She felt compelled to go to her friend in her time of need. Bex would need to tell Maude she would be gone for a while. Maude would need to know how to contact her since she was now a landlord with those type responsibilities. And besides, she was beginning to think of Maude like *family*, like a second mother.

The next morning Bex showed up at the café early. She wanted to talk with Maude before the regulars arrived and it seemed Maude wanted to talk with her too.

"Maude, I'll be out of town for about a month on *business*. I'm not leaving until next week but I wanted you to know in case there's a problem and you need to contact me. You have all the emergency contact numbers for utilities and so forth. And you have my cell phone number."

"That's coincidental, Ms. Hargrove. I was going to tell you I'll be gone for a time too. The bungalow will be empty. Anything I need to do before I go?"

"No. I think we're fine. We both have each other's contact numbers. Be safe on your trip. Everything okay?" Bex asked.

"Oh yes," Maude replied. "You have a safe trip, too."

"Yes, I'll be visiting a friend but not sure if I call it a leisure trip. I've got a lot to do before I leave," Bex replied.

And with that the two parted. Neither could give an approximate time when they would be returning.

Maude had placed a temporary sign outside on the sidewalk. It read:

CLOSED FOR ONE MONTH

Bex looked at the sign and started to go back inside to speak with Maude again, but decided against prying into Maude's privacy.

*A month is a long time. Why the hell didn't I ask where she was going?* Bex thought.

Maude had not offered the information so maybe it was too personal to share, Bex surmised.

Neither woman had pried. And ironically both women were bound for travel outside the United States.

Maude had already purchased her plane ticket to her destination. She was due to catch a flight out of Chicago the next morning.

Bexley still had to schedule her flight through Greg Randolph's travel agent. Bex could not fly out until the next Friday, just as Greg had requested.

Neither woman knew each would be traveling north—far north of Chicago.

# Part II

# Alberta, CA
# 1867 to 2017—150 years
*During Grand Elder Obigon Sakawa's Time*

**Indian Land Treaty 1867**- Many historians date the development of the Canadian land treaties back to the confederation of Canada in 1867. Treaties were signed before the confederation of Canada and included those from 1764-1862. The Numbered Treaties, though, came in two waves: Treaties 1 through 7 from 1871 to 1877 and Treaties numbers 9 through 11 from 1899 to 1921.

The first wave was in consideration of the new *Canadian Pacific Railway*, the second was for *Resource Extraction*. With the second wave of treaties, the First Nations people and other Indigenous people in Canada were guaranteed the use of the land in perpetuity for hunting, fishing, farming and the lands used for resource extraction would be returned to its original state when finished.

The government did not anticipate such a rich source of oil reserves to be found under these lands. Instead of returning the land to its original state, there has been a steady, unending excavation of such magnitude that the lands can never be returned to its original state, even though some investing users tried, proving it to be cost prohibitive. In the 150 years since the *first* signing, environment pollution has steadily destroyed the people's ability to make a living off the land. Instead this has been an "***environmental genocide***."

**Indian Act of 1876**- was a consolidation of previous regulations pertaining to First Nations people in Canada (*previous known as Indians*). The Act gave greater authority to the Federal Department of Indian Affairs; it could now intervene in a wide variety of internal band issues and make sweeping policy decisions, such as determining who was an Indian. It was amended nearly every year between 1876 and 1927. Since 1867, when the *development* of the Act began, the Canadian government has been in charge of Indigenous/First Nations affairs. This control has been described as genocide of a heritage by a combined effort of church and government to assimilate them into the Euro-Canadian culture, a "***cultural genocide***."

# 9

## Obigon Sakawa Sr.
## One Hundred Years Old

Obigon, *Obi,* as everyone called him, loved to sit in his chair by the window. When he knew it was time for Snowbird, his great-grandchild, to come for her nightly lessons, he would turn on his table lamp so she would know it was okay to come on in. Most of the times, he snoozed until she arrived.

That was just one of three things Obi loved to do each day. The second was to spend time with his good friend, Kinoo Kiyasew, to whom he was devoted. But the third, and most precious part of each day, was the time he could spend with his great-grandchild, Snowbird, helping to prepare for a student competition in hopes she would win a college scholarship.

Obi went to the kitchen and pulled out a few sprigs of witches' hair to make tonight's tea. He would teach Snowbird about food tonight. If meat smelled like garlic and was a bit slimy, it had gone bad. He would explain that healthy fish do not have lesions or boils on their scales and that no healthy fish was born with deformities like two mouths. Obi was not quite ready to discuss the fish he and Kinoo had caught that morning.

The First Nations people were seeing animal carcasses and fish go belly up in the lake. Moose, caribou and goats floated in the waters in the off season. As the years went by, the people began to understand their water was not as healthy as it once had been. It smelled bad and was not clear anymore. The people had had to get used to these changes and they began buying bottled water to keep from getting sick.

But bottled water, trucked into the little hamlet, cost money. And storing it was inconvenient. Public water from the faucet for bathing and grooming still came in contact with their bodies. They would forget at times and drink the faucet water, bathe in it or cook in it and even melt the snow to use it, which they had been warned not to do. Whether it came from the faucet or the environment, there were issues of contamination.

More people were getting abnormal cancers and dying. These illnesses *and unemployment* were certainly behind much of these people's alcohol abuse, depression and drug abuse. These problems were rapidly becoming a vicious part of First Nations people's lives!

Obi coughed in his slumber. It jarred him a bit; he opened his eyes. Snowbird had not arrived for her lesson. He had not heard her knock. He looked for his red bandana to wipe his mouth after his coughing spell. He was feeling the urge to urinate more often. When he did, he noticed his urine was dark. He vomited more often using his rag to clean his mouth, stuffing it in his pocket most times. He was trying to remember to drink from the bottled water purchased from the Hudson Bay Trading Post. His cough seemed different lately. *It must just be the cold draft*, he thought, as his great-granddaughter opened the door.

She went over to him and kissed his forehead.

"Welcome child! Come in from the cold. Fix us some good hot tea with the sprigs I laid out on the counter. Then cover up with the furs. We have two days left before you go to your competition."

Snowbird nodded and fixed their tea. She nestled cross-legged on the floor, covered with beaver pelts, enjoying Obi's teaching stories.

*Narrow Road to Obi's home.*

*Obi's Home*

Suddenly Obi announced their evening was over.

"You need to go home now and get some sleep. I must walk down to Kinoo's home and check on him."

Obi hugged Snowbird and watched her leave. He wrapped a fur around him and walked outside. It was not late, but maybe too late to catch his friend awake and sober. He didn't want to stand outside in the cold, even though he was used to frigid weather. All the warm coats and wraps this evening would not have been enough. Obi felt chilled to the bone as he stood on the steps of Kinoo's home waiting for his old friend to answer the door. He coughed and drew the leather ties of his hood tighter, then put both gloved hands over his face to stave the chill. His skin itched constantly. He knew Kinoo was inside. But he felt his friend must be drunk, passed out, unable to hear his knock. Kinoo had the problems with firewater; he was sad to have his best friend succumb to that demise.

Obi was unwilling to wait longer. He turned and walked home frustrated. He was trying to help his friend with his problem the last couple days trying to ensure he would be sober enough to drive his great-granddaughter to the airport to catch a flight to Calgary for her competition. He had recently begun a routine walking to Kinoo's house after Snowbird left in the evenings to check on his progress.

People in the community relied on the wise ones, the Wisdom Council. Obi, the oldest member, intervened on the people's behalf speaking to the Great Spirit in his shaking tent ceremonies. He would ask the Great Spirit for guidance and safety for his people, to watch over the drunkards, to provide jobs and provide basic needs for all. This wish, he knew, would be a dual-edged request; there didn't seem to be an answer to his people's problems.

Obi hoped Snowbird might be his greatest legacy, to prepare her for her future, maybe for the future of their people. He hoped her greatest legacy would be to prepare her children and teach them the First Nations people's heritage during her lifetime. This was important to Obi. He hoped it would be equally important to her.

# 10
## Snowbird

Snowbird was just twelve, and plenty resourceful and mature for her age. But she could not possibly shoulder the murders that had begun before her time, back when her people attended the residential Indian schools. At an early age, she was about to be tested how she fit into the outside world beyond her little hamlet on Lake Athabasca. She would soon be asking questions why that outside world had allowed such deaths.

She called her great-grandfather Obigon Sakawa Sr., simply, *Obi.*

Snowbird coughed as she trudged along the icy path each night to her great-grandfather's place.

"I see you," Snowbird called out to the pack of coyotes in the distance.

Suddenly she pulled back as an eerie light reached out and touched her shoulder. It had raced toward her in lightning speed then just as quickly as it had thrust toward her; it flickered then retreated, melding into the night sky.

"Ooh," Bex responded losing her balance, feeling chilled as she stared across the vast frozen lake—the Ice Road.

Maybe she swallowed the cold wind too hard and its harshness had stunned the back of her throat. Maybe the fairies, or little people from the hoodoos, had come with a purpose suddenly entering her body again as she knew they could and had before.

"Oh, you're here," Snowbird cried out as another faint-blue flickering caught her attention then dimmed in the southern skies in the direction where her parents worked—almost a 170 miles south in the oil sands projects.

Snowbird swallowed hard again trying to resolve the lump she felt lodged in her throat. It could be anything; even an emotional reaction to missing her mother and father. She rarely saw them after they began working in the oil sands. A rumbling quickly festered in her tummy. Maybe she was just nervous about the upcoming student competition in Calgary.

She gazed pensively toward the dark southern skies, beyond Lake Athabasca where her parents worked in the project. She tried to imagine the little rental houses where they lived part time.

Little did she realize she was living downstream of the Alberta Oil Sands Projects where her parents worked all day for a company that was digging into the earth, extracting a composition of oil and sand. Then the companies processed it into oil for energy resulting in residual toxic chemicals dumped into the waters or leaching from holding ponds right into the Athabasca River, which in turn flowed into Lake Athabasca, every day, making their way toward her little hamlet.

Snowbird felt a gripping sensation of something evil looming nearby. If it was not for Obi, she felt she would be swallowed up by loneliness. Obi was her best friend. She lived to be with him during the evenings; he was her guiding light.

Snowbird also felt the comfort of the blue flickering lights at times when she walked to Obi's house or was awakened after a nightmare. When Snowbird saw the blue flickering light, it immediately calmed her; she wondered what it was yet she knew there was something always around her, protecting her.

The little people and the fairies watched over Snowbird, grooming her with strength and courage, guiding her—charged with the duty to keep her safe.

Snowbird leaned back, instinctively opening her mouth, hoping to inhale the essence of the blue light as she walked this night to Obi's shack. It was as if on some level, she knew the fairies and the little people were with her but she had never actually met them or been properly introduced. She somehow knew that would never be possible.

She was the chosen one but they had never told her.

Obi knew this child had a special energy about her, a special glow that illuminated even more when he was around her. He believed in her future. The little people and the fairies *had* told Obi in the shaking tent that she was a chosen one! *He* had a duty, then, to also teach her and protect her.

This evening, Snowbird sensed Obi was preoccupied with other things. He was. He harbored a deep secret that he had not wanted to share. He had been thinking recently of his days attending the Holy Angels Residential Indian School. He had had an awakening recently, an experience with his friend, Kinoo, that was still haunting him.

"Obi, I will fix a plate of dried moose meat, caribou and dried fruit tonight to go with our tea," Snowbird offered. At times, while she fixed a bite to eat, Obi would doze. Sometimes he would doze during his lesson. She wondered what he was thinking or dreaming.

"I'm sorry. I was dreaming how I was made to eat the *white man's* food prepared in the *white man's* ways at the school when I was a child," Obi replied.

"This is good food, my child, that you have prepared," Obi said and leaned back against his chair.

"Your hair is so beautiful," Obi said.

Snowbird beamed up at him with admiration.

She had no clue Obi was imagining how awful it would have been for her to have attended the same schools he had, to have the nuns cut off her long beautiful black braids as they had done to his hair often while he was there. He remembered how the nuns had wacked his hair constantly as it grew and had seen them toss it the trash. What a blow it had been to his manhood.

"Child, I was three when I went to that school. The nuns never allowed my hair to grow long. I was sad about that. Our people consider long hair a symbol of maturity, growing up and becoming wiser. Long hair is sacred to our people."

"One lesson I'll share with you today, Snowbird, is that you should never cut your hair. It is taboo to cut your hair," Obi said as he lovingly caressed her braids.

Obi shivered at that moment.

"Obi, are you cold?" Snowbird asked as she wrapped his favorite blanket around him a bit more securely.

Obi dozed again then snorted. It startled him that he had fallen asleep then awakened with Snowbird sitting there patiently waiting.

"That's okay, Obi, I know where you were in the lesson," she would say and get him back on track. She was only twelve, but Obi had taught her many things and had repeated the lessons so often, she knew many times what he was going to say next.

Obi taught her about Christianity and how it differed from their beliefs.

"Child, at first I thought Christianity was a violent faith. I was confused at first. Every night I stared at a man nailed to a wooden cross hanging on the wall above my bed. I was afraid. I did not know about Christianity, why this man, Jesus, had to die on the cross," Obi explained.

"Then the nuns told us that Jesus was the Son of God similar to our people's Great Spirit and that we would go to be with God one day," Obi said.

"If we believed in him," Obi added, "We would be in the Mystery of the Sky, child," Obi continued. "We would be with God in His Heaven forever and it would be a good thing."

"Snowbird, dear one, our people believe in love and respect for all living things. Our faith, now, is a combination of two beliefs, actually *many beliefs*. I believe in Christianity and Mother Nature. I believe the Great Spirit and the Christian God are important among our people," Obi shared.

"It was troubling, child. When I came home after being in that school, my family thought I was evil. I was trying to teach them the *white man's* ways; they told me I could not speak of such things to them, that it was taboo. The other students told their families the same things. They were told to leave the family. There was trouble in the families, much violence. Our people did not accept their own sons and daughters any more. The grown children left or fought their families."

Snowbird looked at Obi in horror.

"The students were ashamed of their family. They had been taught by their new school teachers to be ashamed of their people's heritage."

"When I graduated from the school, I was much older than the others," Obi said, "but my family took me back. That was good. I was lucky," Obi said.

"But it was not good for my family. I hadn't been taught survival skills in the wilderness in school or how to help my family. I was a burden to them. I had not been taught those things in school by the nuns," Obi explained.

"Obi, you have taught me so much about our people. I'm so glad. I want to know all you will teach me so I can teach others."

"It is important," Obi replied.

"Snowbird, when the students graduated, some could not readjust to their old world any more. They had forgotten or were conditioned to think differently. Many wandered off, took their own life," Obi said.

"We are not sure what has happened to your grandfather, or to some of my friends who graduated with me and to many others who have since graduated in the last 150 years or so. I have lived a long time and have seen much."

"I know, Obi. I hear this too and talk to my friends at the good community school who have parents who attended those same bad schools," Snowbird said.

"I fear the people who went to the bad schools are still angry and sad. They've gone to the firewater, drugs and fight each other and it's getting worse."

"I have seen times when all was well within the families and now our families are greatly troubled! It will take many moons and many generations of our people to work through this problem."

"My dear, it is quite different today than when I was growing up in Fort Chipewyan and for you, our culture, your life today; it is still considered quite different by those outside our world."

Snowbird kissed Obi's hands and told him she had to go home now. She had school the next day.

"Obi, I'm glad the Community School has good teachers!"

Obi hugged her and watched her go.

When she left, Obi opened a leather bound book he usually kept in his medicine bag. He took a pen and wrote a memory he had almost forgotten. He wanted to tell Snowbird of these things. But he felt she was not mature enough to hear such horror. He could write in English; but sometimes it wasn't as important to do so as other times. This time it was important.

*—The nuns cut the hair off both the boys and girls. They even shaved the boys' heads. They poured thick, black oil substances on our heads. It stank. This was done to get rid of lice but it was done to all of us whether we needed it or not. They told us we stank, were ignorant and worthless.—2017 Obi.*

Obi remembered something else he wanted Snowbird to know when she read this book one day:

*—Dear Snowbird, the nuns took our things. They took a pair of my moccasins and a pair of leather pants with beads that my mother had made for me and threw them away. I was young, but I remember. They replaced them with a uniform of a shirt and pants with a number sewn onto it. I was number 9 and*

*it was marked on my sheets, toothbrush and cup.*

*Snowbird, I am the oldest living person in the hamlet. I remember when the nuns, with their funny hats, came to my parent's teepee in the bush and took me. I was pulled out of my mother's arms and put into an open wagon pulled by a truck. There were other children on the wagon with me. My mother screamed for me. I remember hot, stinging in my eyes and seeing my mother growing smaller and smaller as the wagon drove away. The nun with the big hat held me down with great strength. — 2017 Obi.*

That was enough for tonight. Obi put away his book. He put it back inside his medicine bag. He lay back in his chair. He remembered how he had never taken to the school food. He had not been accustomed to such different food. Obi shuttered remembering how the nuns had made him eat his own vomit when his stomach would not accept the *white man's* food.

# 11

## Obi's Childhood: 1920's
## Fort Chipewyan, Alberta

Snowbird was confused about her great-grandfather's childhood attending the Holy Angel Residential Indian School.

"Why didn't your parents come to the school to get you out, Obi?" Snowbird asked.

She was distressed about Obi being abused at the school. She sipped on root tea waiting for his answer.

"I did question my parents later when I came home at nineteen years old," Obi told her. "I didn't see them from the time I was three until the time I was nineteen."

"They said the Great Spirit had whispered to them if they protested too much and showed too much anger, they would be thrown in jail or be killed."

"Many children tried to run away. But it was too cold and they had no place to go. So they always came back. When they did, they were beaten more for running away," Obi replied.

Obi tried hard not to show weakness. But there would be more of these times when his eyes revealed he was still holding back great pain and more secrets.

Obi told Snowbird about marrying his *Sôkòm* (Cree name for *wife*), her great-grandmother. Obi told Snowbird how her great-grandmother had died of tuberculosis. Back then little was known of that disease.

"We had only one child together—your grandfather, Sakawa II," Obi had exclaimed. "And the one who laid with him, your grandmother, wandered off, too. After that, your dear grandfather went sick in head. He turned to firewater in a bad way. He never saw his good *Sôkòm* again. She never came back to the bush. Now, we rarely see him; don't know where he is."

Obi talked for hours that night about his dear *Sôkòm*.

Snowbird knew he was lonely despite his grand elder status in the community. He was lonely in a deeper way. Yet his belief in the Great Spirit—his God, comforted him.

Obi would glance lovingly at the knitting needles sticking in a vase in the corner when he talked of his *Sôkòm.*

"We never asked why; it was not like the moon, which always rises after the setting sun. She was just gone; she never returned," Obi said. "First Nations people do not talk about the dead. It is not our custom. You can't bring back the dead,*"* Obi told Snowbird.

"When people asked about your grandmother, we just said she wandered off into a dark place. She went crazy in the head, went to the Great Mystery in the Sky. We often pray for her soul to come full circle. But we pray in silence, child," Obi told her.

"Same with your grandfather; he might have wandered off never to return."

Snowbird finally revealed a secret of her own. She told Obi she was beginning to have nightmares that her people had wandered off and left *her* and that she had been taken by the governmental Indian Agents, forcibly taken by the church nuns, hauled off to that bad school and abused. She told Obi her nightmares were also about her hair being cut off, that the Great Spirit was displeased with her because she no longer had her braids and had chosen not to protect her any longer.

Snowbird told Obi she felt for her braids each morning upon awakening to make sure they were still there.

"Snowbird, don't think badly of your grandfather. He had the firewater habit because he saw too much at that school. He probably has wandered off, might not ever return. Be prepared for that. But you have people here who love you, will take care of you and guide you if that happens and if I have gone to the Great Spirit…your braids are still there," he confirmed as he gently pulled on them, smiling at her.

# 12

## Little People and the Hoodoos
—◄—

It had been over ninety years since Obi had attended the Holy Angels Residential Indian School, he told Snowbird.

"The school has gone through many name changes. The building has fallen down and been repaired many times. I believe it was the Great Spirit that guided those to close its doors forever. That was many moons ago."

Snowbird refilled their cups numerous times with tea that night and would many more times in the nights to come.

"Your parents and grandparents went to that same school," Obi told his great-granddaughter. "They had their stories about this school, too."

"Child, the Indian Agent came for you one day, as well. We told them they could not take you. We told them you knew the English ways because your parents worked for the *white men*. We explained we were sending you to the Community School. You were blessed not to have to go to that residential school. They had all but closed its door anyway. But you could have been shipped off to somewhere else in Canada."

Obi paused.

"Understand my words?"

"Yes," Snowbird always answered. "Why didn't you become one of the Community School's teachers? You would have been a good teacher, Obi," she said.

Obi smiled. He was not sure how to answer her.

"*White man's* ways are still strange for me and I don't understand all they do and say. My head is too full of what I need to teach you. That's enough."

They both laughed.

Snowbird's parents did have good jobs; therefore, it was highly probably Snowbird would go on to further her education and be self-supporting. She did speak English fluently and also her native tongue, *Cree.*

When Snowbird was not in school or at Obi's house, she was outside playing in the little hamlet at the water's edge or roaming in the grasslands. She dared venture into the hoodoos though. She was also careful not to walk out onto the Ice Road when she thought the ice was melting. She knew that meant trouble, especially for vehicles that might fall through the thawing ice.

Sometimes the truckers dared to travel on the thin ice at the end of the season. Snowbird would ride down with Obi in his truck to the edge of the Ice Road to watch the excitement when they heard a big semi-truck had fallen through and was stuck. She knew how important it was to get the trucks out quickly. It was a huge catastrophe when this happened because the truck was usually bringing their community's supplies, especially their drinking water. It was quite a spectacle to witness a truck sinking into the lake and more of an event to see it pulled out. It was quite expensive to pull a truck to shore.

Depending on the size of the truck and how far the tow truck might have to cut a trail through the ice, it could cost upwards of five grand and many hours to pull it out of the water. It was an incredible feat to watch. Her great-grandfather knew just how close he could park his car at the edge of the frozen lake and watch. But now, Obi didn't drive anymore.

"You can't fool Mother Nature," the elders would say to the surprised drivers whose trucks sank through the melting Ice Road.

"You must respect thinning ice," people in the community would say to the truck drivers as they shook their heads at the travesty.

The people in Fort Chipewyan were proud to be able to read the signs of Mother Earth for survival. Their people had survived off the land for some 10,000 years reading the signs of nature. They would successfully hunt caribou, moose, beaver, buffalo, and catch fish. But things had been changing for years.

3

https://i.cbc.ca/1.3477888.1457217547!/fileImage/httpImage/image.JPEG

Nature was showing a more devastating change was underway. There was nothing anyone could do to stop the change, either, just like trying to halt the digging in the oil sands.

Each night when Snowbird met with Obi, she followed the same path walking between the houses to block the wind. She trekked onward to Obi's home each evening, pulling her hood around her head for more protection against the fierceness. The winds gusted off the frozen lake with nothing to stop it from picking up the chill of the sub-degree, frozen-lake surface temperature. She headed uphill. She glanced back once more across the grasslands toward the Ice Road. The sheer flatness gave rise to the hope she would catch a vision of the coyotes' silhouettes this evening.

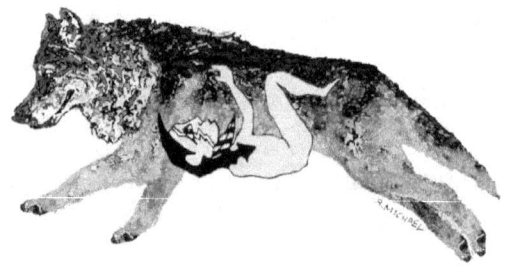

6

6

Snowbird could smell the air, the scent of their movement in the wind. She could sense things were happening in the hoodoos.

© Darby Sawchuk / dsphotographic.com 5

Obi had taught Snowbird how to hone her senses like the coyotes. She had learned to tell if food was inedible. She knew when fish and fowl were not fit to eat. She knew when medicinal berries and mushrooms were ripe for gathering. She noticed when there was nothing to hunt, no fish to catch, and when plants were unhealthy. She knew something was wrong in the air when the witches' hair on the tree trunks hung slight and limp that the environment was unhealthy.

Snowbird could tell the air smelled foul many times; a smell seeming to come downstream from where her parents worked.

Snowbird coughed. If Obi had any witches' hair left, she would surely make a cup of tea for them as soon as she reached his home.

*It would help her cough and his,* she thought.

South of her hamlet, 170 miles from where she stood, many trucks were busy carrying tons of bitumen, *black cake*, as they called it, digging it up from huge, deep holes in the earth. The process to separate this oil and sand cake mixture into fuel released a foul petroleum-gas smell.

More importantly and unknown to Snowbird was the fact her parents were playing a part in all this digging. They were extracting this cake, that black gunk out of the earth; scratching and scourging the surface reducing it to a semblance of the moon's surface— such extreme and vast excavation evidencing evil and destruction! And yet she had never visited the Alberta Oil Sands Project. She had seen pictures of the moon's craters and Obi said the place where her parents worked looked just like that. Her parents had not talked much about the oil sands project other than to say the ground was black and that huge machines, with tires three times their height, dug into the earth all day long, making deeper and deeper holes. They had given Obi pictures of the moon saying it looked like that. They were silent about the project. It was as if something was dead and their people didn't talk of the dead. They were embarrassed and ashamed to admit their jobs contributed in the ruination of Mother Earth and went against their cultural beliefs.

Looking out over the blanket of ice-covered snow, Obi thought Snowbird would have a problem forgiving her parents for their means of employment; they had downplayed the truth of their jobs. Obi felt Snowbird's world was still very innocent of what their people had to do to survive.

But Snowbird was growing up; she was becoming wiser to the world around her. She knew her people had mixed feelings about the oil sands projects and that it had become a hotbed of heated talks and arguments within in her community. It was where most of the people in the hamlet worked 24/7.

The big companies in the oil sands furiously worked to retrieve and refine as much bitumen they could and get out of the project as quickly as they could when resources were depleted. These companies often left the land in ruin. Few companies took steps to reclaim the land to what it used to be. But it could never be like it once had been.

Snowbird wanted to know more. Obi taught her the seven sacred teachings of their culture: Truth, Humility, Honesty, Wisdom, Respect, Courage and Love. Obi taught her by using little story-lessons how it was important to always be mindful to complete the Circle of the Sacred Seven.

—◄—

Snowbird noticed a tickling in her throat. She tried to clear it by coughing again.

"The little people must be trying to communicate with me, playing magic within my body and head, giving me these thoughts," Snowbird whispered.

Snowbird saw Obi's home in the distance. In two days she would be taking her first plane flight. She was so excited about her upcoming competition in Calgary and so thankful for Obi's guidance preparing her for this performance. She said a prayer as she approached Obi's shack each night: *Thank you, Great Spirit for my great-grandfather. God bless his wise soul. Keep him with me until I am ready to fly and he is ready to go.*

# 13

## Holy Angels Residential Indian School

—◆—

14TRC

Fort Chipewyan-
Holy Angels Residential Indian School *(H.A.R.I.S.)*
Circa 1900s TRC Report

$S$nowbird knew the waters of Lake Athabasca well; the lake was situated in the northern quadrant of Alberta, Canada. She had explored its banks as a child ever since her family would allow her to wander off alone and play. She had learned the rules, her boundaries, regarding that grand lake in all its seasonal mysteries, dangers and beauty. The lake and the grasslands had become her friends. She continually felt she was watched and protected by the Great Spirit, the little people, and the fairies of the hoodoos while she roamed through the little hamlet alone. She was right. The little people were right there, the whole time, watching her, watching *out for* her.

Yet, she knew, in her parent's absence, not to attract

attention. She still thought she might be thrown into the wagons and hauled off to the bad schools. Her fears were unwarranted in that respect, though. When the school closed, the abuse became just sad memories—secrets. Those nuns were probably dead.

The bad schools, like The Holy Angels Residential Indian School in her hamlet, had been closed, abandoned since the late 1990s. Just a few similar schools were operating into the 2000s. Those abusive teaching methods trended further into the foster home system after the residential schools closed.

But it wasn't just nuns that had become frustrated and abusive toward these children. It was religious teachers from many denominations and the government entities such as the Royal Canadian Mounted Police, the Methodists, the Presbyterians, the Anglican Church, Roman Catholic Church, Congregation of Women Religious, the Jesuits, and the Mennonite and Brethren. This type abuse had become commonplace, a way to control and assimilate these First Nations' children and their families.

Snowbird's parents—Sakawa, III and his wife, her grand-parents—Sakawa II and his wife, and even her great-grandparents—Sakawa Sr. and his wife, had attended the Holy Angels Residential Indian School of Fort Chipewyan. Being a mandatory boarding school for their people, there were consequences for not obeying the national laws back then and as late as in the early 2000s with other area schools still operating: either the students attended the schools, learned English and the Euro-Canadian ways or there would be dire consequences for the students and their parents.

Obi still warned Snowbird not to go near the school area—a manifestation of his own fears.

"Those are evil grounds. There are bad spirits still roaming the ruins," Obi would say.

Obi had grown up in that school and had lived in the hamlet his whole life. Few of his classmates had remained in Fort Chipewyan. Most had already died. Many had been shipped to any one of some two hundred other such schools scattered across Canada and nobody ever heard from those students.

Obi was the oldest person in the hamlet and the oldest student from that school still living in the area, to his knowledge. His soul had been troubled with what he had seen there and he struggled daily with the memories for almost a century.

Snowbird sensed his melancholy mood at times when that school was mentioned. She was fearful, yet curious. She yearned to find out what secrets that school held and what else her great-grandfather had not told her. She wanted to know the mystery of the schools as well as the mystery of the place where her parents now worked.

Snowbird had secretly visited the abandoned school. Cold chills had swept through her body one day while wandering through the hallways. She felt shadows were suffocating her, pulling her into the walls, down into their essence.

She felt like a truck stuck in the melting Ice Road when she had wandered through the hallways. She vowed never to return.

2

Legend was that ghosts lived there and roamed the hallways of the decaying structures especially during that in-between-time just after dusk and right before dawn. Those were the hours when the northern lights could play tricks on human eyesight. Shadows of figures and dancing lights were seen in the school's hallways. That was when coyotes would run in packs and stories were told of them running through the abandoned school at night when the moon was out and the Northern Lights danced in the sky. Snowbird knew not to wander in such places for there were surely more tales yet to be told and unknown dangers yet to unfold!

# 14

## Obi's Medicine Bag

Snowbird was excited after last evening's lesson. She was a quick study and thrilled to have Obi guide her in the competition details. She had had to submit an application to compete with the theatre group in Calgary and part of the application included writing a play to summarize her research.

Since Fort Chipewyan did not have a theatre coach, her great-grandfather and her Community School teacher had offered to help her. The prize was a college scholarship. She knew she could do this. She knew so much about her culture. The topic for her group was none other than *RESPECT EARTH*.

Snowbird had listened to the elders talk; she knew the problems facing the environment. She had incorporated the plight of her people and the environment into her skit. She was one of many competing in a group from Alberta. The groups were to fly to Calgary and perform their skits in the Saddledome. It was a grand opportunity since the stadium was normally used for much larger events. Each year there was a small window of opportunity to use this space and N-GerDon Corporation had always been given first choice with this venue.

The prizes were substantial and each student would have a chance to win money towards a college scholarship. Such a prize would radically change Snowbird's life. She was thrilled to compete and confident in her abilities.

Obi had helped Snowbird all he could. When she left for the competition, he and Kinoo would have many things to do before she returned. One duty was to seek the guidance of the Great Spirit regarding the bundles under his bed thinking only *they* knew of their existence. Obi wanted to involve Snowbird in the ritual of the shaking tent but knew she would be away performing her own ceremony. He had taught her a little of that ritual, and had discussed the medicine bag, but had not wanted to involve her in the details of this particular ceremony. Obi did not know she had actually seen him with the elders and had seen him crawl inside the shaking tent to do his part. She had never said anything.

"I know you will be in Calgary when we shake the tent. But you listen tonight while I show you important things in my medicine bag that I use in this custom. Then I will teach you the rest of what to do at a ceremony."

"Obi, I have to admit something. I have already seen and heard you in the shaking tent. I hid in the bush. I knew I shouldn't have been there. But I watched often from nearby just wanting to learn all I could about our people. I want to be like you one day and shake the tent. I sneaked out of the house one morning right before the sun rose—like you and followed you. You didn't see me and it was easy since my parents were not around. I wanted to learn; I'm sorry."

"My child, that was dangerous for you. It is not allowed. You're too young and don't have the wisdom to understand. There is danger outside the protected area where you hid in the bush. You need to be wiser in the future. I'll tell you when you can perform the ceremony. You'll be a wise woman soon. Your time is coming. The world is changing and you'll be considered important and equal to a man one day."

"Obi, I forgot. Kinoo gave me this message. It is from my parents. My *Nikâwiy*, (mother: Ni-gah'-wee) said to give you these instructions about the trip."

Snowbird reached into her coat pocket and retrieved a piece of paper.

"My parents are flying straight to Calgary and they'll meet me there. I leave by plane from here. It'll be my first time on a plane! I'm so excited!"

Snowbird handed the piece of paper to Obi that listed her parent's itinerary, flight number and hotel.

"I'm going on a sea plane. Not the Ice Road. That takes too

long to drive, our teacher said. I wish you could come. I know your spirit will be with me, though."

"I hope you'll win your scholarship. Then you can teach like me one day. You will be a big teacher in a big city and will do great things in the future. I'll give you my medicine bag one day; then you can help our people. You will dance, tell good stories like me, teach people our ways. They'll learn from you. Calgary has good schools. You'll win a scholarship and then you can support me! Maybe you will buy me a better fishing pole!"

They both laughed.

Obi placed his hand on her shoulder and looked at her with admiration.

"You've learned our ways, well. You'll make our people proud. Show the world our culture and be proud of your heritage, your *Wahkohtowin* (Cree culture)."

"My child, hurry to my bedroom and pull the medicine bag from under my bed. I'll teach you the meaning of the feathers tonight. It's time. It'll help you when you wear your costume."

Snowbird jumped up and ran to get his medicine bag and quickly returned. Obi took the medicine bag and opened it.

"These are wren feathers. They have protective magic," Obi said as he took two feathers from the red pouch inside his medicine bag. He took feather after feather explaining their importance. Snowbird reached out to touch the feathers. Obi pulled her hand back quickly.

"NO! You are not to touch, yet. These are sacred feathers! Only I can touch these. I use them in the sacred shaking tent. I, alone, will pass them down to you in time. I'll say a prayer first, then, I'll give them to you to use one day to perform in your own shaking tent."

Obi put his finger to her lips to silence her.

"These feathers protect us from bad things, illness," he continued explaining the swisher feathers.

"The fairies use them in the between-times after the sun hides and before it appears again in the morning. The fairies come during that time to warn our people of many dangers. The fairies guide us with these feathers. We sleep and go to a different world. The fairies and the little people swish the feathers across our cheeks to protect us and remind us what we should do," Obi said.

"Yes, Obi, I have heard the tales of these little people riding bellies of the coyotes searching for lost souls; I listen at night while sleeping. I hear the fairies in the trees outside my window and sometimes I think I see them hiding in the bush. They live under mushrooms when the snow melts. The new season warms the wet ground and that's when I begin to see the mushroom fairy circles growing."

Obi smiled as he looked into Snowbird's dark brown, inquisitive eyes.

"You remembered," Obi inhaled deeply. He smiled.

"These are the greatest of the feathers."

Obi carefully showed Snowbird the feather of the Snowy Owl.

"Its feathers are the whitest of white and the owl sighting is rare," Obi told her.

"For wisdom and the messenger," he said laying the feather on the floor in front of him. "Many people fear the Snowy Owl because at times it can mean the death of a family member or someone close to you. It is the communicator, it can bring a message that it's okay to lose somebody or something you cherish; the hard time of life is over and something good is coming!"

"Great Horned Owl. For seeing the future," Obi said.

"Great Bald Eagle. Able to talk with the Great Spirit." Obi continued.

Obi carefully put those feathers back inside his pouch. He laid two aside.

"These I give you tonight. One is a wren feather and one is that of the swisher."

"These are for guidance and protection while you are away. You'll do well, my child."

Snowbird sat reverently as her great-grandfather chanted a few words, then circled the air with his palm and let out a brief hollering, a quick repetitive sound. Then he became quiet. He turned to Snowbird.

"Stand, my child," Obi commanded softly.

"Wear these in your costume during the performance."

Obi picked up two more items: a bone fragment from a caribou and a smooth stone from the hoodoo mounds.

"I'll make a necklace with these."

Obi took a piece of leather from the medicine bag and wrapped the bone and stone expertly encasing them in leather crossties, knotting it on one side and making a loop to fasten to the other. He stuck the protective wren feather and the swisher feather through the braiding and gently placed it over his great-grandchild's head.

"Care for this, my child. Spirits of the caribou have protected our people 10,000 years. The caribou is the reason for our people's survival. Hoodoo spirits will keep you safe under their watchful eye."

"Before I go, I want to know if my name came from the Snowy Owl. I've never seen one, but hope someday I will!"

"I don't know, my child. I don't know if your mother or father ever saw a Snowy Owl. I have only seen one."

"It has such grand wing span," Obi said spreading his arms out wide.

"Like this," he said, pretending to soar with his arms spread wide like the bird.

Obi twirled around the room.

"My child," Obi's eyes brightened as he continued, "The owl's head and body have little black and brownish speckles like little stars in its own universe. It eyes are as yellow—brilliant as the sun and glow at night. Its pupils are as black as your hair, my dear."

"I saw the owl the day the sky darkened and the Northern Lights disappeared. It was early 1979; a big black eye came from the South crossing over the middle of Canada. The little people and the fairies went crazy trying to calm the wildlife. The birds and coyotes went silent. Then they began to howl and the birds that we see at night came out and flew about in the daytime hours. The sky darkened here too and we lost the beautiful lights we see all the time from twilight until dawn. It's the bursting of sunspots on the sacred sun that cause our sky's Northern Lights. They were strange that day."

"But the most beautiful sight I saw during that time, my child, was when the Snowy Owl perched on my front yard fence for a moment then took flight across the sky headed for a tree in the bush. Its wing span had been at least five feet, dear, about as wide as you are tall." Obi laughed as he spread his arms again and turned sideways to measure her from head to toe with his outstretched arms.

Snowbird hugged Obi. "Your hair is the whitest white like the Snowy Owl, Obi!"

Obi laughed and nodded.

"Will I ever see the Snowy Owl?" Snowbird asked.

"You can't trust your eyes. You must be wise to your surroundings and listen for Mother Nature when she talks to you. If you hear a strange barking in the sky that is out of place or a strange hoot like nothing you've ever heard; when you hear the sound of clicking or knocking, like when you press your tongue to the top of your mouth locking it in place then suddenly letting go making a sound. If you repeat that fast so it sounds like clapping—if that is what you hear, you know you are in the mighty midst of a great Snowy Owl."

"Child, we are finished with our lessons tonight."

Snowbird hugged her great-grandfather's neck and gathered her things.

"We have one more night before you go to Calgary," Obi said. "We must go now. I will walk you home."

Snowbird was silent during their walk. She remembered Obi saying the Snowy Owl comes out to warn the fairies and the little people of the hoodoos that someone special will die soon. But when they die, something good always follows.

# 15

## Kinoo
## Gone Ice Fishing

Snowbird would perform soon in Calgary. She would wear the necklace Obi had given her last night. She needed to pack just as soon as school was over so she and Obi would have time to meet for their last lesson. Kinoo needed to get a good night's sleep, too, so he could drive Snowbird to the small airport.

This morning would be special then. Obi had all day to spend with his friend before Snowbird would arrive in the evening. He and Kinoo had special plans. They wanted to go ice fishing hoping to catch dinner to celebrate Snowbird's upcoming performance.

Kinoo Kiyasew was Obi's most loyal friend. They had spent many days enjoying ice fishing on the frozen Lake Athabasca. The sun would glisten off the ice-encrusted landscape. The two took their portable, fold-up aluminum stools and placed them inside a makeshift teepee hut with a little portable propane heater. They would normally hide out all day fishing protected from the sun and cold sitting around a hole they had dug in the frozen lake surface. This was a typical pastime during old age. The two men had shared much time together—about 36,500 sunrises and 36,500 sunsets.

Today was supposed to be fun. They wanted to celebrate and pray for the child's success. But it was not a day they would remember as being joyful. In fact, it would change their lives forever! The day had gone horribly wrong. The two of them would have to make a decision that day how to keep the day's events a secret and hide what they found until they could decide what to do with what they had encountered.

—◁▷—

They had been fishing for a short while. The warmth from the heater had felt good. They shared and chuckled over some community gossip. Even if nothing had been biting, they were enjoying each other's company like always. For a time they had laughed and carried on like young fools.

They were taking turns making up stories. Kinoo had the better imagination putting the evil spirit twist on the made-up tales to warn the people of danger. Obi had always been better with including the Great Spirit's teaching morals at the end of each story. So he kept adding an ending to each tale that gave him the last word, which made Kinoo mad so he would start again with another story! They made a fun-loving, good team, these two old friends!

Kinoo and Obi had been part of the community's Wisdom Council and Elder Council for decades. The hamlet was small. Emergencies were handled within the family, possibly by the one doctor or a handful of staff nurses at the one clinic, which operated on a 24/7 rotating shift.

The one doctor rotated through the territory and was there once a month for five days. Other than that, many people still practiced home remedies gathering herbs and mushrooms to use for medicinal purposes learned from their ancestors.

There was one trading-post type grocery store, two gas stations, one restaurant, and the one community school. There was no Walmart in Fort Chipewyan; the nearest store like that was the Hudson Bay Store, the trading post grocery and supply store (HB) with limited items, not like a Walmart store. The nearest Walmart was 170 miles south in Fort McMurray.

The two old friends had bought bait that morning at the HB before heading out onto the ice to fish. They used colored maggots, which had never failed them; they wondered whether Walmart down south even sold them.

Suddenly, interrupting these old men's comradery was a recognizable sound—an undeniable squeal of their rod and reel's fishing line. The whiz-at-will was orchestrated by a fish obviously outbound like an underwater missile without a destination; the getaway fish was pulling freely under the ice. The two men knew which line the fish was stealing; the freewheeling line on the reel seemed to whistle.

All of a sudden the line pulled taut against the ice cutting into the edge as the line zzzzz'd again with greater gusto. It looked as if the line might rip open the ice hole.

"Maybe we'll fall in!" Obi laughed.

"And be dragged all the way to the Arctic Ocean!" Kinoo continued thinking about their people's legend.

The men's hullabaloo echoed across the flat surface of the ice on the one side bellowing to infinity. On the other, their echoes repeatedly bombarded the banks of the little hamlet, reverberating within the hollows of the abandoned buildings behind them with an unknown audience of long ago spirits hounding them to bring home the prize! This fish would be a whopper if they could just get it up through the hole. How that fish had thrashed about bumping the underside of the ice as Obi and Kinoo reeled it in.

It was the thrill of the catch that was so much fun! The sedentary blood in their legs begged to keep up with their dance. Obi and Kinoo laughed so hard their faces turned red. Kinoo ended up on his rump with outstretched legs straddling the ice hole pulling on the reel! What a tale. His butt was wet and the cold was creeping up through his core!

*Prize for dinner? Not, not this strange thing flopping about.*
Neither elder wanted to touch it.

# 16
## Wolf Willow Bark
## Loblolly Pine Resin
—❦—

Lake Athabasca drained into the Athabasca River, which drained eventually into the Arctic Ocean through several waterways. Fishing had been good in the past, but not so good in the last decade and always more of a challenge through the ice. Kinoo and Obi had had a good day just being together as good friends. They had decided the day would end with them creating a big fish story usable for teaching their people. But they had to bring home the fish first or tell the legend of their ancestors—the excuse when they had come back from an unsuccessful fish outing. The two friends decided they would bring home the fish but not to eat it or talk about it. That meant they had to tell the age-old legend excuse to Snowbird and any others:

> ...that all the fish in the lake had been swallowed up by the big one that got away and it had taken the lake's entire bounty with it in its belly downstream through all the rivers and waterways and dumped them into the Great Arctic.

That would have been the excuse their ancestors had told their people if the hunters had come home empty-handed without anything to feed the family. Then they would have to go into the reserves of dried fish and canned goods. Not bringing home fish or game for the family would never have to be their fault if their imagination in storytelling had been good enough. The stories became more colorful and imaginative through the generations.

Obi and Kinoo had been joking while they struggled to reel

in the fish. They had been so excited. But on this day their euphoria had been deflated.

"Kinoo," Obi said. "Do not touch it. It's bad luck for people to touch such a thing. We won't tell anyone," Obi said.

"Hold the fishing pole and line. I'll unhook it. This creature should not be in these waters. It's a sign, Kinoo! It is an evil sign," Obi said.

Kinoo started to kick the fish back into the ice hole in disgust. He leaned over it to look again. Its two mouths had odd, curling lips doubled back over each other, twisted and flattened against its body. The two mouths took up most of one side of the body. It looked like intestines hanging out. Actually the fish did have two mouths. It was a horrible sight.

"Don't kick it back into water, Kinoo," Obi cried out.

"We will keep the deformed part of this fish for its cleansing ceremony and burn its good part so it can go back to the Great Spirit. We cannot give up this fish to the waters again like we do when we eat wildlife and return their bones to the water in gratitude prayer. We cannot return any portion of this fish to the water," Obi said.

"Kinoo, spear it with your knife and put it out of its misery! We'll cut off its head—the part with the two mouths—and wrap it up for later. We will surrender it in the next shaking tent ceremony when we pray to rid us of this evil. We will also be praying to the Great Spirit at that time regarding the giant companies who pollute these waters. The Spirit is angry with them for what they are doing," Obi said. "We will add this evil thing to our prayer list and show it to the Great Spirit as evidence of wrongdoing."

The two men took their hut down. They made their way to the lake's edge. They cleared an area on the icy bank right down to the barren frozen earth and set about gathering as much dry kindling they could find.

"This day has turned out badly," Kinoo said.

"Yes, my friend. But we have to do this deed."

They ignited the twigs with the Bic lighter Obi used for his cigar. In a few minutes they had a mini campfire on the frozen river bank. As the flames began to burn steadily, they watched the little smoke trails disappear into the sky.

Obi pulled out a cherished cigar. Sacrificing it, he took his knife and stripped it of its cinnamon-flavored wrapper. He pulled his red bandana from around his forehead and stretched it out carefully on the bank to dampen on the icy ground. He laid frozen leaves to thaw on top of the brown cigar wrapper on the bandana. He placed the whole fish squarely in the middle. He cut it in two carefully so as not to cut the cloth and scraped the good half of the fish body off the cloth to the side leaving just the deformed head with the twisted mouth.

He pulled two corners of the bandana and tied them in a knot. He pulled a wren feather from his shirt pocket. The wren feather had magical, protective qualities. He slipped the feather into the knot and formed the peace sign with his fingers, moving his hand quickly back and forth over the bundle. He looped the other two corners of the knotted bandana pulling them through his belt buckle and secured it. It smelled like cinnamon for now.

"*Papayatik*, peace with you," Obi whispered patting the fish bundle.

"*Papapyatik*," Kinoo repeated as he touched his collarbone to calm his soul.

This was his way of paying homage to the deformed fish soul.

Kinoo whittled the top of a branch into a sharp point and thrust it through the remaining fish body Obi had laid aside, skewering its carcass. Sitting down beside Obi, he held the stick over the little campfire. The two listened as the body sizzled and crackled over the flame watching it brown then blacken into a sooty, charcoal lump glued to the middle of the stick. Kinoo waved the stick in the air a few times watching the curls of smoke he created surrender to the sky. The smell of fish disappeared along with the burned out twigs now resigned to plain ash with just a glint of a final cinder.

Kinoo pulled an old handkerchief from his pocket and wrapped it around the small black clump glued to the middle of that short stick. Kinoo found some Wolf Willow bark and resin from a Loblolly Pine tree and crushed it between his fingers and sprinkled it into the handkerchief. He tied its corners.

Kinoo extinguished the last cinder with the sole of his boot turning the ash to a greyish slush within seconds. The sacred lump, the cremated remains of half the fish, was securely wrapped in Kinoo's handkerchief. They had to find a place beside the frozen lake to bury it and pray for it before going home! They stood and walked up the bank a bit where the bush began.

Obi's bandana was wrapped securely around the other part of that fish—its deformed head and double mouth. That evil bundle dangled from Obi's belt loop. The gravity of the moment still haunted them and bumped against Obi's thigh. It was a constant reminder as he walked that he was tired, he needed to rest. This had been a stressful day both spiritually, physically and emotionally. He was ready to go home!

# 17

## Like Nubs of Teeth

---

Obi and Kinoo stopped about a hundred feet along the bush from the lake. They discovered a place where a group of rocks were stacked in a circle around a tree, buried under seasons of decayed leaves and barely visible. The rocks looked like the nubs of teeth sticking up through the icy ground.

Obi stared at the rocks then looked around to see exactly where they were. The century old, abandoned schoolhouse stood behind them, just a shell of a building. Obi really didn't want to be there. He was beginning to feel anxious remembering his childhood at that school.

He turned and began digging into the surface of the frozen ground to make a shallow grave for the cremated lump Kinoo held. That was their purpose and he hastened to finish. A great icy wind, a *(kistin),* blew in where they were digging.

The sudden gust had caught the two elders by surprise and both struggled to catch their breath. They wiped the icy film that had blasted their faces. In the brief moment, both men felt a mysterious presence, a swishing against their cheeks. Both men knew the feeling. Both had experienced the fairies coming in the between times to remind them, to warn them of what they must do. Neither said a word while resuming the task at hand.

The circle of rocks appeared to be beckoning them to further investigate the area.

*Dig deeper, dig deeper,* the fairies encouraged as best they could through the magic of suggestion.

The ground was revealing itself. A slight witches' hair growth appeared on the tree trunk above a carving and its entire trunk began to glow.

The fairies watched with a discerning eye as the two men

continued digging. The fairies were afraid the two men might stop digging in frustration and wander away without finding what they were supposed to discover.

*There's more, look around,* the fairies whispered through the rustling of tree branches alerting the two men to look up at the tree trunk. The men stood awestruck with the magic of the moment.

"Kinoo," Obi said. "We are on sacred grounds, I feel it. I remember now. The fairies whispered in my ear last night. We are supposed to be here. We are close to something. But what? I can't remember."

Kinoo and Obi turned to step lightly out of the circle, respecting the area. Just then another gust of wind blew them backward into the circle again. The last of the ice magically peeled away from the earth unveiling the rest of the barren ground with the circular, strange rock formation. It began to glow. It was unmistakable now that a person, not animal had arranged them and that a bigger force was at work here too, they thought.

"Obi, we were meant to find this place," Kinoo replied.

"Yes, Kinoo. Spirits tell me something special is here within the circle, below the ground," Obi said quickly.

They found branches hidden away in the nearby bush seemingly purposed for this task. They began to dig deeper inside the circle. Kinoo was the first one to notice something being exposed as Obi dug up a frozen mass, a dirty cloth bundle of reddish material tied in a knot. The rest of the bundle still lay unearthed.

"Whatever this is, Kinoo, it has been here a long time, I think."

"Obi," Kinoo called out, "Look at this. This is a knot, tied by human hands. There is something in here that someone has carefully buried."

Kinoo reached to pull the bundle up by the knot when both noticed there was a sewn part around a slit in the material, like a buttonhole in a piece of clothing. Obi leaned down and saw that a wren feather was stuck in the remnants of the knot and it had been purposely placed through the buttonhole.

"This bundle is protected," Obi said as he quickly withdrew his hand.

Obi remained motionless in a kneeled position.

"It has the sign of a wren feather—the sign of our people's custom to protect this bundle."

Obi stared into Kinoo's eyes. He looked down again, pulled the single wren feather from the knot then continued to dig around the frozen mass.

"What is it, my friend?" Kinoo asked.

"I don't know yet," Obi said.

Just then, Kinoo looked up noticing the glowing on the tree trunk behind them. There was a pathetic specimen of a witches' hair clump barely visible above what appeared to be a carving on the tree trunk. Obi and Kinoo dug faster to loosen the bundle from the hole. They left the bundle sitting there and stepped up to the tree that was glowing from within so intensely they could not ignore its calling. They leaned in close to read the carving.

"Are they words? Cree? English? Symbols, Kinoo?"

"I think it's a circle with the English *number 9* carved in the middle," Kinoo volunteered.

"Under it looks like the *number 10*," Obi said. "I see a name here, too, I think."

"Kinoo, your eyes are better than mine. Read what that says."

Kinoo stared at the name.

"Obi," he cried out. "It spells *M-E-R-I-N-D-A. It is Merinda!"*

"Obi, maybe this is where my Merinda is!" Kinoo called out again.

Chills went up Kinoo's spine and he pulled his long, wet grey hair back and tucked it behind his ears to look again.

"My child, it's my child! She went missing from this school! We never found her! I think she's here."

Kinoo fell to his knees crying.

"Obi, I remember the fairies told me when I slept last night that I'd find this place. I remember this in my dream. But they whispered Merinda is not with the Great Spirit. I don't understand, my friend," Kinoo said.

"Obi," he said sadly. "Do you think this is her grave? And that bundle over there?" Kinoo pointed to the cloth mass not yet unwrapped, "What's in the bundle?" Kinoo asked.

"Bones?"

"Kinoo, was your daughter *number 9 or number 10?*"

Obi had a dreadful hunch about the numbers he did not wish to share with Kinoo, just yet.

"Oh, I remember how we were given numbers, now," Kinoo cried out. "I had a number too. Oh, do you think my Merinda was *number 9*? But then who is *number 10*? Maybe Merinda is a third child," Kinoo commented, horrified at the thought.

The two men broke through the frozen dirt with sticks but did not find another bundle. At that moment, Obi turned his attention back to the decayed cloth-wrapped bundle they had set aside.

"Kinoo, this is protected, sacred ground of the dead."

Obi looked more carefully at the frozen mass.

"Ugh," Obi grunted in a low fearful manner as he carefully peeled away folds of aged, fragile cloth. He pulled the mass completely out of the ground and looked at it. The layers of cloth had flaked away like icy shavings leaving lengths of something still stuck to the material as he pulled. He felt another mass within the same bundle. It was small, round and hard. Just as he turned the mass over, something slipped from the bundle.

"Feels like more bones and…"

Obi gasped.

Suddenly through fragments of the frozen cloth tumbled a small skull—that of a child. The material was so frozen and hard, yet brittle when he started peeling away its surface. The separated skull had fallen through the threadbare substrate. Several disconnected bones were entangled in the matted cloth, clinging mercifully to the material—as if to maintain their self-worth, their dignity, as if to hold on to any last thread of hope to prove its identity as once being a human being.

Obi sat back on the frozen ground in shock holding remnants of the tattered, fragile bundle that had come apart.

"Oh my Great Spirit, what have I done? These bones are of a dead person. A small child! This is a skull! These are human ribs? Bones of arms and hands. Where is rest of child? Oh, Great Spirit? I don't see the rest of the body! No legs! No body below the ribs. Poor child!"

Obi frantically searched the grave and found it empty of anything else.

"What happened to all of you, my children? Are these the mixture of two or more children, headless, no feet and no legs? Oh my Great Spirit, help us!"

Obi cried out looking upward in the sky with overwhelming grief—shocked with horror—wondering what to do.

Just then Obi heard rustling in the trees again and a bluish smoke encircled the two men. Obi drew back his head and breathed in through his mouth. He recognized the incoming magical aura as fairy guidance.

"Oh the little people and the fairies tell me the story of this place," Obi said as he closed his eyes and raised his head toward the sky with outstretched arms.

He tilted his head back again taking in all the special magic. The bluish smoke immediately filled Obi's mouth and the long trailing disappeared down his throat.

Kinoo sat there, stunned. He had watched Obi come out of the shaking tent before with a similar bluish smoke rising from his head, coming out of his nose and mouth after speaking with the Great Spirit, the fairies and the little people. He had heard Obi talking like this when he prayed loudly. But he had never seen the spirits actually enter his body like that.

Kinoo bowed down to the Great Spirit in the Sky chanting with reverence. He moved closer to Obi and touched his friend's arm. This startled Obi. He jerked and opened his eyes.

"I was seeing the truth in my mind. You interrupted my vision, my friend. Yes, it was no animal that did this, the spirits tell me. I have wisdom inside me from the Great Spirit and the fairies. These bones were carefully wrapped, protected by the wren feather. This wren feather belongs to someone else. It is not easy for one of our people to give up their wren feathers. This person will surely return to this place to retrieve these sacred bones one day. These bones were placed in this hole under the witches' hair and tree for a purpose. Someone has arranged this circle of rocks to mark this sacred spot so they'll know where this grave is. This is not a proper grave though, not a final grave. This mystery person knows that. They will come back to make this grave right, make the souls, whose bones these are, right with the Great Spirit."

Obi stumbled over his words.

"This, dear Kinoo, is part of a school uniform like the girls wore in the school we attended..." Obi paused, "Over there," Obi continued with horror turning to point to the abandoned school he and Kinoo had attended as children almost a hundred years before.

Kinoo had recognized the uniform, too, but had not wanted to say anything—fearing the worst. Now he remained quiet, waiting for Obi to tell him what they must do. Obi gathered up the bones and the fragments. He tried to wrap the bones. Then he hesitated.

"Obi, these might be bones of more than one student," Kinoo said.

"There is a student number on the uniform," Obi said, pulling back some of the fragment to get a closer look at the number.

Obi turned pale. He could make out the number on the remnants of the cloth more clearly, now. The *number 9* was sewn into the ragged, dirty material. Tattered and old, it was certainly the *number 9*.

"Kinoo, my friend, the Great Spirit guides us to this place, where the *number 9* is on this child's uniform. My number at this school was also *number 9*. My friend, this is a sign I am the one to protect these bones and bury them properly. We must take these bones home with us so we can perform a ceremony in the shaking tent and pray the Great Spirit will complete the circle and reunite the souls even though their bodies have been separated. I am not sure how many children's bones we have, though."

"The fairies tell me to take your knotted handkerchief, wrapped around the cremated lump, and put it in the hole where the bundle of human bones were buried and cover the hole again."

Kinoo followed Obi's instructions. After they buried the knotted handkerchief, the two men smoothed the ground's surface and placed the branches used to sweep the ground back on top of a bushy area.

"The good essence of the fish now rests in a proper grave by the waters."

Obi uttered a quick, but reverent prayer as the Great Spirit would expect him to do. The tree glowed brightly again then dimmed.

Obi tried to ignore the bundle wrapped in the bandana tied to his belt buckle. That bundle held the evil part of the fish. Obi did not feel right with the evil bundle resting on his body as they walked. He had given up his wren feather to pull through the knot of the tiny bundle they had just buried. They careful stepped out of the circle of rocks. They would be home soon and he would pull another wren feather from his medicine bag to stick behind his ear for protection.

Both men turned away from the school and headed home. Kinoo carefully carried the fragile bundle of child's bones. Obi's bandana held the evil fish head bundle; it was tied to his belt and bumped against his body continuously as he walked.

They quickly bypassed the ruins of the school. It was shrouded with overgrowth—a horrible reminder. The windows had been shattered over the years, the doors missing. It was an evil giant in their eyes. Neither knew each was harboring a deeper secret. They were trying to concentrate on finding something more substantial on the ground or discarded in the bush with which to wrap the child's bones more securely.

Kinoo found a piece of frozen cardboard on the ground, stable enough to hold the fragile cloth bundle so he would not have to touch the dead. And if these bones were those of his daughter, he had to bury her bones properly.

# 18

*"Much4ch4k"*
Protect, Drive Away
⸺⬥⸺

**O**bi and Kinoo walked in silence but were troubled with what they had just uncovered.

"My good friend, if these are Merinda's bones, the bones of your lost daughter, she must be part of the mystery why these bones are here. But we do not know when these bones were placed here or if these are bones of more than one child."

Obi opened more discussion as they walked.

"How old would your Merinda be today?" Obi asked.

"She must be sixty-something! I don't know if she is dead or alive," Kinoo said as he shook his head in bewilderment.

"You ever hear from Merinda? After she went missing from the school? Think she actually ran away? Did you hear from her at all after she disappeared?" Obi asked trying to figure if the grave was that of one, two or three children since there was only one uniform remnant with a number.

"The Indian Agents came to our home, Obi, looking for my child when she disappeared. Our people knew nothing. She just vanished. The school said they believed us. But they did not do anything about it. I never knew what number my Merinda was," Kinoo admitted apologetically.

"Do you think the Indian Agents killed my daughter? Do you think she killed herself? Do you think the nuns killed her? Our people were afraid for a long time and never said anything. We never heard from Merinda again," Kinoo said.

"We never talked about her after that either. We were afraid to. Today friend, I tell you. I fear the nuns killed her; but I do not know that. I just saw too much evil at that school. And I don't know if she was *number 9,* but I can't be sure she wasn't either since her name is on the tree," Kinoo replied. "There's just one name there—but two numbers."

"Obi, there are records of student rosters with names and numbers, somewhere—surely!" Kinoo exclaimed.

"Yes, there should be. But I'm not sure where. We'll try to find out! It's strange that I was *number 9* too; and we found the uniform with a *number 9* sewn into the fabric. I have to think about this. I'm not good with dates any longer. I think I was born in 1917. I was told the Indian Agent took me from my home when I was age three. I graduated when I was nineteen."

"I never told anyone what I saw or experienced at the school," Obi mumbled.

"Now, I remember. It was 1936 when I graduated. They said I had to leave, that I was too old to stay there. I went home. It's been years since then. Many students have come and gone from this school since it opened. And now it's been a long time since it's closed. Many students could have been given *number 9* in all those years. I don't think many rosters could have the *number 10,* the *number 9* and the name *Merinda*. What do you think? I also think since I am *number 9,* too, that the Great Spirit must have guided me here to find this place to help these lost spirits."

"Obi, but *number 10's* bones are missing too and maybe Merinda's bones too; there is no number for Merinda unless she was *number 10*. I was not allowed to visit Merinda when she was at the school. They wouldn't let us. I think it's significant that there are two numbers found together in this one spot. The two must know each other, like us. Friends maybe, right?"

Kinoo's suggestion that the probability the two students were somehow associated was reasonable. He thought this might make it easier to find the student numbers on the same roster with one being the name, *Merinda—if a roster exists.*

"True, my friend, if this Merinda person, or this *number 10* person, comes back looking for the bundle with the *number 9,* they will find this knotted handkerchief wrapped around a stick with a charred lump and an unharmed wren feather. It will certainly be confusing," Obi replied.

"Yes, the bundle of bones left had a wren feather, but it was soiled and old. It will be confusing. Maybe they'll think someone burned the bones properly and wrapped them with this handkerchief," Kinoo replied.

"It was so long ago, my friend. A lump on a stick is not a person's remains. They would not think that—I don't think. It might be too frightening to think that."

"Obi, Merinda knew our people's ways; she was old enough to know our customs. If she ran away or disappeared, somehow, she'd know it was wrong to leave the dead this way. It would bother her. She attended the school for two of the *white man's* years. She must have met up with trouble herself somehow. Maybe there *is* a fourth person to consider!"

"Kinoo, we will take this bundle of bones with the feather home with us. We'll go to the Hudson Bay Trading Post and look for the student rosters. It is oldest place in the hamlet. That building dates prior to the school being built some 200 years ago. There might be records dating back 100 years stored there."

Kinoo whispered the Cree word for evil spirit, *much4ch4k*, and drew a deep "X" into the circle of rocks.

"Protect this place; drive away the evil spirits," he whispered.

Obi and Kinoo looked at each other. Obi touched his friend's shoulder. Both recognized what each other's secrets had been. Obi hung his head and tightened his lips trying hard to be strong.

"Obi, I, too, saw evil things," Kinoo said as he broke down and cried. "Classmates—my friends, went missing. The nuns beat me. I was a slow learner but I tried to learn quicker. I remember the hard painful strap," Kinoo said hanging his head again.

"Me too, my friend. Me too," Obi said as he laid his hand on his friend's knee to comfort him.

The two hugged each other tightly and swayed back and forth, chanting and singing songs of their people. As they swayed and hummed, they called out to the Great Spirit to take away their pain.

"Kinoo, you hold tightly to the bundle of child's bones," Obi replied.

"Instead of the shaking tent ceremony being just about the oil sands project down south, we will also pray to reunite these souls with the Great Spirit, the spirit of the bones of the children and the spirit of the deformed fish to join with its good half. We will pray for all to be made whole and good again in the eyes of the Great Spirit," Obi explained.

"We must get back to my home now, though. I think the Great Spirit will accept the good part of the fish body we buried today; it was a proper burial. I'll pray tonight for guidance. We must hurry, my friend. I'm supposed to meet Snowbird this evening. I don't want to tell her we didn't catch a fish. Tonight I will convince her of our people's legend when they don't catch any fish. That will be our story. Okay? We will stick to that story. I will tell her we have nothing to show from our day of ice fishing!"

Obi began coughing long and hard as he wiped his mouth with the back of his hand. Kinoo saw the blood Obi wiped on the side of his pants in lieu of his bandana; neither had a second handkerchief for Obi to use.

"Obi, we must pray for you too in the shaking tent. You must rest when you get back. You're not well. Send Snowbird home early this evening. She needs to pack for her trip. I will pick her up tomorrow morning and make sure she boards the plane for Calgary," Kinoo promised.

"I sent her home early last night and went to your home to see if you were all right," Obi commented. "You did not answer the door."

"I was sleeping," Kinoo said and walked on without further reply.

The two continued along the narrow path toward home. Kinoo put his free arm around his friend's shoulder and gently hugged him again.

"I'll check on you tomorrow. Here is the bundle of bones."

"Kinoo, remember to take Snowbird to the airport! Don't get into the firewater this evening!"

Kinoo didn't reply. *I'm trying*, Kinoo thought.

# 19

## Under Obi's Bed
—◈—

It had been a long day. Obi reached his home, wearily climbed the few steps to his porch landing and opened his door. He was exhausted but he had a few more errands to do before Snowbird's lessons. She was due any moment.

"I must find a place to hide these bundles," Obi mumbled as he walked around his home.

He decided to hide the bundles under his bed. He placed them on the floor, took one of his walking sticks and pushed the bundles as far under his bed as he could with both the stick and his foot.

"Where is my jug of Wolf Willow bark and Loblolly Pine tree resin; where is it?" He mumbled as he shuffled about the kitchen.

He found it, pulled out a handful of herbs and began crushing them with his fist. He stuffed them into an old worn-out moccasin and shoved it under his bed to stave off the stench of any thawing decayed remains and fishy smell. Between the resin, bark and the cinnamon flavored cigar lining around the fish head, he felt that was enough to disguise any foul smell until he could perform the ceremony.

Obi prepared a small plate of dried moose meat and dried fruit for Snowbird. He walked back into the other room with the plate of food placing it on the side table and sat in his favorite chair. He turned on the table lamp to alert Snowbird to come in when she arrived. For now, he would lay back in his recliner to wait.

He needed to remember to tell Snowbird the legend of their people when they go hunting and aren't successful. He must tell her they would have to quit early so he would be able to check to see that Kinoo remained sober. While waiting, he fell asleep. He tossed and turned in a fitful slumber. He struggled with a nightmare gripping the sides of his chair rocking it back and forth in the powerful dream. It was as if he thought he was in the shaking tent praying to the Great Spirit.

Snowbird had knocked on Obi's door a few times. She didn't get an answer. She had walked on in having seen the light of the table lamp. She saw Obi snoozing in his chair. She saw his arms flailing as she approached. Obi grabbed her arm holding on to it for dear life, still dreaming, mistaking her arm for the bent wood of the shaking tent structure.

"Obi, wake up, it's me, it's okay, you're safe. You can let go," Snowbird said softly.

Obi had still been dreaming he was hanging from a low tree limb and that he was looking at a smattering of blue, shimmering light above him twinkling in the trees letting him know he was safe and that he could let go. He was holding fast to the tree limb thinking it was not time yet to let go. Then suddenly he opened his eyes aware something was shaking *him*.

Obi looked up at Snowbird. He blinked for a moment to get his bearings.

"Obi, this is Snowbird. I'm here, now. Everything's okay," she said. She held his hand to comfort him seeing he had been dreaming, thrashing about in his recliner as if fighting something.

"Snowbird, I was dreaming that I was in the shaking tent speaking with the Great Spirit," Obi replied.

"Yes. Well, I'll fix tea, Obi. It will calm your nerves."

"Good, make it hot. Fix one for you too."

Snowbird scrambled into the kitchen, found the bottled water, poured it into a saucepan and quickly heated the water to a boil. She pulled a small portion from the clump of witches' hair Obi had placed on the counter. She placed the clump into the saucepan to flavor the water. She had rinsed it under faucet water, *forgetting she was not supposed to use the water for cooking* even if she had boiled it. She poured the tea into two cups. She put a little bit more witches' hair in each cup, dunked it below the water line with a spoon and pressed it against the side of the cup to release its good healing powers.

Obi took a sip and sighed, "Good!" he whispered.

"Obi, I would like to see the feather of the Snowy Owl again—the one that stands for wisdom and is a messenger of good things to come. May I see the feather of the Great Horned Owl too? The one that allows you to see the future? I'll get your medicine bag."

Obi swallowed hard after his cough. Before he could stop Snowbird, she had bounded like a jackrabbit to his bedroom, plopped down on the floor and had crawled halfway under his bed to pull out his black medicine bag. It was way under the bed this time so she swung around and hooked the loop handle of the bag with the toe of her shoe and pulled it out. She reached for the handle and pulled it toward her. But out came more than she had expected.

Snowbird had hooked the medicine bag but it had dragged two other bundles with it. They were too interesting to ignore. In fact, they were frightening at first. Both bundles were wrapped mysteriously and both smelled of dampness, decay, but of a strange combination of musk and spice. Since she knew Obi had been ice fishing that day, she couldn't wait to see if this might be something from their day ice fishing in the lake. It was too tempting for a twelve-year old with an imagination!

One bundle was wrapped in a cold damp cloth. Snowbird frowned. It smelled a bit musky and fishy. She was torn between taking it out to Obi so he could show her the fish he and Kinoo had caught; but something told her not to. She thought she would take a quick peek and then not tell Obi she had seen the fish, if that was what it was, so she wouldn't be telling a lie. She was curious. She felt a little heady as she began to open it. She wasn't sure the feeling was from being disobedient or from the intense smell of cinnamon, sweet fruit, Wolf Willow and pine resin.

Snowbird squatted on the floor cross-legged with the first bundle set squarely in front of her. She lifted its damp cardboard flap covering. It looked like Obi's red plaid bandana was tied around something. Did she dare untie its corners? Her curiosity got the better of her and she struggled with the knot to see what was inside.

"Oh," she gasped. She looked at it closely. Her eyes sharpened as she studied it. It didn't scare her. It was disgusting and smelly, though.

"*Kekway,* what is it?" she whispered.

She grabbed the two cloth corners in each hand taut and bounced the bandana a bit so whatever it was would flip over. She did not dare touch it. She studied the other side in the dim light of his bedside lamp.

*It was one disgusting bloody fish head*, she thought. The rest of the fish body had been lopped off. She didn't think they would be having that fish for dinner or the other part wherever that was. She stared at the unrecognizable, twisted, cord-like lips of the fish mouth. It looked like the intestines of something. But the intestines were strung out along one side of the head on the outside surface. She'd never seen anything like it. It looked so deformed—so wrong—so evil. She studied it again. Even at twelve years old she knew the fish was not a healthy fish. It looked as if it had two mouths.

*What was Obi doing with it? And why was it under his bed? What sort of shaking tent ceremony was he planning? Did it have anything to do with these things?*

She quickly tied the bandana again, closed the damp, cardboard flaps as best she could to conceal her intrusion and shoved the bundle back under the bed with her foot. It had left a damp spot on the floor. She tried to wipe it with one of Obi's rags from his bedside table where a bloody one already lay.

She looked at the other dirty bundle and wondered if it was the same thing. It was much bigger. She took it and placed it between her outstretched legs and stared at the dirty white cotton material which felt freezing cold and damp to the touch. It looked like the contents were thawing out under Obi's bed. Nearby, she noticed an old, single moccasin was full of herbs.

She recognized the scent as that of Wolf Willow bark and resin, herbs and medicinal fragrances used to ward off animals. She was curious about this too, yet a bit alarmed at what she might find in *this* bundle.

She hesitated then carefully began unfolding its wrapping. The cloth was fragile and old. It was matted, muddy and appeared as if it had been left outside and had frozen—now thawing. Something began to stink as she opened the bundle. Bits of the same Wolf Willow bark fell onto the floor. It was the bark of a yellow flowering tree shrub—its flower was yellow on the inside and silvery on the outside with a sweet musky smell. The bark though, more potent, was beginning to permeate the bedroom. She struggled with it a bit trying to wrap it back up hoping Obi would not smell the pungent Wolf Willow she had released when disturbing the wrap.

Suddenly she gasped. One object she recognized as a small human skull and beneath it the disconnected bones and partial rib cage—skeletal remains of human decay with horrific stench. She sat back stunned. She quickly tied the bundle with the leather and haphazardly pushed the wren feather back through the knot. She pushed the bundle way under the bed and stood up. She wiped her hands on Obi's rag again and held onto the bedpost to regain her composure. She smelled her hands and wondered if Obi could smell the Wolf Willow *or death*.

She forced a smile and quickly returned to the other room with the medicine bag. She didn't know what to think. But she felt she was not supposed to have seen these objects. It had frightened her, yet intrigued her.

She tried to act as if she had never seen them when she came back into the room. She held the black medicine bag under her arm and forced a conversation concerning the upcoming competition trying to distract her thoughts.

Obi was fearful Snowbird had found the bundles, but it appeared she hadn't. She had returned with the medicine bag and never said a word about the bundles. Obi felt assured she had not discovered what he and Kinoo had uncovered that morning. He was glad. He thought he might be in for a long night of explanations. And this was the night before Snowbird was to leave for Calgary. He would not have wanted her to leave without explaining the bundles if she had found them. He still had yet to tell her he and Kinoo had not been successful in fishing that morning. He would check later to see if the bundles were wrapped and tied as he had left them.

"Obi, I'm going to the competition tomorrow. What are going to teach me tonight?" she asked; her voice a little shaky from having confronted a human skull and partial skeleton just seconds before under Obi's bed.

She did not want her great-grandfather to know that *she knew about his secret bundles*.

"I do wish you luck, my child," Obi lightly pounded his heart with his fist, "here inside you and inside me."

Obi pointed to his head, eyes and heart, "Wise spirits guide you. Our people will pray for you."

"Kinoo and I went ice fishing today but we were not lucky. Do you remember the legend our people tell when they're not successful in fishing or hunting?"

Snowbird knew the story. But she did not want to hear him repeat it tonight because that would mean he was lying to her. So she just said, "Yes, Obi, I guess the Great Arctic Ocean has more fish in it now since the big one got away after swallowing the rest of the fish, swam away and spit them out into the big Arctic Ocean!"

Obi laughed, looking at Snowbird's face, still unsure whether she had not found the bundles.

Snowbird never said a word and was now convinced more than ever that something was very odd about Obi not telling her about these things. He had not lied to her, but in a way he had not told the truth of the day's fishing, either.

"Let's get those two feathers out of my bag again so you can see them once more," Obi said, thankful Snowbird had ended that subject rather abruptly.

Snowbird listened quietly as Obi repeated the previous

night's lesson. Tonight, the feathers meant more to her. The spirit of the wisdom feather had already shared a secret. She was indeed wiser than others knew. The spirit of the Snowy Owl feather was still a mystery though. *Out of hardship comes something good.* She wondered if it meant she would win a scholarship and be able to go to college. She hoped so!

Snowbird thought the feathers would change her life but she only had a glimpse of part of the story. Her life was about to change in ways she would have never imagined. Her courage was about to be tested in ways no twelve year old should ever have to experience.

Obi advised Snowbird to get a good night's sleep and told her he would walk her home then go see about Kinoo.

Snowbird walked inside her parent's home wishing they were there. She longed for their comforting hugs and encouragement, too. But she would see them soon when they came to her competition in Calgary.

She had never been afraid to be alone before. She hated admitting she was afraid of anything. Tonight, she felt something was aligning with the evil spirits. She was anxious. She gently touched the caribou necklace Obi had given her to calm her nerves.

She couldn't shake the images of the human skull and disgusting fish head with the double mouths wrapped in the bundles under Obi's bed.

*How many others knew about this secret?*

Snowbird was not sure whether it was the night breeze, which chilled her soul or whether it was the chilling reminder of what she had seen that sent shivers through her body. Her great-grandfather, her *Nimosôm, (Ni-mo-soom), Obi,* had said there was something troubling his people. Snowbird decided the shaking tent ceremony must be about those bundles. She felt light headed again. She hoped the feeling would subside before she left for Calgary on her first flight.

Snowbird hoped Obi had found Kinoo sober and had warned he must remain sober to take her to the airport. She knew about the firewater, knew how it affected him and hoped he could shake it. Actually, Snowbird knew much more than Kinoo and Obi were giving her credit.

# 20

## First Flight

—◆—

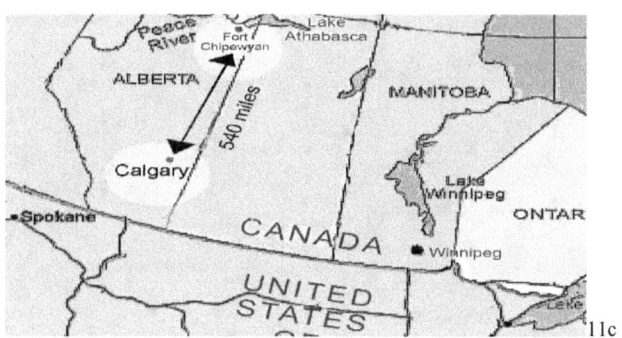

Obi awoke early the next morning. He had not slept well after he had walked with Snowbird part way home and had checked to see if Kinoo had gotten into the firewater. So this morning, feeling anxious, he decided to confirm his friend had taken his great-grandchild to the airport.

Obi put on his warmest coat and walked down to Kinoo's house to make sure his friend was up. He knocked on the door again. Nobody answered. He hoped Kinoo had already gone to the airport to deliver Snowbird as promised. He walked back home.

Snowbird would be gone for four days. She was thrilled to be flying like a bird and her head was glued to the window of the plane looking out over the vast wilderness and seeing the pockets of civilization below.

Before Snowbird knew it, she was in Calgary five-hundred miles from her home.

"We will be on the ground in ten minutes," the pilot announced. "Buckle your seatbelts, stow all personal items overhead or safely under your seats and prepare for landing. I hope you have a wonderful stay in Calgary and please fly again with us soon."

The plane was at the terminal in minutes. A female from the theatre held a sign reading, "Snowbird, Fort Chipewyan-Student Competition."

Snowbird walked toward the woman holding the sign who was her mode of transportation. As soon as they arrived at Snowbird's hotel, the child looked to see if her parents had arrived—they had not.

She had noticed an itinerary in her room which acknowledged *N-GerDon Corporation* being the main sponsor of the competition. N-GerDon had also been the company to pay for her entire trip expense through a foundation grant.

Snowbird read where N-GerDon would be awarding the educational scholarships to winning students and felt honored to be there. She was supposed to meet the other students in the hotel lobby in an hour. It was still fairly early. When the time came, Snowbird still had not heard from her parents, so she left word with the hotel desk attendant, as suggested by her group leader, Mr. Hamilton. The attendant promised to advise them, when he saw them, that their daughter would be in rehearsal for the majority of the evening.

Snowbird had one small luggage bag; she had carefully packed her costume in it. She was wearing jeans, a heavy hooded sweatshirt and tennis shoes on the plane. She hung up her costume in the hotel closet.

Snowbird went over to the window and took in the view. She was amazed how large a city Calgary was. She would be competing with student groups across Alberta; there were no other students from Fort Chipewyan. The theatre coach had visited Fort Chipewyan and had chosen Snowbird due to her academic performance, her community involvement, and her knowledge of the people's heritage. She would be competing in a group comprised of several towns and cities in northern Alberta. This year's scouting efforts had included the hamlets of the First Nations for the first time.

Hopefully Snowbird's parents had had a good flight from Fort McMurray but she still wondered where they were. She had not heard from them and she was getting worried.

Scotiabank Saddledome

Snowbird's thoughts wandered to Obi and Kinoo. Would Obi be lonely without her? She hoped Kinoo was keeping him company.

Obi and Kinoo were involved in a little secret drama of their own thinking Snowbird was unaware. Snowbird knew more than she had let on. She knew about the bundles.

But Snowbird had forgotten all about them; her thoughts now were on her competition and her parents.

Kinoo and Obi's thoughts were focused on the competition but divided their attention between that and the bundles stowed away under Obi's bed that were in desperate need of prayer and sacred ceremony.

Obi had rested the whole day Snowbird was traveling. He had not heard from Kinoo after he was supposed to have taken the child to the airport. But that was okay. Obi had slept all day himself in his recliner and well into the evening before going to his bedroom. It might have been that Kinoo had come by, didn't get an answer at Obi's house because Obi was sleeping.

*Kinoo would have had a good laugh over that one!* Obi thought.

But now Snowbird would be in Calgary.

Obi fixed a bite to eat and thought he would call the B&B to track down Kinoo. Before he could find his little cell phone, Kinoo was knocking at the door.

"Good afternoon, my friend."

"Did you get Snowbird to the airport on time?"

"Yes, as promised."

"Want to see if the HB has any record of residential student rosters?"

"Okay by me."

The HB did have some records. But there were notes in the files that said the schools could destroy records every six years. That stumped the men and deflated their enthusiasm.

"Friend, I'm not sure where to turn. We can take this to the Wisdom Council as a group. That might open up more questions than we want. We don't know where this might lead us. We might be going down a good road or a bad road, one that would be trouble for our people."

"Let's think about it and try to remember those days to fill in the gaps. Let's talk to each other about what we saw at the school. This might help us. Let's not tell anybody of this just yet. We'll also need to perform the ceremony soon because my bedroom has a strong smell coming from the bundles I put under my bed."

"Obi, I have some work to do for the B&B and then later I must pick up some groceries for them. Do you need anything?"

"No," Obi said. I think I'll start on the ceremony plans."

"Okay, then I'll see you tomorrow."

"Yes."

Obi spent the day working on the shaking tent attaching the animal skins to its framework. Kinoo contacted the elders who normally attended the ceremony and told them one was being planned in a couple days to pray for their lands and to stop the oil sands project from polluting their water. He did not tell the elders about the bundles yet.

That evening was quiet. It was day one for his great-grandchild. She would either win or lose tomorrow at the competition.

Day two was equally slow. He had a cup of tea in the morning with Kinoo who told him the elders were ready for a ceremony. Kinoo went on his way and Obi continued with the plans.

Day three came and Obi hoped his great-grandchild would be celebrating with her parents and having fun sightseeing. Obi counted down the hours when Snowbird would return the following day.

Day four came. Obi had not been able to sleep. He had spent most of the night sitting in his chair thinking back on the past week and dozing as best he could. A bloody handkerchief rested on his knee. He had drooled in his slumber. Blood was smeared on his chin. He thought about walking down to Kinoo's house; his reason was motivation enough to remind him to pick up Snowbird tomorrow and to get some fresh air from his rank smelling home. He thought about it too long, though, and fell back asleep.

# 21

## Merinda, the Runaway, 1962

Indian Agents had scouted the little hamlet in 1962. A wagon, which they hauled behind a truck, rumbled along the paths of Fort Chipewyan looking for babies and children. The agents stopped at all the shacks and houses thought to have young children and asked about children living in the bush. They were looking for all young children who needed to learn the *white man's* ways.

The Indian Agent had come to the bush looking for a young First Nations child, *Merinda*, who was eight years old.

"No, you cannot take her. No."

"Move along. She has to go. It's the law," the Indian Agent said and pushed the father aside.

"Father, what's happening? Do I have to go with this woman on the wagon?"

"Father? Father? No, I don't want to go. No! No! Don't take me. Don't take me."

Merinda's father stood back as their people warned him; he had no choice if he wanted to live.

"You will be killed, you must let her go. They will make trouble for you," the band people told him.

The First Nations father was devastated. He didn't know what to do as he watched the Indian Agent take his daughter away; tears rolling down his cheeks. His wife had wandered off years before and now he was losing his daughter. He whispered to the Great Spirit for help but remained quiet.

Merinda watched her father. She yelled his name over and over.

"This is best for you, child. You will have opportunities and will learn the *white man's* ways," the nun had said. "It will be better for you. You are ignorant and we will teach you…and make sure you are clean. We will teach you about God."

Merinda looked at them. She didn't understand a word they said. She did not speak English and she did not like the funny, large white hat the lady wore.

———

Time passed. By now Merinda had attended the Holy Angels Residential Indian School in Fort Chipewyan for almost two years. She was ten. It had been hard for her to get used to her surroundings at first. She had been brought there against her will. She had not wanted to leave her father especially since her mother had gone and he was all alone. But she had had no choice. The women with the big hats had taken her away.

The Grey Nuns had also taken her beautiful beaded tunic and moccasins the morning she had arrived at the school that had been handmade for her by a grandparent. The nuns had replaced them with a uniform of a white shirt and dark skirt, and had sewn the *number 10* to the front panel of her school-issued shirts. They had given her a strange new name as well. It was a *white man's* English name, *Maude Johnson*.

It had taken her a while to respond to that new name. It sounded strange when the nuns called on her in the classroom. But most of the time, she was called by just *number 10*. It confused her. She already had a special name, one given to her at birth, one she had earned as she grew older, *Merinda Kiyasew*. But from then on, as a student living at this new place—this school, she would have to forget her former name and remember, *Maude Johnson.*

—⊶—

About 150,000 First Nations children had been forced to go to one of 200 residential schools scattered across Canada after the 1876 Indian Act was enacted. It had been a practice that had continued as late as 2009 with most of the schools closing down in the late 1990s. When the schools first opened, the treatment of the First Nations children had progressively gotten worse. The program evolved into a situation where these children were being taken by force, in most cases, in a fierce attempt to enroll them into the residential schools or later foster homes to subdue their Indian ways, *to kill the Indian in them.* What had started out as a humanitarian venture to ensure the First Nations children would have a chance to survive in the modern world, being taught the *white man's* ways, had gone horribly wrong!

—⊶—

Little Maude had made only one good friend at the school. That friend had had a tough time. She had not learned to read the English words quick enough for the frustrated nuns. Nor could she speak the English language. This angered the nuns. When the friend continuously stumbled with her lessons and reverted to using her native tongue—the Cree language, the nuns would rap her knuckles hard. Even slap her, or worse, for forgetfulness.

One day in their frustration, at the end of their patience, a nun grabbed Maude Johnson's friend, *Number 9,* by her uniform. They dragged her from her seat yanking her by the ear and pulled her out the door separating her from her classmates.

*Number 9* had looked straight into Maude's big black eyes in horror as she was being pulled down the aisle. Maude had remained quiet, hot tears burning her cheeks. She watched her friend being punished harshly and carried off.

A second nun was pulling her classmate's bangs directing her out the door—scolding her for being stupid. All the other students heard her yelling and crying in the hallway. The unexplained thuds and banging against the wall and the blood-curdling cries grew fainter. Then suddenly everything became silent as if the commotion surrounding *number 9* had been taken outdoors perhaps. A third nun remaining behind with the other children, seemingly unnerved to such episodes, continued on with their lessons.

Maude was forced to say her new name, Maude Johnson, daily and follow with saying, *number 10,* so she would learn to speak it correctly. She did not want to succumb to such punishment like her friend had suffered. She followed instructions daily then whispered her real name, *Merinda Kiyasew*, so she would not forget that either.

The episode with her friend had been imprinted in her memory. In fact, that day had been the last time Maude had seen her friend alive. The young Maude had just turned ten around the time of her friend's disappearance.

Little Maude was smarter than most of the other students. She knew more than the nuns thought she knew. In fact, Maude had seen what the nuns had done late that same night after her friend had been taken from the classroom. She had watched from the upper windows of the residential boarding house. She had climbed up on a chest and peered from the window ledge out over the school grounds to the place where the students were not allowed to go.

The moon had been full and the other students were asleep in their bunk beds. Maude often climbed out onto the rooftop to think even if it was just a moment in the frigid cold. It seemed to energize her, snap her back into reality.

Maude saw something that night she would keep as a secret for a long time, never speaking of it until decades later. She had seen the Grey Nuns burying something. And it had horrified her. She had kept what she had seen to herself during the months that passed into years and then into decades and then to half a century!

Maude began to see other evil things back then. Biting her tongue, she had been dutiful and compliant, but sad and secretly determined she would find a way to escape that place. She had planned what she might do to avenge her missing friend's suspected murder. She would escape when the timing would ever become possible.

An opportunity arose to carry out her plan. She had the nerve to follow through. One early morning she had awakened hours before dawn as often she would. She had taken a deep, long sigh remaining in her bunk bed quietly thinking through every detail of her plan.

She would only have this one chance, she had thought. And she would have to carry out her plan under the cover of darkness when the others would be still sleeping in the school house dormitory.

She had turned her head and looked at the bed where her dear friend had slept for two years. She had looked at the new classmate sleeping in that bed. She had not liked her but had not really given her a chance, understandably. How could she? The new girl had taken her friend's place and had been sleeping in her bed as if her friend had never existed.

Maude had not finished grieving for her friend the entire time the bed across from her had remained empty. And staring at the new student, she had had to come to grips with the fact her friend was never coming back. But she knew that at some level. She had rejected the new girl, and had withdrawn from the others.

Maude said a prayer of strength. She reached under the bed mattress that morning to retrieve her secret wren feathers, hidden there from the nuns, and placed them in the buttonholes of her uniform. She finished dressing quietly under the sheets.

It was early in the morning and still dark outside. She had taken great care not to wake the others. Having stripped her pillow of its cotton casing she quickly stuffed her shoes inside it and slipped quietly out of the lower bunk. In socked feet on the cold floor, she tiptoed to the back rear window. She managed to stand on a chair and climb up on a rickety chest and open the window sash as she often did and climbed out onto the roof.

She had taken one last look across the line of bunk beds occupied with sleeping children. She exhaled slowly. Satisfied nobody had seen her, she had slipped out into the cold. She had closed the window quickly behind her forbidding any cold from blowing into the room that might suddenly arouse one of the students. She quickly donned her shoes and stood up looking out over the vast snow, the lake, the Ice Road. It was frigid!

*Can I do this? I have to*, she thought and jumped. There was no turning back.

There was no way to get back inside anyway without alerting everyone once she was on the ground. The doors were locked from within. She threw the pillow case over her shoulder and ran for her life. Luckily, she had not broken anything in the jump.

Everything seemed so much larger, more ominous from the roof; the land spread out as far as she could see joining the scarlet heavens of the dawning. The faint bluish northern lights were fading. It was so cold. *She must not think of that now.* From the ground, everything seemed so closed in.

Maude quickly ran to that sunken place where she had seen the nuns struggling that night—where she thought they had buried a body. She had seen the nuns digging a hole in the moonlight struggling with a bundle about the size of what she had thought might be a body, the size of a child, a student—her friend.

She could not be sure of it. She just had a hunch it was her friend in that hole. The nuns had stomped on the bundle and had hit it continuously dismembering it with the shovel pounding it deeper into the hole. The nuns had gestured the sign of the cross over their chests and had quickly hurried off.

*Whatever it was in the ground, the nuns had obviously not wanted anyone to discover it,* Maude had thought.

It had not been a proper grave, though, she feared. It was not in a holy place. She had looked at the area often in the days following the incident. She studied the ground from the second story dormitory window not wanting the nuns to see her looking.

Students were forbidden in that area. Play was organized and the nuns monitored where the students went on the school grounds during the day. From where she was allowed to play, she could see a spot that had been freshly disturbed and a small depressed area. She knew that was the spot.

Maude had memorized that spot over the years in her mind's eye. It was on the school grounds near the edge of the woods that lined up with the school not far from the lake's edge and near the biggest tree around, she remembered. She had noticed there was a natural grouping of very large permanent bolder type formations nearby to mark its whereabouts. And there was a great tree about a hundred feet down a ways toward the lake with a good stand of witches' hair flourishing year round. She had walked off the area with her feet and knew about how many of her feet it had taken to get to the suspected location.

Tears had often run down Maude's cheeks when she went outside with the other students. She had never said a word about what she had seen that night to anyone!

Maude's intentions that early morning had been to escape from the dormitory, run to that place, look for the tree branches she had hidden nearby during the day. She would grab any natural tools like rocks and those branches and dig into the earth at that spot until she found what she was looking for, what she expected to be buried there. She had thought she might not have to dig too deep but also knew she would not have much time for digging at all. She would find her friend's bones, put them in her pillow case and run. Just run as far away from there as she could.

Maude had been taught when you take the life of a living thing for the purpose of sustaining another life or person, you must pay respect to that living thing, animal or plant for giving up its life. You pay homage to its remains. Her people had routinely taken the bones of a caribou, muskrat, moose or fish bones out to sea in a sacred manner saying a prayer of gratitude that it had given its life so her people could eat, could survive. These were the type respectful ceremonies her people performed. The souls of those who had once lived were thought to return to Mother Nature from whence they had come. She did not know how to deal with this sort of thing regarding her friend. But she knew her friend was due at least the same and she suspected she was certainly not in a proper grave.

Fifty years later, memories of that morning still haunted Maude. She was still using the name the nuns had given her— Maude. *Poor scared Merinda,* Maude thought about the girl she used to be.

Maude felt safe in the United States, now, and was going by the name *Maude* permanently. She never thought about herself as being Merinda anymore. Maude had grown into a very spiritual woman at 63 years old. She had been taught the culture of the First Nations and she still honored those teachings; especially the completion of the soul. She had recurring dreams, nightmares seeing images of her friend without a head, imagining the howling of coyotes constantly running at night—looking. She imagined the little people riding the bellies of the coyotes throughout the lands of the hoodoos searching for the rest of her friend's body. Maude was the only one who really knew both places where the bones of her friend had been buried. The nuns were probably long gone, probably dead by now, she surmised.

She had not been able to pull up all her friend's body from the hole. In fact she had thought it would be just bones she would find. To her horror, the human decay of her friend had not been bones at all—it was a shock to see her remains. This image had weighed on Maude ever since. She had tried to dislodge that wren feather shaft from the dirty buttonhole of her friend's uniform that night to kiss it—decay and all. But she had not been able to budge it. The ground, the cloth, the bones still heavy with decaying flesh had been too frozen.

Maude had feared wildlife might have found the two graves over the last fifty years. She had hidden bark of a Wolf Willow tree and resin of a Loblolly Pine for a couple weeks at the edge of the school grounds prior to her escape back in 1964. She had put this fragrant mixture into the pillow case with her friend's body. Her people had taught these plants and other natural herbs were useful. The fragrance would help ward off preying wildlife that might smell decaying flesh and dig up the graves. Maude had not wanted her friend's bones dug up a second time. She had thrown a couple handfuls of the bark into both graves. One grave was where she had been able to exhume part of her friend's body. The second makeshift grave where she dumped the rest of the herbs on top of the remains she left behind. It had been the best she could do.

She had buried that pillow case with the grotesque looking remains in that second grave under a marked tree a hundred feet farther down toward the lake's edge near the bush. That unique tall tree was marked with a fullness of witches' hair on its trunk. Maude had carved a circle and then her friend's *number 9* inside the circle. Below that she had carved her name, *M-E-R-I-N-D-A* and the *number 10*.

She had hacked away at that tree trunk hurriedly with a sharp rock. This was a second grave, a makeshift burial place for her friend—under the tree with the witches' hair, along the banks of Lake Athabasca, the base of the tree encircled with rocks the size of a shoe stuck in the ground. Maude was proud she had learned to write in English. She was sad her friend had not learned the language.

She had left quickly so as not to be caught that morning. She had had to leave right then. *She had had to go!*

"Kihtwám ka-wápamitináwáw," Maude said softly to her friend in Cree.

"Until-we-meet-again," she murmured, enunciating the words slower a second time—in English.

# 22

## Maude Johnson, the English Name

—◀‖▶—

$M$aude had had to get used to being called by her English name, *Maude Johnson*, the name the nuns had given her, instead of her birth name, *Merinda*. Deep down, she was still Merinda being respectful of her Cree name. But that was in the past.

Maude sat on an end stool in a café she now owned. Chicago, Illinois was where she had lived for fifty years. She stared out the window, not really looking at anything. Inside, customers sipped their coffee minding their own business. Her thoughts, most days, crept back to her childhood in Fort Chipewyan, Canada, her land of origin near Alberta. Her people had lived in the bush in the 1960s. She thought about the two years attending the Holy Angels Residential Indian School and escaping and how she had been blessed to have come to live with a married couple living in the United States. They had treated her like a daughter. She had been a lost and lonely child when she had escaped from that school, so thankful to have survived the jump from the window that night, to have been able to dig up her best friend's bones before she ran even though she could only exhume part of them. She had to return to Canada one day to finish what she had started. She loved Chicago. She had grown to love her regulars at the café. But Canada was still tugging at her.

Her beloved, deceased mother, her *Koogum*, had told her many stories of the need for souls to come full circle and rise up to be with the Great Spirit. Her mother had wandered and left Maude puzzled as to what had happened. She was haunted by her mother's soul too. She felt an intense obligation to her classmate whom she knew in her heart had to have been murdered.

Maude felt paralyzed sitting in her schoolroom desk when the nuns had dragged her friend out of the classroom kicking and screaming that day. She felt her friend's soul was unsettled and she had felt guilty about leaving Fort Chipewyan. Maybe animals had found her friend's remains by now. She had to know. She had to reunite the two graves of her best friend as best she could.

Maude blinked hard sipping her coffee. She had bloodied her fingers chipping away at the tree trunk, digging frantically into that hole and pulling on that frozen bundle that night. She remembered that horrid quick snap, hearing the crack and feeling the give. The release of the bundle from the hole had sent her reeling backwards in horrid realization that she had pulled her friend's body apart. She held her ribs and skull in her hands and part of the cloth bundle. She realized later that the friend had already been dismembered as the nuns must have beaten her down into the hole. That was why the body had broken apart so easily when she pulled on that morning to rescue it. Not because she had the strength to dismember it with her unlikely child strength, but that it had been frozen together in such a fashion that her adrenaline had been enough to separate the broken frozen parts. She would not have been physically able to do that as a child.

Maude shuttered again at the thought. She placed her coffee cup on the counter, laid her hands flat on her knees, breathed in deeply to calm herself. She whispered, "Please forgive me, dear friend." Maude frowned, fiercely biting her lip to keep from crying as the memories came flooding back. She had sat on the frozen ground, in the darkness of the wee hours before the dawn, feeling for her friend's lower body, her hips, and her legs. The body parts she had found had not been an entire body. To her horror, the body had not been just bones. The body had not had time in two years to turn to a skeleton as she assumed it would be when digging. Instead, Maude remembered—even fifty years later—how the body had been a frozen mass of human flesh, stiff tissue decaying in a school uniform. The nuns must have broken her apart somehow Maude had imagined thinking back on how she had seen the nuns raising the shovel over and over in the moonlight with the Northern Lights dancing in the background.

Maude breathed in slowly. Nobody had seemed to care. Not that day, the next, that month, *ever*. No church, no government entity, no teachers, no parents had inquired—the whole incident was shrouded in silence forever. But then again, how would she know that? She had escaped well after the incident. She had only been there two years; but she had been there long enough to know that days, weeks, two years had passed without a single inquiry or mention of student *number 10*.

*Nobody cared about that missing child—her friend! She had wondered what the nuns had had to report when two girls went missing: student number 9 and number 10. Vanished!*

Maude had been picked up by a truck driver the night she had escaped. He had driven some two thousand miles down the Ice Road eventually making his way to the States. She had arrived safely in the States by miraculous measures probably before anyone knew she had disappeared.

Nobody ever traced anything back to Maude connecting her with her friend's bones, a grave, a death, or any murder. Not even a whisper about what she had carved into the tree trunk, or her name. But then, how would they know where to find her? She had been fortunate to escape thousands of miles from that place.

Maude had heard most of the residential schools had been

closed down some thirty years later. It was a relief to think the Holy Angels Residential School, where she attended, might have been one of those to have closed permanently.

Maude sat thoughtfully holding her coffee cup with both hands. She swiveled her barstool from side to side. The customers always left that seat open for her. She sat in silence thinking about her real parents. She knew her mother and father had gone to the schools. She suspected now that her father had probably been abused in the school thinking back on his behavior before and after his wife's disappearance. Things had just gotten worse. She wondered if that had caused her father to go to the firewater. They say her mother had been affected in a bad way having gone to that same school and maybe committed suicide. Some said tuberculosis. Maude sighed, thinking about her drunkard father and how he had probably wandered off too by now. She was lucky to have escaped all that.

But had she? She had been greatly affected! She had not married. She had spent fifty years thinking about that school. She wanted to marry and have children. She had never had the opportunity. She was happy in the confines of her little Chicago café. It was her safe haven. But she was missing something—a family.

Maude whispered a prayer at that moment in memory of the dear truck driver wherever he was. He had found her on the side of the Ice Road and had taken her away from all that. She had managed to run that night in the frigid weather as far as the Ice Road at the edge of the little hamlet. She had fallen down just where the frozen lake began. She remembered seeing a huge truck sliding toward her with those blinding headlights! The truck had come to a stop and a man had hopped out and had come running toward her.

"I saw you fall, then get up," the truck driver had told her.

The man had seen her running and tripping appearing frantically trying to escape from something. He had seen the look of terror on her face and didn't know whether it was that he had almost hit her or whether she was afraid of something else.

"I almost ran over you, young girl," he said.

The truck driver leaned over to help, then physically picked up the little girl and carried her back to the truck. He offered a rag to wipe her bloody hands and a blanket to warm her.

The truck driver had been in a hurry, running behind on his schedule during the wee hours of the morning. He was speeding, trying to make up for lost time, when he had come to a sliding stop in front of Maude.

The truck driver had said she looked like an injured Snowy White Owl flapping its wings trying to fly away. When he realized it was a little girl, he had told her he knew something was wrong.

The driver was a father himself and his heart had gone out to this child for whatever reason she was out on the remote Ice Road at such an hour in the freezing weather not wearing appropriate clothing. He could not leave her behind but was on a tight schedule. He thought he would contact the Royal Canadian Mounted Police, but that would be in Edmonton— miles away in the wrong direction. His home was Chicago in the U.S., not Canada, and he was uncertain of the runaway laws. He knew she was running away from something or someone and needed help.

That had been 1964 and Maude had vague memories of having told the driver how the nuns had killed her friend. She didn't think she had told the driver she had dug up her friend's bones and had tried to rebury them somewhere else. She still thought that was a protected secret. Maude was lucky the man had been a decent, compassionate person who had taken her to safe place in the States and had not taken advantage of her.

*Oh Great One, thank you for the truck driver that stopped that morning and rescued me. Thank you that he was in a hurry and had to get back to the United States. Thank you that he was on his way to Chicago. I would not be alive today if all this had not been so. Thank you Great Spirit for sending the little people and the fairies to tell that driver I was there on the side of the road in trouble.*

The truck driver had been on a seasonal delivery on the Ice Road to remote areas of Alberta, all the Indian reserves and to service little population clusters on route purposed to replenish limited provisions during their winter months. After finishing his deliveries, he was deadheaded back to the States, to Chicago.

The Weidners had adopted Maude soon after she had arrived in Chicago. The couple had heard from a halfway house that a child needed a home. The Weidners were also Catholic, like the Grey Nuns. They took little Maude to catholic mass   every week. It had taken years for Maude to feel safe attending that church. She would clutch her American mother's hand when in the presence of priests and nuns for a long time. But as the years passed, she realized not all nuns were bad.

In fact, she had finally confided in the Weidners about her experience in the school with the bad nuns. They were horrified she had experienced such things and had taken her to the church nuns to discuss her experiences.

The nuns had been devastated for her. They tried hard to dispel her fears. They were very patient, kind to her and explained that not all religious people were like that. They told her that Christianity was about love not hate, peace not anger and kindness not cruelty. Yet they also commented to Maude's parents that little girls tend to have very creative imaginations and they found it hard to believe her story about the Holy Angels Residential Indian School's nuns being abusive.

Maude believed in Jesus Christ and that Jesus was the Son of God. She believed one part of this new religion in one respect but she still held on to her former beliefs. Many times attending a catholic mass with the Weidners, she would touch her wren feather necklace for the Great Spirit's protection.

Maude had worked in the café with her adopted parents for as long as she could remember—she was certainly Americanized. The Weidners had tried to track her real family. It would have been almost impossible to do that in the 1960s, even if anyone had wanted to try. It had now been over fifty years since that time and the Weidners had passed away.

Additionally, the name changes had been so confusing. In the States, she was known as *Maude Weidner*—legally adopted daughter of the Weidner couple. By 2017, she had been a Chicago café owner tax payer for decades!

—◆—

Finding Indigenous children who had attended those residential schools was tough back then and tough today. The name changes were an obstacle. That had been one major reason families lost touch with their children who had been taken from them, especially those students who were relocated to schools thousands of miles from their homes in another part of Canada with different names.

The First Nations people had had to register under the Indian Act, later renamed the Indian Registry. But the schools were allowed to destroy their attendance records after six years. Some did, some didn't. Many students, later in life, were able to locate kinfolk using this source and in 2016, more relatives were being discovered using online computer resources. But most of these grown students were leading much different lives now. They would surely be lost to obscurity in any search for kinship. Most grown students did not want to remember.

Many First Nations children were eventually placed into white families back in the 1960s and 70s by agencies such as religious organizations and the Bureau of Indian Affairs (BIA). Many children were often placed without the proper papers. These were lost children when they aged out of the program. They had no place to go and the religious agencies and the BIA had to find homes for these graduating students and were eager to pass them on. Most of these students were still minors.

It was a massive undertaking to place thousands of graduating children. The families did not want them back even if they could be located. Sending these children back home from remote places scattered all over Canada was costly. Many anthropologists and sociologists feel this dumping of thousands of graduating students from these programs spanning some 150 years back into society, was the early beginning of mass human trafficking problems in the Americas.

—◁▷—

When Maude's American parents passed away, few letters concerning her childhood were found with their personal effects. No letters from any Canadian relatives were found except her adoption papers dated 1966, two years after coming to the States. That identified her as a legal U.S. citizen.

Maude had scrutinized every scribble and every marking on those adoption papers. Someone had to have contacted the Holy Angels Residential Indian School at some point, she thought, since the adoption papers listed that school. It had been the Canadian authority that had officially placed Maude with the Weidners in the U.S., back in 1966, which was customary and normal during those times.

The date of the adoption papers, though, was well after Maude had run away—two years. Since the schools wanted to get rid of these students, they also were lax in finding the parents. There was not a system in place to handle that.

There was a notation in Maude's adoption papers that Maude had Indian Status with the Indian Registry and was a member of the Cree tribe of the First Nations band from Fort Chipewyan, Alberta Canada. She was lucky to even have such papers. The last name of her real father though, was illegible.

In most cases, First Nations peoples back then could not write in English. So it is fair to say, perhaps, that blanks were filled in carelessly or with just an "X". The signature on Maude's papers had been scribbled maybe as a means to divest from any real association with a legible name especially since the religious ordinances and the government mandated the given names of all First Nation's students be changed to an

English name.

There was no monetary receipt found among Maude's adoption papers, so she figured no money had changed hands, which was a common practice. She had no U.S. birth certificate, of course, but had U.S. adoption papers that provided citizenship. The similar document for Canadian citizenship would be her Indian Status. She had dual citizenship. And the Weidner's will had given her the rightful ownership of the Chicago café as beneficiary.

The Weidner family had told Maude she had spent some time in the care of a medical facility when she first came across the border in 1964. The truck driver had known some friends at the truck depot who had called upon a halfway house. They had allowed Maude to stay a couple nights. Fate had found the Weidners. They had owned the café down the street from the halfway house and had been looking to adopt a child. Word of mouth trickled down to the café of a child available who needed a home.

The Weidners made an inquiry. They took the child into their home in 1964 and adopted her in 1966, two years later. Maude had traced her adoption papers back to the Bureau of Indian Affairs, which back then, was promoting a program of adopting Native American Indians into white Caucasian homes with the help of the religious sector and the residential Indian schools. Those two agencies had been noted on her adoption papers. She had read about the Aboriginal Rights Doctrine, allowing passage across the Canadian border, and about the Immigration and Nationality Act, which she had trouble understanding where she fit into that equation. Canada seemed to view the same law differently than the States.

So Maude found herself wondering what she might run into once she left the U.S. and whether she would be able to return to the States. She thought just the Indian Register with her name on it would give her full Canadian citizen rights. Her adoption papers would give her full U.S. citizen rights. She hoped so. She paid her taxes and felt protected being in the

States no matter her ethnic background.

A customer had found an interesting article rummaging through a relative's attic and had given it to Maude. She had posted it on her café bulletin board. It was a photograph of a family with a white husband. The article described him as a retired army soldier and his wife—a Cree Indian princess and a small male, *half Indian* child. It said nothing of their personal life or the life of this child.

The customer's relative had said he remembered his grandmother living near that mixed *Indian* family. Supposedly the husband allowed the *Indian* wife to keep a teepee erected in their front yard. The article had been hanging on the wall in Maude's café for over a decade. It was posted there to remind her of her roots and too, that she had planned to return to Canada one day. She also felt she might be related to this princess somehow. Everyone could see she had similar features. Maude felt she had heard the name, *Princess Natawee*, from somewhere in her past. *The mansion was probably torn down by now*, Maude thought.

Maude was reluctant to go back to Canada. She felt she had no family members still alive. She felt the duty to her friend, *number 9*, was reason enough. *Number 9* was definitely a link to her past.

# 23

## Maude Weidner

The temporary A-frame sign, erected on the sidewalk outside Maude's café, read "Free Coffee until 3 p.m." No reason was given. The day wasn't special to anyone except Maude. It was Maude's private celebration. Ever since she had come to Chicago from Canada as a child, she had felt *freedom* was as good a reason to celebrate as any.

There had been several articles clipped from newspapers in her American parent's possessions. One article addressed the child from Canada:


### HOMELESS INDIAN CHILD
### PLACED WITH CHICAGO COUPLE


The article was a short human interest story the Tribune had run back in the mid-60s when she had first come to Chicago. It had simply called Maude an *Indian*, the article read. And nobody put much value on such people or occurrences at that time. The story was rather boring. Nobody seemed to care. She was just an insignificant child—only important to the Weidners and that was about the size of it, plain and simple. Nobody inquired further and so life went on. Maude was accepted by the café customers. They adored this bright, dark haired child who was very helpful, could speak English and competent with her chores. *This* human interest story she kept in her private personal folders.

But the article, given to her by that customer, was just as important. The article showed a family of three. That article mentioned a Princess by name, the Great Blackfoot Chief Elder's daughter, *Natawee*. It briefly mentioned her husband was a former fur trapper and a major in the Army. So the café gossip was that Maude had a long lost relative who was a princess and everybody joked with her calling *her* princess from time to time as well. Maude thought there might be some truth in that story, somewhere, but she wasn't saying just yet.

Maude had vague memories of her *squaw* mother telling her about how the fur trappers would come into the camp and traded provisions for *Indian* women (as they were called).

Maude took great pride in her jet black, long hair. She wore jewelry much like that of her Canadian Blackfoot, Cree ancestors: a little turquoise, a little silver, leather braiding in a necklace donned with specific wren feathers that held great meaning for her people. She had come to the United States with few personal belongings as a runaway. The truck driver had bought her a *white man's* dress so she did not have to wear the soiled uniform he had found her wearing that horrid morning.

She often visited the closest library looking up the Cree band names. She had managed to find some last names while studying her adoption papers and comparing these. She thought her last name might be something like, *Kiyasew*. She had spent some focused time scrutinized the illegible scribbling on those papers.

She had looked up the meaning of that name, *Kiyasew*. It meant, *Bright Eagle*. And her given name, *Merinda,* meant pretty woman—that had delighted her. She liked the meaning of her whole given name: *Pretty Woman, Bright Eagle.*

She had been known as *Maude*, for so long now that the Indigenous names sounded odd.

Maude's American parents had written a letter to her one Christmas and given it to her with a few presents. She had read it often since their deaths.

*Dear Maude,*

*We loved you the moment you came into our lives. We listened to you when you told us about what had happened to you at the school. We are a Christian family. We were so anguished when you told us how the nuns in the school mistreated you. Please do not judge Christianity, nuns, or school teachers for what they did to you. They were missionaries only trying to help—Godly people, for the most part, just trying to teach God's love.*

*We are so sorry for what happened to you. Even Godly people lose their way at times when they get frustrated with their mission. These people sinned, yes. The way they went about teaching you our ways was wrong. Please open your hearts to people who try to help others and try to understand their circumstances. When you are older, you will understand. Our hopes for you are that you see the love of God and His people and how His people try to help one another in their community.*

*We wish for you to grow in the faith of Jesus Christ. We hope you will never forget your past and your time with us as the years go by. We hope we will be able to show you love, acceptance, protection and provide you with more opportunity than you would have had otherwise.*

*With love on your third Christmas with your American parents. We wish you the best. Always,*

*The Weidners,*
*Christmas, 1969*

Attached to the letter was a curious memo:

*Fur trader unknown, Indian girl pregnant, married him. Traded nine horses. Male child given back to band in a promised horse trade.*

Maude had wondered for years, after reading this notation, if that male child and the olive-skinned woman in the photo were related to her. The note and article her American mother had kept and the one a customer had given her were so similar in the details and definitely associated.

Why had her American mother attached this notation to that Christmas letter? Maude had played with the notion these people were her people. She wondered if the princess could be her great-grandmother and the male child perhaps her grandfather—if they were related at all. She just remembered her people talking about *Natawee*. Her people placed great importance on names.

She knew what her given names meant. She had looked them up. She had a complicated string of names now though:

*Merinda-Kiyasew, Maude-Johnson, number 10, Maude-Johnson-Weidner…and often called Princess by the café customers.*

The string of meanings attributed to each of those names in succession: P*retty Woman- Bright Eagle, Powerful Battler- Son of John, number10, Powerful Battler-Son of John-Hunter and of course, then princess!* She just preferred, *Maude*.

Her café regulars called her Maude. They were abiding customers for the most part. Maude loved to listen to them while pretending to mind her own business! But she thought they might be worried seeing the sign out front so she just told everyone she was visiting family. Then at closing that day, she locked up the café for one month.

She caught her flight out the next morning.

# 24

## Little Hamlet

1s

$B$ex knew Maude was going out of town and so she didn't have to worry about her needing anything. Bex was now a landlord. That job description had never interested her. But she thought the bungalow might be a good rental investment. At least it was rented. Maude had rented it. Now her tenant would be gone for a month. And so would Bex. Or at least that long; her high school friend Shinski might have other plans for her.

Bex felt an obligation to come to her friend's aid; that was the only reason for her coming to the remote hamlet of Fort Chipewyan. The *North B&B* sat at the edge of the upper frozen grasslands, near a limited airport. The B&B's brochure featured a few, self-contained, quaint and charming *suites,* if one could call them that. By U.S. standards, it was a place that had the typical accommodations for a B&B: bedrooms, the Gathering Room, the Dining Room, and the Media Corner to handle Internet capability.

Bex had had a long flight from Chicago to Fort Chipewyan in Alberta. The flight had not been direct. It had originated in Chicago—CHI by Northwestern Air Lease Ltd. then on to Fort Chipewyan—YPY; the entire trip had taken over ten hours.

The reservation host suggested, was Greg's company's travel agent. Bex was glad the agent had found a float plane with skis capable of landing on the ice. Otherwise, it would have been some twenty-two hours to come by the longer route, which she understood was called the roller-coaster route. Bex completely agreed with Shinski's comment about this being wilderness.

It was not the first time Bex had been on skis but definitely the first time on a plane with skis.

A nice old man, who looked to be about a hundred years old, picked up Bex in a two-tone, white-and-red, old truck. It had a front bumper apparatus that looked like a jungle gym. The front of the vehicle was adorned with curling pipes and huge rubber bumpers. The apparatus was used to pull people out of the snow and the frozen lake.

"Good afternoon. My name is Kinoo. I'll take your luggage. It's not far to the B&B. You have to wait long? Like the plane ride? You're here sightseeing? Friends? Family? No? Yes? Welcome to our community."

"No, visiting a friend; well, yes and no. Maybe I'll do some sightseeing too," Bex replied laughing.

"Yes. You travel light, miss," Kinoo said nodding.

"Hope you brought a heavier coat," he commented as he opened her door.

"If not, you can purchase a heavier coat at the Hudson Bay Trading Post a couple blocks from here. It's the only store here."

"Thank you," Bex replied shivering as she began to realize Canada was going to be *colder than even her Chicago wardrobe could handle.*

Kinoo helped unload her luggage when they arrived at the B&B and then said goodbye.

Bex checked in and found her room—*second floor at the back*, which was an acceptable room but in no way did she consider it *quaint, luxurious or even classy.* The room had a king size bed. The bathroom was adequate with an oversized window seat, but with a table, chair…and *lamp?* She hung up a few things and went back to the front desk, located in the Gathering Room. Shinski was there waiting for her.

The two old friends hugged each other for a long time. Bex noticed Shinski's eyes were red; she'd been crying. The long embrace represented a lifetime of friendship and coming to each other's rescue over the years, even though they had not seen each other for some time prior to the recent class reunion.

Bex saw signs of desperation in her friend who immediately began a tearful rundown again of everything gone wrong in her life. Bex sat down in one of the arm chairs in the Gathering Room and listened while Shinski flailed about in dramatic fashion.

"And on top of everything else, they don't have good coffee in the B&B. We'll have to bring some back from Chicago when we fly back and do the Michigan Avenue routine again. Greg can get us a flight. And then maybe, from there, we'll fly to NYC to see a play on Broadway and shop the major stores all next week," Shinski commented.

"And then we can go skiing at Whistler in the eastern part of Canada and after that shopping in Montreal, Quebec..."

"Hey, slow down."

Bex put her hand in the air, palms upright motioning her to stop talking.

"I just got here. I'm not too keen on getting back on a float plane with skis and going back to Chicago or anywhere else right now. It takes hours and hours to get anywhere from here."

"You just wait. You'll get as bored as I am very quickly. I'm so unhappy here, Bex. The thought of spending another minute here is unbearable. I want to support my husband but I cannot stay here."

After Bex and Shinski had had a little chat in the B&B Gathering Room, Shinski said, "Well, I'll show you the suite. It's small compared to what I'm used to. My bathroom at home is bigger than the whole suite."

Bex followed Shinski as she headed to the room where Bex had just put *her* things. She held her breath awkwardly anticipating a misunderstanding as Shinski opened the door with her key.

"TA-DA! This is the room. Yes, *our* room."

Bex, halfway listening, immediately commented, "Oh, I'm so sorry, I put my things in your room. But the attendant said my room was to the left of the stairs at the top landing. And this is the only room at the..."

"Uh, yes, I didn't want to tell you. We are sharing a suite. All of us. This *our* room."

Shinski opened the door wide and led the way to the interior of the suite. Bex stood behind her waiting for further instructions.

"The couch pulls out, Bex. I'm so sorry, but this is their *luxury* suite. This is the best of this B&B," Shinski said getting ready to cry again.

"But you said it was a suite?" Bex questioned Shinski looking for another door or some trick wall that moved exposing another room.

"Yes, the bathroom is really big. I think that is why they call this a suite. It has two vanities, a window seat, a chair with a table and a lamp. I guess the big oversized sitting area in the bathroom is considered, well, maybe considered a suite."

"A chair, table, lamp, vanity and tub in a bathroom are considered another room? They want to call it a suite?"

Bex laughed.

"Well, I hope there is not another person occupying that *suite* area when I decide to carry on my personal business in there!"

Bex laughed again. She was happy to hear Shinski laugh too.

"Greg is never here; it will be just the two of us staying here most of the time," Shinski said in an upbeat tone hoping that would satisfy Bex.

"And, heck, we can sleep in the same bed like we used to and never have to pull out the couch. I don't even know how it works. I've never slept on a pull-out couch before."

"Oh, Shinski, it's okay. It's bigger than my whole…"

Bex stopped. She was going to say it was bigger than her entire apartment. But she had not told Shinski anything about her new life, new job, and moving out of her penthouse condo, the bungalow and living in a small apartment. She was saving her woes for later.

Shinski sat down hard on the king size bed and started crying again.

"But you'll have to sleep on that pullout when Greg comes. Until then, you and I can share the big king, if you want. It'll be fun. I promise."

Having tried to remain upbeat, she sighed in complete disappointment and burst into tears again. "I didn't think you'd come if I told you how bad it was upfront."

*Sounds like a Greg stunt*, Bex thought smiling at Shinski.

"Shinski, you have to stop crying. You'll get sick and we can't sightsee and travel if you get sick. I'm here, now. And I am just happy to have a place to stay with friends. Heck, I would have been happy to sleep in the bathtub in the suite."

Bex laughed trying to cheer her up.

Shinski stood up again and hugged Bex.

"Thank you, Bex. You saved my life!"

"Hey, we'll work it out. It's all good!"

Bex hugged Shinski again. The two walked down to the B&B Dining Room to grab a bite to eat. The common dining table was set for six yet only five were present.

Bex was used to American food, French fries, Chicago street-vendor's warm donuts and Starbucks coffee. She looked around at the others eating heartily. She filled her plate with little dabbles of this and that and took a bite of the food prepared by the B&B owner. The setup was served family style with big platters of food placed on a huge table with room for everyone to sit together. Bex looked at the meat with a questionable expression.

The owner asked if anyone would like coffee. Bex of course nodded. The owner looked down at Bex's untouched plate of food.

"That's moose-caribou barbeque. Ever had moose or caribou, ma'am?"

Bex and Shinski looked at her politely and shook their heads. That was the meal! They could take it or leave it. Both thought about the reunion specials that night for dinner back in Port Washington when the waiter had offered fresh catch of salmon out of the local waters and the unique entrée flown in from Canada—caribou, moose and bison. Thank goodness there were enough side dishes to sustain their appetite.

Shinski spoke as she ate. Bex listened.

"Bex, I know you wanted to see the oil sands project where Greg is working. But I have to warn you. It is not my favorite place. Anywhere else in this world would be better than that place. I've been there once. I hated it. I ruined a good pair of Italian heels there. I'm not too crazy about going back. But I know you want to see it. So we'll go. We'll call Greg and he'll arrange a tour for us."

"Okay, let's walk outside after dinner before it gets too late, and before the temperature falls below zero. I want to get my bearings and figure out where south is, where the oil sands project is. You can just point. And, Shinski, you wouldn't happen to have a heavier coat I could wear would you?" Bex asked as they walked toward the front door.

Shinski ran back to her room and appeared with one of Greg's heavy down-feather coats.

"It's a bit big, but it will keep you warm."

Shinski was wearing a warm, Lynx, fur coat.

"This is the one thing Greg brought me that has been really nice to have in this frigid climate."

"Wow, Shinski. That's some fur coat. Where did you get that? I don't think I've ever seen a Lynx or a Lynx fur coat in the United States. And you said there were no good shops up here!"

"Greg bought it for me while we were in Spokane, Washington, vacationing a few years back. It is an expensive coat, a really nice coat, Bex. You cannot get anything like this up here. It definitely keeps me cozy warm in this awful place."

Bex read the label, "Proudly Distributed by Spokane Fur Company, Canadian Lynx."

"Shinski, the coat was assembled in the States, in Spokane, Washington. But the *fur* is from here in Canada."

*Part American, part Canadian*, Bex thought. *Ironic!*

"A Canadian Lynx gave up its life for you to stay warm. It was trapped right here in Canada! Hey, there is another tag." Bex read it aloud: "Hertzberg Furs, Raleigh NC, Kiszely Creations."

"So, it's Canadian fur, but definitely a USA design and assembly!"

"Okay, Bex, I guess I have to thank some animal up here for giving up its life for me to stay warm. But I have to go to the U.S. to get it? Greg paid fifteen grand for it. Lynx is better than mink, you know."

Bex smiled thinking of her favorite afghan throw—the faux mink coverlet she always used watching television back in her Chicago apartment. She thought she may have paid $69 for her faux fur and it was wonderfully cozy warm.

"Some owner did quite well in the transaction, I'll admit, Shinski; and if it is keeping you warm and making you happy, it is worth every cent!"

Bex looked at the label again. She flipped the bottom up to check the reverse side or to see if there was a second label stitched with gold thread or something.

*Who would pay that kind of money for a coat? Greg must really be trying hard to keep Shinski happy these days!*

"Fifteen grand, huh? Ouch!" Bex said aloud. *Not even full length!*

"Shinski, do they get mad up here when people wear fur? Is it politically correct in Canada or just necessary to stave off the frigid cold?"

"Bex, don't you ever read high fashion magazines? Fur is coming back! France, NY! Fur everything is all over the covers of *Vogue, Elle, GQ, Harper's Bazaar*—even *Architectural Digest* shows ottomans made out of real fur. Don't you read the posh magazines anymore? You never did! The top designers are dying expensive furs in the most elegant, *tres jolie* colors with chic names like *Pouty Lip Pink* and *Peacock Plumage Blue* and *Key Lime Essence* and *Arctic Circle White*. Lynx is exquisite, luxurious, and warm! This one's called *Lynxurious Lady Gold*."

"Yes, I know about the activists' side of it too; but Canada is really cold. Fur and leather is all they wear when it is really cold. And it gets really cold up here, Bex."

Shinski paused a minute before she continued with a profound statement.

"I think you'll find a lot of things up here will rattle your chain much more than whether anyone will get mad at you for what you're wearing. People up here are mad as firecrackers over so much more," Shinski began.

"Like whatever Greg is doing here…well, let me just say, Greg says the people in this area are mad that N-GerDon Corporation and others are digging for something he calls black cake. I saw so many signs in Fort McMurray stating, *Go back home, Get off our land, Stop the Project!* and so forth. The people were complaining to Greg they are worried about the safety of what they eat, breath and drink. They think these oil cakes are poisoning them or something! Heck, I'm worried. I am wondering how healthy it is to live in a place like this. I drink bottled water and I use bottled water to wash my hair. I even wonder about the meat we just had tonight," Shinski said.

"You mean, what I ate tonight might kill me? What exactly is caribou and I don't think I've ever seen a moose. I just know they are big!" Bex commented.

"Caribou is a type of deer, I think. Maybe a moose or *mooses* or is it *meese* are just bigger than *deers* or is it *deer* or maybe even Santa's *Rudolph*. Heck, I don't know. I've seen a moose in a photo. It is a wild looking, monstrous thing!"

"So you're saying Canadian wild meat is bad for you?" Bex

asked.

"No, Greg told me that's what the people are saying," Shinski replied.

"Remind me not to eat any more wild meat while I'm here. So we have bottled water in the room? Have you tasted the faucet water?" Bex asked.

"No. I just want to be safe and use the bottled water." Shinski replied. "We have cases and cases of it in the closet."

"Great. So we use it to take a bath, brush our teeth and wash our hair? So, no showers then, right?"

"Oh well, don't worry about it. But the attendant downstairs, though, did mention something about using bottled water instead of the faucet water. I was the one wondering about taking baths, that's all. I heard Greg talking about it," Shinski said.

"Well, I can say this. I wondered why there were four cases of bottled water sitting in the bathroom suite. I thought you had just bought it for your bubble bath like you said."

Shinski turned to Bex and responded curtly, "No, it was delivered to the room when I arrived. I thought it was a kind gesture, until I read the accompanying note, *we suggest you drink and cook with bottled water.*"

# 25
## Serendipity
—⊣⊢—

After dinner, Shinski led Bex around the B&B for a few minutes waiting for Kinoo to come back from taking a guest somewhere. They could walk where the snow had been shoveled which wasn't far. Kinoo dropped off a guest and circled around to the B&B signage where the women were standing.

"Hope you didn't have to wait long. I just dropped off a nice woman; she's from Chicago, too. Where would you two like to go?"

"Oh, we just wanted you to drive us around the little hamlet so my friend can get her bearings this evening—while we can still see—before it gets late. Then we'll come right back," Shinski said.

"I can do that," Kinoo nodded and pulled away from the curb.

"Happen to catch the lady's name?" Bex asked.

"She came to the B&B not long before you. Um, forgive me. I'm not good at remembering names," Kinoo apologized.

"I'll ask her next time and write it down. Oh! I remember, now. Name is something like *Wy-dee-nor*!"

Bex asked Kinoo to repeat the name. "Did you say Weidner?"

Kinoo's face brightened and he smiled, "Yes. Yes. Do you know her?"

"Know her? If it's Maude Weidner, she's the woman living in my house in Chicago," Bex cried out in astonishment.

"What, Bex?" Shinski asked, interrupting their conversation. "Who is Maude?"

"It's a long story, Shinski," Bex turned to her friend. "I'll explain later."

"Did you say she was staying at the B&B?" Bex asked excitedly.

"Yes. How is it that a woman is living in your house in Chicago and you don't know she has come to this place? That is strange!"

"Kinoo, she is renting my house in Chicago. I moved to another house. She is living where I used to live. Well, it's a complicated story. Where did you take the lady?"

"Bex, have you moved?" Shinski asked still focused on Bex's earlier comment.

"Shinski, I'll explain that later," Bex replied.

"She went to the edge of the lake to the old abandoned school house. I just dropped her off at the B&B entrance. Then I picked you two up standing in the snow at the front signage," Kinoo replied. "She's at the B&B now."

"Kinoo, if you just dropped her off, would you mind taking us back to the B&B now? I'd like to find her," Bex said.

"Shinski, I can't wait for you to meet Maude. She is the owner of the café I've been telling you about. She's renting my house so that I could take a sabbatical with you to clear my head. I didn't update you on my life yet, but I quit my job, Shinski. Yes, my law career. Maude gave me a half-year's rent money upfront, which was amazing and awfully generous of her. That will carry me for a while. I can pay my apartment rent in my new place and she pays me to rent my old house."

"But Bex, you were making a six-figure income. Sorry, I wasn't supposed to know that. Greg looked you up; he has connections that way," Shinski replied, embarrassed for having revealed such personal information.

"That's okay, Shinski. I just got fed up with big business. They're always thinking of the bottom line and never the little people—the victim! They say they care. But employees are just numbers. The only numbers the employers care about are the ones that have dollar signs in front of them. Don't get me started, Shinski."

Kinoo arrived back at the B&B and the women thanked him

for the mini tour.

"Shinski, let's hurry inside so I can find Maude."

Bex went up to the front desk attendant.

"Ma'am, would you ring a guest for me?"

"Ms. Hargrove, the rooms at this B&B do not have individual phones. Who are you looking for?"

"Maude Weidner."

"Well, I just took some bottled waters to her room and she wasn't there."

"Would you mind giving her a message then, ma'am?"

"Be glad to."

"Tell her Bex Hargrove is staying at the B&B in Room 2 and please call me on my cell phone or leave me a note so we can meet. I think that will do it, thanks."

"Shinski, let's go upstairs. I want to try to text her or call her on my cell."

Bexley tried a few places in the room to get enough bars on her cell phone to make a call and wasn't successful. So, she ended up sitting in the chair in the bathroom suite trying to get enough bars to make the call. Now she understood the bathroom suite idea. Obviously management knew this was the sweet spot for cell phone connection and a chair and table would be useful! *The sweet spot in the suite! Now that's quaint!*

"Shinski, I'm not getting an answer. I'll leave her a text message and we'll just have to wait to see if she responds."

Bex and Shinski woke up the next morning and were eager to see if Maude had responded. The two walked out into the hallway headed for the Dining Room and saw a note Maude had left on the floor just under their door. It read,

Ms. Hargrove—In Alberta too, quite the surprise.
Meet tomorrow at breakfast 8AM — Maude Weidner

Bex and Shinski hurried down the stairs to the Dining Room. Bex spotted Maude sitting at the table alone and quickly walked over to join her.

"Maude, I can't believe we're here at the same time. How funny we both ended up in this place in Alberta Canada, such a remote place."

They hugged.

"I couldn't get you by text last night. I thought about how I should have told you where I was going that last day when I came by the café. But then when I remembered you saying you were leaving the next day. Well, there was no time. I knew you had my cell phone number if you needed to reach me. Since you were not going to be in town either, I didn't think it mattered. Then I find you here of all places. May I ask why you're here?" Bex turned to Shinski.

"Oh, where are my manners? I want to introduce you to my friend."

Shinski was staring at Maude's long black hair, leather tunic top hanging low over a long printed skirt. The olive-skinned woman wore leather boots with fringe, a turquoise necklace and a leather coat with a hood trimmed in fur. Shinski was trying to determine what animal skin it was.

"Shinski, this is my friend, Maude Weidner, the woman who owns the café in Chicago and the one renting my bungalow. I had no idea we would be in Alberta at the same time—in Fort Chipewyan at that! I still find that amazing odds," Bex exclaimed.

"Maude, this is my friend, Amanda Randolph. I call her, Shinski. She's staying here with her husband, Greg Randolph, who is currently working in Fort McMurray with N-GerDon Corporation. He's involved with the oil sands projects. I hope you will be able to meet him while we're here. Oh, Maude, this is such a coincidence."

Maude smiled and graciously shook Shinski's hand. She was thankful Bex had not pressed her wanting to know the reason for her trip. She had not wanted to explain the reasons yet. She did not want Bex following her around, either. This was her private crusade.

Yet Maude had had some success that day and had wanted

to share it with someone but she felt she had to be careful who she brought into her secret realm and dared not speak of what she had found out quite yet. She felt she had located the big tree with the carving and the circle of rocks. She had been ecstatic over that. She was still trying to locate the first grave, though, with the rest of her friend's bones. The snow and ice was about two feet deep and it had been hard to find anything. Maude was there on a mission and still wanted her privacy during her visit. She was very happy Bex was here with a friend who would certainly keep her occupied.

"What are you going to do today?" Bex inquired while the two women poured themselves a cup of coffee and devoured some fresh hot muffins the B&B owner had placed on a side buffet.

"Oh, I might go to the town meeting hall and see what locals do here," Maude answered. "And you?"

"Well, I think we will be trying to contact Shinski's husband trying to schedule a tour of the oil sands project south of here. You're welcome to go," Bex offered.

Shinski remained quiet. She was staring at Maude's feather earrings.

"Ma'am, forgive me for staring. I love the feathers on your earrings. Do they have a story behind them?" Shinski asked wondering who would wear such ridiculous clothing and accessories.

"Thank you, Mrs. Randolph. Yes, they are wren feathers. They protect us. My people passed them down to me. They are probably a hundred years old. They came from this little hamlet."

Maude looked at Bex to see what her reaction might be.

Bex turned to Maude and stared in disbelief. The comment had not fallen on deaf ears.

"Does the necklace you gave me as a housewarming gift have anything to do with this place? Do you have family here, Maude? Was the friend you said you lost a long time ago from here?"

Maude had forgotten how much she had told Bex about the necklace, her lost friend and she was amazed how quickly Bex had put together some conjectures.

"I used to have family here, Ms. Hargrove. I think I spoke to you about my Weidner family in Chicago who adopted me long ago in 1966. I was twelve years old then. I lived with them until they died. It's a secret I haven't told many people. Maybe I'll locate family or relatives here."

"Maude, I'll help you if you want. When Shinski and I return from our tour, I'll help," Bexley offered.

Shinski shot daggers in Bex's direction hoping to deter Bex from making arrangements for that sort of activity while in Canada. That would cut into their time together. Tagging along with a woman dressed like she was and wanting to spend time traipsing around abandoned schoolyards in the freezing cold was not her idea of a good time.

"That's awfully kind. But I think I have to walk this journey alone. If I find something and need help, I'll find you. Being that you are a writer, my purpose here might make a good human interest story for the *Tribune,*" Maude said.

"Yes, but I'm a lawyer, too, and I can help you, legally."

"You're a lawyer and a writer? Were you not good at being a lawyer?" Maude asked innocently.

Bex laughed. "Fair question, actually I am a good lawyer. I am taking a break from the rat race." Bex laughed. "I guess all of us have personal journeys we must travel and long stories to share when we're ready!"

"Coffee isn't good here. I'll bring good coffee back or herbal tea. I found some witches' hair while I was out on the school grounds. I used to make tea from it and it's good, it's different. You should try some."

With that, Maude rose and walked to the B&B front desk and asked if the attendant would buzz Kinoo for a ride to the other side of the little community.

"Good day," the two women said in sync as Maude walked away.

"Yes, nice to see you again, Ms. Hargrove and to meet your friend, *Shinski,*" Maude replied nodding to both women.

"Shinski, this is the strangest coincidence. I'm shocked she and I are here at the same time. I think she's here because it has something to do with a photo I saw on the back wall of her café in Chicago—and a necklace she gave me. I think she's a distant relative to a Princess Natawee if not a princess herself. The princess might be from here. I can't believe how our lives are so intertwined at times. Let's contact Greg and see about that tour before we start thinking about stalking my friend."

"Princess?" Shinski asked with ears perked. She was a little more interested in this olive-skinned lady, renting Bex's Chicago bungalow, now that she might be a real princess!

Maude did not want to divulge where she was going or that she was focused on the Holy Angels Residential Indian School at the edge of the bush near the lake. There were few buildings in the area and many of the houses were old—more shacks than anything else. The hamlet was small but maybe too big to totally walk its perimeter sightseeing. It was too cold anyway. So she had to rely on Kinoo for transportation. She didn't want Kinoo asking too many questions either or following her around, waiting for her on the school grounds or watching her from his B&B truck.

"Shinski, we need to call Greg to line up the tour."

The two women went to the Gathering Room. Shinski called her husband on her cell phone. Maybe the hour of the day and a different spot in the B&B would provide better reception.

"Greg?"

"Amanda? Has Bex arrived?"

"Yes, she has. She wants to schedule the tour to see that place down there and then we can go have fun somewhere other than around here."

"Amanda, I'm not sure you…"

Shinski cut her husband off in mid-sentence.

"Bex wants to see the place. It's her idea. She wants to see the place you keep talking about."

"I'll have to get clearance for her to do that, hon. You sure you want to come down here again?" Greg asked his wife. "You freaked out last time."

"If Bex comes, I think I'll be fine."

"When did you both want to come? If it's this week, I can't take the time to join you on the tour but I'll be able to arrange it for you both to go with a visitor's group," Greg said. "I'll call you right back. The tourism center promotes a general tour. Remember this time to wear old shoes or tennis shoes so you don't ruin any expensive ones again. Love you."

Just as promised, Greg called right back. "Amanda, let me speak to Bex, honey, okay?"

"Okay." Shinski gave her cell phone to Bex.

"Yes, Greg?"

"Bex, take this website down if you have something to write with. Ready? This will give you all the information about the tour."

Bex wrote the website on the back of the B&B brochure she had grabbed from their lobby.

"Okay, Bex, look it up and whatever you need to do, I'll pay for it. Have Amanda call me back if you need me. Have fun. See you soon, I hope. May I speak to Amanda again?"

With that Bex gave the phone back to Amanda and heard her reply, "Love you too, baby."

"Bex, do you have your laptop?" Shinski asked.

"Yes. I brought it with me. I'm a writer now, remember?"

She turned to Shinski and smiled.

"Shinski, I need to get my computer and bring in back down to the Media Room so I can figure out this oil sands tour scheduling. If we're lucky the Internet connection in this room will be working better than the cell phone connection around here."

With that, Bex and Shinski went back to their room, picked up Bex's laptop, a few bottled waters and headed back downstairs. They looked around for something to munch on. There wasn't anything like popcorn, ice cream, key lime pie or

Godiva chocolates. But they managed to find a few individually wrapped cookies and sat down to plan some sightseeing. Bex googled the website Greg had given her and read pertinent parts of the oil sands project info:

*"Fort McMurray is located in northeastern Alberta, the jumping off point for major industries in the region... tours and activities including informative oil sand tours, challenging golf games, exciting outdoor adventures and thrilling winter activities... accessible by land or air... take time to tour the Athabasca oil sands also known to be a piece of prehistoric history dating back 110 million years. A mixture of sand, water and bitumen, the oil sands hold a potential 300 billion barrels of recoverable bitumen with today's available technologies. The tours also look at the restoration process...after the bitumen, often called, black cakes, has been removed and the sand is reclaimed by the earth..."*

Bex turned the computer screen around so Shinski could see the images.

"I've seen them already," Shinski replied after a quick glance.

"Shinski, this place is gigantic—like the moon's surface!*"*

Within an hour, Greg had called back and had given Bex the information for the tour.

"Okay. Bexley, I've made the arrangements for you two to pick up tour tickets at the gate day after tomorrow..."

"Oh, Wow. I told Shinski you couldn't get anywhere from here but I guess I'm wrong."

"Well, if you have a private jet, you can travel pretty quickly anywhere up here. N-GerDon Corporation has private company jets that are used to hopping around between main hubs like a taxi. We have to coordinate who's going where but it works pretty well. And I just happen to fit you two in for day after tomorrow. I have left an itinerary on your email. So see if you can pull that up, look at it and get back to me, I would appreciate it. I have some company business to attend to in Calgary during the same time. So I just wanted to make sure everything is taken care of with you two before I leave. I'll meet you at the tour gate and visit for a few minutes before I have to leave. Call me after reading the email."

Shinski was listening to the plans.

"I hope Fort McMurray has a Starbucks and good restaurants."

"You know, Shinski. I was laughing that Starbucks was truly on target setting up cafés on every corner in America. But I'll have to tell their Mr. CEO, Howard Schultz, they missed a corner—Maude's Café, in Chicago and I doubt there's one in Fort Chipewyan or Fort McMurray. He must not be talking about all of North America!" Bex scrolled down through more info on the computer.

"Hey, Shinski, I take that back, I just googled it. They do have a Starbucks in Fort McMurray and guess what? It's on Hargrove Street! OMG! How coincidental is that? Maybe I have relatives in Canada that I don't know about!"

They laughed. Bex read the email Greg sent her. It was a great itinerary. She called Greg to confirm.

Two days later, the women were on an N-GerDon company jet hopping over to Fort McMurray. Kinoo had taken them to the airport and it was as simple as that. They took just a few items with them and Shinski was wearing sneakers! When the plane landed, the first place Bex and Shinski went, by taxi, was to get a latte at the Starbucks on Hargrove!

"Well," Bex had noted. "I am impressed with the names of the streets in Fort McMurray, Canada!"

Shinski had received a text message from Greg that after the tour, the company limo driver would be able to take them wherever they wanted to go. But it would not be available until after their tour.

Bex and Shinski were to be gone for just a couple of days.

Kinoo had watched the women board the company plane and said they should call the B&B when they returned so Kinoo could pick them up. Getting around in the remote areas of Canada was pretty easy if you knew the right people, Bex teased Shinski *as the princess of the oil sands who had access to private jets!*

No sooner had their jet taken off than a smaller one landed. Kinoo received a buzz from the B&B. Another visitor to the community had just arrived at the airport. Kinoo had seen the plane land. He remained at the airport looking for his new passenger.

# 26

### David Drury- Detective for Hire
### Royal Canadian Mounted Police
### *RCMP*

—⊪—

David Drury, a detective, was a freelance case worker often assisting the Royal Canadian Mounted Police, *RCMP*. He was usually contacted when there were special projects that might involve complicated issues in remote parts of Canada, too involved for the RCMP to handle efficiently. He had been assigned to the Calgary car accident involving the Sakawa family and N-GerDon Corporation employees. Coincidentally they all had connections to the little hamlet of Fort Chipewyan in the northern remote area of Alberta.

It had been about a six hour flight from Calgary to Fort Chipewyan. First on his list of things to do was to find the elderly Mr. Obigon Sakawa Sr., who was about a hundred years old. Drury feared he would be senile and unfit to be a guardian for a minor child also assigned to him.

Drury had compiled a list of people involved in the case. He had been instructed to find the next of kin to the deceased Sakawa couple (*Mr. Obigon Sakawa III and his wife*) and two more relatives with the same name. At that point he would proceed with finding custody resolution for the minor child,

Snowbird Sakawa. The case involved the First Nations culture.

The hamlet of Fort Chipewyan was even smaller than Drury expected as he looked out the window of the plane. Upon landing, David had contacted the North B&B's front desk attendant. He had been instructed to ask for a Mr. Kinoo, the driver, to transport him to the North B&B.

It had not taken Kinoo long to spot his passenger and help him with his luggage. He was the one looking for Kinoo's red and white truck. In fact, Mr. Drury found him!

"Where are you from?" Kinoo asked Mr. Drury trying to be friendly.

"Calgary. Here on business."

"Oh. I dropped off a child last week and watched her board her first plane flight to Calgary to attend a student competition."

"From here?" Drury asked.

"Yes, she's the great-grandchild of my friend, Obi. We have not heard from her in several days. But we hope she won her scholarship."

"You work for the B&B? Did you say your name was Mr. Kinoo?"

"Yes. If you need to go someplace, you call the B&B and they will buzz my beeper. I'll pick you up. My name is just Kinoo. I'm easy to find. Our little community is not that big."

"Okay, Kinoo," Drury noted.

"What's your friend's last name?"

"Sakawa."

"Is it Obigon Sakawa? Is he about a hundred years old?"

"Yes, he is the oldest and wisest in the community. You know him?"

"No, but he is one of the people I have come to see."

"Well, I need to pick up another person after I drop you off. I can take you to see him when you are ready."

"Great." The two drove on in silence.

David Drury had made his first contact in the case. This had to be the minor child connection. *This will be easier than I thought,* he decided.

"We have arrived. I'll help you. Then I have to go pick up a woman at the school grounds. She's staying at the B&B, too. Her name is Maude. She's from the United States. I'm the only taxi driver around so, I must go pick her up and bring her back. Maybe you two will make friends while you're here? Yes?"

"That would be great. I'm here on business but I think it will be an extended stay. It would be nice to have other people to talk with."

Kinoo left Mr. Drury at the B&B and headed to the school.

Mr. Drury settled in and busied himself working on the details of the case. He figured he might be bringing sad news to families. He wanted to brush up on some cultural details and review pertinent words in the First Nations Cree language. This was a complicated case. But he had his first contact, Kinoo, and they would talk again soon to arrange to see Mr. Obigon Sakawa. He would prepare his papers and buzz the front desk to contact Kinoo and then ask him if he would drive him to Mr. Sakawa's home.

---

Obi had not heard from his great-granddaughter; it had been days since the competition. He knew she had planned to go sightseeing with her parents the day after the competition and then return to Fort Chipewyan. Her parents would fly back to Fort McMurray. But neither Obi nor Kinoo had heard a word from anyone regarding the competition or when to pick up Snowbird from the airport. Communication was scant at best in these remote areas. Kinoo and Obi figured she and her parents decided to stay a few more days and if she won, maybe there were other things she had to do regarding that. They weren't worried yet but eager to know the outcome of the competition.

Obi rose early this morning. He prayed to the Great Spirit hoping for the safe return of his great-granddaughter and Snowbird's parents. His grandson, Sakawa III and his wife, should have returned to work in Fort McMurray by now, Obi thought. All the festivities were over and whatever the outcome, he would be proud of his great-grandchild.

Obi and Kinoo had always enjoyed a morning routine spending time over a cup of coffee or tea. Obi had buzzed Kinoo and had not yet heard from him. He knew he probably had a few guests to transport on his taxi route. The community was less than four square miles. The two customers Kinoo had taxied to the airport a few days ago had been Ms. Hargrove and Mrs. Randolph. Earlier this morning, Kinoo had taken Ms. Weidner again to the edge of town to the school grounds. She had told Kinoo she would stay for a good part of the day. Obi didn't know there was a new guest in the community that had just arrived.

*No matter that Kinoo is late. He must be busy*, Obi thought, as he sat alone sipping his tea.

There was a knock at the door. Obi had never known Kinoo to knock. He got up from the table and looked through the window and saw a strange man standing on his porch—looking right at him. He was holding an official looking document in his hand. Obi thought he knew everyone in the little hamlet. He did not know this person; Obi opened the door anyway.

"Looks important, sir," Obi said as he nodded to the man.

The man shuttled quickly past Obi into the room eager to get out of the cold.

"Sorry for barging in on you, but it is so cold standing out there. I think snow is two feet deep and frozen solid," Mr. Drury admitted explaining his intrusion.

"Yes, I don't go out much," Obi said as he motioned for the man to sit down.

"Sir, your friend, Kinoo, dropped me off and said he had to transport someone to the school and would be back to join us soon."

"He didn't tell me I would have a visitor. Care for some tea?" Obi asked.

"Yes, hot," the man replied. "I'm from Calgary and it is just as cold there but somehow the winds coming off the frozen lake here seem to make this part of Alberta feel much colder!"

Obi fixed the stranger a cup of hot tea.

"Why are you here?"

"Obigon Sakawa Sr.?" the man asked as he stood to read the document he had brought.

"Yes, there are three of us by that same name still living." Obi managed to make humor of his name sakes. He was the senior Obi having two other family relatives with the same name, his son, the II (*the drunk*) and his grandson, the III, Snowbird's father. He immediately wondered whether this man was here to notify him that his drunkard son had been injured, died, or found frozen to death. He feared trouble.

"Sir," the man said a bit shaken by Obi's last comment that seemed to be making fun of his relatives.

"Uh, sir, my name is David Drury. I'm here on behalf of the Royal Canadian Mounted Police with some regretful news. You are next of kin, I suppose, to a Mr. and Mrs. Obigon Sakawa III of Fort Chipewyan. They were employed by N-GerDon Corporation in Fort McMurray?"

Obi stood there, sighing heavily, and feeling confused. It was not his drunkard son he was talking about.

"Sir, did you hear what I said? Can you hear okay?" The stranger was confused now trying to figure if the old man could hear or maybe there was another reason for no response. He scrutinized Obi trying to determine his age—*definitely over eighty years old for sure.*

"My son is a drunkard, gone for months. No telling if he is alive. Do you speak of my son or grandson?" Obi asked.

The official looked even more confused. He went on with his duty to advise next of kin.

"Sir, does he work in Fort McMurray? I regret to inform you that…" David Drury started again with purposed resolve.

Obi staggered a bit as the man read more of the official document. He realized the stranger was talking about his grandson who worked in the oil sands. Then it hit him the stranger had also mentioned his grandson's wife—this was Snowbird's parents. *Both of them!*

Obi slumped into his favorite over-stuffed chair with the comforting, padded arms. He listened as the official read that the couple had been killed in a car accident three days ago in Calgary.

In those split seconds, Obi tried to process this man's news. Was his entire family dead? The stranger further explained that contact information had not been readily available. And since the accident happened five hundred miles away, and the victims had listed two addresses: a temporary one in Fort McMurray and a permanent address in Fort Chipewyan, and having so many individuals with the same name, it had been difficult to identify and contact family members.

The stranger continued, "Their car was broadsided and had caught fire. Sir, emergency teams were not successful. The flames engulfed the car and the victims. This is not the normal manner to communicate such things. Normally, a doctor at the hospital or a policeman would call a family member to meet our officials. Being as remote as this is, we had to improvise. I am so sorry to come to you in this way. I had hoped your friend, Kinoo, might be here with us while I delivered this news."

The official paused. Obi motioned with one hand, waving it circles to continue on with what had happened as he stared at the floor.

"It had been difficult to identify the bodies until the family could be located. Sir, I am sorry for your loss. Your age was noted in the report but…"

"Snowbird?" Obi suddenly yelled. "Is she alive?"

"Is she your daughter, or, uh, your great-granddaughter, sir?"

The official frantically searched for that information as Obi spoke.

"Yes, my great-granddaughter," Obi said.

"Yes, she is alive and was not involved in the accident."

"Oh, I give thanks O' Great Spirit. Thank you."

"Yes, but Miss Snowbird is a minor child. The law prohibits a minor child, for her welfare, from physically identifying the bodies or being involved in this type investigation since the bodies were burned beyond recognition. I am so sorry."

"Since she is First Nations decent, there are additional legal and cultural considerations. Miss Snowbird was able to give us enough information of her parent's itinerary that checked out with their flight arrangements, a car rental and hotel reservations found in the name, *Sakawa, III*. Sir, I am so sorry about all this detail."

"This is also a fact-finding mission. Fault has been determined. I'm here on the behalf of the child, too, finding out about your living arrangements and to confirm identities. I've been instructed to follow up with N-GerDon Corporation that employed your grandson and his wife. There will be additional paperwork needed to transport the bodies. And there will be insurance claims; I can help you regarding the requirements of the province and your people's council."

"Sir, it is good to have a friend who can comfort you in this time of need while I discuss this. Is your friend, Kinoo your caretaker, someone who stays with you? Does he handle your affairs?"

"Sir, I can take care of myself. I can also take care of Snowbird. Her parents work far away."

Obi slumped again.

"*She has no parents now*," Obi whispered to himself.

"Snowbird is a student. She hoped to win a scholarship to college. The competition was in Calgary. And you said you are from Calgary?"

"Yes, sir, I've been dispatched to inform you of the accident. I don't know anything about whether the child won a scholarship or not. I'm here to assist in the funeral details as well as confirm the identities of the bodies, and placement of the child. I can help you with the customs of your people regarding the deaths. I'm here to determine who will be the legal guardian of the child. I'm an assistant assigned to you in this situation and your people's Wisdom Council has also been notified."

"I'm *on* the Wisdom Council," Obi whispered.

"The parents traveled to Calgary to see their daughter perform," Obi mentioned again.

"Sir, I'm here to find out as much as I can. Right now, I can't answer all your questions," Drury said.

"Sir, we need signatures that allow us to take care of details making sure we abide by the customs of your people and Canadian law."

Obi sat tall and straight in his chair looking the young man dead in the eyes, listening more intently.

Drury's face was drawn and solemn but he continued.

"When the minor child's parents did not show up to see their daughter's performance, the child informed her theatre coach. The theatre coach contacted the stadium security who eventually contacted the Royal Canadian Mounted Police. They could not locate the parents either. It seems the car accident had taken place just outside the Scotiabank-Saddledome where the student competition was being held. It was unknown at the time the fatalities in the accident involved the child's parents."

Obi reached across the table for the written itinerary Snowbird had given him. It had all the necessary information regarding flight numbers and hotel accommodations.

"Sir, calls were made to nearby hospitals trying to locate the child's parents. Due to the complicated nature of the case, the Calgary City Police contacted the Edmonton RCMP. They have a working relationship with Calgary Child Welfare. They took the child in temporarily. It would be best for the female child to remain there for a while, sir, uh, due to her age and *your* age. She will be staying in a residential school until we can sort this out. I was brought into the situation at that point."

The man pointed to another document.

"Sir, there are some more papers we must sign now."

ANNE MICHAEL

The detective looked at Obi who was obviously distraught.

"Sir, Child Welfare *will* take care of the child, I promise."

Obi sat dumbfounded looking up at the man.

"It's in the best interest of the minor child that she stays in the residential school," the man reiterated.

Obi went white. "NO! NO! She will not go there! No. Not ever! *Please!*"

Obi cried out to the man, "Sir, my good friend, Kinoo will be here soon. He will agree with me! I will not speak to you any more on this matter. You do not know what's best for my little Snowbird's future."

Obi began to tremble.

"She is my blood. She belongs here with our people. I know nothing of this school where you've taken her. She's a special child, very talented. She has a good future. She will not survive in those bad residential schools. NO! You will not take her there."

Obi began coughing up blood and bent over in pain. He cried softly holding his side and wiping the saliva drooling from his mouth.

Drury sat silently. He was trying to be professional, courteous and compassionate. But this was a new experience for him, too. He thought the old man might die right in front of him. He waited for Obi to speak.

Obi thought about the school of his childhood. He did not know whether the schools today were any different. He was crushed thinking Snowbird might now be in a type school like he had attended; he had worked so hard to prevent that.

"Sir, I was not allowed to bring your great-grandchild with me without knowing your health or whether you could care for her properly since both parents are now deceased."

"Yes, it appears you are not an invalid, but you are living alone and please forgive me, but you appear to be quite ill at the present time."

The detective had seen the blood on the side of Obi's mouth after his coughing spell. Obi seemed to be in pain.

"Sir, is your friend coming back? You need medical assistance. I am here to help. Should we call him?"

At that moment, Kinoo, Obi's friend, opened the door. He called out softly to announce his arrival.

"Sorry I'm late. Any more tea left?"

Kinoo felt tremendous tension in the air. He looked at the stranger then Obi, who was leaning forward and groaning softly. He saw blood on Obi's mouth.

"Obi, my friend, are you hurt or in pain? Do you need to go to the clinic?"

Kinoo turned to the stranger for explanation.

"You said you needed to talk with my friend. Why are you here, sir? I forgot to ask you when I dropped you off. You have obviously upset my friend."

The man shook his head helplessly as he looked at Kinoo then Obi. He tried pulling the document gently from under Obi's leg. Obi grew angry and leaned forward to keep the man from retrieving it.

Obi caught his breath and said, "NO, you cannot take the child."

"Obi, take who? Are you hurt?"

Kinoo was stunned and confused. He turned to the man demanding to know what was going on.

"My friend is angry. That makes me angry, too. State your business, sir, or go."

"My name is David Drury. I am a detective and have been hired as a case worker for the Royal Canadian Mounted Police. I'm here on official business and I have given your friend a next-of-kin notification of the deaths of Mr. and Mrs. Obigon Sakawa III. Normally, this is not how this is done. But this is a complicated case. It involves numerous individuals living in Fort Chipewyan. Due to the remote nature of the area, I have been sent to investigate this case and facilitate a resolution. This involves a minor child and her parents. It involves First Nations customs. And I need to confirm associations with N-GerDon Corporation."

Kinoo slumped into the chair beside Obi.

"Next of kin? Fatalities? You mean killed? Does that mean the child and her parents?" Kinoo asked.

Kinoo could see Obi had collapsed under the news.

"Sir, I need to get my friend to the clinic. Give me the papers and I'll read them at the clinic," Kinoo demanded.

"Sir, the child is in a residential school. We need to obtain your signatures *here* and *here…*"

As soon as Kinoo heard the words, "*residential school,*" he bent over collapsing his head into his palms. He shook his head back and forth then looked up quickly. He had to be strong for his friend. Both men were too old to receive this type emotional news. He had to find courage and seek medical attention for his friend, Obi.

"Sir," Kinoo replied, "I must take my friend to the clinic. I can't sign papers now. Dr. Pathway is only here certain times. We must go to the Nunee Nurses Station. Now! They'll see Obi. I have the truck outside. I'll take your letter with me. Where do *you* want to go? I'll take you back to the B&B."

"Sir, that's fine but I do need to bring you up to speed with this case. There were two deaths involved. Another man is critically injured in a hospital and the child…uh, I need you to sign this release form so I can reveal the details of this case with you. You are not related and your friend here is incapacitated."

The man spoke louder with more authority insisting Kinoo sign the document. Kinoo quickly looked at the single page document, which the man had just read to him, and scribbled an "X" on the form. Obi clung to Drury and Kinoo as they assisted in getting Obi into the truck. Drury used the time riding in the truck to continue updating the two men; his time for questioning would be cut short with Obi's medical condition.

"Kinoo, another N-GerDon employee, critically injured, has been admitted to the Foothills Hospital in Calgary. Obi, your relatives have been sent to the morgue in Calgary. The child is in the custody of the Calgary Child Welfare temporarily assigned to a residential school there. Here is my card with my contact information number—it is my cell phone. It also lists the number for the RCMP, the Calgary Morgue, N-GerDon Corporation—if you should need that, Calgary Child Welfare and the residential school. Again, I am here to assist you with all the details of the burials and through any legal matters. You will need me. I apologize for being so blunt with my delivery. This is a complicated case and I needed to tell you as much as I could. I am so sorry about your loss. Truly. Again, I apologize if I have come across insincere or unsympathetic. I have traveled a long distance to get here and have been authorized to assist you in any way I can. I can also be a mediator with the N-GerDon Corporation and can help with your Wisdom Council intervention. I will be staying at the B&B. Contact me as soon as you can so we can get started with protocols and procedures. Mr. Obi, I hope the clinic can help you. I am truly sorry for your losses and we will take care of the child."

Kinoo dropped Drury at the B&B.

"Kinoo, so we will plan to meet tomorrow, is that correct?"

Kinoo nodded.

"Perfect. That is perfect," Drury said and hurried inside.

Kinoo nodded in frustration, glad to get rid of this annoying man. He drove Obi to the clinic.

# 27

## The Only Clinic

——

Kinoo had all the necessary documents for Obi to be admitted to the clinic. Obi had his big warm coat on with additional beaver pelts around his neck for added warmth and a fresh handkerchief in his hand. They hoped to see someone on the staff of the Nunee Nurses Station quickly. Perhaps a nurse practitioner, a paramedic or someone on the team of nurses if Dr. Pathway was not there. If Obi was lucky, he had timed his medical need within the five consecutive days a month in which the doctor was there.

Kinoo arrived at the clinic. Often their front door was frozen shut and patients had to ring their buzzer to get the nurses to let them in.

Kinoo helped Obi take his shoes off and place them with the others at the front door, which was their rule. An attendant saw his condition and took him to the back of the clinic for some quick determinations. After a time, the nurse came back to talk with Kinoo.

"Sir, your friend, Mr. Obi, has a very high temperature and is coughing up blood. He has pain in his stomach, a rash on his body and says it itches terribly. We need to do some tests. Dr. Pathway will be here tomorrow morning about 8:30 a.m. We will allow him to stay overnight due to his age and living alone since he is running a temperature. Can you come back tomorrow afternoon? Are you next of kin?"

Kinoo did not want to hear that and just answered, "Yes," he lied. "Yes, kin! Good friend, too. He...I take care of him now," Kinoo said.

Kinoo did not know what to say. Obi was in the middle of a family crisis at the moment and Kinoo was worried for his friend and his entire family.

"Need my 'X' mark permission to talk with my friend?" Obi asked.

The nurse smiled and turned to Obi with some forms.

"You sign here, first, Mr. Sakawa Sr., so I can give your personal health information to your friend, here. Thank you."

The nurse witnessed Obi signing his "X" mark on the form and turned to Kinoo.

"Okay. We'll see you tomorrow after the doctor has had time to see Mr. Sakawa; but he will be staying overnight until then, as I said."

Kinoo decided to stay at Obi's house so he could be contacted by anyone if needed. Kinoo sat in Obi's comfortable chair. He struggled to read the document Mr. Drury had given him.

Tears streamed down Kinoo's face. He was an old man too; this was no easy time for him either. The tears were not caused by what he was reading in the document; he had not read that far into the first page yet. Kinoo felt suddenly overwhelmed with the events of the week. Catching the deformed fish, finding the bones of a child in a makeshift grave on the school grounds, covering them back up, wondering if his own daughter, Merinda, was alive and what might have happened to her, who might have buried the bones under the tree, the tragedy of his friend losing his family. Now Obi was sick and what were they going to do about Snowbird?

Snowbird was in limbo. She had been their hope, their people's chosen one. Kinoo felt so discouraged.

He was devastated to find out Snowbird was in a residential school for children in Calgary. There would be burial plans to work out regarding the child's parents, considerations of their customs and the laws of the Canadian provinces. There was the unfinished shaking tent ceremony still in the planning stages. There was the deformed fish head and then, of course, the bones of a child hidden somewhere in Obi's house—under his protection; one bundle wrapped in Obi's red bandana and the other wrapped in dirty, old material covered with damp cardboard.

Both Obi and Kinoo were trying to deal with all these issues—such a heavy, emotional burden at their ages. Kinoo sighed and laid his head back on Obi's chair with the cushioned headrest. He just wanted to close his eyes for a moment. He knew he would be buzzed before long by someone needing his taxi services.

The B&B had a full house now and Kinoo was the only taxi and tour guide in the hamlet. He had many guests to keep up with and continuously thought about the passengers and where he had last dropped each one in the community. He had taken the two women to the airport days ago. They would be away for a short time while on a trip to Fort McMurray. They would need a ride back to the B&B when they returned. The one woman, Ms. Weidner, was still on a schedule going to the abandoned school grounds each day. Mr. Drury was his newest customer and Kinoo promised to meet with him tomorrow.

Kinoo constantly churned the B&B's guests' schedules in his head. It was a little ritual—a game he played all day long to keep tabs on everybody, to keep his mind sharp so he wouldn't forget. It was something to do in his old age.

Kinoo began to wonder if the woman from Chicago, who kept going to the schoolyard, would eventually stumble onto the sacred place under the witches' hair and the circle of rocks, and the grave where he and Obi had buried his handkerchief with the charred lump of fish remains. Surely, the woman would find this place if she kept walking the grounds and poking through the snow and ice—*if she was looking for something like that and knew where to dig.* Kinoo was afraid the sacred ground would be disturbed again. The people believe the land and water held on to what they hear and what happened there. Hundreds of years from now, those songs, chants and the violence that had taken place in those locations would haunt those who crossed the land. The little people hunt for lost souls that have been disturbed or cannot find their way home to the Great Spirit. They try to bring the souls full circle to journey home to their Maker.

*What was this woman looking for anyway? Why would anyone want to walk around on those abandoned school grounds? There was nothing there to see with the ground covered in snow unless she knew something was hidden beneath.*

Kinoo sighed, closed his eyes for a moment. But he could not rest. He picked up Obi's eye glasses and resumed reading the document Drury had given him.

It was strange to read about his people in this manner. Everything was laid out on paper. He read as best he could the heading: PERTINENT DETAILS.

The documents mentioned the minor child, Snowbird Sakawa, and the fatalities: Mr. and Mrs. Obigon Sakawa, III. The child was designated as a *Code Adam*. The Saddledome Security had contacted the authorities who had assigned the child temporarily to the Calgary Child Welfare who had placed her in a residential school in Calgary. Kinoo did not know exactly what a *Code Adam* meant. He thought it had something to do with lost children or lost parents...lost Snowbird.

Kinoo's eyes welled up as he read about his friend's family and the remarks about Obi's health and tenuous state of mind.

The summary briefly stated action was needed; custody determination regarding the fitness of great-grandfather Mr. Sakawa Sr., his mental capacity and caretaker ability at age 100. His *age was a negative factor in child placement*, the summary stated. There were a few comments regarding the First Nations Aboriginal Indian cultural sensitivities, the need for transportation of the bodies from Calgary and their burials to be decided by the Wisdom Council. Life insurance policies were noted but only that they existed. There was a note that Snowbird's financial expenses for her temporary care *were being covered by the residential school budget, not the Alberta Province.* Snowbird's admission identification was number *26*.

Kinoo remembered his number had been *30*. Obi had been *Number 9*, Kinoo's fear was that the name Snowbird would be dropped, that the child would be known as Number *26* and that she would be given an English name as well. He shuttered at the thought.

A RCMP progress report form was included for Mr. Drury to complete and a check off list including: death certificates, option for completed adoption, school placement and addresses to confirm. The summary was extensive with multiple pages of forms to complete.

Kinoo sat up straight not sure he quite understood all the words and what they meant. He knew it would separate the family and greatly affect Snowbird's future.

Kinoo's buzzer went off; he had been expecting the taxi request. It was time to pick up Ms. Weidner. She'd spent the whole day on the school grounds again. Kinoo had decided when he dropped Maude off at the B&B, he would park his truck and find Mr. Drury. Maybe he could speak to him today rather than tomorrow, as planned.

The document had listed a *Greg Randolph*, an American citizen working for N-GerDon Corporation with a wife, Mrs. Amanda Randolph, address: North B&B, Fort Chipewyan, Alberta.

Kinoo thought he knew that name; it was the same as Ms. Randolph whom he had taken to the airport recently with the woman from Chicago, Ms. Hargrove. He remembered they were going to Fort McMurray. This bothered Kinoo all day.

—◆—

Kinoo picked up Ms. Weidner at the school. "Good day for you, miss?" he asked her.

"Yes, I found what I came for, I think," Ms. Weidner replied.

The drive to the B&B was quiet; neither talked. Both were trying to make some sense of the day.

"Here we go, Ms. Weidner. I'll park over there, today. I'm meeting a man who is staying at the B&B. Will you be going to the school tomorrow?" Kinoo asked and seeing Maude nod, he agreed to pick her up at the same time the next morning.

Kinoo found Drury relaxing in the Gathering Room. He sat down and asked if they might have a chat. "I think I have some information that might be helpful," Kinoo began.

# 28

Maude Makes an Emergency Phone Call
to Bex In Fort McMurray

—◆—

Kinoo introduced himself again to Mr. Drury and the B&B guest reciprocated.

"I am sorry. Yesterday, my mind was on my friend, Obi. My name is Kinoo and I think I have some information that will help you."

"Okay, let's talk. People call me *Drury*."

"You gave me a document yesterday," Kinoo began. "I read it last night while I was staying at my friend's house. Obi was kept overnight in the clinic for observation. So much has happened," Kinoo said.

"Mr. Drury, you spoke of a *Greg Randolph*. I took a woman by that last name, *Randolph*, and her friend, *Ms. Hargrove*, to the airport days ago. They spoke of a *Greg Randolph* on the way to the airport."

Drury was all ears. He straightened up in his chair taking out his laptop and cell phone.

"So you know these people? And how do you know them?" Drury asked as he began typing on his laptop.

"They are all staying here at the North B&B. They went to Fort McMurray to see the oil sands project. Oh, there is a third friend. She is the woman from the United States who lives in Ms. Hargrove's house in Chicago. She is here to see the abandoned school grounds. I take her there every day. She did not go with the others to Fort McMurray."

While they talked, a woman had come down to make herself a cup of tea. It was Maude. Kinoo did not see her coming and Drury did not know her. Maude looked over and noticed the men in deep conversation. She thought she had heard her name mentioned, having keen ears like the coyote.

Being a covert busy body, she slowly walked to the end of the buffet bar so she could better hear their conversation.

The two men mentioned her name again. Then they mentioned her friend's names, *Ms. Hargrove* and *Mrs. Randolph*. Maude did not know what to make of it. She moved closer pretending to be looking at the individually-wrapped cheese Danish and the assortment of cookies on the buffet. She definitely heard the name *Greg Randolph*, then the words: *Calgary, car accident,* and *Foothills Hospital*.

She decided to call Bex just to ask how the two women were doing, if everything was all right and whether they were enjoying their tour. Maude also felt she might need some legal assistance since she had found what she had come to find but not sure what to do with what she had found.

Maude took out her cell phone and moseyed over to the far side of the B&B's Gathering Room near the front door searching for privacy and a better cell phone connection.

She called Bex.

"Hello, Ms. Hargrove?"

"Yes?"

"This is Maude."

"Oh, my. Hello, Maude. Is everything all right?" Bex asked. "I did not expect to hear from you! Are you back home in Chicago?"

"No. I'm still here in Canada. Just wanted to see if you were safe."

"Yes, why?"

"Well, there is something strange going on here. I heard two men at the B&B, just now, talking about your friends. I heard them mention the name *Greg Randolph*. I heard them say *car accident in Calgary and Foothills Hospital*. I was worried. I also wish to talk to you about some lawyer matters—the burial of First Nations people, maybe even a murder. The main thing reason I called was to see about Mr. Randolph."

"Wow. Uh, I don't know. Are *you* in trouble? You mentioned murder? Oh my God. Greg! We have to find out about Greg! We just saw him just the other day before we went on the oil sands tour. He had to go out of town. To Calgary! He went on company business to some student competition his company was sponsoring. Maude, I understand now. I get it, oh my God, I've gotta go."

Maude's cell phone abruptly disconnected.

"Ms. Hargrove? I'll stay here and wait for you to come back to Fort Chipewyan. I need to talk to you about my problem and a possible murder, which is scaring me. I told you about Greg Randolph but I have more to discuss. Ms. Hargrove? Are you still there?"

Maude realized she had lost the connection. She put her cell phone in her pocket.

While David Drury had been walking Kinoo to the door, the two men had passed Ms. Weidner and had overheard the last part of *her* conversation. Maude nodded politely as the gentlemen passed. Maude turned to leave but was politely stopped by a hand touching her arm.

"Please excuse me, Ms. Weidner," Kinoo commented. "You were just talking about a man named *Greg Randolph*?"

"To my friends, yes," Ms. Weidner replied.

David Drury spoke up. "Were you talking to your friends about a Greg Randolph—the U.S. citizen?"

Ms. Weidner frowned, but nodded cautiously.

"May we speak to you a bit, if you don't mind?" David Drury asked gesturing the three back to the Gathering Room for a private conversation.

David Drury introduced himself to Ms. Weidner informing her why he was in Fort Chipewyan and why he had taken an interest in her conversation. Ms. Weidner was growing more anxious and concerned by the moment.

"Forgive me, but we heard you mention the name *Greg Randolph, First Nations, burial* and then *MURDER* all in one sentence."

Maude looked at the two men.

"Again, madam, forgive me if I seem a bit curious. I am

here to investigate a car accident, which involves Greg Randolph. And then we heard you mentioned *MURDER* in the same sentence."

Mr. Drury told Ms. Weidner it was imperative he get in touch with her friends to whom she was speaking, that Mr. Randolph had been critically injured in a car crash and had been taken to the Foothills Hospital in Calgary and not expected to live.

"My friends will be on the plane soon coming back to the B&B," Ms. Weidner replied appearing a little shaken that her conversation had been overheard. "Here is my friend's cell phone number."

Drury dialed the number but could not get through to Ms. Hargrove. He left his contact information in a quick message. He felt that just the name *David Drury* and a cell number, appearing on her caller ID log, would not mean anything to her since she did not know him.

Drury turned to Ms. Weidner, "Madam, I work with the RCMP. But if you need any help with anything else, perhaps I can assist you. Did you say *murder*?"

Maude looked at the two men and sensed both were looking for an explanation for her strange comments. She decided to tell them about her phone call.

"My English is not good sometimes," she lied. "I called my friend to tell her about the car accident you were just discussing. I apologize. But I first overheard your conversation a moment ago. I knew my friend was visiting a guest here by that last name and her husband has supposedly been working in Calgary the last few days. I thought it might possibly involve the Ms. Randolph I met recently."

"I think I might have said the word *matter*, not the *murder—discuss the matter*," Maude lied.

She was hesitant to tell the men about the murder, about the bones in the school yard, the graves and to admit she had used the word, *murder,* when she asked Bex for legal help.

Kinoo said he had to leave to see about his friend, Obi, in

the clinic and excused himself.

Drury wrote down Maude's address, cell number and then he excused himself. Ms. Weidner nodded and watched the men walk away. She tried Ms. Hargrove's cell phone again without luck.

Maude was left alone in the Gathering Room. She sat down in a chair by the fireplace and gazed at the roaring fire. She listened to the fire popping and crackling. She watched as flames shot up from the chunks of wood casting elongated shadows out into the room, their silhouettes dancing up the wall and across the ceiling.

*They look like people without an identity*, she thought.

# 29
## Unfinished Business
—◦—

Maude finally went back to her room. Her day had certainly been eventful and emotional. She had finally uncovered part of the secret she had kept for fifty years. She did not have all the answers but was getting closer. She had found the tree with the hanging witches' hair and the circle of rocks at the foot of its trunk and had been successful in digging up something from one of the makeshift gravesites. *Or at least she thought she had.* It was just a strange clump on a stick wrapped in a handkerchief, but no bones yet and didn't know why the bones she had buried had disappeared and replaced with this *thing in the handkerchief.* The school grounds had been deserted every day she had visited the school. No person had followed her that she could tell. Had someone been watching her?

The school had been closed for at least two decades. It had falling down and was abandoned. She could see that nobody would have had a purpose to be at the school and yet she had seen the place under the tree had been recently disturbed. The snow had been trampled with fresh footprints around the circle of rocks. But within the circle, the ground had been recently swept neatly, yet covered, to look like the rest of the area. Maude was keen to such signs.

Kinoo, the driver, had said it was not a sightseeing destination and people were afraid to come to the school grounds. She had seen depressions like footprints all along the bush, from the lake, about a hundred feet leading up to the area near the circle of rocks.

*So who might have come to the school grounds recently?* Certainly, no nuns would have come back! Or if they had, were they feeling guilty wanting to make things right by the murdered child? Certainly the nuns, who had killed her friend, wouldn't be returning; they had probably died of old age by now, anyway.

Maude had poked around the brush for days until she had finally located both graves, she thought. One was still just a depression and she had not disturbed it again, just located it. It had been fifty years since she had been there.

What she had wanted to find within the circle had been the decaying pillowcase with the remains of her friend's body she had buried there so long ago. Instead she had found just a small fairly new handkerchief with its corners tied around a little lump on a stick and a wren's feather stuck in the knot—a *fresh* wren's feather.

*What was that in the handkerchief?*

She couldn't figure it out. Someone or something had taken her friend's bones from this place. But what was this that someone had buried in their place?

Maude felt frightened that maybe someone had been watching her! Someone in the little hamlet might have the bones she had come to locate. Someone had already dug them up. Someone now knew about the partial human skeleton; maybe this person had already guessed the child had to have been the victim of some savage crime. Did they think *she* murdered this person? If anyone saw her digging in the area, would they come for her?

*Why would anyone want to take the bones? Why would they put this handkerchief and a fresh wren feather in the dug-up grave? Those feathers are sacred and hard to part with. The feathers stood for "protection." Who would do that? What could be the explanation for all this?*

# 30
### Into the Firewater
---

Kinoo was driving back to the clinic. He was afraid for Obi who had obviously been sick for a while now, he realized. He thought about this Greg Randolph person being the husband of the American woman staying at the B&B. That he had been critically injured and was in a hospital in Calgary. He thought about Snowbird and her parents. Her family was like *his* family. Kinoo was distraught.

*Too much suffering!* Kinoo sighed as he drove. *Too much loss! So much evil!*

Kinoo felt depressed thinking about his daughter now. He never knew what had happened to her but had never forgotten her; he had just tried to make peace with the loss and tried not to discuss it. A shaking tent ceremony had been performed in her honor fifty years ago by his friend, Obi, who had prayed for his lost daughter's spirit to come full circle.

Kinoo's daughter had been so young when she had been taken at age eight. He had given his daughter the name, *Merinda*, which he knew meant: *the pretty one.* The Indian Agents had forced her to go with them. Kinoo could not even remember what his little girl looked like except that she had long black braids and a curious smile. The loss had saddened him all his life. He had not been able to watch her grow up. His wife died of tuberculosis or wandered off in a depressed state. Losing both would be losing his entire family.

Kinoo grieved for Obi too since it now seemed he had lost his entire family.

Seeing the name, *Merinda,* carved into the tree had brought back so much sadness. Maybe the bones of his daughter were stuck in a hole too somewhere like the bones of this child he and Obi had just found. Kinoo broke down crying. He longed for his daughter. He tried to imagine what she might look like today. *Merinda* was gone but she had remained forever in his heart.

Kinoo thought about his wife. Her body had never been found. That had been so long ago. It had been difficult for Kinoo. His wife had disappeared. Then Merinda had disappeared. Their names had never been mentioned until he and Obi had talked the other day. The first time Merinda's name had been spoken in fifty years. The hurt had been too great.

*It doesn't get any easier, Obi*, Kinoo had admitted to his friend.

*It makes us stronger, maybe. We must live with it, my friend. You learn to live without loved ones and hope to be reunited someday in another world*, Kinoo remembered Obi saying.

Obi had taken Kinoo's hands and sandwiched them between his—squeezing them for support and had whispered, *Kinoo, children are resourceful and stronger than we think. Merinda will find her way. The little people, the fairies, the Great Spirit will keep her safe and guide her. She'll come full circle one day, if she hasn't already.*

Kinoo had many thoughts like these as he drove to the nurse clinic. Drury was talking about making burial arrangements for the ones killed in the car accident. Snowbird was now living in some residential school. It just seemed to be one bad thing after another. Evil had certainly settled in his little hamlet.

Kinoo felt alone. He looked over the front seat into the back floorboard of the truck, where he would hide things. The truck belonged to the B&B but he was really the only one who drove it. Some days, Kinoo would stop on the side of the road or find a good view of Lake Athabasca and sit for a time. He would look out over the ice or the great water when the ice had melted. He would roll down the window in better weather and listen to nature.

It was frigid cold outdoors this day; but Kinoo stopped the truck when he found a good view of the frozen lake and rolled down his window. He was overwhelmed. Then he opened the door and swung his long skinny legs around to the side and dangled them over the edge of his seat. He wanted a drink so bad. He wanted the entire bottle. He knew one bottle was already open tucked under the driver's seat from the back side. He couldn't remember when he had opened *that* bottle. That was a good sign but he longed for it now!

Kinoo sat there. Would he lose Obi too? What if they could not bring Snowbird back home? What if she was stuck in Calgary? What if those teachers in her new school were abusive to her?

Everyone had worked so hard to ensure Snowbird would never end up in a residential school like that and now she was in one by no fault of her own *or theirs*.

Kinoo reached into the back of the truck and pulled the bottle from its hiding place. He held it tightly looking at the label. He had not touched it in a long time. He closed his eyes and could savor the memory of its taste. The bottle rested on his thigh with his fingers locked around its neck.

Kinoo's other arm was hanging limp across the open truck window and his head was resting on that arm. He felt old and tired.

*I have lived too long.*

He heard a truck coming but he didn't look up. In a few seconds, the idling motor was constant. He knew the truck was sitting right there; he could see its tires and even reach out and touch the driver, yet he did not look up. He heard music playing on the radio inside the other vehicle. Kinoo remained motionless. He didn't care who it was; he'd been crying and he was filled with shame, grief and fear.

"Kinoo, my friend, don't do it," the other person finally said. "Too many people depend on you. Too many of us have gone too far with that firewater. You know that. I know you have trouble with it. But you're needed, my friend. You need to be strong for many people, for Obi."

The man reached over and laid a hand on Kinoo's arm.

Kinoo looked up. He nodded. His elder circle friend gently reached for the bottle. Kinoo held tight for a second locked in a tug-a-war, then loosened his grip. His friend raised the bottle gently out of Kinoo's hand but did not take it away quite yet. He just held it high in the air. Both looked at it and saw a Snowy White Owl pass over in the sky, a rare sighting during the day.

The man still held the bottle high and Kinoo looked at it for what seemed an hour or until the owl disappeared. Suddenly he jumped up, closed the truck door and jerked the bottle from his friend's hand. He dashed it to the frozen ground on top of some rocks. The bottle shattered against the hard surface.

The two men were shocked. Neither had expected the bottle to explode in that manner.

All of a sudden Kinoo started laughing. Then the friend started laughing. Kinoo patted him on the back. They hugged.

"Good friend. Good friend. I needed a friend. Great thanks to you! I'm okay. I've got to go see Obi now. We've got to get Snowbird back. I'm going to take Obi home today from the clinic. Don't forget we've got that shaking tent ceremony to do, my friend. You are right, people need me."

Kinoo looked at his friend straight into his eyes—down to his very soul and nodded.

"We need each other," the friend said, made a fist and lightly pounded his heart.

"Good friend. Good friend," Kinoo replied.

Kinoo watched as his friend drove slowly down the road. He looked out over the frozen grassland and the hoodoos looking to where the Snowy White Owl had flown and nodded. The little people had sent a wise friend and fowl to watch over him and to alert him. Kinoo touched his shirt pocket. Obi's protective wren feather was still there from the day before.

Kinoo climbed back into the truck and drove on to the clinic. He met Dr. Pathway who ushered Kinoo to a private room to talk. Dr. Pathway told Kinoo she had screened Obi for cancer and had found quite a few abnormalities and requested that Obi go to Fort McMurray immediately for more testing. She told Kinoo that Obi's symptoms: stomach pain, headaches, overall itching, constipation, coughing up blood, temperature, congestion and pain in the lungs were troublesome. His difficulty in breathing, inability to go to the bathroom, dark stools and elevated white blood cell count pointed to a likelihood of several cancer prognoses. She did not want to alarm Kinoo, but she said the family needed to prepare themselves for the worse and that Kinoo needed to be strong for his friend.

"Kinoo, this area where you live is showing more cancer incidents than normal—especially for bile duct cancer. Obi is surely a candidate for further screening in Fort McMurray. With his age, and these symptoms, my guess is they will test for that. He's showing elevated levels in a lot of areas and inflammation in the body. We cannot rule out additional cancers of the blood, lymphatic system and lungs from my initial reading."

Kinoo was devastated.

"I knew he was sick. I just didn't know how sick. Is he in pain?"

"Kinoo," Dr. Pathway replied, "Obi says he's not in that much pain, but I've given him pain medicine. This is a limited facility. Obi is in the North Zone for the Alberta Health System (AHS). Do you know what I am talking about? That means we live in the healthcare area north of Red Deer. The plan of action, for Obi, is that he first goes to Fort McMurray, about a 170 miles south of here so he is still in the North Zone for insurance purposes. They have a larger facility and can do more in-depth screening. If they detect cancer of any kind, they will allow him to go out of the North Zone to the Edmonton Zone. I will approve that. You can contact the others in the Wisdom Council since Obi might be in a healthcare facility a long time. I think this is your best plan," Dr. Pathway said.

"Obi is sick, my friend. I'm sorry. I'll make an appointment for him at the Fort McMurray facility today. You will need to sign a form if you are the one who will be taking care of him. I think Mr. Sakawa, *Obi,* signed it yesterday and said it was okay to tell you his condition. But if you can, would you try to sign your name? I need your signature too."

"Yes," Kinoo said with renewed conviction.

Kinoo knew how to sign his name. He had just gotten lazy and had reverted to using an "X" to sign all things. Nobody had questioned him. Kinoo took a pen and wrote in clear letters,

K I N O O   K I Y A S E W

"Mr. Sakawa, your friend here, Kinoo, will take you home, now. I am setting up more tests for you in Fort McMurray. I'm going to let you rest tonight at home with your friend, Kinoo, who will be staying with you. We will make plans for your transportation to Fort McMurray and will contact the AHS and the Wisdom Council to guide you through the policies and procedures."

Obi had a strong will and had helped his people many times through similar situations. Today, he allowed big tear drops to fall on his pants leg.

"We must get Snowbird home first," Obi mumbled.

"Kinoo, sir, give Obi these medications. Can you read?"

"Yes, with Obi's glasses."

Dr. Pathway helped Kinoo take Obi to the truck and the doctor nodded to Kinoo. Neither Obi nor Kinoo talked on the way to Obi's home.

Obi felt comfortable in his own bed and glad Kinoo was staying with him overnight.

Kinoo felt like the strong one now. He suddenly remembered the evil bundles that needed full circle ceremony. *Where were the bundles, the one with the deformed fish head and the other bundle with the child's bones?* He walked softly into Obi's bedroom.

"Obi?" he whispered.

Obi answered with closed eyes, "Yes, my friend?"

"Where are the bundles?"

"They are under my bed," Obi replied.

"Okay, my friend. Okay."

"Kinoo?" Obi asked in a whisper.

"Yes, my friend?"

"Snowbird." Obi murmured as he fell asleep.

Kinoo looked at his friend, "I know, Obi. I promise."

# 31
## Shaking Tent

*Wake up! The Sun is coming.*
*The birds are already singing.*
*How beautiful this land of ours is.*
*It must remain good for all.*

*Waniskâ! Pêtâpan ôma...*
*âsay piyêsîsak kî-nikamowak...*
*ê-miyonâkwan kitaskînaw+*
from the Cree Literacy Network

♫

Just before sunrise Obi awoke. He felt stronger. He called out to Kinoo, "Friend, I am better. I will perform the shaking tent ceremony tomorrow."

Kinoo came into the bedroom.

"Rest, Obi, rest."

"No, must do tomorrow. There are too many souls in limbo. You must gather the elders."

Kinoo saw his friend was stubborn but that he did appear stronger with renewed strength. The shaking tent ceremony was important. Kinoo nodded.

"Okay, my friend. I'll tell the others to get ready."

Kinoo left his friend, rounded up the elders instructing them to bring the shaking tent from the bush and set it beside the fire pit. He informed the band the ceremony would take place the following dawn at the fire circle.

Kinoo walked back to Obi's home.

"My friend, we are ready."

"Yes. I have the bundles. I have the Great Spirit in my soul. The little people clung to the bellies of the coyotes last night and ran through the grasslands. The fairies told me it is my time. I feel rested and we will get up early before the sun comes up tomorrow."

The next morning, Obi was ready. He and Kinoo put on their ceremonial dress with the correct feathers, leather-beaded pants, jacket, and retrieved the bundles from underneath Obi's bed. Obi brought his sacred medicine bag and Kinoo drove them to the fire circle. The rest of the elders were already there. The fire was ablaze and felt warm in the chill of the morning. It illuminated the faces of all Obi's long-time friends.

A tired, yet positive, Chief Elder Obi sat cross-legged with his right, high cheekbone and heavy forehead reflecting the soft deep-orange glow of the fire and the uncertain timing of the dawn. His other cheek was lost in the darkness. There was a soft whispering among the elders.

Obi's grandfather had been a Great Chief Elder of the North American Blackfoot Cree, one of the First Nations people, the Aboriginals of Canada, a mixture of Indian, Inuit and Métis. His grandfather had performed many ceremonies on the banks of Lake Athabasca in that same shaking tent.

Obi was among his people this morning and felt comforted. Their loving spirit encouraged him to prepare for the ceremony and to make requests for their welfare. The skies were still dark but they warned the time was coming for the dawn's light to reach that breaking point when the ceremony could begin.

Obi held the smudge pot ceremoniously over his right shoulder and closed his eyes. He added damp sweet grass to the pot, dabbing it with his finger flattening it against a live ember. Smoke curls trailed from the pot as he lifted it. It was a sacred moment. His fellow elders in the circle would soon waft the smoke with the palms of their hands, directing it to their nostrils and face. The elders inhaled the fumes to cleanse their minds of evil as the pot was passed among them.

Obi began the cleansing. He dipped his calloused, tall finger into the hot charcoal pot, scooping a bit of mixture, and ceremoniously smudged his handmade pipe. He stuffed the remaining lump of mixture into its chamber. He lit that mixture too. He nodded in acceptance of the honor and passed the charcoal pot. The adjacent elder nodded his bowed head, repeated this procedure and passed the sacraments to each their brethren. One by one they fueled their instruments, inhaled the sacred smoke and mumbled prayer in a tradition of faith, hope and respectful request of their Great Spirit.

*Free Snowbird. Do not orphan her to face this world alone.*

Obi did not pray for himself rather he prayed for another leader to emerge.

Obi closed his eyes, chanted a prayer to the higher spirit.

*"Mamuskachi^tew," thanks to the Great Spirit who works miracles.*

Obi slowly rose, leaving the others, and crawled into the shaking tent. He would be the one to request many things of the Great Spirit this morning.

The remaining elders sat close in a circle around the fire pit. Kinoo was now the oldest elder of the circle. When all the members had inhaled the religious perfume of the sweet grass and cedar, one elder reached into the pouch of his ceremonial garment and withdrew pictures of all the Sakawa family members that had just died in the car crash.

They whispered for the big companies to stop their destruction and to stop poisoning the earth. They whispered for the poison to leave Obi's body. They whispered for the evil to leave the deformed fish.

Kinoo took the pictures of the family from his brethren elder and chanted words looking up to the Northern Aurora Borealis Lights as sunrise began to peek through the heavens. Obi had obeyed tradition. He was engrossed in ceremonial customs, shaking the tent as the dawn broke.

Daylight transformed Obi's silhouetted figure. The elders could no longer see it. The light of the dawn made all Obi's motions disappear. Yet he was still inside praying. The elders could hear him rapping, mumbling, and the tent seemed to come alive as it swayed from side to side and a bluish glow rose from the top of the tent.

The elders calmly waited for the lull, mumbling something as a group when they heard Obi howling. They joined in with a low humming. The elders gingerly placed the hand drawn image of Snowbird's likeness at the edge of an ember. They watched it catch fire and burn disappearing into a spray of flittering cinders.

The family images burned steadily until there was nothing left but ashes as the elders hummed softly. They watched with hopeful sentiment as the last of the live cinders took flight in little flits of light hovering above them then vanishing.

Finally there was a call out to set Snowbird free and bring her home. It was a call for the evil among them to leave their hamlet, for the Great Spirit to take it away.

Kinoo had brought both evil bundles. He took the first bundle, unwrapped the remains of the fish head and gawked again at its hideousness. After mumbling, he took a pointed stick and pierced the eye of the fish head and held it up toward the sky. He cursed the fish head and rammed the stick into the flames as he let out a howl. This was the signal for Grand Chief

Elder, Obi, to respond with chanting and shaking the tent again. In his native tongue, Obi asked the Great Spirit what had made this fish sick. Then Obi asked for guidance.

The fate of the community was unknown. The fate of the surrounding waters was unknown as was the same for the surrounding land, the wildlife and the air. The elders hoped something would soon be revealed in the transparency of daylight. Obi was chanting as the Great Spirit was telling him the evil was in the land, the air and in the water and now inside the animals, plants and the people.

The Great Spirit continued, "And now Obi, the evil is spread throughout your body."

Outside the tent, Kinoo heard Obi's wailing and took his cue to perform the purification of the precious child bones wrapped in the tattered cloth remnants.

Kinoo took the cookie sheet, the one purchased from the trading post, and reverently placed the partially wrapped child's bones, the arm bones and partial ribcage carefully in the middle of the metal pan. He gently laid that platform onto the blazing angry coals. He took a prepared stick and rammed it into the ground at the fire's edge. He pushed the small child's skull down onto the stick and watched as flames seared up through its eye sockets blackening the hollow edges transforming the head into a masked entity.

Kinoo's mumbles were followed by more of Obi's wailing as he continued his ritual inside the shaking tent. The people knew even the center of a blazing bonfire normally 800-900° was not hot enough to burn bones, but it was a ceremonial ritual. When the bone fragments on the cookie sheet finally seemed to glow, the elders chanted in singsong reverence, raising their arms to the sky wailing and chanting. The metal platform with the purified bones would be handled by the Wisdom Council.

The ashes among the bones seemed to take flight caught up in the swirls of smoke from the fire pit and curled higher into the sky. This child, *number 9,* was great in their eyes! This child was now with the Great Spirit.

"The light will reveal," Chief Elder Obi replied as he stepped out of the shaking tent in a sweat that glistened in the dawn's rays and the remaining firelight of the pit. There was a bluish flittering of light exhaling from his mouth as he stood up. The people waited for answers from Obi and what the Great Spirit had told him. He stood with a blue glow illuminating his body shape and slowly addressed the elders:

"The full face of North America and its great problems meet the unmistakable dawning light and the worry shows on the face of you wise ones and the faces of the giant companies. Truth has been set into motion and will rise up in the end against evil."

Obi paused.

"We must be patient."

In the height of the ceremony a mysterious drama played out in the dawning of the morning. Suddenly it all disappeared in the light of day. The dark evil was still unknown, the fire had extinguished itself, but determination was fiercely present.

"This is a day of great sadness and great gladness. We begin a long journey. The Great Spirit says the giant among us is causing our problems. I prayed for our people's welfare and the return of my Snowbird." Obi paused to catch his breath.

"The Great Spirit and I have shaken the tent. The Spirit says we must not let the *white man* take our lands or our children. We must fight for our land and that it provides again. The giant must clean up the land and make it pure. Our people grow sick and die at their hands."

"We must pull together strong! The four races of people of all lands, you know: all Asian, all black people, the different nationalities of white, and of First Nations. The Great Spirit put us all here for a reason. Look for the signs to protect you. The Great Spirit will send a messenger by the Great Snowy White Owl. We will suffer; but good will come. Our children must not forget, they must keep our people's ways but must learn the ways of the *white man* too. Together, it is possible to make everything good again."

Great cries followed low guttural rumbling. The elders waited until the embers died. Obi patted his pocket; the piece of material with the *number 9* was safe. He could not bear to see it destroyed a second time. It would be like destroying himself.

# 32

### Greg Randolph
### Alberta Oil Sands

$T$wo days prior, Bex and Shinski were standing at the McMurray facility entrance waiting for Greg.

"Alfred, there they are. I'll be right back. I need to speak with my wife a moment and make sure she and her friend are all set for the tour…and to apologize to them for not being able to join them."

"Right, chief, I'll be right here, waiting."

Greg ran up the entry walk to where his wife and friend stood.

"Amanda, I'm sorry that plans got changed. I received a call at the last minute to do this thing in Calgary for Mr. Stelman. He called me personally asking me to present the scholarship awards at the Alberta Student Competition in Calgary. He asked as a favor, darling; I couldn't turn down the boss."

"I know. I understand. I have Bex here for company."

"Well, Alfred has offered to be your guide, your chauffeur

—everything while you're here. He's a prince of a guy!"

"Well, dear, I'm off to Calgary, a city where a good portion of $200 billion has been spent as a caveat of the energy industry in Alberta. I'm excited to see it! We'll all see it together one day, I promise! Be good sweetheart!"

Greg kissed Shinski and ran back to the limo. Of course Greg would be flying today to Calgary in a company jet in first class fashion, jump into a nice company limo when he arrives, be whisked off to a five star hotel, dress in cocktail attire and be chauffeured to the Saddledome in style for the competition awards!

"Shinski, did Greg say that the whole energy industry brings in a couple hundred *billion* dollars to Alberta? That's a good chunk of change. I guess Calgary might just rival New York if Alberta has that kind of revenue to enhance its cities."

"Well, shall we have lunch then?" Shinski asked.

"We have about an hour before the tour starts and there's a little café inside the facility that's so-so."

Bex and Shinski ate a quick lunch. The limo returned within the hour as Greg instructed to pick up the women and transport them to the tour gate. Shinski was bored the moment the tour started.

"Shinski, let me get some pictures and see a few of these instructional films, get a look at this bitumen black cake substance you kept talking about and we can leave. Okay?"

"This is *your* day, Bex, whatever you say."

That did not sound convincing to Bex. But she was interested in the oil sands project. She did have quite a few years under her belt: studying environmental effects on the world, graduating with an environmental science degree, having spent years as an environmental inspector and a corporate lawyer in Chicago mainly defending environmental violators!

Shinski knew that. But she also had learned recently that her best friend had walked away from the whole environmental scene and from a six-figure income to become a freelance writer for the Chicago Tribune. *So why were they there?*

—//—

Bex was an advocate for the environment. She was captivated with the little video on the oil sands project the tour provided—aghast with what she was seeing, appalled the oil sands project had ever gotten off the ground.

She was saddened to see such destruction of planet Earth. When she heard Greg mention Alberta having benefitted from the oil sands projects to the tune of a COUPLE HUNDRED BILLION dollars as of 2017 and as much as 1.2 TRILLION DOLLARS by 2038; the victim-syndrome scenario raised its ugly head once again within her heart and soul. She just kept thinking in order for an industry to make that kind of money, there had to be a downside, a ginormous victim side to all this!

She could see who the victims were by looking around. They were the poor residents and anything living downstream of these projects and these holding ponds she was noticing on the tour. She had been dealing with these type toxic cesspools for decades. They were nothing but huge pools of toxic waste with the likelihood to cause problems with the environment: leaking and leaching into the soil and waterways.

What had that fisherman in Port Washington told her? What was that phrase again he used? *Oh yeah,* Bex remembered, *power plants are nothing but chemical plants that produce energy!*

Bex could see all sorts of problems with the set up across the oil sands of Alberta. There could be thousands of victims physically suffering from illnesses caused by the toxic levels of chemical waste discarded by these oil sands processes. *These people need a lawyer.*

*No, I am not going to be anyone's lawyer in Canada. I'm through with that type law! I'm sure this place retains enough lawyers to fill up the U.S. fleet,* Bex admonished herself.

Bex wondered what the difference was in U.S. law versus

Canadian law regarding environmental infractions and ordinance irregularities. *What was Canada's equivalent to the U.S. EPA?*

That interested Bex. She knew Illinois State law. She knew federal (EPA) laws would also apply. She knew nothing of Canadian law concerning the environment or whether it was as inclusive as the States. But she did know what a class action lawsuit might shape up to look like regarding what she was seeing and suspecting.

The stuff going on here in Canada with the oil sands project was looking like the craters of the moon. The holding ponds were the colors of the rainbow and looked like they could glow at night like the Northern Lights. All this was potentially harmful to everyone downstream if there were toxic levels of chemical waste in the water as she suspected. Bex felt she should keep those thoughts close to her chest especially since Greg worked for the area's largest investor.

Amazing what politics and money-hungry corporations can do and how much power and control they can wield over victims—*poor ignorant, suffering victims*, Bex thought.

—•—

As long as Bex had been an advocate for protecting the environment and then ironically ending up jumping ship and defending those who pollute the environment, she was aware of the *Keystone pipelines*. But she had had no dealings with a case pertaining to them. She had never heard of the Alberta Oil Sands. She knew regulations had been placed on that type industry as early as the 1960s and 70s. But the boom of that industry normally follows the cycle of the price of a barrel of oil, which fluctuates with the Dow Jones, what the U.S. President or the Chairman of the Federal Reserve might say or *the weather*!

Now that she was being introduced to this madness in Canada, she felt she also had to be somewhat politically sensitive with her comments because of her best friend's husband, Greg, working for N-GerDon. He held an important position with that investor and was *on the fast track to becoming their next CEO one day*, Shinski kept telling her. Bex was perplexed as she continued listening to the tour guide's presentation.

"The oil sands project, in the Athabasca reservoir, is not only a large project of the magnitude you see here in the display wall photos," the tour guide said, "but it is the largest known reservoir of crude bitumen in the world and the largest of three major oil sands deposits in Alberta…" the tour guide continued.

The oil sands territory was impressive. It was expansive, black, deep and barren with what looked like little black ants running around carrying black specks to bigger places with smoke stacks!

Those specks were actually oversized dump trucks with tires as high as twenty feet tall carrying truckloads of black hunks of bitumen (cake-like clumps, a mixture of sand, clay, tar and oil). Hundreds upon hundreds of trucks were being filled up with these black cake chunks being dug from the holes and hauled away for processing. The holes in the ground were miles wide and looked to be a few hundred feet deep. The oil sands project was a massive expanse of real estate with nothing but one-mile wide craters one after another with these large machines eating away at big green spots (*trees*) as if it were all one gigantic Pac-Man game eating away at a huge green game board. It bothered Bex when she discovered only 3% of the bitumen could be mined, that the other 97% of the bitumen was too deep in the earth to ever be mined.

Waste ponds holding toxic chemicals were scattered around. Huge buildings were positioned strategically among these holes spewing smoke, busy puffing away, processing the cakes by separating the oil from the sands and other impurities to make fuel for energy.

There was the larger issue of how to transport the oil to its destination. That's where the other controversial issues had arisen. The industry plan was to lay a grid of pipelines throughout Canada and then route pipeline across the U.S. border to the Gulf of Mexico. From there, the oil would be shipped all over the world. A large part of this oil sands project was routing pipelines through towns, under lakebeds and through sacred Indian burial grounds.

*So this is what all the people are picketing about,* Bex determined. This is what is causing so much sickness among the people, their lands, their wildlife, the air, indirectly into the food they eat then probably affecting their DNA passed to future generations. This is what is leaching into the water.

She nodded completely understanding the people's plight. *Big problems,* Bex thought. She pursed her lips trying to wrap her head around a couple hundred billion dollars for just the Alberta Province and what that type money could do for these people. It was an interesting situation, a Catch-22.

"Shinski, let me grab a few brochures and view a bitumen cake up close, read a bit more on that display over there and we'll call it a day."

On accompanying headphones, Bex listened to the tour guide finish describing one area and then identify a photograph. She quickly studied a piece of bitumen cake in a display glass, gazed out a huge viewing window of tempered glass across a horizon of curling smoke, black holes, huge craters, huge holding ponds, hundreds upon hundreds of trucks, huge bulldozers and a score of temporary housing that looked like a government project itself. The oil sands industry had put Canada on the map—certainly Alberta!

Bex was beginning to understand the human dilemma in all this: these people were in a no-win situation. They were torn between the decision to protect Mother Nature or having employment for survival to pay for basics like a home versus living in the bush—in 2017!

There were limited fish and wildlife fit to eat and the plants were not healthy anymore. The toxic byproducts of the oil sands ventures were of such levels to poison everything, killing living things, causing illness, cancer and death in humans. The toxic byproducts were unhealthy levels of arsenic, cadmium, selenium, chromium and other chemicals.

If the First Nations people could not follow in their ancestor's footsteps and learn to survive off the land because what they would hunt, fish or breathe were being poisoned, then they would have to go to work for the oil sands projects to make a living. Even then, the poisoning of their environment was physically killing them and emotionally and spiritually destroying their culture. If those companies paid them to dig up the earth to make fuel for the world and leave the earth an ugly mess, this inevitable, ultimate choice was stressful and disturbing. Was the cost of this endeavor worth all the risk to humans and the environment? If only 3% of Earth's bitumen, in this area, could be mined versus the cost associated with its process and waste disposal being prohibitive—*if the truths of the hidden cost were known*—who approved this?

Or had that waste removal cost aspect been moved to the bottom line of another report filed away somewhere and not mentioned again as a cost factor? Had that bit of knowledge not been communicated when initially trying to convince the public how efficient certain power ventures were? Was the cost of waste removal now being passed on to unaware, hardworking citizens? *Of course it is,* Bex thought. Had it ever been communicated that the process has potentially deadly side effects for living things, humans—*like probable death*?

This industry offers salaries upwards of sixty thousand dollars annually, which is a lot of money for people who have practically nothing living in the wilderness of Canada. How can they turn that down? But are they told the truth? When would they be told the truth? And if then, what are their options at that point?

By 2017, the oil sands investors were so entrenched in their process having already ruined 54,752 square miles of oil sands area—just about the size of the State of Illinois, bigger than

Tennessee or Virginia or Pennsylvania. It would be extremely difficult to return this expanse of land to its original state (as per the Indian Land Act). The First Nations people continue to picket citing the Land Treaties of the 1870s going forward were supposed to protect their lands in perpetuity, that the government is in violation of these treaty agreements and ignoring their rights.

The situation seems futile for the victims, primarily the First Nations community folks who do not have the resources to fight. It does not seem to matter if there are ongoing appeals in the courts with cease-and-desist rulings to halt the digging. *Possession is nine tenths the law* the people are being told when they complain.

The First Nations people criticize the government that they have sold or leased the land illegally to other countries for the mining of the bitumen. Additionally, it appears improbable for these investors to reverse the damage done to the environment; the investors would just reply they had leased land from the Canadian government and to take it up with them, that their transactions are with the *government, not the people.*

So the treaties and agreements of 1867 and 1876 and those that were signed later between the government and the First Nations people were being virtually ignored. The government says *sooner or later it was inevitable the lands would be developed* and seemed to cast the agreements aside as nuisance treaties.

*How has this egregious display of contempt of the laws gotten so out of control breaking the protective land agreements with the First Nations people?* Bex thought, shaking her head. Her heart went out to the victims as it always had in similar legal cases she had tried in U.S. courts.

Bex could understand both sides of the issue. She knew the big business mentality, especially if backed by the Canadian government. She knew too well how big business normally wins in court in the end. She knew loopholes are the key to legal tactics. She knew interpretation is a slippery slope in a court of law. How many lawyers do the oil sands investors retain? How much legal representation can a couple hundred billion dollars buy? And weren't the treaties changed every year by the government from 1876 to 1929, more than fifty times consecutively and maybe even a few times after that?

First Nations people or anything living downstream of the project didn't stand a chance, it seemed!

# 33

### The Other End of that Emergency Phone Call From Maude in Fort Chipewyan
—◆—

On the day Bex and Shinski were to return to Fort Chipewyan on N-GerDon's private company jet, they had reflected on the previous day's sightseeing in Fort McMurray starting with Greg not being able to go with them on the tour. How fun it had been thinking back on when the two of them had tried to sneak out a locked side door of the tour facility like they had done so often sneaking into theatres in Chicago through the side doors when they were teenagers. The hotel accommodations had been just so-so. The oil sands tour itself had not been particularly memorable to Shinski the second time as the two women decided to skip the remainder of the tour.

"Okay, Shinski. Done with the tour! Are you happy now?" Bex asked as she put away her cell phone, zipped up her camera case that had almost been confiscated, and put the headphones back in their tour display holders.

Bex stuffed the brochures, which she had procured from each plastic box along the tour corridor, into her coat pocket. The two women had bowed out of the pro-industry, guided tour group, walking slowly backwards in covert manner distancing themselves from the other tourists. They were looking for the nearest side exit. And just before they opened an alarmed door, a human blocked their exit. The intervention by a rear tour guide, stepping in front of them, did not go well. He had not been amused with their antics. The two had been escorted out the main entrance and surveilled as they walked down the sidewalk.

"I'm glad Greg wasn't with us," Shinski admitted. "That was fun but pretty childish."

"But we're free!" she had exclaimed running to the limo

where Alfred was waiting. Bex had followed shaking her head; *never grew up*, Bex had chuckled looking at Shinski in her moment of childish display.

Alfred had suggested a place for them to have dinner, waited while they ate, then had driven them to a hotel for the night. The women had not thought much of Fort McMurray's hotels either. Certainly not the resort city Shinski had envisioned for her friend, Bex.

Mid-afternoon the next day Alfred picked them up on route to the corporate hanger where the women were to board the private company jet destined to return to Fort Chipewyan. Sarah had squeezed them in on the flight manifest.

"Understand you are leaving us today. It has been a pleasure serving you two princesses," Alfred replied with a smile.

"Back to Fort Chipewyan, so we can pack and go play in LA or somewhere else!" Shinski said. "We're through with the oil projects, Fort McMurray and Fort Chipewyan! We're going to plan some fun!" she replied.

That's when Bex's cell phone had rung. Bex was about to receive the emergency call from Fort Chipewyan. Bex looked down at her caller ID. It had been a couple days since they had left the B&B; they had finished the tour, spent one night in Fort McMurray, and were ready to leave those black cake craters forever headed back to the B&B in Fort Chipewyan!

—————

Bex looked at the caller ID on her cell phone.

"It's from Maude. I hope it's not an emergency. What on earth could she want?" She commented to Shinski.

"Hello, Maude?"

"Hello, Ms. Hargrove."

"Is everything all right?" Bex asked. "Did not expect to hear from you. Are you in Chicago?"

"No. Still here in Fort Chipewyan at the B&B. Just wanted to see if everyone was all right there. I had overheard some disturbing news."

"What?"

"Are you still in Fort McMurray?"

"Yes."

Maude began to inform Bex what she had overheard when eavesdropping on Kinoo and Mr. Drury in the Gathering Room. As Maude was speaking to Bex, the two men coincidentally were now passing by her unintentionally now able to eavesdrop on *her* conversation with Bex. The men suddenly realized Maude had overheard their conversation about the car accident and talking about Greg Randolph. They heard Maude continuing to tell Bex what she had heard the men say. Maude had tried to turn around for some privacy to explain she was worried about Greg Randolph.

Shinski had been sitting beside Bex in the limo while Alfred was driving. She was trying hard to discern what was happening from what she was hearing from Bex's side of the conversation. She understood something was wrong as she caught her husband's name, that there had been a car accident in Calgary, but was perplexed when Bex repeated the word, *murder*.

"Wow. Uh, you okay? Murder? Uh, I don't know, Maude. Are you in trouble? We'll check on Greg from this end. Gosh, thanks so much. We saw him just the other day before the tour began. He had to dash off on business. He set up the tour for us and the hotel but said he had to go to Calgary and we would reschedule a fun trip to Calgary another time, something about a student scholarship program sponsored by his company and he having to present some awards and would be gone for a couple days."

Bex thought a moment. "Oh my God, Maude, I understand now! Hey, I have to go. We have to call Greg to see if he's okay. Car accident? Oh, my. If you plan to stay longer in Canada, at the B&B, I'll catch up with later."

Bex hit the call-end button abruptly cutting Maude off in mid-sentence. She turned to Shinski with a blank expression.

"Shinski, I don't know what to make of what I just heard."

Bex looked at Shinski, then the limo driver, and then back at Shinski.

"Oh Shinski, something horrible has happened, I think. Maude overheard Kinoo talking to a man about a serious car accident in Calgary and Greg's name was mentioned…"

"Oh no, not Greg! Not Greg." Shinski wailed. "I heard you mention murder. Was he murdered, in a car accident or what?"

"Alfred, can you get us to Calgary? Greg Randolph, we think, is in critical condition at a hospital there; something is terribly wrong! Can you call there and confirm if Greg has been admitted?"

"Shinski, don't worry. Maude did not say he was murdered. She just mentioned a murder and I don't know what that's all about either. Let's just see if Greg has been admitted to a hospital in Calgary or find out where he is and if he is all right."

"Yes, ma'am, I'll call right away," Alfred replied.

He decided to let corporate know first and called Sarah, the president's executive assistant. She would know what to do.

"May I speak with Sarah, please? Thank you."

"Sarah, this is Alfred. There's a possibility Greg Randolph has been in a bad car accident in Calgary. The friend of Ms. Randolph just received a disturbing phone call about a car accident involving Greg Randolph. Mrs. Randolph is with me. She wants the company to fly her to Calgary rather than Fort Chipewyan. Do we have another jet available at Fort McMurray with a flight plan for that? Can we confirm Mr. Randolph has been in an accident first? Sarah, *you* tell me what to do."

"Alfred, take them to the corporate jet hanger as scheduled and wait there. Don't board, yet," Sarah replied.

"Give me some time to check this out. We won't be able to get them on our jet this afternoon for Calgary anyway. We're not going there again today. I'll check commercial flights tonight or in the morning. I'll see if we can find some availability on anything else. I'm scrolling through commercial, sea planes and float planes right now. It looks like it'll have to be on corporate. I don't see anything else. I'll get back to you."

"Ladies, your luggage is in the limo's trunk. We might have a slight change in plans. I'm going to close the limo screen divider for a moment, if you don't mind."

Shinski was crying and wringing her hands, "I just don't know what I'll do if Greg's been hurt. I just don't know. I waited so long to get married. He is just so perfect for me. We love each other so much. Oh, God, please don't let him be dead. Please keep him here with me. I'm not strong. He's the strong one. Dear God. Please."

"Alfred?" Shinski asked, rapping on the divider. "Alfred? Do you know what happened?"

Alfred lowered the glass divider while pressing a button to end speaker phone mode on the conversation he was having with Sarah.

"No ma'am. I'm afraid we're all finding out together. But corporate knows now and they'll handle it from their end. My instructions are to get you to the hanger at the N-GerDon air strip. We'll get you there as soon as we can, Mrs. Randolph."

"Don't worry Shinski. Alfred will take care of us. Just pray," Bex added trying to comfort her.

Bex held Shinski tightly and said a quick prayer. She squeezed Shinski's hand and hugged her. Shinski was sobbing, unable to speak.

"Alfred, is the divider screen up?" Sarah asked when Alfred resumed their conversation. He looked in the rear view mirror at Shinski's horrified look before he raised the screen.

"Excuse me ladies, I'm going to have to put the divider up, again."

Shinski doubled over into Bexley's lap and just wailed. Bex did not know what to do. She just held her friend waiting for some miracle.

"It's worse than we thought," Sarah replied. Her voice cracked; she tried to remain professional.

"Greg is in serious condition, not expected to live," Sarah said softly.

"Mr. Stelman had always described Greg like he was his son... heck, we all adored Greg. He's a winner in our eyes. He worked his heart out for this company," Sarah said softly.

Sarah was trying hard not to sob.

"Alfred, we need to get Mrs. Randolph to Foothills Hospital in Calgary as quickly as we can. I understand she had previous return flight plans to Fort Chipewyan and that her friend has been authorized with Mrs. Randolph to expense their travel and accommodation arrangements. Please ask if her friend can travel with Mrs. Randolph to Foothills Hospital in Calgary. We're trying to work out something from this end on one of our jets."

Alfred lowered the screen.

"Ms. Hargrove, will you be accompanying Mrs. Randolph to the hospital? I am..."

"Absolutely," Bex interrupted him."

"Excellent. We should be at the hanger in about twenty minutes. You'll board with your luggage. A Mrs. Dilworth, the plane attendant, will meet you when we arrive. If you'll follow her and board quickly, I'll need to speak to the pilot and make sure he understands your circumstances. Restroom facilities and some food will be available on the jet. If you need to use your cell phones, please do it now. There will be a limo driver in Calgary waiting upon your arrival."

Alfred raised the divider screen.

"Shinski," Bex said lifting her friend's limp body up for a minute. "Listen, I must call Maude in Fort Chipewyan and leave some contact information."

Bex dialed Maude. It had worried Bex when the divider screen went up again; she knew something was really wrong.

At that moment, Sarah called Alfred back.

"Alfred, Greg was pronounced dead on arrival at the hospital. I can't believe this. I understand there were two other fatalities in a car explosion and that the scene was horrendous.

They're trying to identify those victims now. The plans have changed for the women," Sarah paused. Alfred gasped.

"Alfred, seems Ben was driving Greg to the awards ceremony. Ben T-boned the car with the two fatalities. Ben's all right; he wasn't hurt badly. He's the one that called to update us," Sarah said. "But the car he hit exploded and those individuals died." Sarah sighed.

"Alfred, I'm relaying this to you as it's coming off the police report-feed simultaneously being aired on television in a general statement to the public. I'm watching a live streaming of the incident on the area news. That means it's on the Internet and Twitter now too. Mrs. Randolph will be able to see this on her cell phone. They have not released names yet, but I don't want her finding out this way. She'll suspect who it is right away, I'm sure. Oh, my God. Don't mention this to them yet," Sarah commented.

"Alfred, Mr. Stelman is buzzing me. I'll get back to you. If you have any problems at the hanger, just call. Your party has been cleared for boarding. I'll keep you posted. Goodbye."

It was hard for Sarah to accept her favorite employee was dead. She had spoken to him a couple days ago and had given him this assignment. She wished Mr. Stelman had not sent one of his employees to award the scholarships. It was not that Sarah wished Mr. Stelman such a fate; it was that the company had not needed to send a representative at all. One of the judges, already there, could have easily presented the awards on behalf of the company. Sarah knew that. *Now their favorite, rising-star employee was dead!*

# 34

## Saddledome Assignment

Sarah had been the one two days prior who had called Greg Randolph on behalf of the CEO, Harold Stelman. She had communicated his request to change Greg's itinerary, which cancelled plans with his wife and her female friend. Greg had been asked to represent N-GerDon in the college scholarship awards ceremony in Calgary. Greg had caught up with his wife at the front entrance to the Fort McMurray tour facility to explain the change before dashing off to Calgary. The women had been disappointed but decided to make the most of the two days they had planned.

Greg had hardly been aware of the trip to the corporate hanger on route to catch his plane to Calgary; he had been busy thinking about the student awards, a phone call he had needed to make to the theatre director at the Saddledome and work on a report Mr. Stelman was expecting regarding the leaching of Holding Pond Number Three. He had been daydreaming what he might do in the future to surprise Amanda and Bex with another trip to Calgary for fun since he had had to reschedule today's plans with them. He had already boasted Calgary was on the same level as New York City. He hoped it would be!

"Good afternoon. My name is Greg Randolph. May I speak with the coordinator of the student competition being held at the Saddledome today? I'm going to be delayed getting there," Greg said.

"Yes, I'll connect you, sir."

"Greg, how are you? Looking forward to your company presenting the awards again this year and we are so thankful for your company's generosity. I understand you will be arriving a little later than expected? Know what timeframe? We can certainly make a few changes to the schedule until you arrive, so don't worry. Be safe and see you later this afternoon."

"Well, again, I apologize but I'm just leaving Fort McMurray on the company jet. Depending on traffic when I get to Calgary, I should be there by three o'clock for the awards—at the latest."

"Don't worry. We'll see you when we see you."

Greg pushed the end button to complete the call and resumed some last minute finishes on the holding pond report.

"Alfred, you're a good man. Thanks. See you soon," Greg waived to Alfred getting out of the limo and boarding the company jet.

Greg took a seat on the plane and resumed business. There were many obstacles concerning community acceptance of the oil sands project. One of his jobs was to smooth public outcry about their environmental safety concerns, answer their questions and get this project back on course without any more hiccups meeting barrel production expectations. He was trying to resolve the leaking of the holding ponds into the waterway. That was an ongoing problem!

His wife was becoming a big emotional concern as well. He knew Amanda was not going to be able to handle this remote lifestyle much longer.

*Thank God Bexley is here for her now. Crisis averted temporarily!* Greg thought.

Greg was in Calgary before he knew it and had finished up typing some more reports on his laptop and working on some expense reports he had brought with him. He spotted Ben, waiting for him, leaning by the company limo.

"Hello, Ben, so you're down here now with our company limo fleet. Like it?" Greg asked.

"Yes, sir, there are five limo drivers here now. N-GerDon stays quite busy with their employees and visitors flying in and out of Calgary. Some city, sir! You'll enjoy it here. Alfred told me this is your first visit."

"Yes."

"I hope it will not be your last."

"I feel sure I will be visiting here again real soon. I'm planning to enjoy the city with my wife and her friend next time—in grand style. I'll be scouting out some good places to take them. I'm here on business this time."

"Yes sir."

Greg sat in the back seat with the limo's privacy glass divider closed so he could conduct some last minute business scheduling for the next week. From the back seat, Greg was still able to hear the occasional profanity slipping out of Ben's mouth as he drove. That surprised Greg since it was certainly not professional of Ben. He looked out the window as they darted in and out of unanticipated heavy traffic. Greg tapped on the glass screen divider.

Ben lowered it.

"Say Mr. Ben, my man, anything wrong up there, champ?"

"No, sir. Just fast moving, heavier traffic than normal. Lots of it today! Trying to find some shortcuts, sir. Didn't mean to bother you! I'm trying to hurry."

Greg was getting a little anxious about the time as well and seeing Ben driving a little recklessly had captured his undivided attention for a moment. Greg could see the Calgary Scotiabank Saddledome in the distance, though, through his side window and that was reassuring! He smiled at the grandeur and magnificence of the architecture then returned his attention to his papers and laptop screen.

*What an awesome sight*, he thought, as he continued typing an encouraging response letter to an oil sand's protest group. He had just finished the letter and closed his laptop when the limo swerved violently and Greg heard Ben's most profane comment yet.

Greg's computer toppled to the floorboard and Greg bumped the limo's side door hard. He reached for his seatbelt to buckle it up as he tapped on the glass divider screen again.

"Ben?"

Greg didn't hear if there had been a response; the sound of blaring horns, people screaming and the sudden implosion from all sides heightened his senses. His body was thrust forward initially in one frontal impact with the glass divider screen and shattered it, then his head jerked back as the limo was hit from the side and started into a sideward spin hooked with the other car. Greg sensed being turned upside down as he blinked to make sense of images flashing by. He was facing the floorboard sprawled out on the back seat. There was a sudden damning impact to the other side of the limo jamming him into the floorboard, head first, like a spear into its target. His nose hit the floorboard hard and then he felt pain shoot through his whole midsection.

Another vehicle had locked with the limo crumpling into its metal entangling three cars that came to an abrupt halt. All Greg remembered hearing were horns. For a split second his eyeballs scrolled upwards uncontrollably as his brain tried to reset the senses. He blinked again trying to identify the blankness of the floorboard.

There was another sharp, undeniable pain in his left leg, groin and stomach, now. Then he felt nothing. He knew he was injured and trapped. He heard Ben calling him then he passed out.

Ben had bruises and his head was bleeding. He climbed out of the driver's window sideways through the busted-out door window framework and ran from the vehicle fearing a second explosion. He looked back at the limo and saw it had been ripped apart and twisted between two other vehicles. He saw the vehicle he had T-boned when he sped into the intersection was now upside down across the street on the sidewalk engulfed in a ball of fire.

He had seen Mr. Randolph trapped inside the limo with the glass divider shattered and that glass had impaled his passenger. He had heard nothing when he called out for Greg. Ben had crawled out of the limo and had run from the wreckage to where the bystanders were. He had blood all over him from a broken nose and saw a medical team member running toward him.

Ben called Sarah Lance to update N-GerDon on the incident. She was his go-to person at the Fort McMurray corporate offices. Then Ben let the medical assistant attend to his injuries.

Witnesses standing on the sidewalks would later report they had seen cars spinning and sliding into the intersection at terrific speeds colliding with side road traffic and had pointed to the man from the limo, Ben, as the one who had caused the pileup.

Many bystanders had immediately run to assist the injured passengers anyway they could. This group of people impeded emergency vehicles responding to the critical center of the mayhem where there more serious injuries.

"The car just exploded, sir," a bystander told the city police.

"Flames shot high! The car doors were crushed and mangled and we couldn't get them out," they said pointing to the limo and the car that had exploded. The car had burned right before everyone's eyes and there was nothing they could do but watch it burn right down to charred remains of the body frame.

The two bodies in the car were incinerated in the intense fire within minutes. People were stunned with shock.

Greg Randolph, critically injured, was pinned in the back seat of the limo. The vehicle landed cockeyed in the middle of the intersection causing the pileup.

"Sir, can you hear me? Sir?"

The response team tried to solicit a response from Greg as they tried to figure a way to get him out.

In a labored breath, Greg said, "Tell Amanda...tell her I'm sorry. Tell her I love her." Then he slumped into unconsciousness again.

"Okay folks, move back," the medical crew yelled.

"Get a wrecker crew over here! We've got someone trapped and unconscious. Need crowbars and a torch! Pull this wreckage off the side here so we can access the side door!"

A tow truck had driven up on the sidewalk and had attached a chain to the one car and pulled it away from the limo and a good portion of the damaged limo came with it. A fireman took a small blow torch to the side door and frame in two places, then took a crowbar and pulled it away for access and carefully removed a portion of the divider cavity that had previously held the limo's glass privacy screen. It had prevented their access to free Greg's body which was face down, twisted in an unnatural position forced into the well of the floorboard with his legs doubled back. Part of Greg's body was jammed under the limo driver's seat. Shards of the broken privacy screen had pierced the core of his body. Blood was everywhere. When they checked his neck there was still a pulse but it was weak.

Greg's injuries were extensive but the medical crew was able to free him, place his body carefully on a gurney and board him in a fly car while running back to attend to more of the injured. Flashing red emergency lights and screaming sirens alerted everyone there were emergency vehicles trying to exit the area; but the sirens were useless in forging a pathway. The fly cars crawled through the vehicular entanglement on route to the nearest medical facility, the Calgary Foothills Hospital.

There were two large black zippered body bags lying in the street near the charred car. They contained two bodies.

"Oh, God, my God," the people screamed.

The Calgary City Police moved quickly to section off the area. Hindering the emergency team efforts were the rubber-neckers causing a bystander delay.

The medical crews, the Coroner, and the Calgary City Police scurried about performing necessary duties to help clear the wreckage, attend to the injured victims as best they could and direct traffic away from the accident.

Tow trucks worked diligently to remove cars that could not be driven. It had been a long process to exchange identification among the drivers involved in the fender benders, the more serious cars damaged and those with personal injury.

Greg had been pronounced DOA at the hospital. His body was processed and toe tagged with cause of death being listed as fatally injured in a car accident. His legs were broken and his core organs lacerated from large sections of broken plate glass, which had been the limo's privacy divider screen.

The body was taken to the city morgue in Calgary. The police attempted to call the contact numbers Greg had had in his wallet upon arrival at the hospital. There was an emergency contact number for his wife, *Mrs. Amanda Randolph* and an N-GerDon corporate staff member, *Sarah Lance*.

Ben, the limo driver, had been taken to the same hospital with non-life threatening injuries and released with a broken nose. He had given his contact information to the police and had stood guilty as charged by a group of bystanders pointing to him as the original offender who ran the red light and going too fast.

Ben called corporate with the devastating update regarding Greg and to ask Sarah if she would arrange for another corporate limo to pick him up and take him home. It was a difficult conversation since Ben knew he was responsible for having caused Greg's death. *Or that the corporation would be since he was an employee driving on company business.*

Thank God for corporate liability insurance.

—◦—

Greg Randolph never made it to the student competition. The accident happened near the Saddledome. When Greg didn't arrive as expected and it became apparent he would be too late to make his presentation, the theatre staff implemented alternative plans and the ceremony continued without a glitch. One of the competition judges simply stepped in to take Greg's place. But the staff was growing increasingly concerned as to his whereabouts when he *never* showed.

Two Saddledome security guards, who regularly monitored traffic updates, had heard a call come through alerting them of a major wreck near the stadium. They had made necessary updates to their log and had remained alert to whatever they could do to alleviate expected traffic congestion in the area.

Their job now was to make sure stadium visitors could easily access their cars and maneuver the accident scene to attend scheduled events. Another show was due to commence within the hour.

The Calgary City Police had contacted Edmonton RCMP regarding the case since the incident transfers to their jurisdiction when fatalities are involved. The RCMP began contacting next of kin. They had tried unsuccessfully to contact Mrs. Amanda Randolph with information of her husband's death. An urgent message and phone number had been left with the B&B attendant in Fort Chipewyan.

Greg was a United States citizen, killed in Canada, which would add a layer of red tape to the procedure when the time came to transport the body across the border.

The RCMP officer also called Sarah Lance, the executive assistant at N-GerDon listed as an emergency contact.

"N-GerDon Corporation," Sarah Lance answered, "Ms. Lance speaking. May I help you? Mme Lance parlant. Puis-je vous aider?"

"Ms. Lance. I'm calling in regard to a vehicular accident involving a Mr. Gregory Randolph. This is the RCMP, Edmonton. I'd like to confirm his employment with N-GerDon Corporation in an effort to contact next of kin."

"Yes," Sarah slowly answered. "We're aware of the accident. The limo driver, Ben Reese, who was involved in the accident, contacted us."

"Yes, ma'am, we've tried to contact a Mrs. Randolph on a cell phone number given. She was one of the contacts on a list found in Mr. Randolph's wallet. He had this company number as well. But we haven't been successful in reaching his wife. If you have an alternative number to assist in our effort, that would be most helpful. The address Mr. Randolph had appears to be a temporary residence; at a B&B in Fort Chipewyan. There were no other phone numbers. Here's my badge number, name and phone number if you think of additional information."

Sarah Lance was still shaking as she jotted down the contact information. She had asked if there had been any more news about Greg and the officer had hesitated. Sarah knew what that meant and started to cry.

"I am sorry, madam, truly, very sorry," the officer replied.

Sarah hung up the phone.

She could not believe it. *Their fair-haired boy, DEAD.* She started to buzz Mr. Stelman. Instead she walked back to his office to tell him personally.

"Mr. Stelman, *Harold,* our dear boy, *Greg,* is dead."

Sarah collapsed in a chair next to his desk.

"Greg is dead!"

Sarah disbanded with all professionalism, and slumped in the chair next to Mr. Stelman's desk. She had been Mr. Stelman's executive assistant for thirty years following him from city to city as a loyal employee. Today, she was vulnerable, grieving and needed Mr. Stelman's consolation. The two had grown quite fond of Greg—their rising junior executive star groomed for Vice President, eventually even CEO.

Mr. Stelman stood immediately, walked over to comfort Sarah, leaned down and put his arms around her for a moment in sincere sorrow, then stood erect.

"Sarah, we need to find Mrs. Randolph," Mr. Stelman said softly steadying himself with his hand on her shoulder. "Is she still a guest at the North B&B in Fort Chipewyan?"

"Yes," Sarah managed in a bare whisper, "she and her friend. I told Alfred to take them to the airport hangar and that I'd call him."

"We need to make plans to get her out of Fort Chipewyan. Had they bought a house yet in Calgary?"

"No."

"We need to get on this ASAP. She'll probably want to go back to the States, I suppose. We need to help her in any way we can. There're quite a few logistics in this we need to focus on. Find a hotel for her in Fort McMurray for the meantime; I understand she's not happy in Fort Chipewyan." Mr. Stelman paused. Then, Sarah, it looks like we're facing substantial liability here. Call our insurance agent and our man in the legal department. Get a hold of Ben Reese and tell him he's to take a week off. We'll deal with that later. For now he has a lot more to worry about than his job. We have quite the task before us too!"

"Sir, Mrs. Randolph's accompanying friend's expenses are also being paid for by the company, per your prior approval."

"That's an issue. Do what we need to do to honor Greg. But we can't continue that forever," Mr. Stelman commented.

# 35

## Same Last Name
—◆—

The coroner in the medical examiner's office was busy with the three fatalities that had arrived from the *Saddledome accident* (as it was being referenced). There were two unidentified fatalities in the explosion taking precedence over their other work and Greg Randolph's body had now arrived and had been toe tagged.

The charred remains of the two bodies from the car explosion would take a little more time and effort to identify; there was nothing much left of the bodies except skull, some skeletal remains, some hair, charred belt buckle and jewelry. The coroner was noting bone structure while examining both bodies trying to ascertain decent. Noted were the high cheek bones, large front teeth with a slight gap, lack of the Carabelli cusp on the maxillary first molars (a little bump which is missing in Native Americans but not always due to racial integration) and the two bony lingual nodes protruding from the jaw bone under the tongue. Noted also was the inverted breastbone indentation, the little toes that lie under the next one and the extra ridge of bone along the outside of the foot. To be sure, there would be a need for further confirmations such as dental records if any existed. Then any evidence collected at the accident scene would be helpful. It appeared both bodies were of First Nations decent from the coroner's first evaluation.

The RCMP solicited the CCP's help in going to the impound lot looking for any identification in the charred framework, the only thing left of the car itself.

—◆—

"Hey wait, the license plate is burned to a crisp, but I think I can make out the raised numbers on what's left."

"Yes, hey, take your cell phone, snap a photo of the license plate at an angle to capture a shadow from the raised edges."

"That worked! I can see the numbers."

"We'll run the plate numbers when we get back to the station. The photo angle shows the numbers clearly."

The police identified the vehicle as a car owned by a rental company reserved at the Calgary airport location under the name, Obigon Sakawa, III. There were two addresses given on the rental application. One for Fort Chipewyan and the second in Fort McMurray.

RCMP conjectured the second passenger might be the wife due to the coroner's report of a burned 14K gold wedding ring with a raven designed on it still on the skeletal ring finger. The size of the skeletal frame was that of a female versus a male. The present assumption was that the driver and passenger were probably husband and wife.

Working backward, the scheduling for flights coming into Calgary, at the time the car was rented, listed two individuals on the Fort McMurray flight manifest being a Mr. and Mrs. Obigon Sakawa III. The rental application listed employer as N-GerDon. For now, the RCMP felt they had a good lead to follow.

The officer had just called the company's executive assistant asking about Greg Randolph. But he had two more employees, he thought. He redialed the number to speak with Sarah Lance again.

"Ms. Lance. This is the RCMP Edmonton headquarters again concerning the Saddledome Calgary accident. The investigation has turned up two other fatalities involving a second car driven by another employee of N-GerDon Corporation."

"We have evidence verifying two other individuals both, we think, by the same last name, *Sakawa*, and need confirmation of employment to help with their identification. Would you mind verifying a *Mr. Obigon Sakawa III* as an employee of N-GerDon?"

"That name doesn't register with me. Wait one moment while I run an employee check. I can do that from here. Well, yes, we do have that name listed, husband and wife actually— both employed here. Yes, now what did you say was their involvement in all this?"

"There were three fatalities in the same Calgary vehicular accident, Ms. Lance. They all were employed by the N-GerDon Corporation, it seems, from what we've been able to ascertain in our preliminary investigation."

Sarah was silent trying to comprehend.

"Madam?"

"Yes, I'm here. Bizarre! You mean there were three employees involved in the accident in Calgary all in different cars?"

"Yes ma'am. Well, no, just two cars. We are having difficulty identifying the two victims in one car. So if you will assist us, it would be appreciated."

"Yes, I understand. The Sakawa family is First Nations, Fort Chipewyan. They have customs to consider."

"I think we have a Mr. and Mrs. Sakawa III, then, as two more victims. Do you have contact numbers for them?"

"Well, no, it looks like each listed the other as contact. But I see they have family in Fort Chipewyan and a daughter in Ft. Chipewyan. I have a phone number for an address. You might reach the daughter, there."

—⊰⊱—

The RCMP was well rehearsed in such matters. This situation was looking like it would involve sensitive issues with culture, two individuals with residences in both Fort Chipewyan and Fort McMurray, one individual with a temporary address: Fort Chipewyan and a previous one in Port Washington, WI in the States.

The RCMP was now ready to contact a special agent—hire a detective they had used at times in special instances such as these. The case was looking like they would need some help with someone who could travel to Fort Chipewyan, have bilingual ability, and time to focus on the details. The RCMP division officer researched the flights with Air Canada. There was an early 6:50 a.m. flight out of Calgary YYC arriving Fort McMurray YMM at 8:20 a.m. tomorrow morning. It would be tight but possible to make the 9:00 a.m. connection on Hahn Air System to Fort Chipewyan. It was a forty minute flight from there.

The officer knew just the person for this assignment. He called David Drury, explained the case, the complications that could arise and then maybe some unforeseen ones he should expect and asked if Drury was interested in the case.

David Drury accepted the assignment and by ten-thirty the next morning, he was knocking on the door of a home in a remote Canadian hamlet—one of the addresses of the three Sakawa individuals—the address for the hundred year old elder Sakawa, the one that was still alive.

Drury had checked into the B&B. Kinoo, the hamlet's taxi driver, had dropped Mr. Drury off at Obi's house. He would return shortly to join the stranger, Mr. Drury, and his friend, Obi, in their meeting.

Kinoo had not inquired as the nature of Mr. Drury's visit to Fort Chipewyan. But he had planned to return within the hour and figured he would find out soon enough.

Kinoo had left the man standing on Obi's porch knocking on the door.

Drury had stood in the freezing cold hoping someone would answer the door quickly.

Obi thought it was Kinoo and wondered why he was knocking when normally he just walks right in. Obi got up and looked out the window and saw a man staring right back at him with papers in his hand. Obi went to the door and opened it.

"Looks important, sir," Obi had said to the stranger.

# 36
## Calgary Competition
## Excitement and Turmoil
—◁▷—

Snowbird took a deep breath. She had been lined up backstage of the Saddledome for the last ten minutes with her Alberta drama-class group, ready to perform in this year's *Alberta Canada Theatre Group Level Two: Ages 12 through 16—Scotiabank Saddledome Student College Competition.*

The student performers had been selected from previous tryouts at each of their local schools. Fort Chipewyan Community School had been fortunate to be included in this year's competition.

Snowbird's group topic was "RESPECT EARTH." Her group met the night before the performance to finish up loose ends making sure all the props and costumes were set to go. Now they were ready to perform in front of the judges, family and friends.

Snowbird stood in line with her group dressed as an Indian chief holding a large round ball painted like the Earth. The others were in costumes as well. They were standing in line behind Snowbird scheduled to start their performance at three in the afternoon. Her group had been the last scheduled.

Snowbird was nervous, but ready. She patted her collarbone to relax, touched her caribou necklace with the two feathers intertwined in leather thinking how Obi had been so supportive in giving it to her for protection and wisdom. Without Obi, she would have never been able to compete. He had taught her all about loving Earth, protecting it, not polluting it, so Mother Earth would in turn provide for all.

Snowbird walked on stage single file leading her group. She was pleased to hear the applause as her group performed. She was confidant and the response indicated her group was certainly the audience favorite.

N-GerDon Corporation was the main sponsor for the event and had been graciously welcomed back each year. A company representative was set to announce the 2017 winners after all groups had performed.

The executive of N-GerDon Corporation, Greg Randolph, was to have personally awarded the scholarship money to the winning students. Large bank-check mockups were ready for a dramatic presentation emphasizing N-GerDon's generous financial contribution to these students' future education.

Snowbird's group concluded the student performances and applauses for all lasted several minutes.

There was a brief delay. Then one of the judges came forth to announce the winners of this year's competition. The audience didn't seem phased a bit that the N-GerDon representative hadn't shown. They were too busy waiting for the announcements of the winners to notice the change in the program.

Snowbird's group of ten had come in first place. The performers went wild when they heard their names and ran out on the stage to bow. The audience clapped vigorously for Snowbird, still dressed as the Indian chief. All the groups were praised for their outstanding performances and then were asked to take their seats for the closing remarks by one of the judges.

"As you know, N-GerDon is one of the largest energy corporations here in Alberta. The industry as a whole contributes about $200 billion to Alberta. N-GerDon Corporation and other industries have made it possible for students, like you, to attend institutions of higher education. Our previous winners have gone on to become highly productive citizens with successful careers making our world a better place in which to live, work, play, and raise families. We want to thank all the sponsors for their continued support of this annual competition."

"And now, I would like to present the educational awards to this year's winners. Let's give a round of applause again for

Team 9, from Red Deer North, for their wonderful performance regarding their topic, *RESPECT EARTH,* and the winners of the 2017 Education Award."

"As I present the award checks to each student, if parents and friends in the audience would please hold their applause until the end, it would be appreciated."

Snowbird scanned the audience looking for her parents. She did not see them. Everyone cheered wildly as she and her group walked out individually to accept the oversized award checks. She beamed with pride for herself, for Obi, and for her people as she cradled the 2' x 4' foot cardboard display of the mock check for $2500—the perfect photo op.

Snowbird looked around feverishly for her parents. They were still not there. Afterwards Snowbird went up to her theatre coach, Mr. Hamilton, and told him her parents were supposed to have come but she could not find them anywhere. The two waited for thirty minutes after the competition ended then Mr. Hamilton located the stadium security.

Snowbird explained her parents were supposed to have flown in from Fort McMurray and that the three of them were to stay overnight, sightsee the next day and fly home the following day.

"I can't remember the name of the hotel where they were staying. I gave that piece of paper to my great-grandfather, Obi," she exclaimed.

"Okay, Snowbird," Mr. Hamilton said. "We'll find them."

Mr. Hamilton asked the security guard, *Fitz,* if there had been any messages left for the theatre group, specifically for a *Miss Snowbird.*

"No, sir, I'm sorry."

"Well, it seems I have a student with no parents, no information about where they are staying, or what airline," Mr. Hamilton said looking at his watch.

"Well, the only message here is for you stating a car is waiting for you at Gate 4 to take you to your next competition. But nothing for Snowbird; and your last name, again, miss? Is it Sa-ka-wa?" the guard asked.

"Yes," Snowbird replied pronouncing it correctly for the guard.

"Okay, young lady, let's see what we have here—a copy of your contact information. Okay. Cell phone, work numbers in Fort McMurray for your parents! Wow, you're a long way from home, my dear. Okay. Oh, you're from Fort Chipewyan. You've traveled a good distance to come here. We'll find your parents."

"Mr. Hamilton, go on, you have another event waiting for you. Leave Snowbird with us; she'll be fine. I know you have a taxi waiting at the South Entrance and with our concert getting ready to start, you'll want to move your taxi otherwise you will get bogged down in concert traffic. We'll take good care of Miss Sakawa. We have your contact information and her competition application listing her emergency contact numbers."

"I'll check back with you tomorrow, Snowbird. Thank you Fitz," Mr. Hamilton said and reluctantly left Snowbird with stadium security.

"She'll be okay, go on to your next competition," Fitz waved him on again.

Hamilton ran to catch his taxi. His group would be getting antsy hoping they would make their next event on time.

Snowbird sat down with the guard and told him as much as she could remember again about her parent's itinerary.

The guard nodded.

"You sit right here," the guard said.

Fitz kept the child within sight while he made a call to the Calgary City Police. Snowbird still had on her Indian chief costume. The police had said to give the parents an additional hour then call back and they would issue a Child Protection Alert, *a Code Adam*. Fitz promised the child would be fine for the time being in his charge. He hoped the parents would show up at the stadium since this was their intended meeting place.

Fitz called a few more places while he monitored duties for

the stadium's evening performance that was underway. He was not willing to contact Child Welfare just yet.

Fitz had begun calling the hotel where the theatre group had stayed the night before. There was not a reservation for Sakawa except Snowbird Sakawa. The guard called the Calgary airport's main phone number and asked for airport administration assistance to check the manifest for flights from Fort McMurray that day.

"Sir, thank you for your security status credentials," the attendant said confirming the guard's badge number and security station location.

"Sir, the only flight from Fort McMurray had two passengers with that last name—Sakawa. But that flight arrived on time about six hours ago."

"Thank you," Fitz replied. He finished his conversation, looked dismayed as he glanced at Snowbird. He had reconfirmed the manifest and the arrival time and sighed.

"Did you want to change back into your regular clothes?"

Fitz smiled gently tugging the fringe on Snowbird's pants in a friendly gesture.

"I couldn't find my regular clothes when I went backstage to change. I spent too much time looking for my parents and lost my clothes," Snowbird explained.

"They were in a white plastic bag with my shoes," she sadly admitted looking down at her moccasins.

"Okay, I'll call maintenance and see if they've found such a bag," the guard replied.

"Yes, yes, okay, thanks," Fitz replied and hung up.

In a short while the head of maintenance came into the office.

"Sir, we have looked everywhere. We did not find a bag with clothes, shoes, anything. We're so sorry. The stadium is open to the public for the current show, so I'm not sure we'll have another chance to look further until after the event ends late tonight. Perhaps someone will find it and turn it in before then. Let's hope so. I think it's more probable it has been accidentally thrown away," the staff member replied and left.

Snowbird watched as the maintenance director walked out of the security booth.

*At least I am wearing the necklace Obi gave me,* she thought. *I'm glad I didn't lose that!*

"Hmmm, we aren't done yet, young lady. Let me think. Are you thirsty? There are some water bottles in the small refrigerator there and some crackers."

The guard walked around the corner to speak in private to a guard by radio, "Hey, Brad, you there? Brad?"

*Static*

"Yeah Fitz, what's up?"

"Got a Code Adam and need your help. I know this is not your job. But can you call four hotels in the area asking if a Mr. and Mrs. Sakawa III are registered and get back to me? These are the numbers."

Fitz rattled off the names of four other hotels besides the one he had just checked.

"And then would you check out the Foothills Hospital to see if any party by that name has been admitted today? We're just covering all the bases…"

"Fitz, did you say Sakawa?" the patrol officer interrupted.

"Yes, why?"

"Wow. You just come on duty, man?"

"Well, a little over three hours ago, maybe. Why?"

"There was a whopping wreck just a few blocks from the Saddledome about six hours ago. One car T-boned another car and it exploded. Guys on duty said the flames were intense. Think there were three fatalities. Surprised you didn't see the road blocked off when you reported to work."

"I just noticed on the log that there had been a wreck and traffic was under control."

"Yes, just cleared it up in the last few hours. That one car was totally destroyed by fire! A complete loss! I saw the car up on a tow truck trailer bed. Man, those people didn't survive that. Yeah, but listen Fitz, that name, I think that was the name of the couple that was in that car. Or something like that name. It was a funny name. Hold on, I think they were able to find out the license plate and a name."

Brad fumbled a minute as if checking the name and then replied, "Fitz, yeah, the name was Sa-ka-wa. Two people by that name, we think. The other car had an individual that was critically injured. Took him to the Foothills Hospital; don't think he made it, though. We got there late but bystanders said they saw a male crawling out of one of the cars, the big limo, I think it was. He was alive and ran from the pileup. Don't know which party was in which car actually. The report doesn't have all that, yet, Fitz. It was a hell of a mess out there though! The two cars with the most damage had two passengers each. The shorthand version of the police report only reads *two cars collided in intersection causing ensuing major pileup.*"

"But two bodies went in black body bags to the medical examiner's office. What's left of their car is in CCP's (Calgary City Police) impound, maybe both cars. We were on site for about an hour then were called back to the station. I'll call to see if I can get those names officially released and call you back. The spelling might not be right on this report, but I think it is your party, *Sa-ka-wa.* They might release the data if I tell them there is a minor child stranded in a strange city without family and we suspect the two victims might be her parents. I'll check the other police reports too and get back to you—*910— over.*"

"Okay. Thanks Brad, over."

Fitz walked back around the corner. Snowbird had started on a second package of peanut butter crackers and sipping from a bottle of water.

"Miss, you'll need to stay here with me for a little longer. Let me show you where the restrooms are."

The guard accompanied Snowbird down the hallway and pointed to an indention where left was MEN and right was WOMEN. Snowbird went inside the women's restroom dressed in her Indian chief costume and moccasins. Other event guests were staring and laughing. Minutes later Fitz led her back to the security booth.

"My parents aren't coming are they?" she asked slowly looking up at him in sadness.

"Let's go back into the security booth. I'll have a staff lady take you to the Saddle Room Grill for something healthy to eat."

"No thank you. I'm not hungry."

Snowbird sat in her costume quietly until the guard's radio buzzer startled her.

"Fitz here, yes, Brad. I understand. Right, I'll call right now."

"Miss Snowbird, there's a young woman coming to meet you; she's with our customer service. Since it's getting late, she's made arrangements for you to spend the night in a nice place. There are other children there. I'm sure all of this will be cleared up for you. You're a smart young lady. We're so proud of you for winning that college scholarship. The large cardboard there leaning against the wall is not really a check or money. It's just a prop. The N-GerDon administration will be sending the actual money award to your parents or to the school you choose. That's what they do; you can just leave that thing here. I'm so proud of you."

"Well hello, Mrs. Corvaire," the guard said announcing the arrival of a woman from the Saddledome Customer Service. A second woman stood next to Mrs. Corvaire.

"Thank you for coming. This is Snowbird Sakawa. She is one of our student winners today of the Alberta Canada Theatre Group Competition. Please take care of our little Indian chief here! She's a promising young lady!"

Mrs. Corvaire took the lead and turned to Snowbird to introduce the second woman.

"Snowbird, I want you to meet Ms. Childress. She's a representative of the Calgary Child Protective Services in Alberta. You'll be going with her tonight."

"Fitz, we'll be releasing the child to Ms. Childress with

CCPS (Calgary Child Protective Services)," Mrs. Covaire replied.

"Fitz, if you'll sign the Stadium Liability Release form, Ms. Childress has there, legally transferring our Miss Snowbird to the Child Protective Services, we'll be all set."

Fitz turned to the little Indian chief.

"Snowbird, I have enjoyed meeting you. You are special and I hope you have a good future at whatever college you decide. I wish you well."

He hugged the child and watched her leave with the lady. He hadn't wanted to say anything about the probability of her parents having perished in the car accident, and now she quite possibly was alone in the world. That would have broken his heart; he was sure he wouldn't have been able to maintain his composure. He watched them walk down the corridor that led to the gateway exit.

The two stopped; Snowbird turned and looked back. She lifted her hand and waved slowly.

Fitz waved back, a tear rolled down his cheek. He would always remember the *little Indian chief...princess.* He watched as his little princess disappeared around the corner with the woman.

Ms. Childress led the child to where she had parked her car. She requested Snowbird buckle up in the back seat. Mrs. Childress made small talk with Snowbird to make her feel more at ease; however, she had to make some phone calls. Snowbird sat quietly listening to the one-sided conversation.

"Yes. So you have a definite confirmation matching name and address? Will you fax that police report to my office? I should be there in about twenty minutes. My secretary is still there. She knows I'm coming. I know it's late. We have had a heads-up on this situation since early afternoon and many people have been checking with local authorities."

"Yes, a minor. Child Welfare. Maybe start an IPPA (Interprovincial Placement Agreement) case management. Fort McMurray and Fort Chipewyan. Yes. Okay, let me look."

Ms. Childress glanced through the application papers the stadium guard had given her which was the only identification Snowbird had.

"Okay, from what I can determine, she is full Indian Status, First Nations. Okay. Okay, contact them too. It's a temporary placement status. It's a residential facility-PT (placement temporary). Her expenses? Yes, I know. Well, if the Canadian government doesn't, we'll have to assume that responsibility as the servicing provincial territory having present custody. Okay, just check her in as, *Child Protection Investigation Not Concluded,* and go with that for now. I don't know about the living arrangements or family arrangements or next of kin right now. Listen, I'll call you back."

Ms. Childress looked in the rear view mirror meeting Snowbird's eyes intently staring at her with a straight face. Ms. Childress needed to make one more call before arriving at the center but she decided to reassure Snowbird by engaging in a little more light conversation.

"Snowbird, tell me about your competition today. I understand your group won."

"Yes, we did."

"I'm so proud of you."

"Thank you," Snowbird replied softly then looked out the side window again.

Ms. Childress wanted so much to say her parents would be so proud of her, but she was not sure what might have caused their delay hoping nothing bad had happened and thought it would be better not to mention the parents. She tilted the mirror at bit to avoid Snowbird's sad gaze. It broke her heart. She had seen so many of these type situations. She picked up her cell phone and made that last call.

"Hey, yes, we're on the way. Will you call the Saddledome guard and update him?"

It was after hours when Ms. Childress pulled into the parking lot of Calgary Child Protective Services. *During times of crisis, the doors of this agency are open 24/7 to protect the children*, Mrs. Childress thought, as she took Snowbird's hand.

Snowbird followed along beside Ms. Childress. She looked up at the woman and asked, "Ma'am, are my parents dead?"

# 37
## Taken Away
—◄╟►—

Snowbird told Mrs. Childress she was very worried about her parents and that everyone was being closed mouthed about them. She had heard enough of Mrs. Childress's conversation to feel frightened. Snowbird had followed alongside Ms. Childress as they walked to another office of the Calgary Child Protective Services building and was introduced to yet another woman.

"Snowbird, you'll be staying in a residential school facility temporarily. A case-management worker will be assigned to you tomorrow," the woman said.

"Miss, are those your only clothes?"

When Snowbird nodded, the woman left the room. She returned with an armful of folded clothes and a pair of slide-on shoes and a pair of socks.

"Snowbird, you may try these, if you wish. I think they'll fit you and look nice. I'll take your clothes and…"

"My *costume*, ma'am?" Snowbird asked, interrupting the woman.

"Yes, your costume. I'll place them in a bag for you."

"I don't want to put them in a white plastic bag," Snowbird said curtly. "That's how I lost my other clothes."

"Okay, I'll see if I can find you a bag with our agency name on it; one with a space for you to mark your name."

The woman took note of Snowbird's reaction and understood she would have to be a little more sensitive and alert to such apprehension. She glanced toward Ms. Childress.

"Do you have a sister, cousin or grandparents," Ms. Childress asked trying to get Snowbird to relax.

"Just Obi; and I think he's in bed by now," Snowbird replied.

Ms. Childress laughed as she completed her paperwork admitting Snowbird to the residential school facility. She stood up, hugged the child and explained she would drive her to the school herself. When they arrived, the administrator, who had agreed to meet them after hours, admitted Snowbird and showed her where she would be sleeping that night.

"I'll return tomorrow, dear. Good night," Ms. Childress said and waved goodbye.

Snowbird nodded without saying a word. She wondered how long she might have to stay in this place. She thought about what Obi had told her regarding the residential schools and wondered if this place was like those places. Obi and her parents said they had been forced to attend residential schools where the teachers were mean. She remained quiet not sure what tomorrow would bring.

*How long will I have to stay here?* She asked herself as she lay in bed that night looking at the other children asleep around her. Her fist gripped tightly around something she was hiding under her pillow. It was the necklace Obi had given her.

*How long will it be before I can go to my college and leave this place?* She wondered as she drifted off to sleep.

That night she dreamed about Obi, her mother and father, the little people and the fairies. She dreamed she was the one riding the belly of a coyote. She awoke in the middle of the night thinking she had heard whispering.

Snowbird thought she had heard voices, *"You are safe, princess. We are with you!"* She felt her cheek; she had suddenly sensed a tingling there.

"Are you here?" she whispered to the fairies. She hoped so.

"Obi, I wish you were here with me, too," she whispered clutching her fist even tighter around the leather strands of the necklace.

"I need you," she mumbled pitifully as she fell asleep.

Early the next morning Ms. Childress contacted the RCMP concerning the Code Adam, the temporary custody placement of the minor child and additional information of a great-grandfather still alive—a guiding influence in the child's life. Ms. Childress reported he was living in Fort Chipewyan but was very elderly. The RCMB response was encouraging.

"Hello, Ms. Childress, I did some searching in our recent police files about your *Snowbird*. The name matches information in our system. I have noted it and will be giving the additional information to an individual already assigned to this case. You know him. It's someone you've worked with previously—David Drury. I'll tell him about the minor child. I think he already has the name of her parents and this is probably related to the Code-Adam-Snowbird you have at your school."

"Oh, great, he's good. I hope so. I've heard our little Snowbird is such a talented young lady."

"Yes, we've sent David Drury to her home in Fort Chipewyan to handle the case and provide assistance to the family. I didn't know about the misplaced child until now. We are dealing with three fatalities who lived in Fort Chipewyan all employed by N-GerDon Corporation in Fort McMurray. The child, Snowbird, is caught up in this, it appears, and is stranded in Calgary. It's going to be a complicated case."

"Yes, I can see. The child will be perfectly fine with us until we can determine what's in her best interest," Ms. Childress replied.

"Agree. Like I said, we've already dispatched Mr. Drury. With you having a working relationship with him, I think we can come to a resolution on this case quickly."

"That's great! It looks like we'll be footing the financial expenses to care for Snowbird. I want to make sure we do what's right for her but also what's financially feasible for our bottom line. This case does not necessarily fall under any one category; it involves many issues. We have it listed as *Child Protection Investigation Not Concluded* on the IPPA. Keep me posted. Thanks."

# 38
## Complete Disclosure
—◆—

Kinoo heard his buzzer go off meaning someone needed his taxi services. He called the B&B and was requested to pick up Ms. Weidner at the school grounds.

"Thank you, Kinoo for picking me up. I wanted to ask some questions about your people's culture," Maude commented as soon as Kinoo arrived to drive her back to the B&B. "Are the stories about little people riding bellies of coyotes at night superstition? I've heard stories at the trading post and not sure what they mean. Do little people really roam at night? Maybe they're just homeless children," she said.

Maude did not wait for Kinoo's reply. She plowed on with other questions fearing she would lose her nerve if she stopped for Kinoo to respond.

"I have ancestors in the area, Kinoo. I'm from Fort Chipewyan too. I left when I was ten years old back in 1964. I attended the school here, the one that's abandoned now."

"Is that why you've been visiting the school grounds, Ms. Weidner? Are you searching for something?" Kinoo asked.

Maude hesitated then decided to confide in Kinoo.

"I ran away from this school fifty years ago. I don't remember my family. I do remember my people's customs, though. I vaguely remember the little people and the coyotes; I remember them helping the lost souls complete their circle to the Great Spirit. I came back to finish some personal business and to see if any of my family was still alive. I was adopted in 1966 and lived with a family in Chicago until they passed away."

Kinoo looked at Maude in the rear view mirror. He was stunned by her words. He studied her features, wondering about her age and decided she could not possibly be his long lost daughter—this woman's name was Maude Weidner. He was curious, though. His feeble mind began to churn thoughts of long ago when the Indian Agent had taken his daughter.

*She is dead*, Kinoo thought.

"You should talk to our wise one, Obi. I'll speak to him. I'll tell Obi about you. What's your name again? Is it a married name?"

"No, I'm not married. My name is Maude Johnson Weidner," Maude replied.

When Kinoo dropped Maude off at the B&B; she thanked him. Kinoo promised to talk to Obi and to plan a meeting soon.

Maude decided not to go directly to her bedroom. She wanted to relax by the inviting fire blazing in the Gathering Room. She thought she'd enjoy a cup of coffee and nibble on the fresh sweet rolls the attendant had laid out on a side table for guests. There was a self-service coffee pot on the table. She had to laugh. *Now I have to make my own coffee.*

She fixed a cup of freshly brewed coffee, walked over to the stone fireplace and found a cozy spot in a chair beside the warmth of the fire.

*I must be the only one here this week.* Maude had not seen anyone coming or going even though the attendant said there were no vacancies in the B&B; it was totally full. Maude was disappointed she had not told Kinoo that her given name was *Merinda Kiyasew.*

Maude did not know if she could trust Kinoo yet. She felt it would be confusing to tell him all her names since birth: *Merinda, Kiyasew, number 10, Maude, Johnson, and Weidner.* She had left that little girl, Merinda Kiyasew, in the past some fifty years ago. She was feeling anxious remembering she had also been called, *number 10.*

She recalled more things about her childhood sitting there in front of the fire acknowledging there were many more things she couldn't remember. She couldn't place her father's face, certainly not her mother's face since she had been too young when her mother had wandered off. People change over fifty years and she could not be sure she would recognize anyone *or if anyone would recognize her.*

Her memories at the school were more vivid than her family life before that. And she had had no contact with the place since she left. Clearly she remembered the horror of the two years she had attended the school. And more vivid than anything were the events of that morning when she had run away.

The thought of that awful day made her sad. She regretted she could not remember her friend's actual name. She just remembered seeing the *number 9* on the front of her friend's uniform day after day.

Maude sipped her coffee. She was still alone in the room; it was a good thinking room!

*Maybe Kinoo would want to help me make sense of what I've found in the circle of rocks,* Maude thought.

She had placed those rocks in a circle so long ago under the tree where the witches' hair grew. She had not found what she had buried there. She had found something quite confusing.

*Would Kinoo think badly of me if I told him the reason I came back to Fort Chipewyan was to find the dead body of my friend?* Maude wondered.

Maude wanted to reunite the bones of her friend so her soul would be at peace.

*Would he believe me? Would he get suspicious if I keep going back to the school grounds? Would he report me to authorities?*

Would her friend's skull and bones even be there anymore? Could someone have buried them somewhere else on the school grounds?

Maude remembered how the rest of her friend's body had been too far down in the first hole, too frozen in the dirt to pull out.

*That unholy grave dug by the nuns!* She shuttered.

Would she get into trouble if she told someone after all these years that her friend's bones had been buried in two graves?

What would happen if she told someone what she had seen the nuns do that night? She could not be sure about customs and laws in Fort Chipewyan or Canada.

If she keeps going back to the school grounds and is caught digging up human remains, could she be arrested for the murder or seeing the nuns bury her friend? And not telling anyone?

Maude wondered if there were any attendance records or student rosters. The Holy Angels Residential Indian School had even changed its name over the years.

*There probably aren't any records now*, she thought.

She would have to befriend Kinoo to help her. She had time. She had a month before she would need to be back in Chicago to open her café again. Heck, she had waited fifty years. *What would a few more weeks matter?*

Maude realized questions regarding who might have attended the school could be answered by the oldest members still living in the hamlet. Kinoo was old enough. His friend, Obi, was one hundred years old and that would certainly be old enough. If the two had lived in Fort Chipewyan all their lives, they would certainly know about the Indian Agents taking the children and forcing them to live in the schools apart from any contact with their family.

Maude knew the practice had been ongoing for well over a hundred years even up through 2000, even until 2009 in foster homes after the residential schools were closed. Obi and Kinoo would have attended the Holy Angels Residential School, she thought; they might have seen similar things the nuns or other teachers had done. She wasn't sure if there had been other religious missionaries that might have come to teach. The school appeared to have stayed under the Catholic mindset. The reason she had been able to roam freely over the grounds is because the school was abandoned and she could poke around undetected. Kinoo was the only one who knew she had spent all her time at the school since the day she had arrived.

*Maybe the two men wouldn't remember anything being that*

*it was so long ago. Maybe they were too senile. Maybe they would report me to the police if I told them such a wild story.*

That was a possibility.

*I have to understand I have U.S. citizenship now. I have papers that say I'm a U.S. citizen and a citizen of Canada too,* she thought.

Maude kept reassuring herself she was safe having adoption papers noting her Indian Status; she was so afraid of being in Canada again and not being allowed to re-enter the States.

Kinoo was on time the next morning to take Maude back to the school grounds. After he dropped her off, he drove over to visit with his friend, Obi. Kinoo told Obi about Maude visiting the school every day and how she seemed to be so obsessed with it and had revealed she had attended the school back in 1962.

Obi reassured Kinoo there were many students researching their pasts since there had been two hundred similar residential schools scattered across Canada that many families were interested in their ancestry, their true identity, *especially* those students that had been shipped to the other schools.

"Obi, my friend, this woman, Maude, told me her last name is Weidner. I don't know any First Nations people with that last name," Kinoo said.

"She said her last name was Johnson, too," Kinoo added.

"There are no names like that in our community," Obi said.

"Obi, remember how we were given a number as identification and also English names? I can't remember my English name, can you?" Kinoo asked.

Obi thought, "If they ever called me by an English name, I don't remember it. I just remember my number. It was *number 9* for nineteen years and I was one of the first ones to go to that school. I think it opened in 1902. Some children were shipped off to other schools somewhere else. I don't know what my English name was. That was over 90 years ago."

"Kinoo make us tea. I need to take my medicine now."

"Obi, I was *30*; that was my number," Kinoo replied. "I'm

like you; I cannot remember my English name either. I've been just Kinoo for so long that I have a hard time remembering that I have a last name at times."

"Obi, the strange woman wants to meet you. I know you don't feel well. But she wants to ask you some questions."

"I'll meet her, I don't feel too bad. I'm just tired," Obi said.

—⧈—

Kinoo picked up Maude the next morning and started out toward the school grounds as she requested.

"Ms. Weidner, my friend Obi said he'd like to meet you. We can go to his home first if you wish or do that another time. If we go this morning, it will give us time to talk and give you time this afternoon to go back to the school yard."

"I'll be happy to meet him. Thank you."

"He's not well, though, so we cannot stay long," Kinoo said as he turned onto a side road and headed toward Obi's house.

Kinoo and Maude went inside and greeted Obi who was resting in his favorite chair.

"Obi, how are you today?"

"The same."

"Obi, this is the woman I told you about, *Ms. Weidner*. She wants to ask you some questions. We won't stay long."

"Good to meet you. Kinoo told me you two have lived here all your lives. I was born here, too. I've been gone a long time though. So I don't know if my kin would still be around. Too many years have passed," Maude replied.

Maude looked at the two men surmising if they were as old as she thought they might have to be to know the answers to the questions she wanted to ask them. Maude felt she had to trust someone and it may as well be these two men.

"Sir, I have a story I'd like to tell you," Maude said. "I'll try to talk fast. Actually, my given name is Merinda Kiyasew."

Maude had barely finished saying the name when Kinoo jumped up and threw his arms in the air chanting and dancing in the way of his people but acting like a crazy man. He cried as he twirled around making a whooping sound.

"Woman," Kinoo cried out. "I knew it. I knew it. I thought it might be true—and it is! I knew it!"

Kinoo could barely contain himself lifting his knees jigging along in a little happy dance and wiggling his fingers in the air in delight.

Maude sat back with her mouth open wide.

Obi wasn't sure what this meant but was thoroughly enjoying his dear friend's entertainment this morning.

"I think you are my daughter. I think you are my *Merinda*."

Kinoo sang a bit of a song making it up as he went along just as happy as could be ending his little jig with a diddly song *...♫ after two days- three days... coming out to see, I loaded up the truck and my daughter to be...♫.*"

"I lost my daughter, Merinda, many years ago. I don't know what happened to her when she was taken by the Indian Agent."

Kinoo hobbled over to Maude, losing his balance and stopped to stare at her features. He wanted to touch her. He wanted to hug her and dance.

Maude was stunned. She sat motionless trying to take in what he had just said, trying to add up the years determining if his age made his claim plausible.

"I have pictures at home. Not good ones, but I have a picture of you when you were young. I have things that belong to you, my Merinda. You want to take a look? I have clothes you wore and a doll you made out of sticks and grasses, remember?"

Maude wanted so much for this to be true. She was so apprehensive. She finally broke down surrendering to the possibility she had craved all her life. She jumped up and gave Kinoo a big hug. She shook with tears. She wailed. Fifty years of loneliness, wonder and sorrow flooded her memories spilling out now in joyful, hopeful tears. She let Kinoo whirl her around a bit then she sat down and continued her story.

"I had to run away. I saw terrible things. I was so afraid.

Why didn't you come get me, Kinoo?"

Kinoo grew quiet and through tears he began to answer but Maude kept talking as if someone had wound her up.

"I was adopted later by another family," Maude explained. "I own a coffee shop now in Chicago. I grew up with American parents. I don't remember my real mother. I don't remember my father's face. But I remember how you used to hug me. I remember your hugs!"

"I've been looking at you these past few days and something in you seemed familiar. I wondered why you were so interested in the school. *My Merinda*!" Kinoo replied again.

"I have more to tell you," Maude interrupted.

"I've been going to the school grounds trying to find the bones of my friend. She was buried there and I found the graves but no bones. They were temporary graves; she was buried in two graves. I'm so ashamed. I have to make her soul right so she can go up to the Great Spirit. I have to do this. I need your help. I buried her in a second grave. The nuns buried her in the first grave."

Maude broke into such sobbing and hugged Kinoo again.

Obi sat up as best he could and inquired again due to his bad hearing what she was doing looking around the school grounds.

"Did you say looking for bones? At the school?"

The two men looked at each other. Both remained silent.

"Why were you looking for these bones?" Kinoo asked.

"They are the bones of my friend," Maude sobbed. "My dear friend," she said softly.

"The nuns murdered my friend. I don't remember her name. She was just *number 9* to me."

Obi and Kinoo were the ones now remaining speechless. Obi sat back to catch his breath and coughed hard.

"Kinoo, I need to rest. I need rest. These words make me feel drunk."

Kinoo held his hands to his face trying to hide tears of pain.

"Oh, my soul and my spirit are numb," Maude exclaimed not sure what to do with all this revelation.

"Kinoo, I'm shocked. I don't know about all this. You really think I'm your daughter, Merinda? I disappeared fifty years ago? Yes! I attended the Holy Angels Residential School here. And your daughter disappeared too? I ran away. That's why I disappeared! Was your daughter related to Princess Natawee?"

"Oh, Great Spirit, Great Spirit," Kinoo chanted again.

"The Great One has brought *my Merinda* home to come full circle with our people. *Princess Natawee*, my child, is my grandmother, my *koogum*. She had one child. The child's name was *Moose Jaw*, my father! She was traded for nine horses, our people say, and she had to give back her first born child—Moose Jaw. Our people told me my grandmother left with a white man many moons ago, a fur trapper, and crossed the border into the United States to live."

Maude sat there, tears flowing down her cheeks. She could not move. She looked at Kinoo and shook her head in total amazement. The newspaper clipping posted in her Chicago café seemed to suddenly loom larger than life.

Obi sat staring at the two of them. He was happy for his friend, Kinoo. But he was sad, too. He was witnessing a re-union of father and daughter; he *was* happy for them. Yet he had just lost his son and daughter-in-law. His great-granddaughter was being detained in Calgary. That weighed heavy on his mind.

Obi was worried he might not ever see his Snowbird again. He just wanted to bring her home. He was not sure how much longer he had to live.

Meeting this woman was short and sweet, he needed to rest. He was interested in the woman and her mission but his mind was on Snowbird.

"Child, we saw these same things at the school back when we were there. We've never spoken much of this to anyone," Obi said through his tears.

This was bitter sweet news to Obi. He had a coughing spell and choked with emotion. He suddenly felt uncomfortable sitting there with itchy skin, feeling as if he had a fever and wanting to vomit.

He shut his eyes; he was grieving and his stomach ached. He wiped blood from his mouth again with the corner of his denim shirt and hid his soiled shirt tail from his guests sticking its soiled corner in the edge of his chair.

Obi had another coughing fit and clutched his stomach. He was in pain leaning forward trying to get the words out as best he could.

"Child, I've been silent too long! What happened to you happened to me—to us," Obi said looking at Kinoo.

He swallowed hard as he said Kinoo's name. He looked as if a tremendous weight had been lifted from his shoulders but still a dark cloud lingered over their people.

Kinoo got up and walked over to his friend, Obi, and kneeled on the floor. The two looked at the ground and held each other's hands tightly.

Maude stared at the men. Tears streamed down her cheeks. She got up and leaned her body into the realm of the two men hugging, seeking their comforting presence.

The two men opened their arms to embrace Maude and held her tightly in their huddle.

For so long they had been adults holding back such deep sorrow and fear regarding their childhood. After a few minutes, they sat back and heaved great sighs then were silent again.

Obi spoke first breaking the silence.

"Oh dear ones, the truth is out. Good. Good. I must rest, though. I am so tired. But one last question. How did you get to the States, dear child? Please tell Kinoo. He will tell me later."

Kinoo and Maude kissed Obi.

"Obi, we will come back tomorrow."

"Just find my Snowbird and bring her home. That's all I ask of you," he whispered and closed his eyes.

Obi was a broken man, a tired chief elder of his people. He was weary beyond his years and had hung on far longer than he had imagined he would. Surely there was a purpose for his longevity.

Kinoo called to his friend as they left, "Obi, we will find her. We will bring her home."

# 39

### Bones and a Feather
---‖---

Kinoo drove Maude to his home; the two talked for hours.

"Oh, dear Kinoo, I have so much to tell you," Maude whispered softly through her tears.

Maude laid her hand on Kinoo's shoulder acknowledging him as her father.

She told Kinoo she remembered a lot about attending the school and she had remembered her friend, *number 9,* and the day they had been issued those numbers and their English names.

"Yes, I know. I know that well," Kinoo replied.

"You must not tell anyone yet," he instructed.

Maude was rambling on not hearing him, "...then they gave me the English name, *Maude,* and a last name, *Johnson,* and the *number 10,*" she continued.

"So then my name grew even longer: Merinda Kiyasew, number 10, Maude Johnson...then Weidner," she explained.

"Where did Weidner come from?" Kinoo asked.

Maude stopped, inhaled slowly and continued with her story disregarding any of Kinoo's questions.

"I...I saw something I shouldn't have. I...I was beaten at the school. So was my friend. But she couldn't speak English and the nuns didn't like that. They got angry and beat my friend. They beat her many times and one day they took her away. I never saw her alive after that."

Maude looked at Kinoo through more blinding tears. She leaned into Kinoo and buried her face in his chest.

"I...I saw the nuns in the moonlight take a bundle, the size of my friend, and stuff the bundle in a hole they had dug. Then I saw them beat the bundle into the hole with a shovel and then fill the hole up with dirt. The fairies told me where to dig the night I ran away. I was trying to find my friend and take her with me."

Kinoo listened quietly; he hugged her as she spoke. Her story sounded so familiar. It was a similar secret of abuse he had kept to himself for some ninety years.

Maude stopped. She understood her words were greatly affecting Kinoo.

"Did I say something wrong?" Maude trembled.

"No child. No, dear Maude, I am just happy you are home at last," Kinoo said.

"How did you come to be in Chicago and where did the Weidner name come from?" Kinoo asked.

Maude continued with her story about burying part of her friend's bones in a second grave and then had been so scared knowing she had to get away from that place. She told Kinoo how she had run to the Ice Road in the freezing cold and how her hands were bloodied by digging into the frozen earth.

She explained she had tripped, fallen, and was almost run over by a truck speeding down the Ice Road in the early morning hours before dawn. The truck driver had picked her up and had taken her across the border to Chicago and she had been fortunate to be adopted by an American couple—the *Weidners.*

Both remained quiet, lying with their heads propped on the back of Kinoo's overstuffed sofa. Then Kinoo broke the silence.

"The shaking tent!" Kinoo suddenly yelled out.

"I must tell you about the shaking tent ceremony, Maude. Obi just performed the ceremony for these lost souls. The souls of a deformed fish and the bones of children! I don't think too well in my old age. I think the bones we prayed for were the bones of just one child, your lost friend."

Maude looked up at Kinoo.

"You think they were my friend's bones? You found the bones in a grave, the ones I've been looking for!"

Kinoo looked at Maude and took her hands.

"Obi and I thought the bones we found were those of three children in the area of that circle of rocks buried near the witches' hair."

"What? The circle of rocks? Did you dig up those bones in the circle of rocks? I've been looking for those bones every day and couldn't understand what happened to them. I found a handkerchief tied around a stick in the same hole where I buried my friend's body. You found my second grave!"

"We thought there was a child named Merinda buried there or maybe two other children with *numbers 9 and 10* and were trying to determine who those children were."

"I am *number 10* and my friend was *number 9* and I carved the name, *Merinda,* into that tree trunk under the witches' hair. You have answered my questions," Maude cried out.

"And you have answered our questions, too," Kinoo said.

"Maude, we performed a ceremony for your friend's bones so she could come full circle to the Great Spirit. Tomorrow you and I will make sure we have located both graves. We will make sure to complete this journey."

Maude hugged Kinoo.

"I hope so!" She mumbled.

"Kinoo, I know so much has happened. I want to help you, too. I want to help the poor child, Snowbird. She's in trouble. I see you have the same sorrow about your friend's family. Kinoo, my friend who is staying with Mrs. Randolph, is a lawyer. I told her I might need one and now you might need one, too. She is staying at the B&B but is currently in Fort McMurray on a tour. She is due back soon. Her name is Bexley Hargrove."

"Oh, I drove her and a friend to the airport. They were going to Fort McMurray to see the giant, the evil one. I was frightened for them. That is not a good place."

"Father, they have suffered much sadness, too with a friend's death in a car accident the other day."

"That is the way of this world—there is sadness and gladness. We must learn to accept all things. The Great Spirit must be planning something good from this sadness." Kinoo thought about having seen the Snowy White Owl during the day, just recently.

# 40
### The Second Grave

$K$inoo took Maude back to the B&B that evening. They made plans to spend a half day with Obi the following day and then spend time in the school yard searching for the first grave. They also had to plan how to get Obi to Fort McMurray for more cancer screening.

"You ready, my dear one?" Kinoo asked when he picked up Maude.

"Yes, I am stronger this morning and ready to put the past behind me and look to the future for your friend, Snowbird," Maude replied.

"You don't care if I call you *Maude* now?" Kinoo asked. "I know I named you Merinda, but you keep referring to yourself as Maude. So I think you want to be called Maude."

"You gave me the name, Merinda, dear *Nohtawi* (father). I have little memory of that name. I've been Maude for fifty years. Everyone else calls me Maude," she smiled.

"I'll call you Maude, too, then. Let's go to see Obi this morning. Then we'll spend some time at the school and I need to make a doctor's appointment for Obi in Fort McMurray. Dr. Pathway will help us."

Maude and Kinoo arrived at Obi's home about the time he was trying to make witches' hair tea.

"Oh, what a treat! I used to make that tea often when I was a little girl. I forgot the taste. I own a café in Chicago. It's a coffee shop; maybe I'll start serving tea." Maude smiled.

"My friends, I have much to say today," Obi said. "The fairies visited me last night and told me my time is near. I must help my great-grandchild, though. So we must talk today about how to get my great-grandchild back."

Maude and Kinoo immediately became concerned.

"Obi, are you in more pain today?" Kinoo asked.

"No, not pain in my body, pain here in my heart and head," Obi replied pointing to both places.

"My soul is restless!"

For the next couple hours Obi spoke slowly but quite lucidly how Snowbird might be taken care of when he was gone. Many options were discussed. It was a solemn discussion.

Maude talked about the bones in the first grave. She talked about the shaking tent ceremony and how grateful she was the two men had partly taken care of her mission to Canada. But she told the two how she must take care of the rest of her friend's bones from the first grave in a respectful manner so her friend would finally be at peace.

"My dear, I will do everything possible for you regarding this. We'll have to do this in secret, though. We can't tell the authorities," Kinoo said.

"Obi, I've never met Snowbird. But I feel a kindred spirit with her. She's like me. I was forced to go to a school and both of us wanted to escape and go home. I want to help her. I have found my father again. I have found my friend and will be helping her spirit come full circle this afternoon. It's time to help you bring your Snowbird home to family," Maude commented.

"Snowbird knows Kinoo very well. She thinks of him as a second great-grandfather," Obi said, as he turned to his friend and nodded.

"Kinoo, if I should die, will you take care of Snowbird? I do not know this legal term, adoption, but Maude says that's what some families do. Will you be family for Snowbird like that? We take care of our own and take others into our homes when someone dies."

"Obi, do not talk like that; you have more days to live! But I will take care of Snowbird in the future," Kinoo replied.

"Obi, Kinoo," Maude stood and addressed each man. She

spoke up with determination, "I can help take care of Snowbird. I promise to help. I wish to adopt her if you will let me and if she accepts. This is what I want to do!"

"I see this child will have help in the future from each of you. I thank you both and I feel more at peace. But we have to get her back home. I want to see her back here with our people. I want to have these tests in Fort McMurray so Snowbird can come home to me. I'm ready to do that."

Kinoo made sure Obi was comfortable, filled his mug with what remained of the witches' hair tea, then he and Maude left for the school yard.

Kinoo had promised Maude he would go with her to locate and confirm the graves. It was late afternoon when Maude and Kinoo located the exact spot of the first grave. Maude acknowledged the find.

"Yes, this is place. I know it. Yes, Kinoo, you see it too."

Kinoo began unearthing the remains of the bundle. The hole had been dug fairly deep but narrow—not like a proper grave, though, at all. Maude remembered that aspect. She had had to pull upward on her friend's body that night. She remembered that sound—the snap, the dislocation of a part of the body. She remembered tugging on the bundle, what seemed to be the ribs, arms and skull. She pulled them right out of the hole. It was a terrible thing for a ten year old to experience. The body was already dismembered when she saw what she had pulled up.

Kinoo had dug for an hour in the frozen earth when he was finally able to exhume the precious treasure. He had carefully dug around the bundle so as not to disturb what remained of the child's body. Kinoo had gingerly lifted the partial skeleton of the child, still half wrapped in the decayed pillow case fragments and still a frozen mass. But Kinoo could tell the body had been broken apart. What remained was only a portion of what had originally been buried there, the lower half of a human skeleton. He understood immediately that Maude, as a child, could not have dismembered a body in such a manner; it had to have been done before Maude ever dug through the frozen ground trying to find her friend's body that morning, so long ago.

"Oh, my poor sweet friend, I am so sorry!" was all Maude could muster as Kinoo pulled the mass from the ground.

"I'm sorry to disturb you, my friend," Maude said softly.

Kinoo took off his coat quickly, then took off his plaid shirt underneath and quickly put his coat back on. He carefully wrapped the child's remains in his plaid shirt as if the wrapped bundle was that of a newborn baby of the First Nations people.

Maude sat back on the ground just staring at the bundle of bones. She had wondered how she would react when she finally located her friend's remains after all these years. She knew the customs of her people and that it was taboo to touch the body of the dead.

She didn't care. She took the frozen mass wrapped in Kinoo's plaid shirt from Kinoo's grip and held it like a baby. She rocked it back and forth, crying and said prayer after prayer for forgiveness through her sobs.

Kinoo cried with her. He cried for those whom he had known to have mysteriously disappeared from the residential schools.

*Maybe many others had suffered the same fate.*

"Oh Great Spirit, help this child. Help our people. Help this world. Rid this world of evil. Protect us."

Kinoo gently took the bundle from Maude. He did not have the great and wise Obi there to tell him what to do in this instance. He sat with Maude contemplating what should be done.

"Maude, let's take this bundle to the second grave where the circle of rocks are under the witches' hair. We buried the good part of a fish in that grave so the soul could go back to its Creator. I think that is a good place to bury this child, too. We have already had the shaking tent ceremony for the other part of the child's body asking the Great Spirit to complete her soul. The little people have helped us find these bones. The Great Spirit will accept her soul now that we have found her other half but we must bury these bones properly."

"We need to do this and say a prayer to the Great Spirit. This is where you tried to make things right. It is only right that this is where you must finish what you tried to do. You will be at peace."

"That is what I tried to do that night. But I couldn't."

Maude stopped to compose herself.

"What we do today will finally put me at peace with it."

Kinoo and Maude walked the edge of the bush to the trees with the witches' hair to find the circle of rocks. Kinoo found where he and Obi had recently buried the knotted handkerchief with the small remains of the fish body, the same handkerchief Maude had unearthed and had buried it again—herself not knowing just what to do.

They carefully exhumed the small knotted handkerchief with the cremated fish body and laid it aside. Kinoo dug the grave deeper to accommodate the remains of Maude's classmate's bones and the little handkerchief bundle. They sprinkled more Wolf Willow bark and Loblolly Pine resin they found nearby into the hole to ward off animals. They covered the grave with dirt and placed rocks on top.

Kinoo performed a shortened version of the same ceremony he and Obi had done around the fire pit for the child's skull and bones. Maude was calm, respectful and in agreement.

The two hugged each other and swayed a bit as Kinoo chanted a prayer and sang a song from their customs. They listened to the sounds of nature. Maude drew a circle in the dirt.

"Oh, did you hear that?" Kinoo asked.

"Hear what?" Maude asked.

"Must have been wind in the trees, I heard. It sounded as if someone in the trees said, *Aashaa monetoo*."

The fairies sitting on the top limb of the tree, high above Maude and Kinoo, smiled among themselves. They were satisfied the soul of the child had been respectfully buried, its soul reunited.

"Maude, I didn't sleep well last night. I was awakened quite a few times with a sensation of something brushing against my cheeks and I thought I heard voices like just now."

"What does *Aashaa monetoo* mean Father?" Maude asked.

"It means *Good Spirit*, my daughter. *Good Spirit*."

Maude sighed. Maude knew she had finally come to the end of her painful journey. Now they had to focus on Snowbird. Maude put her arm around her *Nohtawi*—her long lost father.

# 41
## Legal Complications
—◆—

The N-GerDon Corporation immediately reacted to the news of the car accident and was conducting an internal investigation.

Shinski and Bex were still in Fort McMurray in limbo waiting for some direction.

Alfred had picked up the two women after their tour and had been on route to the hanger to assist the women boarding the corporate jet for their return trip to Fort Chipewyan.

That's when Alfred had become aware of the news about Greg Randolph, Mrs. Randolph's husband. Instead, he was advised by the corporate offices to ask the women if they would stay an additional night in a hotel so the company could schedule them on another jet. *(Actually to give the company time to figure out something that made sense for the women since remote Fort Chipewyan would not be acceptable to Mrs. Randolph.)*

There had been quite a flurry of communication from all directions about different family tragedies.

Sarah had arranged for clergy and social workers to be available for the two women: Shinski and Bex, as soon as they could be situated somewhere besides the B&B in Fort Chipewyan. Shinski had no family in the U.S. and Bex was determined to tough this out with her friend somewhere in Canada as long as it took.

Meanwhile, when the women were settled back in the same hotel as the night before, N-GerDon was covering their bases using this time to check on their liability, their duty to Mrs. Randolph and consider what else should be done regarding Mrs. Randolph's well-being. N-GerDon employees wanted to attend some sort of memorial service for their dear deceased friend, Greg Randolph.

Sarah had been discussing some of those details with Shinski later that same day when they settled back into the same hotel. Shinski was thankful Bex was there to console and advise her. Sarah apologized repeatedly for the two having to endure a delay in getting them settled somewhere. N-GerDon Corporation was doing everything possible to assist them.

Shinski had asked Sarah to research what was needed to transport Greg's body to Fort McMurray or to Port Washington, in the States. Shinski told Sarah there were no next of kin in the States.

Would it be best to bring the body to the morgue in Fort McMurray? Would it be best to send the body back to the States, to Greg's hometown? Should Shinski fly to Calgary to tend to details herself regarding the body?

"I don't know about how all this is done," Shinski had commented during her conversations with Sarah.

"I just don't know what to do. Please do whatever you think is best. I'm sorry, I am so shaken. I can't deal with this."

Shinski finally conceded in her grief to leave the details up to Sarah.

Sarah had first to call the consulate to report Greg's death. The representative of the Embassy expressed his sympathy and offered his assistance. He suggested the body remain in the Calgary morgue, being sensitive to Mrs. Randolph's emotional state. Sarah agreed when she understood the severity of Greg's injuries thinking the sight of Greg's body might upset Mrs. Randolph even more.

Shinski had turned to Bex for answers. They all agreed the body should remain in Calgary.

Bex and Shinski were drained emotionally.

Alfred had finally received instructions the women would be relocated, temporarily, to one of the luxury efficiencies on the N-GerDon corporate campus for the following night to get them out of hotel rooms. The company still had to find adequate accommodations for the two women. It was a very difficult call as to what the company could or should do. Sarah was putting herself in their shoes and was trying to be fair and compassionate for her friend's wife honoring Greg and his impeccable service to the company.

"Alfred, you're such a dear," Sarah said.

"I'm so glad you were Greg's driver while he worked in Fort McMurray. You've been such a help these past few days with his wife and friend while they've been stuck here. You've been a good, caring employee over the years. Only *you* could have done for these women what needed to have been done. You've transported them wherever they've needed to go. They've both mentioned how concerned and accommodating you've been in all this. Thank you."

Sarah continued, "We've not finalized a plan for them. But, we think it'll be better if Mrs. Randolph remains in Fort McMurray, with her friend, too. We'll make sure they have appropriate accommodations and we want you to stress upon them that N-GerDon is doing everything possible to assist them. I don't think it's fair to put Mrs. Randolph through unnecessary travel back and forth. Greg's body has already been identified, so there's no need for her to go to Calgary. Quite frankly, I'm glad of that, Alfred."

Sarah paused. She shuttered again at what Greg's body might look like after such an accident.

"Please pick up Mrs. Randolph and Ms. Hargrove and bring them to the office. Two nights in a hotel is enough. The facilities here are first rate. We'll take it from here, Alfred, once you get them to the corporate offices. Human Resources have clergyman and social workers waiting for them as soon as they arrive. This has been a nightmare for Mrs. Randolph and everyone else. We need to make things as comfortable for these women as possible, being in a strange city and not liking Fort McMurray much anyway, from what Greg has told us."

"Sarah, Greg was one in a million. I liked him. I'll take care of these women," Alfred promised.

Sarah called Shinski and explained the change in plans. She

hoped this met her approval and said that Alfred would pick them up soon to drive them to the office.

Upon picking up the women, Alfred again offered his condolences and shared what Sarah had said.

"I know, thank you. My poor Greg," Shinski whispered.

Bex was listening to everything trying now to act as legal consultant for her friend.

A human resource counselor and social worker met the two women in a conference room. Sarah was there too and hugged Shinski trying to console her.

"Thank you all so much," was all Shinski could offer.

Two conference rooms had been made available for the women. One room had an adjoining suite; it was a luxury, two-bedroom efficiency with a kitchenette and private bath. Shinski and Bex could rest and perhaps send their clothes to be dry-cleaned. Alfred was at their disposal for transportation and whatever else might be needed.

"Ms. Hargrove, I understand you're a lawyer and Mrs. Randolph has advised me you'll be representing her if she needs legal assistance. We have our own lawyers, which are available to Mrs. Randolph if she so chooses."

Bex thanked her. She knew quite well N-GerDon Corporation would try to persuade Shinski to use their lawyers and that they would say just that: *they could act on her behalf in any legal matters.* Bex knew that tactic very well. She was determined to look after her friend—the surviving spouse of the wrongful death of her husband *whose employer appears to be liable, wants to take care of her needs for the time being even offered to represent her in these legal matters!*

Bex was quite certain N-GerDon Corporation would not be assisting Shinski in any legal matters! Bex felt sure N-GerDon Corporation would be found guilty of the wrongful death!

"Ms. Hargrove, will you be available to meet with our representatives over the next couple days in further discussions?" Sarah asked.

"Yes," Bex replied.

"Oh, thank you, Bex," Shinski hugged her neck and nodded to Sarah.

"Ms. Hargrove, do you have a reciprocal law license in Canada?"

Bex hesitated answering. *Why would she be asking me that?* She felt she knew where this was going. She did not want to tip her hand that she would be contacting a local firm to help them. Heck, she wasn't even employed anywhere at the moment, but she did have an active license. It hadn't even been a month since her resignation from the Chicago law firm. She felt Sarah was really wondering whether she had the appropriate credentials to legally represent her friend in a case such as this. Bex felt Sarah might be cleverly maneuvering to offer their corporate legal department's assistance in handling the wrongful death claim.

*Sure they wanted to handle the case. Like hell they would! Surely Sarah wasn't offering that!* Shinski was in a vulnerable position and could potentially become a double victim if Bex had not been there to advise her.

"My law firm in Chicago has reciprocity," Bex commented assertively. She allowed Sarah to believe she was still employed in a law firm or perhaps still partners in one in Chicago, which neither was true. *But it used to be true.*

Bex watched as everyone left the room. She thanked Sarah for her help.

After Sarah left, Bex sat back in one of the chairs and drank an entire bottle of water. She pulled out her cell phone and called Dan in Chicago.

"Hi Dan, this is Bex."

"Bex, you're back already. I didn't expect to hear from you for a few months. Everything okay?"

"Wow, Dan. So much has happened in the last two weeks. I need you. You remember me telling you I was going to a high school reunion in Port Washington and then going to Canada to babysit a friend in need?"

"Yes, and then when you returned, we would talk about the

water quality report for Port Washington and Chicago you asked for. Hey, just an FYI, I've already received the water report for Port Washington and for your Chicago residence, too, I might add. Been busy on your behalf, my friend, you can thank me later…"

"Dan, Dan. Set all that aside for now."

"Why, what's up?"

"I..she…well, my friend's husband was killed in a car crash in Calgary."

"Oh, I'm so sorry," Dan replied taken aback.

"Yes, it's bad and with thes friend being my best friend, the overlapping of friendship and legalities could be problematical. I'd like you to research Fort McMurray, Alberta, and find a law firm with Cree language interpreters and a firm having reciprocity in the U.S. that can assist me with a U.S. citizen whose death occurred in Canada. I need one that knows U.S. Embassy details, criminal law, and well, all the necessary services in between. Is that too much of a request?" Bex asked summing up their conversation as needing a miracle worker!

"Hold on there, Bex. What are you mixed up in now?" Dan asked.

"It's convoluted. I'll tell you about it later. For now, please find a good law firm in Alberta. Make sure the firm doesn't have connections with the energy industry up here, particularly with the N-GerDon Corporation."

"Well, what little I know about Alberta, Bex. Any law firm up that way will probably be connected with the energy industry in some manner since that's the primary business there. That industry supports Alberta to the tune of a couple hundred billion dollars, I've heard. That some serious moola! It'll be hard to find a firm that's impartial or not connected to that industry," Dan replied.

"Well, just keep that in mind when you look for one. Okay, dear Dan? Thank you," Bex said using all of her sweetness.

"I'll be staying with my friend in an efficiency apartment onsite at the N-GerDon corporate campus. That'll work for the moment; but it'll become a problem, I think. So here's what I'd like you to do for me. I know it's stretching the truth a bit. I'm going to give your cell phone number to Sarah Lance; she's the executive assistant at N-GerDon Corporation in Alberta. If she should call, please confirm I'm a law partner. Or at least tell her what an exceptional reputation I have. Maybe the Internet hasn't picked up any fray about me leaving the firm, yet."

"That'll buy me some time to figure my next move. Dan, I'll be in conference with N-GerDon executives, their legal department and Sarah Lance in the next couple days. I'm going to listen and keep my mouth shut. And you know how hard that is for me." Bex paused.

"I want to represent Shinski, my friend. This case involves the wrongful death of her husband. He worked for N-GerDon Corporation but was a passenger in the limo that struck a second vehicle killing another couple employed by N-GerDon. I don't think it gets any more complicated than that!"

*She hoped not.*

# 42

### Lawyer—Back in Business

The next day's discussions with N-GerDon's legal department's lawyers and appropriate corporate personnel made Bex feel a bit uneasy. Bex was cordial and attentive. She was prepared to jump into fierce lawyer mode if needed. So far, it was panning out to be quite a trouble-free interaction. Bex remained calm, courteous, yet vigilant. She saw N-GerDon Corporation's compassionate side. Greg had been a valued, respected employee and considered highly promotable to corporate management. Now that was impossible; Greg's death was a blow to everyone!

Dan had been prompt with an answer; he had found a law firm for Bex. Kander Law Firm, in Buffalo Woods, nearby, was eager to assist Bex. Their senior law partner, Peter Zacki, had called Bex within hours to discuss her needs regarding the wrongful death and anything else that might arise. The law firm *was more than competent*, Dan had said.

Meanwhile, Bex needed to address Shinski's personal concerns about funeral arrangements.

It did not take long to plan a memorial service. Sarah, the executive assistant, had been prompt, thorough, and very caring with Shinski on the planning. She had consulted a service director to assist them. It was decided Greg's body would be cremated at the morgue in Calgary and a death certificate, needed quickly for various legal matters, would be issued promptly. Bex had been helpful assisting Shinski with her emotional needs; she was Shinski's only family now.

The memorial service would be short with limited guests and without a body since he would be cremated. Shinski was still numb to all that was taking place. She had told Sarah she could not deal with this emotionally and to plan things as simple as possible to be less stressful for everyone.

That evening when Bex returned to the efficiency after the day's discussions with N-GerDon's lawyers, and having had the brief phone call with Peter Zacki, the senior partner with Kander Law firm, things had changed. The situation was becoming very complicated.

Bex told Shinski there was a conflict of interest with the N-GerDon Corporation providing their hotel accommodations, allowing them to stay on campus in the efficiency apartment, and providing Bex the use of a conference room as an office. The idea to keep them under their watch was no coincidence, Peter Zacki had surmised.

Bex informed Shinski she had retained the Kander Law Firm. Its senior partner, Peter Zacki, had decided the playing field had changed; he felt there was a need to be more protective of his new clients. Both sides were becoming more guarded.

Peter had advised Bex to suggest N-GerDon Corporation locate alternative living arrangements for the two women. He supported giving an excuse that *Shinski would be more relaxed and less stressed if she were away from any N-GerDon Corporation environment.*

Arrangements were negotiated to find accommodations off the corporate campus. Bex was playing the part of friend and Shinski's quasi-legal counsel in conjunction with Kander Law Firm.

One of N-GerDon's corporate personnel accompanied Bex and Shinski the next day to a temporary rental house in Fort McMurray. Bex had emphasized, with the lawyers accordance, that Shinski did not want to return to the B&B in Fort Chipewyan. Since she and Greg had not built a house in Calgary, as was their plan, she really had no home. Nor did she have transportation or means to support herself. She was now a widow. In other words, she was in limbo. *Both she and Shinski.*

Bex advised the N-GerDon lawyers that Shinski was alone, unemployed, incapable of supporting herself, and left in difficult circumstances in a foreign country. Bex had been thankful Shinksi had not been there to hear her say her friend was *incapable*.

Shinski and Bex spent that night away from the corporate efficiency, back now in the same hotel once more where they had stayed previously, so the rental house could be cleaned and stocked for them. The plans were for the two women to move into the rental house the following day. The housing solution was easy since the majority of the oil sands employees lived in convenient rental housing subsidized by N-GerDon Corporation. So it was a matter of finding an empty house. Meanwhile, plans were made to move Bex's limited luggage from the shared room in the Fort Chipewyan B&B and what little Shinski and Greg had had living in the B&B, to the rental house. Shinski and Greg had sold the majority of what they owned in Port Washington when they moved to Canada since the cost of moving such items would have been prohibitive. They had been willing to purchase all they would need in Calgary when their house was ready. Greg and Shinski knew their style of living would be limited until the house in Calgary could be built.

That night in the hotel, Bex received another phone call from Maude in Fort Chipewyan.

"Ms. Hargrove, I've been trying to reach you."

"Oh, Maude, so much has happened. I'm sorry I didn't get back to you," Bexley explained.

"The same here, my friend. I've found the friend I had lost long ago; I found her bones in a grave. I buried part of her body fifty years ago. Kinoo helped me bury the other part properly today. I have come to a peaceful place with this experience. It has been a difficult journey. Obi and Kinoo actually found part of my friend's bones by accident before I could locate them. That's why I couldn't find them anywhere I looked on the school grounds. I'll tell you about it when I see you. I also found out Kinoo is my father, Ms. Hargrove, my long lost father, whom I thought was dead. I can't believe it!"

"What? What a minute. What?" Bexley cried out.

"Yes, Kinoo is my father. I am *Merinda*, his daughter, who had run away from the school a long time ago. He knows who I am. He knows the name, *Merinda*. He was sad to lose me years ago and is happy to have found me again. It is wonderful news, Ms. Hargrove. I'm sad to hear about your friend's husband."

"Yes, I'm working on that right now."

"I wanted to tell you that David Drury, the case worker assigned to Greg Randolph's death, is also assigned to the Sakawa family. There is a young girl, Snowbird Sakawa, who is involved in this situation. Seems Mrs. Randolph's husband was in the car that collided with this girl's parent's car. Her parents were killed."

"Who is this Snowbird and did you say your name was Merinda?" Bex asked.

"Yes. But that was my childhood name. And Snowbird is Obi's great-granddaughter..."

"And Obi is?"

"I know you didn't get to meet Obi. Remember the day you and your friend left for the Fort McMurray oil sands tour? Kinoo was going to take us to see the oldest man in the community, Obi. His great-grandchild, Snowbird, had already left for a student competition in Calgary. It's been a nightmare here ever since you left," Maude explained.

"Snowbird's parents were killed in a car accident in Calgary. Their daughter, Snowbird, was supposed to fly home a few days ago. But when her parents were killed, she was stranded in Calgary. Child Welfare took her in and admitted her to a residential school on a temporary basis. She's stuck there. My father and I talked to Obi and told him I wanted to adopt her if he would let me and he agreed," Maude rambled.

"Maude, I mean Merinda, I can't get used to that name."

"No, I'm still Maude to everyone."

"Wow. So much has happened there too. Adoption? But you haven't met the child? How were her parents killed did you say? In Calgary? Maude, did you say in a car accident?"

"Yes. She needs a home. Obi, her next of kin is very sick. I would like to adopt the child," Maude repeated. "I need your help. You're a lawyer, right?"

"Mr. Drury is here from Calgary for a week. He has to make sure the child has a suitable guardian and living arrangements before he can assist in the child's release from the residential school. Our friend, Obi, needs more medical testing in a facility in Fort McMurray and he would be her next of kin, still-living relative, except that he is very sick and a hundred years old and they can't find the grandfather. Snowbird can't be released to Obi if he is sick and because he is too old to be her guardian. We need your help, Ms. Hargrove."

By now, Bex had grasped the urgency of Maude's call. She sensed the gravity of the situation; she understood the complications surrounding the adoption. Maude was her friend, a U.S. citizen, and probably would want to take the child to Chicago. There were just as many problems with Maude in Fort Chipewyan as there were in Fort McMurray with Shinski.

"Maude, I understand. Let me get back to you. I need to talk with some people down here in Fort McMurray and bring them up to speed about what's happening in Fort Chipewyan up there."

Bex pushed the end-call button.

There were so many aspects of this situation and she was just one person. She needed help with this; she needed *Dan's* help. She needed a cohort, a peer, a friend more than ever.

Bex sat down on the couch in the Radisson Hotel suite. She looked at her friend, Shinski, to determine if she would be able to handle another crisis.

"Shinski, I just talked with Maude, the lady staying at the same B&B where you and I are staying. Remember Maude? She just told me the most unbelievable story. I'm not sure where to start."

"Shinski," Bex, began, "Greg's accident involved others who were killed. They also worked for N-GerDon Corporation. And like Greg they lived here in Fort McMurray part time. The

N-GerDon lawyers told me about them today. Their names are Mr. and Mrs. Obigon Sakawa III. I just found out from my friend Maude there is more of a connection to this couple than I could have imagined."

"I understood this couple is First Nations from Fort Chipewyan," Bex said. She wasn't sure whether to go on with the story since it might upset Shinski.

Shinski sighed and looked perplexed with the connection.

"Bex, I am so thankful you are here with me. I don't have anyone left in my family to help me. This is beyond me and I just don't understand it all."

"The importance of Maude's call, Shinski, is that the two other people, who died in the accident, were the parents of one of the students who competed in the competition Greg was supposed to have attended. But Greg never showed and neither did the student's parents."

"The student, barely twelve years old, is Snowbird Sakawa. She has been taken by Child Welfare in Calgary to a residential school for children until they can find a suitable next of kin guardian. She is a First Nations child."

"Shinski, we did not get to meet Obi, the hundred year old man; he is Kinoo's friend. We were supposed to meet him the day we left for the oil sands tour. Kinoo had offered to take Maude and the two of us to meet him. But we didn't have time. Remember?"

"Obi, the old man, is the student's great-grandfather. Shinski, remember Maude? The one who wore the feathers you thought were so strange? Well, it seems Kinoo, our taxi driver at the B&B, and who is Obi's dear friend, is also Maude's biological father."

"Bex, what are you saying? This is overwhelming. I can't follow it all."

"Bex, back up. Are you saying Greg's limo killed this child's parents and that she is an orphan now? Oh my God!"

Shinski started sobbing realizing the significance of the accident. A cloud of guilt was descending around her!

"Shinski, Greg is not at fault; he was just a passenger in the limo, which hit the other car. Maude says her friends need a lawyer they can trust because she wants to adopt the child. She also said Obi is sick and needs to be transported to Fort McMurray for extensive cancer screening. I will need to talk to a Mr. David Drury who is staying in Fort Chipewyan; he's investigating the same accident. He's been dispatched to Fort Chipewyan to assist with these details. There are additional details he needs to update his investigation. I can help with that."

"I don't understand," Shinski stepped back.

"My head is swimming. I'm confused and horrified with all this. I just want to throw something or hide under the covers!"

"Shinski, settle down. This isn't your fault. It's not Greg's fault, either. It was an accident. But N-GerDon Corporation will be held liable, I feel sure. That's why there's liability insurance, my dear friend."

"This is so awful, Bex," Shinski replied.

"I'm exhausted. What am I going to do?" Shinski cried out.

"I'm not sure. Don't know yet. Get some sleep. It'll be all right; I need to get in touch with Mr. Drury."

Bex called Maude and asked if she had Mr. Drury's cell phone number and if she would pass on the message that she needed to talk with him as soon as possible about the car accident.

"I think he's been trying your cell phone for days," Maude said. "His number must be on your cell phone caller ID log."

*Oh, that's who that was,* Bex realized.

"I didn't recognize the phone number the other day. I've been so tied up. You told me about Greg possibly being involved in a car accident and after that, I didn't focus on anyone trying to reach me. I'll check my call log."

Bex scrolled through her phone log and found Drury's number. She was used to juggling a lot of balls in the air as a lawyer, but this case was becoming personal as well as difficult professionally. Her demeanor and stamina were being tested. It was easy for her to be in lawyer mode when she had no personal connection to the client on either side. But there was Maude—her friend with her adoption case and finding human bones maybe involved in a murder. There was Shinski—a dear friend, with the wrongful death case of her husband. There was a stranger, Obi—sick and needing help with getting his great-grandchild out of a residential school five hundred miles away. Everything she was working on overlapped in so many eerie ways. Being in Canada, without her realm of legal familiarity, was daunting and made her feel like a fish out of water!

Everyone seemed to need her. She was in a quandary. She was thinking this would be a vacation. But she had also wanted to help victims. Her victim list just kept growing.

*Maybe God will give me a few mulligans with this group of victims. I need to help them but it this is a tough bunch!*

Bex was empathetic toward First Nations people in Fort Chipewyan, especially regarding the language and cultural barriers. She was there to help her best friend through a rough time, worse than Bex ever imagined.

Bex needed help on all sides. She and Shinski were dependent on N-GerDon Corporation for many things including lodging, food and other necessities. Neither one had a car in Canada, both dependent on N-GerDon for transportation. A limo and company jet were available for their use if they could be squeezed on the manifest.

Bex had to be careful. She was about to embark on a course to sue (*bite*) the very hand that was feeding them, *so to speak.*

# 43
## Obi's Fate
———

$M$aude had told Bex that Mr. David Drury was staying at the Fort Chipewyan B&B for another week and he had been trying to reach her. Bex scrolled through her cell phone missed-call log, found his number and called him immediately.

"Hello, Mr. Drury? This is Bexley Hargrove."

"Oh, yes, I've been trying to contact you."

"Yes, I'm in Fort McMurray. I'm sorry I didn't see that you had called and I understand we have a mutual interest in a company, N-GerDon Corporation, and a car accident resulting in the death of several individuals. I'm speaking of Greg Randolph and Mr. and Mrs. Sakawa III."

"Yes, and a minor child, Snowbird, who is stranded in Calgary and has just been temporarily placed in a residential school until an appropriate guardian can be determined."

"Yes. I just heard about the child."

"It does complicate things, doesn't it? Mr. Drury, I'm a lawyer and a friend of Mrs. Greg Randolph. I've offered my legal services to Mrs. Randolph but if there are other individuals who need my help in this situation, I'd be obliged to assist them any way I can. A friend of mine is interested in adopting the child."

"Well, there are two families involved, the Randolph couple, and then the Sakawa family. There is a senior Sakawa, a junior Sakawa, a third Sakawa with a child by that same last name," Drury said.

"Yes, complicated! When can we meet?" Drury asked.

"Well, I'm in Fort McMurray, as I said, and I need to stay here with my client, Mrs. Greg Randolph. I have Internet, cell phone access and even a corporate jet available for my use, if needed," Bex continued.

"Well, I understand why N-GerDon Corporation is being so accommodating. I've read the police report on the accident and other background on the case and I understand their liability concerns. The company has quite a legal issue on their hands. It's a lawsuit that will probably be settled out of court though. I doubt it ever goes to trial with all the negative environmental publicity on the oil sands projects down there. They wouldn't want any additional exposure no matter the issue. Having so many victims caught up in this scenario, it would not be good publicity even if this situation doesn't have anything to do with the oil sands project," Drury said offering his unsolicited opinion.

"Mr. Drury, these are the pressing issues as I see them. The two are dependent upon the other. One is to get Mr. Sakawa Sr. to Fort McMurray for testing to determine if he can be a fit guardian for the child who has been displaced. The other is the wrongful deaths of three individuals. I see these as our priorities," Bex surmised.

"So what's your strategy to accomplish this?" Drury asked.

"Well, I might be able to arrange transportation for Mr. Sakawa Sr. to Fort McMurray for additional cancer screening by cashing in on a guilty-conscious chit to utilize N-GerDon's corporate jet. I don't want to abuse its use, but if I need to use it, I have their approval and I will—it's needed. We'll investigate the cultural aspects of the burial of Mr. and Mrs. Sakawa III. I understand their people are from Fort Chipewyan and there are First Nations burial customs to consider," Bex said.

"Mr. Sakawa Sr. has nothing to do with N-GerDon Corporation directly. But indirectly, he is associated with everyone I have named. So I will have to talk with the lawyers and Executive Assistant, Sarah Lance, or have Shinski ask Sarah for the favor for the use of the jet."

"Yes, Ms. Hargrove, I have the Wisdom Council working on that aspect now, too. I have contacted the morgue in Calgary and plans to transport those three bodies are underway," Drury commented.

"The body of the U.S. citizen is still somewhat an issue. Greg Randolph's wife is my friend and she's traveling with me. We are still discussing plans for her husband, though, and what to do with his body. Cremation has been discussed."

"Mr. Kinoo and Ms. Weidner have asked me to follow through with the legal matter of adopting the minor child even if the sick great-grandfather, Obi Sakawa Sr., is determined a capable guardian. We are working on that," Bex commented.

"Yes, I have met Ms. Weidner," Drury interjected.

"The minor child has never met the person that wishes to adopt her, I understand, and neither does the child know that process is being considered. I have a friend who works at the residential school where the child is staying. I have not contacted her, but we have a good working relationship. So, whatever plan we devise can be presented to her at the appropriate time," Drury added. "I think she'll follow whatever I suggest is in the best interest for the child."

"Okay," Bex said. "I'll arrange for the company jet to fly Mrs. Randolph and me to Fort Chipewyan to retrieve our belongings at the B&B and ask if we can pick up Mr. Sakawa Sr. while we are there and transport him with us on our return flight to Fort McMurray. That way there won't be additional flight costs since we would be scheduled for the use of their jet anyway. We'll be in Fort Chipewyan two days at the most. The company is planning to move Mrs. Randolph into a rental house in Fort McMurray until future plans can be negotiated."

"Ms. Weidner advised me that Dr. Pathway is performing some medical tests on Mr. Sakawa Sr. at the Nunee Nurse's Clinic in Fort Chipewyan. If you'll assist getting his health records released to the appropriate hospital in Fort McMurray and then advise me of which hospital, I'll ask the Kander Law firm to investigate the adoption papers and possible U.S. citizenship—ASAP. If Ms. Weidner decides to adopt the child and take her back to the States, there will be issues," Bex said.

"That's a lot of juggling, but I'll do it," Drury replied.

Two days later, the jet was ready to take Ms. Hargrove and Mrs. Randolph back to Fort Chipewyan. Sarah hugged Shinski and wished her a safe trip to Fort Chipewyan and to call when she returned to Fort McMurray; that the rental house would be ready to move in when she returned.

Shinski and Bex sat by the window on opposite sides of the plane to view the vastness of the oil sands from the sky.

"Bex, this is a God awful place. I hate it here."

"I know, Shinski, I know."

Bex gazed at the destruction of the landscape below. But within hours she was equally amazed how the land differed across Canada's wilderness. She recalled Greg describing some places in the wilderness of Canada being beautiful while other places could be considered the ugliest place on Earth. Bex had looked out over miles upon miles of moon-crater voids and black muck. *Ugliest place on Earth!* Bex had likewise deduced.

Bex was glad to see Fort Chipewyan as they approached. It was a remote area, but she was seeing it in a different light. *It was better than where she had just come from even though it was more remote. Still too remote for her!*

When Bex and Shinski arrived, they called the North B&B, and arranged for Kinoo to pick them up.

"Hello, my friends. Good to have you home!" Kinoo said.

"Kinoo, please take us to the B&B. We would like for you and Mr. Drury to meet us in the Gathering Room tomorrow morning regarding Obi and Snowbird to discuss a few other issues. Will you be available?" Bex asked.

"Certainly, Ms. Hargrove; will do," replied Kinoo.

The next morning they met to begin devising a plan to get Mr. Sakawa Sr. to Fort McMurray. Sarah arranged for Shinski's personal belongings to be transported to Fort McMurray and finished up those details with Shinski. The bodies of Mr. and Mrs. Obigon Sakawa III would be transported to Fort Chipewyan and would be received by the Wisdom Council for further instructions, as Drury planned.

Kinoo assured Obi everything would be all right, "Mr.

Drury has gathered your medical records from the clinic and given copies to Ms. Hargrove. Several of us will be traveling with you, Obi," Kinoo said.

The next morning, Kinoo met the group in the B&B Gathering Room. This was a big day for everyone. Kinoo had already picked up Obi and the plans were to pick up Shinski, Bex and Maude. It would be a tight squeeze. The B&B said to leave the B&B truck at the airport and someone would pick it up. Kinoo would be going on the plane with the group to Fort McMurray to accompany his friend, Obi. If Snowbird was released, she would be flying to Fort McMurray, it appeared, based on the outcome of Obi's critical medical condition. Those plans were still up in the air.

At the airport, the N-GerDon jet was waiting for them. Kinoo and the women helped transport Obi onto the plane; the attendants took over from there. Luggage was quickly boarded. Bex checked to make sure the other cargo—Shinski's larger belongings from the B&B were designated to go straight to the rental house.

The group would not have to worry about that part of the cargo. Their focus was getting Obi to the hospital. As soon as that was completed, Alfred was instructed to be at their disposal again to transport them to and from their destinations while in Fort McMurray. The rental house would be cleaned and prepared for them when they returned.

While the Fort Chipewyan group would be flying together, there would be no need to reveal Mrs. Randolph's connection with the car accident and the Sakawa family being killed. There was no need to cause anybody any additional grief. Emotions were running high as it was and Bex had enough to deal with.

All this would come to light soon enough.

# 44

Fort McMurray Community Cancer Center
Northern Lights Regional Health Center
Alberta Health Services

—◄╟—

The five passengers were quiet as they flew back to Fort McMurray in the corporate jet transporting Obi to the Community Cancer Center for his testing. N-GerDon had been quite generous with the use of their company jet accommodating the extra passengers given the circumstances and their involvement in the situation. They even scheduled their limo driver, Alfred, on the other end to be their designated driver again. Alfred would be taking Obi and the group to the hospital, to the rental house and then simply be available, upon request, after that.

Bex looked over at Obi when she heard him coughing. She noticed blood on his handkerchief and saw him scratching his arms and chest.

They had a little less than an hour flight if all went well. Bex sat back in her seat and pulled out the copy of Obi's medical file Dr. Pathway had provided. She was stunned. Dr. Pathway's evaluation of Obi's medical condition read like an environmental summary of a polluted waterway. It was not much different than the pig farmer case she had recently argued. Bex looked back at Obi, again.

*His body is so polluted*, Bex thought.

Obi was old. He had lived a hundred years. And yes, it had been a long life. But if he had bile duct cancer and suspected to be inflicted with more cancers, he still had the right to a quality life in the remaining time he had left. He was a fighter. If he hadn't had cancer, who knows how long he would live past one hundred or how much more effective he would have been if he had been healthier in his earlier years.

Bex read the beginning of the toxicology report:

*Obigon Sakawa Sr.—First Nations, Cree, male, 100 years old, D.O.B.–10/24/1916, place of birth: Fort Chipewyan, Alberta, North Zone ABH (Alberta Health Care).*

Bex read the test results that Dr. Pathway at the Fort Chipewyan clinic: *...requires staging of illness with the patient to be performed in Fort McMurray with imaging to determine if cancer cells have spread to distant parts of the patient's body.*

Bex skimmed the report noting the levels of arsenic, cadmium, chromium, polycyclic aromatic hydrocarbons (PAHs), sulfur, lead, mercury, nickel, vanadium, and selenium. She was quite familiar with that entire list. She knew what increased levels of those chemicals could do to living things. The pig farmer case, she had tried in Chicago, had indicated a critical level of those same chemicals *would have grave consequences for the health of humans and living things.*

Bex read Dr. Pathway's report of various levels of chemicals *being significant*; listing the normal levels adjacent to Obi's numbers compared to those *found in the wild.* Bex thought that was an interesting comment for a doctor to make in a medical record. *It must be of geographical importance,* Bex thought.

Bex noted Obi's general physical exam listing his health habits did not appear particularly noteworthy nor did any past illnesses—nothing of significance except his wild meat consumption, especially that of moose meat. Bex had just tasted moose meat recently at the B&B dinner table and vowed never to eat again.

Bex did understand Obi's blood tests for liver function. She knew what his elevated numbers meant. There were high levels of bilirubin and alkaline phosphate present, *consistent with liver disease caused by bile duct cancer.*

Bex flipped through the report and noted a *CEA (carcinoembryonic antigen) and a CA19-9 (tumor marker test) had been performed. Blood, urine and tissue samples had been taken and indicated higher than normal levels of CEA indicative of bile duct cancer.* Dr. Pathway had indicated *an order for a CT scan (computerized tomography- CAT scan) to be given when the patient arrived in Fort McMurray. This would show the tissue of certain areas more clearly. Dr. Pathway indicated a need for an MRI (magnetic resonance image) or a more informative test, a MRCP (magnetic resonance cholan-giopancreatography) that would detail the liver, bile ducts, gallbladder, pancreas and pancreatic duct.*

The list of positive symptoms noted in Obi were: *yellowing of the skin, yellowing of the eyes, dark urine, clay colored stool, abdominal pain, itchy skin, fever, and vomiting up blood.*

Dr. Pathway had written a side remark concerning Obi's risk factor, *Note: patient lives downstream of Alberta oil sands. Note: patient's diet is primarily moose meat, caribou, water, mushrooms, herbs and dried fruits. Note: This clinic has recorded and reported disproportionate number of bile duct disease and this clinic has recorded and reported statistics of higher than normal levels of arsenic (453 times acceptable level of arsenic for this region in moose meat) and heavy metals in caribou and other wildlife with probable link to a disproportionate number of cancers.*

Dr. Pathway had inserted a general description on Bile Duct Cancer being *a type cancer that does not appear in the early stages of the disease.* The bile duct is located deep inside the body; *early tumors cannot be easily detected during routine physical exams.*

Bex continued reading that Obi had tested *positive for a tumor in the bile duct blocking the flow of bile and bilirubin from the liver.*

Dr. Pathway had suspected bile duct cancer all along. In fact she had noted Obi was definitely in *Stage III and with additional staging,* she suspected he might be in Stage IVB which meant the cancer has spread to the organs in the other parts of the body. The final note was an *approval by Alberta Health Care and the Wisdom Council for additional tests.*

Bex lowered the report and looked up. Nobody knew how

sick Obi really was and his prognosis was grim.

She braced herself for another death.

# 45
## Out of the Blue
—◦—

Alfred met the group at the Fort McMurray airstrip; Bex greeted him graciously thankful for his continued services. She asked Alfred to drive them to the corner of Hospital Street and Fitzgerald to the Cancer Center wing of Northern Lights Regional Health Center.

Mr. Drury had already transmitted necessary paperwork from Fort Chipewyan Wisdom's Council to the Indigenous Health Liaison Services to pre-approve Obi as a patient. The medical staff would be expecting Obi's test results from the Nunee Clinic. Bex had brought copies of those tests with her. The hospital had already identified an Aboriginal Health Representative, (AHL) and a Community Health Representative, (CHR) plus an interpreter. Drury had established Obi's Indian Status as First Nations with Alberta Health Care Services, which was preferred, since the medical facility in Fort McMurray was out of Obi's healthcare zone.

"Okay folks. We have arrived at our destination," Alfred nodded at Bex.

"Okay. Maude and Kinoo, would you please assist Obi out of the limo? I'll inquire where we should meet our designated AHL."

Bex disappeared inside the hospital and returned immediately with three attendants. One was the AHL, the other, the CHR and the third individual was the interpreter.

In less than an hour, Obi was a registered patient. The group said goodbye for the time being so Obi could finalize his admission procedures and get settled in a room. They all wished him well with the next day's testing.

Alfred waited for the group.

"Alfred, our next stop is the rental house!"

Alfred assisted everyone with their luggage into the house. Bex had already thought about the arrangements and had preassigned each person to a bedroom. She gave everyone their linens, toiletries and pointed out the bathroom facilities. Bex and Shinski doubled up in the master bedroom, which had a queen size bed. The other two bedrooms would be more private for Kinoo and Maude—each had their own accommodations.

"Brings back high school days with sleep overs in bunk beds," Bex exclaimed when she saw the one bed.

"Beats the heck out of the pullout couch in the B&B!" Bex said and laughed again.

She was glad to have a place for everybody and that Obi had survived the trip and was now in good hands at the hospital. She was glad N-GerDon had furnished the rental with food, fresh linens and provided transportation. Bex was exhausted trying to take care of everyone.

After Bex made sure everyone was settled in their rooms, she walked out with Alfred, thanked him for his help and said goodbye. She went back into the rental and found Kinoo and Maude had already found the television remote. Maude was seated on a barstool similar to the ones in her Chicago café. Bex needed to discuss some things with Shinski and make some phone calls, so she excused herself and walked back to the master bedroom to find her.

"Is there a coffee pot, Ms. Hargrove?" Maude winked.

Bex walked back into the kitchen and located an old model Mr. Coffee pot unit to make coffee when suddenly a chill rippled through her spine. She recalled that part of the legal discussions in the conference rooms the previous day revealed the deceased Sakawa couple had lived in two locations. One was Fort Chipewyan and the other was in subsidized N-GerDon corporation rental housing. She thought her group of four might be staying temporarily in the same residence where the deceased Sakawa couple had lived or where Greg stayed when he came to work in Fort McMurray. Either supposition was certainly plausible.

Would N-GerDon Corporation have done that? Bex couldn't answer that. *Certainly they would have had better sense than to put them up in either of the deceased previous homes.* In any case, the rental was clean and sterile—void of any indication of anyone having ever lived there.

Bex did not have a private place to talk. But Shinski appeared to be in her own world not paying attention to what Bex was doing. Bex just sat down in a chair near the bed in their room and began to make some phone calls. Shinski was still close enough to listen to the conversations.

"Hey, Dan, how are you?"

"I'm okay, how about you? You holding up okay? You have a full plate on your hands!" Dan replied.

Bex began to speak forgetting Shinski was right behind her.

"Dan, you remember the older man, Obi, I told you about, that is sick? Well, he's sicker than I thought. I had a chance to read his medical file while we were on the jet coming to Fort McMurray. It reads like the toxicology report from the pig farmer's case we just tried."

"You're kidding."

"No, and I took a picture of the report with my cell phone, when I thought nobody was looking. When we hang up, I'll send it to you. Read it. Then please delete it. I don't want it floating out there having come from me revealing confidential reports; that's not something I do, *or maybe only do sometimes*," Bex had to admit thinking back on the pig farmer's case again when she slipped evidence to the opposing counsel.

"Dan, I need a second pair of eyes on this report; you would know the consequences of these chemical levels just as much as me. Let me know what you think."

"And I'll tell you what I think right now. The old man is dying. And I don't think he has much time to live. Less than a month, if that long, if you ask me. Dan, I swear, I think he was poisoned by the chemicals in the water and in the wildlife up here. He has eaten moose meat and caribou all his life, the doctor reported. There is a side note from his doctor stating moose meat in the area has 453 times the level of arsenic that is considered acceptable and has higher levels of heavy metal concentrate that is known to cause cancer."

"The doctor already noted in side comments referencing reports of polluted water in the area. She lists concentrated levels of certain heavy metals referenced as critical levels of toxins in the environment coming from the water and indirectly from the oil sands project, as possible, if not probable, contributors to Obi's cancer. Hey, I have to place another call. Are you up for a class-action lawsuit out of our jurisdiction crossing borders into Canada? I think the Kander Law Firm can help us. Think about it, might take years. Talk to you soon. Bye."

Bex emailed the medical report then called Peter Zacki, the lawyer at the local firm.

"Mr. Zacki? Hello, this is Bexley Hargrove, the lawyer from the States—friend of Mrs. Randolph."

"Yes, yes. You retained us the other day to assist you."

"Yes, I would also like to know what's needed for a U.S. citizen to adopt a First Nations, minor child."

"That will take some doing. You have to go through some hoops to do that, but I think that's possible. Just might be lengthy and it could run into some expense. Where is the child now?"

"In a residential school in Calgary," Bex replied.

"And how did she get there if she is from Fort Chipewyan?" Peter asked.

"She was there competing with students from her community for a college scholarship."

"But how did she get there and where are her parents if she is in a residential school? What's that all about?"

"Her parents were expected to attend the competition but were killed in a car accident on the way and never arrived; she is stranded 500 miles from home. She is currently under temporary custody with Child Welfare as an IPPA (Interprovincial Child Protection Alert) situation under the program designation: *Child Protection Investigation Not Concluded.* So, she's in limbo. The RCMP has sent a representative to investigate her home life because the next of kin, her great-grandfather, is a hundred years old, is currently in the hospital diagnosed with possible bile duct cancer, which, as I said, is alleged to have been caused by the toxic water here. That'll be part of another lawsuit I'd like you to consider," Bex explained.

"There is a friend of mine, a woman, Maude Weidner, from Chicago. She is originally from Fort Chipewyan. She wants to adopt the minor child."

"Does the woman have Indian Status papers?"

"I don't know," replied Bex.

"Ms. Hargrove, we may have lucked out. If the person who desires to adopt a First Nations child also has her Status papers and is dually a citizen of the U.S., in good standing, with means to care for the minor child, this might be as simple as signatures and the time it takes to secure them. If the minor child is orphaned, we'll need certified death certificates and her Status papers. But our firm can help with all that."

Bex told Peter she would call him back after she had consulted Maude.

Bex was startled when Shinski spoke. She had forgotten Shinski was in the room. *Hazards of thinking she was still a lawyer with a private office,* Bex thought.

Instead Bex was sitting in a bedroom in a rental house in remote Canada in the middle of a desolate moonscape!

"Bex, I've been thinking," Shinski spoke up. "I want to help this poor girl."

"Okay, wow, Shinski, that's coming from out of the blue! Going soft in the heart nowadays? I didn't think you liked children. First, let me speak with Maude a minute. I'll come right back. Hold your thoughts."

Bex left the room looking for Maude. She found her still in the kitchen.

"Maude, can I speak with you a moment?"

"Yes."

"Can we go to your bedroom for some privacy?" Bex asked softly not wanting to wake Kinoo from his snooze in front of the television.

The two women sat on the edge of Maude's bed and talked. Bex wanted to confirm that adoption was what Maude wanted to do of her own free will without any coercion. Bex was delighted when Maude told her she did have Indian Status and that she had brought those important documents with her so she could cross the border back into the U.S. without complication. She told Bex how she had researched that before she decided to make the trip to Canada.

"We're good then?" Maude asked.

"Yes, I believe we're better than good. I think we can pull this off without a hitch! I need to make some more phone calls. Enjoy another cup of Starbucks blend," Bex winked.

Bex returned to the master bedroom and closed the door to give Shinski her undivided attention.

"Bex?" Shinski asked, "What's involved in making sure this child is set for life?"

"Shinski, don't worry about that right now. N-GerDon will be forced to step up to the plate in the settlement, I feel sure."

Shinski was silent. She looked out the window again.

"Bex, I've been so wrapped up in myself all my life. I'm devastated about Greg. I'm truly not sure what I'm going to do. I've been so selfish thinking of me all the time, though."

Bex was stunned. She had no idea her friend could be this compassionate about a complete stranger.

"Shinski, that's such a kindhearted, compassionate thing to say."

Bex walked over to Shinski and hugged her.

"Shinski, things will work out. It will work out the way it's supposed to."

Shinski began sobbing. Bex wrapped her arms around her friend.

"Shinski, can I get you a cup of coffee? Why don't you lie

down and rest. I'll be in the kitchen."

Bex went into the bathroom and shut the door. Bex turned on the water. She cried. It was her turn to let go. Then she splashed her face with water, looked into the mirror, and sighed. She unlocked the bathroom door, counted to ten, put on her strong, confident face and walked out of the bathroom.

# 46

## What an Earful

—◆—

Maude asked if she could speak to Ms. Hargrove, again, in private. Maude wanted to tell Bex the real reason for coming to Fort Chipewyan and that she had completed her journey. She wanted to explain her reason for possibly adopting Snowbird. The two went back into Maude's bedroom again to discuss it in private.

"Ms. Hargrove, I was forced to attend a residential Indian school in Fort Chipewyan when I was eight years old. The nuns were my teachers. They were abusive and they punished the children who could not speak English well or had not learned the *white man's* ways (description used back then). My father, Kinoo, attended the same school; Obi attended the same school as well as Snowbird's parents and grandparents. Obi, Kinoo and I have discussed some of our experiences in the past week being abused in those schools when we were children. I saw the nuns bury my classmate on the school grounds. I think they killed her."

Maude took a breath and continued.

Bex took a breath and continued listening shocked at what she was hearing.

"Two years after I first came to the school, when I turned ten, I ran away one morning. I tried to take the remains of my friend's body with me. I ran to the place where I had seen the nuns digging and where I thought the remains of my friend had been buried. When I dug in that same area, I found the body. It was all broken up, wrapped in cloth and stuffed in the hole. The bundle was so frozen," Maude paused, looking down shaking her head still distraught with her story after all these years.

"I dug up the remains, the best I could, so I could bury them properly somewhere else. I wasn't able to pull the whole body out of the ground; just part of it. I didn't know what to do with it at that point. I knew I wanted to bury it properly but all I could do was find another place to bury just part of my friend's body. I buried that part in a second grave. There wasn't enough time to dig up the rest of the body. I couldn't stay any longer. The sun was coming up and I had to run. The nuns would've caught me. I promised myself I'd return one day and finish what I had started."

Maude calmed down and continued her incredible story.

"So, then my friend's body was separated and buried in two graves and that has haunted me for fifty years," Maude explained.

"So, I finally came back to Canada to rectify the situation, find the bones from both graves and give my friend the proper burial she deserved that would complete her soul to rise up to the Great Spirit. It gave me final peace. That is our people's custom."

Maude looked at Bex who had been quietly listening and continued.

"Obi and Kinoo had recently discovered the two graves before I arrived in Canada," Maude continued. "It is hard to explain this story, but it has all been taken care of now. I'm glad my friend's bones have been found. Kinoo helped me bury them properly in just one sacred grave."

"The necklace, I gave you, Ms. Hargrove, was the one my friend had given me fifty years ago. It was a friendship symbol, a lasting bond. I gave it to you, recently, as a token of our friendship bond."

"Fifty years ago, when I ran away from the school, I found myself relocated in Chicago. An American couple adopted me. They were a blessing in my circumstance. I want to be a blessing for Snowbird. I want to take her to Chicago with me; adopt her like my American parents adopted me. I want to give her an opportunity she might never have without someone's help. I want to help Snowbird."

"Wow," Bex replied. "I've never heard a more powerful

story. I'm deeply moved. I'd be privileged to help you, Maude. I've helped many clients who didn't deserve help. This is different; this is a worthy cause. What you propose is incredibly honorable, Maude. Here's a chance for me to help someone for the right reason—to help a client and a friend! I feel like I've been given a second chance to find myself in all this and do right by my career choice."

Bex took a moment to comprehend all Maude had told her. She was stunned.

"Maude, I am going to fix myself a cup of coffee. That usually calms me. I'll ask Shinski and Kinoo if they would like a cup. I'll be right back."

Bex got a *yes* vote from the other two house guests and walked to the kitchen to fix four cups of the Starbucks blend coffee Alfred had left for them.

Suddenly she drew back startled. She dropped a coffee cup in the sink—horrified. Her thought immediately focused on that she about to make coffee using water from a Fort McMurray faucet—water that was probably polluted from the place where the black holes are. She had already washed her face in the bathroom just minutes before with water from that faucet. She had consumed a cup of coffee earlier using water from the faucet in the kitchen.

Bex had read Obi's toxicology report. Dr. Pathway had mentioned the area where Obi lived reported moose meat having 453 times the level of arsenic than acceptable.

But Bex thought it probably was not just in moose meat! She knew Obi had spent a lifetime living in the area and certainly during the last fifty years when the Alberta oil sands mining project was well underway continuously polluting the surrounding grounds and waterways flowing downstream to Obi's community. The doctor's report indicated bile duct in late stages, probably IVB and she alluded to the cause—the water!

Maybe Bex was paranoid but she feared drinking the water from the area's public source—Fort McMurray, Fort Chipewyan, Port Washington and Chicago! Anywhere!

Bex picked up the coffee cup and turned the water off. She looked at everyone in the living room. Everyone had been drinking this water. She sighed. She looked in the refrigerator and saw the bottom level fully stocked with bottled water. She began to understand Shinski's fear of washing her hands, her face, her hair, her entire body with water from the faucet or the shower in Fort Chipewyan and Fort McMurray. She took out three bottled waters to make coffee. She could not shake this paranoia of toxic water coming into houses from polluted public water sources.

She had just finished speaking with Dan, her previous law partner, concerning the quality of water in Chicago and before that, in Port Washington, her home town. She thought the fear of toxic chemicals in the Fort McMurray water had merit.

*She had been right in discussing this issue with the Kander Law Firm, too. He probably already suspected Obi's cancer was related to the oil sands project,* Bex thought.

It was clear to Bex, now, what the oil sands project protest signs were all about. Were toxic wastes or harmful levels of chemicals being released into the public water source? Were the toxic chemicals leaching into the soil? If this were so, did that cause Obi's cancer? And if this kills Obi, would it be indirectly responsible for Snowbird being orphaned, alone in the world as a minor? And if that, would Snowbird then have to remain in a residential school, the very thing Obi, Kinoo, and Maude had been so fearful could possibly happen?

Bex's head was spinning. She had victims coming at her from all sides. She had wanted to fight for victims. Well, now she had her hands full.

Bex was determined to resolve this for her friends. She sat down with them in the living room and explained what she wanted to do for them. She said she had retained a local law firm and would be speaking in the morning on their behalf. She said she might be detained for a while and if they needed anything, they should call Alfred.

The next day, Bex called Alfred to drive her to the offices of the Kander Law Firm. She asked if he would check on her friends while she was gone.

When she arrived at the law offices, the receptionist introduced Bex to Peter Zacki, the firm's lead counsel and senior partner. Zacki took Bex into the conference room.

"Ms. Hargrove, hello again. You have more concerns?"

"Mr. Zacki, this case is more complicated involving quite a few people. I'd like to see if we might collaborate in resolving issues my friends have that fall within your Canadian jurisdiction."

Bex began first by telling Zacki she was a corporate lawyer from Chicago. She explained she was on an extended vacation, a sabbatical. She used the excuse she was in Canada helping a friend through a difficult time, which was true. He knew part of that. She did not want to divulge, just yet, that she had resigned from a Chicago law firm; she skirted that issue. She told Zacki about winning a recent case involving a pig farmer who had polluted the waters of Chicago. She told Peter she had won that case.

"Congratulations, Ms. Hargrove," Zacki interjected.

"Thank you. But, I was disgusted that I had won. It's abominable to win these type cases," Bex said.

She told Zacki her client had willfully and knowingly polluted the waterway and was probably still offending, that she fully expected victims in the Chicago area to be forthcoming with health problems suspecting problems from years ingesting polluted water. Toxicology reports had revealed the large quantity of manure, being dumped into the water, was of such highly toxic chemical levels to be known to cause cancer in humans and other living things.

"If you look me up, Mr. Zacki, I have a successful reputation, in the Chicago legal circles, as a good corporate lawyer, especially in environmental pollution. I say that, and yet, I'm tired of defending guilty parties. I'm passionate about the environment. I want to protect it, not be part of the problem by successfully defending those who are destroying it and continue to destroy it."

Bex took a moment to ponder why she had pursued corporate law, in particular—environmental law—to help others. *Was this why she was here?*

# 47

### Kander Law Firm
### Buffalo Woods Alberta

—◁▮▷—

$B$ex and Peter remained in the conference room for the next hour discussing each other's credentials and similar cases argued. Peter's assistant sent out for donuts and fruit. They would spend a few more hours getting acquainted discussing other reasons Bex needed legal assistance.

Bex explained an experience she had faced recently in Port Washington, WI, which she couldn't ignore. She told Zacki she had seen fish caught in the Sauk Creek in the middle of that town, so deformed that she had felt compelled to document them with photographs. She sensed the abnormality might have something to do with a nearby power plant dumping chemicals into the water. She felt this action might possibly become a basis for future litigation, which she might consider handling. Her relentless focus seemed to be on similar causes, trying to find resolution to offenders who pollute the environment. Two reasons for her personal concern: one—she had friends and family living in Port Washington and, two—she lived in Chicago and quite probably was drinking water tainted with large quantities of pig manure dumped into her drinking water source. This dire situation was too close to home to ignore.

She told Peter that since she had arrived in Canada to visit a friend, she realized the pollution of the water upstream of Port Washington and Chicago possibly from Fort McMurray was causing her personal distress. Bex now suspected toxic chemicals from the oil sands projects being dumped into the waterways and leaching into the water source flowing downstream on route to her home in the States day after day. She had followed the waterways to where it flowed downstream to her Chicago home. She shared concerns with Zacki.

Bex changed the subject for a moment. She had other issues to address in a general sense so Peter would understand the scope of her request for his legal assistance.

"Mr. Zacki, that's not the only reason I'm here seeking your help. A friend of mine, from Chicago, *Maude Weidner*, is visiting Canada. Unknowingly, both of us ended up in Alberta at the same time, but for different purposes. I didn't know why she had come to Canada, until today."

"Ms. Weidner told me she had witnessed the murder of a childhood school friend, fifty years ago, when she attended the Holy Angels Residential Indian School in Fort Chipewyan. She saw nuns dig a hole and bury a classmate on the school grounds one night. She suspected they had killed her friend after a punishment episode—a friend she knew only as *number 9*. She tried to dig up the remains to bury them properly but was only partially successful. She was able to recover a portion of her friend's body and she buried those remains in a second grave, nearby. She was afraid she would be discovered by the nuns if she spent any more time digging so she ran away and had just recently returned to take care of unfinished business—fifty years later."

Bex paused.

"My friend was only ten years old at the time, Mr. Zacki. She took on an incredible responsibility that morning, which has haunted her a lifetime," Bex paused and sighed, feeling empathy for her friend, Maude.

"Even though she saw things a ten year old should never have to experience, my friend's life took a hopeful turn, it appears. She told me she was adopted by an American couple, took their last name, *Weidner*, and has been living in Chicago ever since and quite happy, she says, operating her own café. She advised me recently she had promised to return to Canada one day, find those two graves, exhume the bones of her friend and give her the proper burial she deserves. She was able to accomplish that the other day and is at peace with the situation now. However, she is still in Canada. And actually, she is staying with me," Bex explained.

"There will be legal issues identifying that deceased child," Zacki replied.

"My friend is aware of that. She is quite fearful, though, thinking there will be legal ramifications if she were to come forth with such a testimony. She's fearful she will be held responsible for her friend's death, or be punished for the murder or punished somehow for not telling anyone what she had seen," Bex clarified.

"In addition, Ms. Weidner has recently discovered there is a child who has been orphaned. She wants to adopt her. There are complications with this. The orphaned child's name is Snowbird Sakawa. She is the twelve year old minor child, the daughter of the couple recently killed in a car accident in Calgary."

"Peter, I've been thinking about these issues. One of my clients doesn't have much time to live; he is dying as we speak, I fear. There are several cases here and in my opinion each case needs to be assigned to different people."

"One case involves the wrongful death regarding the Sakawa couple and Greg Randolph—*three* victims there."

"Then we have Maude's adoption request. Also Maude will be involved with identification of the child she buried on the school grounds of the Holy Angels Residential Indian School and whether she might face any legal issues. There is another issue of abuse these family members suffered while attending that Holy Angels Residential Indian School. Hopefully, we can address that."

"Third, we will need to address a claim regarding the environmental oil sands pollution possibly causing Obigon Sakawa Sr.'s cancers."

"There is a complication in one of these issues," Bex continued.

She explained Snowbird was the orphaned child of parents who had perished in a car accident.

"The couple had been employed by N-GerDon

Corporation," Bex said. "The Sakawa's car was hit by a limo owned by N-GerDon Corporation and operated by one of their limo drivers, Mr. Ben Reese."

"Mr. Reese survived the crash. But the passenger in the limo, a Greg Randolph, rising executive with the N-GerDon Corporation, did not survive. I told you about the friend I'm visiting. Greg Randolph was her husband. His wife's name is Amanda Randolph. Well, it gets even more complicated. She is my best friend!"

"Woah, stop right there for now," Peter Zacki conceded.

"You have managed to overwhelm the senior partner of this law firm. I'm going to consult the other partners and ask them to join us. Wait right here. Coffee?"

Bex was about to say yes, but changed her mind thinking about what water was being used.

"Do you have bottled water?"

"Yes."

Peter instructed an assistant to bring some bottled waters in and to send out for sandwiches because he expected to be in conference for a while. He asked the other law partners and their assistants with their laptops to join him and Ms. Hargrove in the conference room. Peter made the formal introductions, explained briefly why Ms. Hargrove had approached the firm and set about discussing the issues again to the group.

Peter assigned each of the firm's partners a case portion. The assistants began their files and were soon busy clicking away with details. Bex pointed out where some client issues might overlap.

"As I rethink this," Bex said, "there are actually *five* major issues, not three as Peter and I just discussed. One is getting the minor child out of that residential school whatever that entails. The second issue is the wrongful death suits of three deceased people: the Sakawa couple and Greg Randolph. The third issue is the environmental pollution that has possibly caused the great-grandfather Sakawa's cancer being exposed to toxic chemicals leaching into the water source. The fourth issue is assisting Maude Weidner's adoption request and Maude's possible legal issue with the identification of bones—those of a buried child on the Holy Angel School grounds in Fort Chipewyan. Lastly, there are five clients who say they were abused by the nuns teaching in that school," Bex confirmed and sighed heavily.

The more she thought about it, the more she was beginning to get a handle on the issues.

"I'm not sure where we go with the last issue, Peter. It might be too late to claim abuse. But Peter," Bex said, *"for murder?* There is no statute of limitation. A ten year old witnessed a murder! That's pretty heavy to shoulder at that age and harbor throughout that person's life! "

"Ms. Hargrove, there are recent agreements being processed within the Canadian government that address a portion on your concerns," Peter replied and began to assign responsibility for the concerns Bex had laid out previously. "I'll explain as we go."

"Yes, there are at least five cases! I agree," Peter replied.

"Ken, would you begin working on the wrongful deaths of the three victims? Todd, you handle Ms. Weidner's adoption request and identification issues with the child's bones buried on the school grounds. I'll handle the class action lawsuit Indian settlement agreement regarding the five abused in the schools. And lastly, I will add Obigon Sakawa Sr.'s name to the list in the class action lawsuit our firm is currently working on regarding the oil sands pollution. So, if each team will take notes pertaining to your realm of responsibility, let's proceed."

"Mr. Zacki, if I might interrupt. What is this Indian settlement to which you keeping referring?" Bex asked.

"Ms. Hargrove, there is a government settlement agreement I believe will address the Sakawa family and one of Ms. Weidner's issues. That agreement is known as IRSSA (Indian Residential School Settlement Agreement). It is an agreement acknowledging such abuses as you have mentioned and the government has developed a restitution guideline for students who attended those schools during a timeframe."

"I'm not aware of such an agreement," Bex replied.

"If you don't mind, Ms. Hargrove, I'll discuss that agreement in detail later and also the environment pollution lawsuit we are developing that will address complaints against the oil sands corporations, including N-GerDon Corporation. There are many corporate investors on our list. We will add Obigon Sakawa's name to the plaintiff list. We are one of the few law firms representing the victims. Most of the other firms in the area are on retainers with the energy industry."

"Indeed," Bex replied now understanding she had walked into a hornet's nest stirring in Alberta and was just beginning to understand the depth of the problem.

"You were saying about Mrs. Randolph," Zacki replied trying to get everyone back on track.

"Yes," Bex replied. "Mrs. Randolph is the wife of an N-GerDon corporate rising executive who perished in this same Calgary car crash. She is my dearest friend and the reason I'm in Canada, like I mentioned. She and her husband were planning to build a house in Calgary. She is so depressed having had to move to Canada from the States and I came here to comfort her during a transition period. Now I find I am her legal counsel. She has just lost her husband in that car accident."

"Both she and I are in sort of limbo since I was staying with her in a B&B and all our accommodations were being paid for by the N-GerDon Corporation. There might be a conflict of interest concerning me. I'm not too sure I'm not a victim in all this anyway. As I see it, I'm involved in more ways than one. Seems most everything about my visit to Canada is being subsidized by N-GerDon Corporation in a prior agreement because of my friend's husband's employment. He paid for my flight to Canada and the company is paying for my accommodations and expenses while I'm here. That agreement was approved by N-GerDon Corporation somehow as a perk to Greg who was a star employee. My friend and I were in Fort

McMurray because we were on a guided tour of the oil sands project. We were both shuttled there on an N-GerDon private jet! So you see our downward spiraling dilemma—we are greatly dependent on N-GerDon."

"Thank you, Ms. Hargrove. I've certainly noted that. Please continue," Zacki replied.

Bex continued explaining briefly how she had recently toured the oil sands project with no purpose in mind other than she was interested why her friend and husband had transferred to the area from the States. Bex told the lawyers that she knew Fort Chipewyan and Fort McMurray were not the type place her friend would choose to live permanently; that her friend was just following her husband's career.

Bex told the partners Ms. Randolph had disclosed that her husband's job responsibilities included developing an alternative method and timetable to clean up several oil sands holding ponds' toxic chemical waste alleged to be leaching into the surrounding lands and waterways. Bex told the lawyers that her friend's husband had disclosed he was also responsible for dealing with the negative publicity and perception of the oil sands project. Bex admitted that after she had leisurely toured the site, she understood and agreed with public concerns.

"I was keeping silent on the issue, trying to be objective until I put a set of eyes on the oil sands project. Until then all the negative comments were hearsay. Being associated with an employee, my friend's husband, I did not want to be critical yet. With my background, after seeing the project, I am appalled with what I see," Bex replied. "I'd like to see a chemical analysis of the water over time for this area."

Zacki stopped taking notes for a moment. He looked at Bex and sighed with a half-smile.

"Ms. Hargrove, these environmental protests with the oil sands project represent decades of ongoing complaints. There are numerous law firms, in Alberta, solely dedicated to this issue. Don't worry about hearsay. It is the truth. But as I said, this is a delicate topic since most law firms here have been retained by the oil sands investors as their defense lawyers and certainly could not represent any plaintiff fairly. This is nothing new. Our firm has been addressing these public concerns for some time now. We have not been retained by the energy industry in that regard. We are collecting data from victims' complaints and would-be plaintiffs in our class action suit plans," Zacki interjected.

"I figured that," Bex replied. "Environmental concerns affect us all. Geography means nothing. I've argued similar cases regarding different industries. Remember the pig farmer case I mentioned yesterday, Peter?" Bex asked.

Peter nodded.

"Mr. Zacki, there are a few issues I want to re-emphasize. The Sakawa parents, who were killed in the crash, are the parents of the child, Snowbird. The child is the same child whom Ms. Weidner wishes to adopt. There are additional issues here—the great-grandfather is still living which is the legal next of kin. Ms. Maude Weidner is not related."

"Right, I've noted that. There *are* many issues here. I understand your need for a Canadian-based law firm. Please continue, Ms. Hargrove."

"This puts the child in a precarious situation. Canada Child Welfare has placed Snowbird in a residential school. Her ability to return home depends on identifying a next of kin— abled body and mind, fit to maintain and care for the child."

"Her grandfather, Obigon Sakawa II, is missing—assumed to be an alcoholic as reported and of course her parents are deceased. So, it is a great-grandfather who is the possible relative to consider caring for the child."

"Yes, I think we have those critical points noted, too," Peter confirmed.

The meeting lasted a short while longer. Everyone was ready to end the session for a time so they could digest what had been discussed.

"Ms. Hargrove, are there additional comments before we take a break?" Zacki asked.

"Well, Mr. Sakawa Sr.'s medical situation concerns me. Not only is his age in question being able to take care of the child, but he was admitted to the Fort McMurray Community Cancer Center at the Northern Lights Regional Health Center yesterday with probable bile duct cancer and probable other cancers. I took a look at his medical report. He lives in Fort Chipewyan, downstream of the oil sands project. These type legal cases can be drawn out. He does not have that kind of time, I'm afraid. I don't think he is expected to live out the week. It is imperative we secure his signature on the adoption papers."

Bex looked around the room, tilted her head and frowned. The partners and four assistants, who had been busy clicking on their laptops, stopped and looked up.

"Bex," Peter said. "We are dealing with oil corporations with high-powered, legal counsel worldwide. We are an equally competent law firm. We will begin immediately and should have a direction tomorrow morning when we meet again."

Peter paused.

"These issues don't pose a problem for our firm. We are on top of this and already have resolutions to some of your issues. We might simply be looking at paperwork for the adoption. But we do have to fill out the forms and prepare the documents," Peter replied.

"I understand. I wasn't judging *your* firm over another."

"Don't worry," Peter said. "I was just reassuring you of our confidence in addressing your issues promptly and wanted to remind you of our discussion earlier on the type cases we handle and our many successes, which I shared with you. We have other entities backing us financially on some of these issues. Yes, these cases can be very expensive to handle. In fact, a billionaire from the States has come on board to help fight this environmental issue. So we have substantial financial support."

# 48

## IRSSA

—◆—

Peter looked around the conference table. "As I mentioned before we took a break, I've asked my assistant to make copies of a sixteen page introductory document, *IRSSA*, and will have copies for dissemination tomorrow when we meet again," Peter promised.

"As for *IRSSA*, (the Indian Residential School Settlement Agreement), it's a multi-faceted agreement outlining retribution and reconciliation programs addressing the Canadian government liabilities. You will want to examine the website listed in the packet I'll give you and get a handle on the inclusions. You'll be stunned with what that class action lawsuit reveals. It is a multi-billion dollar, government settlement. It is the largest class action settlement in the history of Canada *against Canada*," he explained.

"Bex, we'll also need to prepare Ms. Weidner for the adoption hearing, so we will make arrangements for her to meet with Todd here tomorrow. He is in charge of that case. As I see it, we should have the minor child returned as soon as we can get this paperwork completed and of course obtain Mr. Sakawa Sr.'s signature. We will make that happen within the week," Peter smiled with pride.

"Peter, Obi does not have that long," Bex reiterated.

"Okay then, Bex. We'll need to secure agreement signatures from him tomorrow. I'll go with you and Ms. Weidner to the hospital. If Ms. Weidner has her Status papers with her, it is all about paperwork from there," Peter replied.

"Okay what do you need me to do?" Bex asked.

"Bex, you and Ms. Weidner meet us at the hospital at ten o'clock in the morning. I think Todd's assistant has a list of who we would like to talk to regarding each of the other issues. So we'll see you all tomorrow!" Peter replied.

"Please call the hospital to advise them of our intentions and to consult with Mr. Sakawa's doctor instructing them to hold off giving him any medications, if possible, so he can sign some legal documents unimpaired. Have any necessary forms provided for such waivers. The hospital will have their waivers, we have ours. We should have plenty of witnesses and there should be an interpreter present."

"Anything else you can think of, Bex?"

"No, I'll see you tomorrow," Bex replied, satisfied with the day's progress.

"Do you need a ride anywhere?" Peter asked Bex.

"No, I can take care of that," Bex replied and called Alfred who was still available for their transportation.

*Bex knew Alfred would not be their mode of transportation much longer.*

The next morning Shinski asked if she could attend. Bex agreed.

"You are certainly part of this as much as Maude and me. You need to come, Shinski, and you too, Kinoo!"

Alfred picked up Shinski, Maude, Kinoo and Bex that next morning and drove them to the hospital. Alfred pulled Bex aside when they arrived at the hospital and told her he had been advised by corporate that this would be the last day he would be available for their transportation. Bex told him she understood.

"Alfred, I was aware of that. I spoke with Sarah yesterday and she told me. You've been so nice. We'll miss you," Bex replied looking at him and smiling. "So, I'll call you later."

"I'll be able to drive you back to the house after your visit at the hospital. But tomorrow, I understand other arrangements have been made," Alfred replied.

"Yes, the law firm will be handling our transportation in the future," Bex replied. "I'll call you later though. Thanks."

Four passengers got out of the car. They waived to Alfred. Peter was waiting at the hospital entrance. There were five visitors: Bex, Shinski, Maude, Kinoo and Peter. The hospital and cultural representatives: (CHL, AHL), the interpreter and Obi Sakawa Sr., were waiting for them in the hospital room. Bex was thankful for the double occupancy room. The group had plenty room to gather around Obi's hospital bed.

Kinoo was Obi's dearest friend and Obi was thankful his friend was there to comfort him. Maude was Kinoo's daughter—she was family now. Bex was Maude's friend and therefore Obi trusted her. Shinski was a friend of a friend and nobody questioned her being there. Peter was head lawyer for the family. Everyone surrounded Obi's hospital bed.

"Obi, my friend, these good people are here today to help. They are trying to bring our little Snowbird home and help find her a good place to live," Kinoo said trying to soothe any anxiety over the number of visitors.

The doctors had been informed in time to hold off on Obi's morning medication. The tests being performed that day did not include any medications that would be problematic with his state of mind to sign documents. If that had been a problem, the patient's representatives, the AHL and the CHL would have had to intervene and more red tape would have immediately delayed the intended purpose for the day. But as it was, all were aware of the medication delay and were in agreement.

The hospital had received faxed copies of signed waivers provided by Dr. Pathway from the Fort Chipewyan's Nunee Clinic. Several forms had already been signed releasing patient information and those regarding Power of Attorney to Kinoo Kiyasew (who had printed his name as his signature) and Maude Weidner. Bex and Peter confirmed the documents and reminded Kinoo he might have to sign other important documents regarding the adoption but that he could be assisted by the AHL, CHL or the interpreter.

Obi did not feel well but also could not hear well, either. So, the interpreter was present at all times. Provisions had been made so there would be no misunderstanding or language barrier concerning Obi's true intent that he agreed to the adoption process for Snowbird to be legally placed with Ms.

Maude Weidner. There were enough people present to act as witnesses to any signatures on legal documents.

"I just want my great-grandchild away from that residential school and back with family," Obi replied.

"Obi, Peter Zacki is a lawyer from the Kander Law Firm. Our friend, Ms. Hargrove, trusts him. She hired the firm. The woman who wants to adopt Snowbird is Maude Weidner, daughter of your good friend, Kinoo. Remember meeting her yesterday?"

"Yes, I remember. I am not senile, I just cannot hear," Obi replied.

Everyone snickered, but when Obi coughed, taking the wind out of him and becoming suddenly quiet, everyone grew solemn again. The group was respectful of the meeting and the severity of his medical condition.

Obi looked at Maude. His eyes welled up. He knew now why they were all there. It was making sense to him.

"Am I dying?" Obi asked in a soft voice.

The AHL immediately approached Obi, taking his hand, saying, "Mr. Sakawa, these people are trying to bring your great-grandchild back for you. The only way they can do that is if you sign these papers stating you are of sound mind and capable of making your own decisions without being coerced in any way and that this is what you want for your great-grandchild. Sir, we talked a little about this yesterday, if you will remember. If Snowbird is adopted by a family member or one with Indian Status, it will be easier to get the child returned to your people. Ms. Maude Weidner has Indian Status and she wants to adopt Snowbird."

Maude came to his bedside and took Obi's hand. She felt helpless as tears streamed down the deep creases of the old man's cheeks. He wiped his eyes with the back of his hand.

"I understand," Obi said. "I understand. I want to see Snowbird one more time before I go to the Great Spirit. I will wait until then. It is not my time yet. I know this decision will be good for her. I feel Ms. Weidner will be a good mother."

"Mr. Sakawa, I am your lawyer, Peter Zacki. I am the local attorney. Ms. Hargrove is your family attorney also. I want to explain why I am here and to explain our plans to get your great-grandchild returned to you. We hope it meets with your approval. We all want the child to be happy, to be taken care of financially and for her to attend college."

"Yes, she will go to college. I hope she won that scholarship and becomes a good teacher," Obi said perking up.

"Yes, I know about the $2500 scholarship award presented to her. We will have that transferred into a trust fund for Snowbird. We are all proud of her. Ms. Hargrove has been in touch with the theatre group's director, Mr. Hamilton, and confirmed her as having won the scholarship. He was very proud of her too and sends his thoughts and prayers to the family. He hopes for the best for Snowbird," Peter said.

"She won! Oh she won! I am so happy," Obi smiled.

"Mr. Sakawa, I am sorry to hear about the death of your grandson and his wife. I want you to know your great-grandchild will be taken care of," Peter said.

Peter was trying to buy some time before he brought up a more sensitive topic he knew would be emotionally difficult for several individuals standing in the room: Mr. Kinoo Kiyasew, Mr. Obigon Sakawa—the patient, and Ms. Maude Weidner.

Peter turned to Ms. Hargrove and whispered that he was going to discuss IRSSA (Indigenous Residential School Settlement Agreement) with the small group and to explain briefly what it was and to warn her that the discussion would no doubt be emotional for everyone.

Bex whispered she had read the summary the night before and agreed it would be difficult to discuss but the revelation should bring closure and peace to the entire family. She commented Obi would probably not have another chance to hear it. She nodded in agreement to discuss it.

Ms. Weidner and her father, Kinoo, were seated in chairs on the other side of the hospital bed where Obi lay. Everyone could hear as Peter Zacki spoke.

"I want to explain something," Peter began looking at each family member. "I've learned recently that you all have shared some things with each other about your childhood days attending the residential schools, in particular, the Holy Angels Residential School in Fort Chipewyan."

"You don't have to feel ashamed or afraid. People know what happened in those schools, now. The Government of Canada has apologized openly for what happened and so have several religious denominations including the Pope at the Vatican—the highest religious leader in the world. Obi, Sir, I want you to know there have been many, many others like you, who were mistreated in those schools. Some 6500 witnesses have come forth testifying about the abuse they encountered in those schools."

Peter noticed Kinoo looking down while he spoke. Obi's eyes were locked in on Peter's—transfixed and unflinching.

"The churches, the RCMP and the Government of Canada apologized in writing and publicly announced their wrongful deeds including abusing so many students—admitting it to the world."

Ms. Weidner grabbed Peter's arm and squeezed it trying not to cry. Her grip was symbolic of thanking everyone, someone—anyone for making this acknowledgement possible. Maude's death grip was extremely uncomfortable; Peter clinched his teeth for a second and continued.

"IRSSA is a $1.9 billion dollar settlement for some 150,000 students attending some 200 residential schools scattered across Canada from 1867 to 2007. About half those students have been awarded restitution in various areas for enduring their abusive experiences and some abuse has risen to the degree that falls under several restitution programs within IRRSA with additional financial compensation. Each of you will receive a copy of that settlement agreement. More importantly, I want you all to know this is the largest class action lawsuit ever awarded in the history of Canada against its own government. The people, *your* people, persisted with their protests, complaints, and testimony. Knowing it would be hard to come forth, to go through the shame they felt in revealing their secrets, these witnesses are honored as your whistle-blowing heroes. You shouldn't feel ashamed or guilty, you should be proud your people fought for your heritage and dignity."

"As a result of this settlement, each of you will receive $10,000 for the first year you attended that school. I will assist with securing your testimony in that regard. So that means Ms. Weidner, *you* will receive $10,000 for your first year. You, Mr. Kiyasew, will receive $10,000. And you, Mr. Sakawa, will receive $10,000 for your first year. The other Sakawa family members, who attended the school, will receive their shares. Snowbird's parents and grandparents will each receive the same amounts and that money will be set up in a trust fund for Snowbird."

"Additionally, each of you will receive $3,000 for every subsequent year you attended. Mr. Sakawa, you attended that school for 19 years. You will receive $57,000. Mr. Kiyasew, you attended the school for 15 years. You will receive $45,000. Ms. Weidner, you will receive $6,000."

"Additional abuse and other circumstances will be handled on an individual basis for additional testimony based on your circumstances. We will be working with you in that regard later. Mr. Sakawa, I wanted you to know this because you are a hundred years old and way past the time of apologies. I hope this news gives you some peace now."

Peter knew the reward amounts were not huge and certainly would not give them back their childhood or the happiness taken from them, but it was something. At least an acknowledgement of what they had suffered. It seemed none of this was registering except a look of disbelief and surprise.

"So, when will we get the money?" Kinoo asked.

Peter did not have an answer since he knew many of the awarded recipients had waited five to seven years or longer for their money.

"We will help your family claim extenuating circumstances

and try to expedite these payouts," Peter replied.

"I am so sorry you endured this. I hope this provides some comfort to you all."

The AHL and CHL nodded then shook their heads disbelieving the complexity in these matters.

"There are additional financial settlements for the Sakawa family regarding Snowbird's parent's life insurance policies. I understand they both had accidental death and dismemberment policies through N-GerDon. Additionally, those financial settlements will put in a trust for Snowbird. We will be taking care of all this in the following days. I wanted to bring you good news. We wanted to get the ball rolling on a happier note when we bring Snowbird home to you—Mr. Sakawa, and your family," Peter stated.

Shinski was standing in the corner not saying a word. She groaned a time or two hearing parts of the speech that troubled her. She looked down trying to be silent so the attorney could continue.

Shinski thought about her husband having spent $15,000 on her designer Lynx fur coat.

Bex thought about all her Armani suits she had hanging in her closet that she had worn to show she was a successful lawyer, to show off to potential clients and cohorts. She thought about her $15,000 desk given to her when she had become law partner. Oh, how she wished she could get back those thousands of dollars and give them to Snowbird's family!

"We are going after those parties who are liable for Snowbird's parent's death. Mr. Sakawa, we will be going after the companies we suspect are responsible for making you sick, for causing your cancer," Peter said.

Kinoo was sitting next to Obi on the far side of the hospital bed trying to remain calm through all this. He had said only a few words to comfort Obi. He spoke up when Peter began talking about Obi's cancer and who might be at fault.

"The evil one, the giant is at fault! The fairies told me this," Kinoo cried.

"Who?" Peter asked surprised with Kinoo's outburst.

Kinoo spoke again, "In our culture we believe the fairies visit us in the between times at night, when we sleep, to advise us of important things."

Peter immediately understood the word *culture* and listened respectfully. He knew some of the local Indigenous beliefs. He knew the First Nations fierce beliefs and their need for recognition of those beliefs. *The IRSSA agreement had addressed this as a major reason for the extensive settlement award.*

"Yes, the evil ones," Peter repeated. "Those are the guilty oil companies I assume you mean. They will probably be the ones to pay for the environmental abuse, too," Peter replied.

Shinski felt sick. She did not want to be in Canada. She wanted to be anywhere but where she was right then!

Bex glanced at Shinski and went over to comfort her.

"Shinski," Bex whispered, "You are not at fault in this. You are a victim, too. Greg did not kill Snowbird's parents. He was a passenger in the limo that caused the crash."

"But he worked for N-GerDon Corporation, and he will be thought of as guilty because of association with the company."

"Shinski, don't forget Snowbird's parents also worked for N-GerDon Corporation. It was Ben Reese who was driving the limo."

"Mr. Sakawa, I must obtain your signature on some documents to complete the adoption process," Peter said.

After the documents were read, witnessed and signatures obtained, it was time to go to the next step. Obi did not seem at all emotionally distraught with the adoption. He lay there with a calm look on his face. He had nodded from time to time as Peter spoke about the award settlement. He wiped tears from his eyes and had remained silent.

"Yes, the adoption papers. I will sign. I'm glad for my family," he smiled. He put his glasses on and wrote his name with a pen—first and last name!.

# OBIGON SAKAWA

"Excellent," Peter concluded. "Well done."

"Friend, I have never seen you sign your name. You have always put an 'X' in the blanks," Kinoo said softly.

"This is too important!" Obi said.

*Finally the papers are signed,* Bex thought, nodding with compassion for all her friends. She excused herself and slipped out of the room. She phoned Alfred to pick them up and drive them back to the rental house. She phoned Drury to advise him the adoption papers had been signed.

Peter, the CHL and AHL representatives, and the interpreter left the room. The family, including Skinski, kissed Obi goodbye saying they would be back later and that Snowbird would be coming home soon. The group reassembled in a nearby room to discuss what time Snowbird might arrive.

"It won't be for a couple days. There are some things we need to handle with Ms. Weidner. Then I need to process these papers today so I can be off to Calgary by late this afternoon. I'll be bringing our little princess home myself," Peter replied.

Kinoo was sitting near the two and overheard their comments.

"Yes, bring her home. I promised Obi," Kinoo cried out.

"Yes," Ms. Weidner replied. "I want to meet my new daughter. I am so excited!"

Peter left. He had paperwork to do. Alfred arrived within ten minutes to drive the little family home one last time. The group hugged Alfred thanking him for his services. Alfred asked if they would give Snowbird a hug for him.

"That's so nice of you. I will," Bex said.

"Wish I could have met her," Alfred said. "I have a child about her age at home and she's special to me too."

The group waved goodbye to Alfred as he drove away. It was a bittersweet parting. But it had to be done. They had to distance themselves from N-GerDon Corporation to avoid inadvertently revealing their strategy. Not that Alfred would intentionally repeat anything to his bosses he heard from his limo passengers while chauffeuring them. But Alfred worked for the N-GerDon Corporation. He was part of the adversarial camp by mere association. Who would know better than anyone, right now, how that feels? *Shinski!*

# 49

### Rescuing the *Princess*

—◄‖►—

After such an exhausting day at the hospital, Bex and her friends: Shinski, Kinoo and his daughter, Maude, wanted nothing more than to relax back at the rental house. It had been an emotional day visiting Obi in his hospital room. Everyone was showing signs of stress, including Bex. She was thankful Obi had survived the flight to Fort McMurray and that the doctors at the hospital were now responsible for their patient. Bex was thinking if cancer did not kill the patient, the emotional trauma of all this plus giving up his only great-grandchild, might. But Obi had seemed okay with it. One *psychological* hurdle was behind them, she thought. The adoption papers had been signed. Another *legal* hurdle crossed.

Giving up Alfred's transportation services had been stressful, too.

Bex was still emotionally reeling over Obi asking Kinoo and the others *if he was dying* and then being so brave in giving up his great-granddaughter to an adoption. It was a gut-wrenching moment in the hospital room. Bex and Shinski talked about it when they got back to the rental house. Not much could be said since Maude and Kinoo were in the limo with them. Nobody wanted to make Maude feel bad. It was an admirable thing Maude was doing, taking on the responsibility of a child *she had never met*.

This adoption was in Snowbird's best interest. Even Obi was not opposed. Yet, the child was not even aware of this arrangement, which would change her life forever.

Peter was on his way to the Calgary residential school to take custody of the child on behalf of the Sakawa family.

Meanwhile, there were other issues needing resolution. Bex and her clients returned to the conference table the following morning to refocus on those issues with the law partners.

—◄|►—

So it was strange to have different drivers the next couple of days—law assistants taking turns transporting the group. Bex's personal entourage was sitting in the conference room at nine o'clock sharp as requested. Ken and Todd had met them in the lobby of the law offices with a cup of Starbucks brewed coffee for each client.

Todd had escorted the three clients: Shinski, Maude and Kinoo, to a side table close by and Bex to a particular seat at the conference table. Todd picked up a packet lying on the table and turned to the first page of the top document. He laid it before Bex and pointed to the itinerary brief as he positioned himself at the head at the table. Bex took a sip of coffee and quickly skimmed the document while Todd began explaining the packet's contents. The law assistants sat primed to take notes. Ken was readying himself to present his part after Todd.

"Peter should return tomorrow. As you know, he is handling the official custodial exchange from Child Welfare to our law firm then ultimately to Maude Weidner."

"Today, we will go over some of the areas mentioned in a little more detail that need further explanation—like IRSSA. The first page summarizes it nicely:

*It is an agreement between the government of Canada and approximately 150,000 Native Canadians who at some point were enrolled in the Canadian Indian residential school system, a system in place from 1879 to 1996. The IRSSA recognized the damage inflicted by the residential schools and established a $1.9 billion compensation package for all former IRS (Indian Residential Schools) students and, in particular, those who had been abused or otherwise harmed. The report states as of December 2012, a total of $1.62 billion has been paid to 78,750 former students.*

"So you can see by the discrepancy between those enrolled

versus those who have been paid, taking into account not all enrolled would have necessarily been abused, there are a number of students who have yet to come forth for a variety of reasons."

"And that brings us to Bex, who has joined with our law firm representing those of you who are eligible to submit complaints under IRSSA. We will need to get your statements and follow procedures under IRSSA guidelines so you can be compensated for your experiences."

"That's almost two BILLION dollars," Bex repeated. "I was stunned when I read that last night, Todd."

"I'd like to end this part of our morning itinerary by letting you all know that IRSSA, announced in 2006, is the largest class action *settlement* in Canadian history—against the Canadian government. It has taken six-eight years to implement the retribution and some witnessing is still occurring with a cut off of date for submitting testimony the end of 2017—this year."

Todd paused.

"Let's take a break."

# 50

## Wrongful Deaths
## Class Action Lawsuits

—◄►—

The group went to the break room while Bex stayed behind to talk with the lawyers for a moment.

"Well, I think as far as the wrongful death of Snowbird's parents," Ken spoke up, "I think it's a slam dunk decision. The corporation will probably offer an out of court settlement. In talking with Peter yesterday, we don't think we should consider any less than $5 million each for the Sakawa couple's wrongful death case."

"N-GerDon Corporation will have a hard time circumventing culpability. The company owns the limo and one of their employees was driving the limo; that employee ran the red light and hit the Sakawa rental car in the intersection causing the three fatalities. Witnesses have testified, in that regard, to policemen at the scene. And the limo driver was ticketed with *reckless driving*," Ken summarized.

"Just five million? I would think $500 million," Bex exclaimed, curtly.

She was angry and emotional. She apologized for her outburst.

"I know it is a number's game," Bex replied. "And it's all about a formula to determine a settlement. It is just sad!" Bex replied.

"I know this upsets you. You're a lawyer. Yet you know these people and you are allowing yourself to get emotionally involved in all this. You have to distance yourself from your cases and go with law and facts, Bex," Todd said.

"I know you think the lawsuit is worth more to your clients, Bex," Ken chimed in, "…but you are too emotionally involved, as Todd said."

"As you know, it's always about the formula: current income, age, number of years working in the field, dependents, future earning capacity and so forth. You've seen the guidelines for this type monetary award. Same as in the States," Ken said.

"Bex, have you seen the value of human life in today's numbers if you live in the United States? I was looking at it yesterday in regard to these cases. Perhaps if Snowbird was living elsewhere, say in the U.S., the VHL (value of human life) would be as much as $8.7 million. If she were an Ameri..."

Todd stopped.

"Say it. Say it," Bex pressured the law partner. Bex shook her head and waved her hand in the air from side to side to cut them off. She glanced at the lawyers. She was disgusted with such thoughts of anyone so ingrained in superior mentality tendencies and generalities—the whole of society.

"I'm just trying to be realistic, Bex, no matter whether it is fair or humane, spiritually correct by whatever religious guidelines. The law succumbs to a legal definition of the value of one's life being a monetary definition and sometimes it appears as if one person is more valuable than another," Ken said quietly.

"Yes, I've read those stats," Bex retorted. "They take into consideration how much money it takes to raise a child, educate a child, feed a child—and basic living expenses for an individual based on where they live. I know the U.S. stats put a higher value on their citizen's lives because they have the ability to make more in a lifetime living in the U.S." She sighed.

"Blah, Blah, Blah. I don't know about Canadian stats. But the human soul, wherever, is priceless," Bex said adamantly.

"We're not the one putting a value on a human life, Bex. But this is Canada, *rural* Canada, not the States. The individuals involved are not U.S. citizens, except Mr. Randolph. I hate to say this in these terms, but you and I know an individual's wrongful death, in the eyes of the court, is compensated using a basic guideline. Those Canadian citizens, who live in the remote parts of Canada, are not able to make a notable salary and their future ability to make a certain amount of money is always considered. In any remote area, the ability to make a living to sustain a lifetime is very questionable. Heck, that's the consideration everywhere, not just Fort Chipewyan. In rural America, the North Pole, a hut in India, in the bush of Australia! It takes less money to feed, educate and live if you reside in ..."

Bex interrupted Ken.

"Well, who took the ability to make a living away from these people?" Bex asked sarcastically in an angry outburst.

Bex was thinking back on the Land Treaties Acts and the Indian Acts and all the propaganda on the oil sands protests she had seen lately through complaints of the First Nations people.

Bex calmed down and whispered, "I know. I'm just so damn mad at the reality of it and the unfairness of it!" Bex sighed.

Bex realized she was acting as if she were debating Dan back in Chicago in imaginary lawsuits switching sides to uncover potential loopholes, any holes in either arguments or to just shout out personal opinions about life. That used to be her pastime activity with Dan in law school.

*But Dan wasn't here with her in Fort McMurray.*

Bex looked at the law partners. She realized she actually did feel victimized by all this and maybe she *was* a victim in this lawsuit as well! She took a deep breath and listened.

"I've run a quick analysis and the five million figure for each, regarding the Sakawa couple, is probably a high guesstimate," Todd said. "But I think it will be something along those lines give or take. If they offer higher, we grab it!"

"Bex, we feel N-GerDon's lawyers might make an offer as much as $50 million in Mr. Randolph's lawsuit as an out-of-court settlement. So Mrs. Randolph needs to be thinking about an offer around that amount and whether she will take it."

"Okay, I'll advise them to take the offers if they are presented close to those amounts. I'm just glad we didn't discuss both settlements in front of all parties today. Just shows a huge difference at first glance in the worth of a human being based on where they live and who they are. I know the formula, the reasoning behind it and what the law states. I know there has to be guidelines for financial restitution. But it just doesn't seem fair at times!" Bex said. *Especially if you're the victim!*

"Bex, Peter wanted Ken and I to submit another idea for group discussion among the lawyers," Todd said.

"In reading the toxicology reports in Mr. Obigon Sakawa's medical file yesterday, we compared the chemical levels to the preliminary findings of others we have obtained for similar exposure. We will be filing for *Negligence and Intentional Injury* on behalf of the First Nations people versus the oil sands investors and will be adding Mr. Sakawa's name to our list."

"We'll want to video Mr. Sakawa's testimony and gather data on his lifestyle, where he lives, what he eats, take water samples from his home and the surrounding water sources and collect his medical records. We'll add his information to the hundreds of others we have collected to prove damages to humans, the environment and creating a situation that has resulted in these people not having the ability to make a living and forced into a recourse that flies in the face of their belief system and signed treaties."

"We're still working on that and the wording of the damages inflicted. Many victims are employed by the company, whose actions they say are damaging them. It's the old problem of being careful who you sue since the oil sands companies are their only source of income for the most part. Difficult case! It is old Pavlovian theory of classical conditioning or even the Stockholm Syndrome; take away the ability to survive and people will do almost anything—including working for the very companies that are destroying the environment and are providing their income source. These people complain of being manipulated, ignorant to what was being signed away—with the aggressive party, knowing the power was skewed, so egregiously, favoring one side over the other—for years. What a vicious cycle churning over the last 150 years! There's an angle there, too, with the longevity of such practices. We've been working on this class action lawsuit for years."

"Bex, if Obi should die before we finish our data, we'll go with what we have. His recent medical records and his recent testing should be enough. We'll subpoena those," Todd commented.

One of the law assistants pulled out multiple stapled pages and flipped through their compiled plaintiff list. It was vast and still growing.

Todd pointed to the list, "For each of these clients, we have a file about an inch thick with medical reports and damaging testimony. So, we feel we'll have enough evidence and testimony representing a massive torte class action lawsuit against the oil sands industry and expect the case to begin in six months."

"I'm impressed," Bex admitted. "I hope you are successful."

"I told Peter yesterday I know this road too well. I've been down it many times fighting so many of these type battles. I don't envy you. I know how long this takes," Bex empathized.

"Bex, we suggest holding off on Mr. Sakawa's individual cancer lawsuit and consider making his case part of our class-action suit including illnesses caused by the pollution from the energy companies. Upon Obi's death, he will become a statistic," Ken commented being realistic again.

Ken looked at Bex who winced at his insensitive remark.

"I apologize if that sounds harsh, but it's true, Bex. You remember Peter saying how hard it is to go after one company at a time alleging they polluted the waters with particular levels of chemicals so toxic to cause cancer in humans. Even if the N-GerDon Corporation is the largest investor in the oil sands, they're not the sole company polluting the waters," Ken said.

The two lawyers nodded looking at Bex.

"Oh, I've argued cases using those exact words in front of so many judges and juries, Ken," Bex quickly replied. "I've been there. I used that same defense in a pig farmer case I argued; I mentioned that case to Peter the other day. Unfortunately for the supposed victims in our case, I won the case with that argument—*for the defense*."

The two partners nodded in recognition of such dilemmas.

"That's why I think we ought to hold out and put Sakawa's name on the class-action suit. We need to consider strategy and the strength being in the numbers," Ken said lifting the hefty stapled plaintiff list again and waiving it back and forth.

"Bex, I think we have a great chance at a large, multi-billion dollar settlement for our plaintiffs regarding the environmental lawsuit."

"Ken, Obi won't live that long. The money isn't important to him. Taking care of Snowbird is important. She is twelve years old. Her future in Fort Chipewyan is limited. The small amount she gets from IRRSA, even if you reach at least a probable $50,000 for her parent's restitution and their life insurance payouts, won't be enough to provide for her future."

"*So therein lies the rub*! She'll end up weighing her options just like her parents did. It'll become that same psychological mental battle of whether to work for N-GerDon Corporation or some other energy company here for sheer survival. And the $50,000 to $60,000 annual salaries, they will earn, weighed against the importance of their sacred beliefs and customs to respect and protect Mother Earth, is a huge emotion decision."

"That industry is a get-in-and-get-out fast industry. Good money for now," Ken continued.

"But these people have to sell out their belief-systems to work for companies in order to have a job and make a living—to survive. What will their children do when the projects pack up and leave…and there are no more jobs and no more land and the water is tainted? What will they do then? At some point the companies will decide to end their digging or the venture won't be financially feasible anymore—whichever comes first. They'll reach that 3% depth of the surface and leave the remaining 97% down in the holes. And then what? The employees will have sold out the land and it will be ruined and there will be people trying to find somewhere else to live, find other work, food, productive lands, and air clean enough to sustain them...somewhere else—further away from home."

"It'll be like a mass exodus to the south where there are already 800,000 undocumented alien immigrants in the U.S. about to be deported even further south to Mexico. So we're just going to kick the bucket of people downstream to the U.S. after the U.S. kicks their bucket of immigrants south across the border to Mexico? Millions of immigrants are already here— many undocumented illegal immigrants among those. The same thing is going on around the world. It's a crazy situation. Did anyone think about that when they took the lands from the First Nations, then lured their people to dig up their respected lands which ruined them, only to dump the employees, after the companies have finished extracting, into uninhabitable places without jobs? Talking about potential ghost towns! Add that to the pot and stir it. And these places aren't called towns or cities. They are called *urban service areas*," Bex retorted. "Fort McMurray and other oil sands projects are called *urban service areas*, not *cities* or *towns* or *communities*. That sounds sterile, futuristic!"

"Sooner or later Snowbird will be mature enough to understand her decision if she chooses to work for the projects and she will have so much more guilt added to the psychology of it. She'll have to decide whether to be really poor trying to live off the land in remote Fort Chipewyan or work for the industry, which in her eyes, killed her parents, her great-grandfather, orphaned her, is killing her environment and might well kill her slowly by polluting *her* body. No matter the car accident that killed her family instantly. They were already physically, spiritually and mentally dying a slow death anyway—working for the oil sands."

"What a decision she'll face soon. Money will not buy her happiness and cannot bring back her entire family or save her dying people and homeland."

All Bex could think about right then was her last day in the

Chicago courtroom when she had turned to her client, the pig farmer, and wanted to spit in his face instead read him the riot act!

*Who was she really directing her anger toward today?*

"Well, I guess that wraps that up," Todd replied after Bex's grandstanding. "So we put Sakawa Sr. on the class action lawsuit or not?" Todd asked being patient with Bex.

"Yes," Bex conceded.

"As for the wrongful deaths, are we good with what we planned if the offers are anywhere near what we discussed, Bex?"

"Yes," Bex calmly replied having come down from her high-horse, done with her soliloquy for the moment.

"Okay, as far as the insurance policies," Todd continued. "We show that Greg Randolph had a separate personal life insurance policy and additionally an accidental death and dismemberment policy through AIG and one with N-GerDon Corporation as well. We show the Sakawa couple also had insurance policies. We'll obtain those policy numbers and they are what they are. There's no negotiation on those as we see it. So, we're set with that situation then, too, right?"

The three lawyers nodded in agreement.

"Okay bring the others back in."

# 51
## The Real Winners
—◈—

The entire group reassembled around the conference table. The day was about over with the last part of the itinerary planned to end the discussions on a happier note, *bringing Snowbird home*. Peter had flown to Calgary and was due back within twenty-four hours. He had the more important task.

The law firm partners began the discussion on Maude's adoption issues. Todd leaned across his folded arms on the conference table, looked at everyone, and began the afternoon's discussion.

"The real winners in all this are the people sitting around the table today. Snowbird will be joining you all soon," Todd looked at his partner and the others.

Ken nodded. Bex nodded. The others smiled. Maude beamed.

"The child does not yet know of the final adoption. Professionals and counselors have been talking to her about the adoption possibility ever since her enrollment at the school. Sooner or later this would have been her course of action or she would have maxed out the age requirements, graduated and had to fend for herself in life. She is twelve, so that would have been in four years. Those schools and foster care are a big problem when kids max out the program at sixteen and are still young adults with no place to go."

"The school administrator and school psychologist have been compassionate, caring and careful in breaking the news to Snowbird. By now she knows her parents have been killed in a car accident in Calgary and that her great-grandfather is gravely ill."

"I expect she will need more mental health intervention once she arrives. The Wisdom Council has been notified and they are working on that aspect."

"Mr. Drury faxed the Child Welfare reports and I have those in front of me. They indicate the director of the residential school did speak with the child about these issues and has worked up a plan for additional counseling which the Wisdom Council will implement."

"Peter and Snowbird are due back late tomorrow afternoon. The report notes you, Mr. Kiyasew, as a friend in the community whom she thinks of as a second great-grandfather. Mr. Kiyasew, we will depend on you to assist with welcoming her home and aiding in the child's transition."

"Ms. Weidner, as a U.S. citizen with Indian Status, do you intend to return to the States with Snowbird?"

"I hadn't actually planned that far ahead. But I guess I had intended to do that at some point," Maude replied.

"If there are plans to eventually take the child to Chicago, I would ask you to consider holding off and make it a gradual transition once you work through the stress of becoming a new little family. Maybe you could live in Fort Chipewyan for a while so the child can get used to the idea having a mother, a new grandfather: you, Mr. Kiyasew, and Obi still in her life," Todd said. "Or, she might just surprise us all and want everyone to move to Chicago," he laughed.

"I understand," Maude replied. She looked at Kinoo.

"Father, you might decide to come live with us in Chicago after all," Maude commented. Kinoo did not answer but he did smile and raise both eyebrows.

"Well, I think we're done here for now," Todd concluded.

He turned to the law assistants and thanked them for hanging in there the entire day. Each person half smiled and nodded. One rolled her eyes. Todd knew what his assistant's expression meant acknowledging long hours.

The meeting was over. A law assistant drove the group back to the rental house.

Actually, Kinoo, chuckled to himself. *Legally, now I'm a grandfather, not a great-grandfather, as it turns out. Young!*

# 52
## Snowbird's Release
—⊩—

$B$ex spent the next morning on the phone talking with Drury at the B&B in Fort Chipewyan.

"The body remains of the Sakawa III couple are resting in the morgue at Fort Chipewyan under the direction of the Wisdom Council. They advised me they would take it from here and handle the burial proceedings per the First Nations customs," Drury told Bex.

"I will call the RCMP to advise them of the final adoption and inform them of Mr. Obi Sakawa's condition—that he is not expected to live out the week."

"So, Drury, your mission here is complete then, since we have an adoption in place for Snowbird. You've been able to identify everyone in the car crash, you've completed the transport of the deceased Sakawa couple and assisted in their burial arrangements," Bex said.

"Yes, I'll be leaving tomorrow headed back to Calgary. It appears my work is done here except some final paperwork that can be taken care of electronically once I get back to Calgary."

"Ms. Hargrove, I just want to thank you for your help with everything. You've been like a Good Samaritan for these people. I'll obtain copies of the adoption papers when I return to Calgary. I do hope everything goes well for you in the future."

The call ended. But immediately Bex's cell phone rang again.

"Ms. Hargrove, this is Sarah Lance, from N-GerDon Corporation. Would you be available tomorrow morning at 10 a.m. to meet with our lawyers? Bring your local law partners as well."

"Yes, that would be fine," Bex replied.

Snowbird was not due to arrive until the afternoon.

"I'll be accompanied by two other Kander Law partners since Peter Zacki is out of town," Bex commented.

Bex called Todd and Ken to advise them of the call. The three lawyers surmised it would be a meeting to discuss possible out-of-court settlements. They had anticipated the quick response. It only made sense; all the parties from the U.S. were still in Alberta. It would be convenient and more economical to handle this case as soon as possible. More importantly, Mrs. Randolph had no place to live, no income, no transportation and no next of kin. She was truly in limbo.

N-GerDon's lawyers understood the company was footing the bill for Shinski's living arrangements and indirectly responsible for Bex's circumstance. Greg had obtained special approval to cover Bex's expenses as a perk for having transferred to remote Canada with the company understanding his wife had not been happy with the move. This was an appeasement perk. Greg had tapped that perk, so the company had that obligation to fulfill and wanted to close that open-ended promise to cover all Bex's expenses.

The two women were residing in temporary rental housing in Fort McMurray near the oil sands project but were getting antsy to move. The Kander Law Firm and Bex had discussed options, timetables, logistics, costs and liability regarding the supposed forthcoming offers.

The next morning the lawyers met. As anticipated, offers were now on the table and it was up to the plaintiff to accept or refuse. The Kander Law firm concluded the meeting with the perfunctory reply: *We'll be in touch*, shook hands and departed.

Todd and Ken called Peter to update him. The case was over as far as they could see except they were all excited anticipating Peter's grand entrance with their little princess.

As Peter had told Bex, the Kander Law Firm was quite competent with an impressive list of successful litigation. Each partner alone was just as competent and the partnership as a whole—unbeatable! Peter had been available every step of the way by phone. He was a veteran at this and believed in his partners. He had wanted to take care of the most important role in this case and that was bringing Snowbird home; Peter wanted to be Snowbird's knight in shining armor!

Decisions to accept the offers were unanimous. Bex called for someone to drive her back and forth to the law offices and the rental house finalizing the offers into settlements with clients' signatures, notaries and then filing the documents. The law assistants transported all necessary filings by courier to the Provincial Court on Franklin Street in Fort McMurray.

—◄►—

In the wrongful death settlement for the Sakawa couple, each was awarded $7.5 million; together—a total of $15 million ($2.5 million higher than expected for each). This was completely converted into a trust fund for Snowbird. Bex had negotiated hard for that one! It felt good to fight for the underdog, the plaintiff, *winning for the victim*! The lawyers would handle setting up that trust fund.

In the wrongful death settlement for Mrs. Amanda Randolph's husband, Greg Randolph, she was awarded $75 million ($25 million higher than expected). The lawyers used the standard wrongful death formula, Greg's age (45) his present salary ($250 thousand/yr) and CEO career-tracking probability (the current CEO made $13 million annually), generous stock options, bonuses, the consideration for the lifestyle with which Shinski was accustomed and the age of a surviving spouse—Mrs. Randolph (42), and the two insurance policies that would be paying off the death claim at the tune of $10 million.

Greg had been the fair-haired boy slated to become N-GerDon Corporation's next CEO! Everyone acknowledged that probability, which had been more than gossip and influenced the settlement. Bex was thrilled for her friend on that one! That promise had been a windfall for the restitution!

"We think these settlements are extremely fair," Ken and Todd both commented. "When we contacted Peter, he agreed."

The group had reconvened at the Kander Law Firm to wrap up some details. Ken and Todd added Mr. Sakawa's name to the class action lawsuit as another plaintiff and again reiterated it would be an on-going legal pursuit. It was still being developed.

There would be future legal proceedings for Obi and if not him, his family. Ken and Todd briefly touched on what that lawsuit might look like. They acknowledged N-GerDon Corporation and other oil sands investors were aware the Kander Law Firm was working on another class action lawsuit but there had been no official public announcements and no official responses.

"Ms. Weidner," Todd continued, "in the case of Snowbird's great-grandfather's death, and the beneficiary being the minor child, you, as her stepmother, also the executor of her trust fund, will be responsible for the management of that fund until she reaches the legal age of 18. That means you, Ms. Maude Weidner, will be in charge of making decisions for the child upon Obi's death."

"This is all quite customary, but complicated. That's why there are lawyers."

All counselors smiled.

"I'll set that trust fund up for you in the States, Maude," Bex confirmed.

"Yes, I once told Peter Zacki that I had become a lawyer to help people for the right reasons. I'm so happy for you, Maude. I'll be there for you," Bex said smiling.

"Peter will be pleased when he returns this afternoon. A lot has been resolved here today!" Bex confirmed with a big smile.

"Bex, we have a law assistant available that will drive your group back to the rental house. I'll join you later. There are some details I need to attend to regarding Snowbird's return, securing Obi's medical test results and other documents to file," Todd replied nodding to Bex who had paved the way for getting copies of those records.

Bex hugged Todd. Everyone looked as if they needed rest. They were satisfied with the day so far, but truly exhausted.

The group thanked all their lawyers saying that without them, they would have been lost in trying to unravel the complicated issues involving both countries and their laws—U.S. and Canada.

Everyone filed out to the waiting car. Bex patted Kinoo on the back.

"Kinoo, you're going to be a grandfather. How does that make you feel? Found your daughter and now you've gained a grandchild!"

Kinoo's face lit up like a bonfire. His eyes glowed and he smiled ear to ear. Nobody had seen Kinoo smile like that in a long time.

The law assistant was waiting to drive everyone back to the rental house. Bex remained behind.

"Our last meeting will be in the morning," Todd said.

"Final documents will be signed. Everything seems like it has worked out as planned. Thank you for your help."

"Has anyone heard from Peter?" Bex asked.

"Oh yes. He's pleased with the settlements. And everything is going as planned with Snowbird's release. It was more difficult to make that happen on such short notice, but if anyone could have done this, Peter would be the man. He has more clout in his little finger than I have in my whole body. He is the only one who could have gotten on a plane like he did and a couple days later bring that child home. We had faith in his abilities."

"Peter said he has the little bird under his wing and should be boarding the plane in an hour and to expect him later this afternoon. He said that Snowbird was excited and he was feeling like a proud new father himself and wondering if he should bring token cigars!"

Bex waved goodbye to the two as she hopped into the car; another law assistant had offered to drive her back to the rental house to join her little family.

Nobody had mentioned Sakawa II, the missing drunkard grandfather, Bex had thought as she rode back with the assistant. She certainly hadn't had the heart to discuss the role of Snowbird's real grandfather with Kinoo or Maude. Nobody had been able to find the grandfather albeit empty liquor bottles had been located in the home two months ago. As is common in the First Nations community, many of their people go missing, wander off and are never seen again. Bex feared one day Snowbird or her people would find the grandfather frozen to death somewhere in the hamlet. It was uncertain how he fit into the IRSSA settlement. That was one unresolved issue. Once Peter was advised he had been missing for over a month, he had filed a missing person's report. As sad as it was, the grandfather had never been capable of being a part of Snowbird's life. The discussion had ended with that; that issue would play out in the hands of the Wisdom Council and local officials as far as the monetary restitution for the grandmother and grandfather. At some point, they both would be considered legally deceased.

The grandfather was born in 1946 and might be alive somewhere but he was certainly incapable of being a guardian. The grandmother was born in 1950 and died in 2000 before Snowbird was born. There were no records of their attendance in the Indian school. That was anticipated since the schools had been allowed to destroy the rosters every six years. The Sakawa family knew the grandparents had attended the schools. Certainly Obi knew and had testified to their attendance. But there were no documents. Nobody knew how long they had attended. Peter was able to warrant the initial attendance year securing each their $10,000 compensation but nothing for the subsequent years since that could not be verified. The $20,000 would also become part of Snowbird's trust fund.

—◆—

Bex and the Kander Law Firm met very early the next

morning. They finalized documents, new passports and travel papers for all family members to cross the border into the U.S. without any trouble when they were ready.

Bex pulled Peter aside after the meeting.

"So, where is Snowbird?" Bex asked Peter.

Peter smiled.

"An AHL representative met our flight last night and Snowbird and I went to their office to sign some papers for reintegration and evaluation. Snowbird stayed with an AHL representative in a hotel last night since it was late. Seems every family member is in Fort McMurray visiting and there were no addresses given in this city for where anyone was staying; that was an issue in tracking down the family. We thought it would be best for Snowbird to freshen up and be rested when she meets all of you," Peter said.

"What are you thinking now?" Bex asked questioning Peter's big curious smile.

"Well, Snowbird wanted to wear something special for Obi, which she felt she could not wear on the plane without causing unwanted attention. She had her special costume in a little bag with her name on it and wanted to make sure it was perfect when she saw her great-grandfather."

Peter leaned forward.

"It's the costume she wore in her competition. She wanted to surprise her great-grandfather and tell him she won the competition while wearing her Indian chief outfit. But don't say anything. Let it be a surprise."

"Oh, that's so adorable. I can't wait to meet this young lady," Bex replied.

"So what are the plans then?"

"Well, we'll drive over to the entrance of the Northern Lights Hospital and meet Snowbird and the AHL representative in about thirty minutes."

"Snowbird has had quite a few welcome-back messages. Her community school teacher called from Fort Chipewyan. Her theater coach, Mr. Hamilton, called to make sure she was safe and back home."

"I personally talked with Mr. Hamilton by phone last night when I arrived. He was devastated this happened to one of his star students. He was so apologetic. He said he had had to call so many places to track down where Snowbird was and who she was with. He had had no success getting in touch with any of the phone numbers for family. He understood why after he finally obtained my number! That was some leg work to accomplish that," Peter commented.

"Snowbird has been through a lot. She is a very smart, very mature young woman for her age. She is going to accomplish great things, I am sure of it. I told Snowbird, I would finish up here and pick her up. I do feel like a proud father," Peter commented. "She is so excited to be home."

"I'm so glad I could finally be on the side of the victims, this time. We won and won big! And big doesn't always mean monetarily! But I think we won in that category too," Bex replied with a big smile.

"Well, let's get going. I have an SUV waiting outside with a driver to transport our little group just around the corner to the front entrance of the hospital complex. I think we have a special princess waiting for our arrival," Peter asked.

"Absolutely!" Bex replied.

"Yes," the others chimed in.

"I don't think we can all fit into that SUV, so you can follow me," Peter said with a chuckle.

"There's an AHL and a CHL waiting at the entrance to take us to a side room where the family can meet privately. That's where Snowbird is waiting. Then we'll go see Mr. Sakawa— Obi. We'll have to pile right back into these cars. But the main hospital has a nice family meeting room waiting for us when we come back," Peter commented as he got into his car.

"Obi's wish is about to come true!" he said under his breath.

# 53
## Until We Meet Again
—❦—

Shinski and Maude had made banners that read, *Welcome Home, Snowbird*. Kinoo had actually signed his name on the banners! When they got out of the SUV, Shinski held one sign and Maude held the other as they walked to the entrance. Peter was searching for the AHL he had met the previous evening.

Peter spotted her. Or rather the woman spotted the group with the signs!

Bex caught up to Maude and whispered, "I have something I want to return to you but let's wait until we get inside."

At the entrance, Bex stopped Maude.

"Maude, I want to return the necklace you gave me so you can give it to Snowbird," Bex whispered as she handed the gift back to Maude.

Maude blinked to hold back tears.

"Thank you, my friend. I gave it to you as a gift of friendship forever. A friend gave it to me—my long lost friend, *number 9*. I hope, now, to give it to my daughter, Snowbird. I'll put it around my neck and then give it to her when we get inside the hospital!"

Bex nodded and hugged Maude.

The group greeted the women representatives and followed them inside toward a private family waiting room. As everyone gathered just outside the meeting room where Snowbird was waiting, the representatives were trying to quieten the visitors like school teachers with their students!

"Okay everyone, when we open the door, you can yell *SURPRISE*. Snowbird does not know all of you are here."

Peter, Bex, Shinski, Maude and Kinoo all succumbed to the fun. They had been just as excited for this day to finally arrive! Shinski and Maude entered the room first with the welcome signs as soon as the AHL opened the door.

"SURPRISE!" the group yelled as they entered the room.

———

It *was* a surprise. There stood their princess. Yet Snowbird was dressed as a little Indian chief with moccasins, and a full headdress of feathers.

Everyone laughed. Was there a little princess underneath all that?

Snowbird recognized Kinoo and ran up to him. She laughed and looked at the welcome signs with Kinoo's name written on them. She took off her headdress.

Maude gasped. *Oh how adorable she is and so full of spunk, like I was at that age,* Maude thought. *Look at those black braids!*

Maude wanted to hug the little Indian chief princess, but decided they had not been properly introduced.

*The first time I have her in my arms, I want to hug her tight,* Maude thought. *I might scare her if I did that right now. She doesn't know who I am, or who I want to be!*

Snowbird looked curiously at everyone. So many people were around that she didn't know! She clung to Kinoo and did a little dance for him in her outfit.

"I won, Kinoo, I won the scholarship. Obi will be so proud."

Kinoo whooped and hollered.

"Who are all these people, Kinoo? I've met so many people in the last week!" Snowbird exclaimed.

The AHL and CHL stood out of their way enjoying the reunion—each donning big smiles of accomplishment!

Bex came forward, introduced herself as a lawyer—Kinoo's friend. Then Bex introduced Snowbird to Shinski, saying she was her dearest friend. Snowbird politely smiled and waved her hand still standing near Kinoo.

Bex gestured to Kinoo to begin introducing Maude. Kinoo first introduced Maude as Ms. Weidner. Then he told Snowbird that Maude was actually his long lost daughter, and that he calls her *Maude*.

Snowbird did not know what to say. She hugged Maude and stepped back.

*Oh how sweet she is*, Maude thought.

"I didn't know you had a daughter, Kinoo," Snowbird said eyeing the woman curiously.

"Dear, I didn't know she was alive. She's been missing fifty years. She'll tell her story later."

Nobody needed to introduce Peter—*he had been the one to rescue her.* Snowbird kissed him on the cheek.

"You look fabulous in your Indian chief costume, dear," Peter smiled and hugged her. "Welcome Home!"

"Where's Obi? I want to see him."

"Then let's go see Obi," Kinoo said.

"Yes. I've missed him! Is he all right, now?" Snowbird asked as her euphoria disappeared.

"Obi is sick, dear one. He wants to see you. He has been waiting for so long and has been asking for you every day."

The group piled into the SUV and Peter's car and drove back around to the cancer center on the opposite side of the hospital campus.

The CHL and AHL again accompanied the group. The visitors hurried down the hallway following behind the AHL, the CHL and the interpreter, to Obi's room. The attending nurse stopped the visitors as they approached.

"People, there are too many of you. Please speak softly. I'll allow you to see Mr. Sakawa, but you cannot stay long. He has had a coughing spell and it has made him very weak."

Snowbird did not stay to listen to the rest of the nurse's directives. She darted right under the nurse's arm, headdress and all, and ran straight to Obi's bedside.

"Obi," Snowbird cried out.

Obi opened his eyes wide.

"Am I dreaming? Who is this little Indian chief? Are the fairies telling me the little people have found my Snowbird? Is this little Indian chief my Snowbird?"

"Yes, Obi, I rode in on the belly of a coyote from the hoodoos and I flew down right here beside you on the wings of the Great Snowy White Owl! Oh Obi, I love you so much. I've missed you. I have so much to tell you about the school and the teachers, my scholarship, seeing Calgary and the plane trip and…"

Snowbird stopped for a moment feeling sad that her parents were no longer with her. She swallowed hard trying to be brave.

"And you know my parents are with the Great Spirit now, don't you? They died in a car crash. They didn't get to see me perform. I didn't get to say goodbye."

Obi tried to change the conversation to a lighter note.

"Snowbird, my little Snowbird, you are here at last. You look wonderful in your costume. I'm so proud of you for winning a scholarship. It is so good, my child. I want you to give me a hug."

Snowbird leaned over and hugged Obi tightly.

"I was afraid at first that the teachers at the school were going to be mean to me. But they weren't, Obi. They treated me so nice, like a little princess. They're not as good at teaching as you are. And I taught them some things, too," Snowbird said, which made everyone in the room laugh.

"I have a whole sheet of gold-star stickers for being smart. They told me they were glad I was there! They helped me find my way back to you. They said I'm a smart girl with a promising future ahead of me. I don't know how they could tell that since they did not have any Great Horned Owl feathers like you use when you tell the future! But I think they meant they hoped I would have a good future!"

Snowbird smiled and gave a big decisive heady up-down nod.

Obi beamed and patted her on the head.

Snowbird turned to Obi after looking around the room at all the women again. She had been so excited to see Obi and

Kinoo she had not paid much attention to anything else.

"Now, who are these people again, Obi?" Snowbird asked. Obi turned to Kinoo for help. Kinoo turned to Ms. Hargrove for assistance with the names.

"Well young lady, maybe we can leave your great-grandfather for a while to rest a bit and we can go to the hospital cafeteria, introduce you to these people and talk."

Snowbird turned to Obi seeking approval.

"Go with them, my child. I need to rest. You have come back to me. The Great Spirit has answered my prayers."

Obi began to cough again which alarmed Snowbird and she turned back to him. She saw the blood coming from his mouth and began to tear up.

"Obi, what's wrong? Are you going to die? Don't leave me."

The representative stepped in to reassure the child it was okay to go with Kinoo and the others and that Obi needed rest.

The group walked down to the cafeteria and sat in a corner so they could talk in privacy. Kinoo spoke first.

"Child, there is much to tell you. First I must tell you Obi is sick. He is not well at all. Obi will die soon."

"I know. I know. The fairies told me this during many nights while I was sleeping," Snowbird admitted.

She withdrew in silence for a moment.

"I want to tell you more about my daughter, Maude," Kinoo said.

"Kinoo, where has your daughter been all this time? She's all grown up!" Snowbird exclaimed.

"I know. She is my grown-up daughter. I didn't know she was alive until recently. She ran away from the bad school long ago. I thought she was dead."

Snowbird stared at Maude.

Maude took Snowbird's hand. Snowbird remained distant but let the woman hold her hand.

"Child," Maude began. "I went to the same school as Kinoo, your family—your parents, your grandparents and your great-grandparents, you know—Obi! I escaped and ran away from school because I…well, I ran away and someone rescued me—like Mr. Peter Zacki rescued you. I ended up in Chicago in the United States. We'll talk later about all that."

Maude debated whether to tell the child the whole ugly truth, then paused deciding to downplay that part for now.

"You ran away? Why? Were the teachers mean to you? Like they were to Obi and Kinoo and my parents?" Snowbird asked.

Maude was taken aback. She didn't know the child knew so much.

"Yes," Maude replied.

Maude paused.

Snowbird nodded slightly and turned to Bex.

"And who are you?" Snowbird asked Bex.

"I'm Maude's friend. My name is Bex and I live in the United States."

Bex stepped up putting her arm around Maude and shook Snowbird's little hand.

Shinski looked at Bex and Maude. She wondered how she would be introduced, if her last name would mean anything to the child and whether the child knew about the details surrounding the limo that had hit her parent's car.

Bex understood the dilemma trying to stay away from mentioning the name, *Randolph,* which might upset the child if she realized it was Shinski's deceased husband that had been the passenger in the limo that had hit her parent's car.

Bex introduced her friend simply as *Amanda,* for now.

Shinski was shocked. It was the first time Bex had ever called her Amanda.

Bex had thought the name Shinski might be a bit hard for the child to pronounce.

"You can call me Shinski; *everyone* does now," Shinski said.

Bex smiled and nodded compassionately understanding her friend's comment.

Kinoo turned to Snowbird. He had been thinking about his

people's culture of storytelling. He was unsure how to tell the child about Maude being her new mother and adopting her. He did not know how the child would take it especially since Obi was still alive and her rightful next of kin. He did not want to press the issue that his friend was dying. He knew Obi would be with the Great Spirit soon.

"My child, sit. I want to tell you a story of our people."

Kinoo had remembered the many years sharing stories with Obi while ice fishing. He remembered something Obi had told him. *KINOO, you have a better imagination to think up the stories.*

Kinoo knew Obi was better with coming up with an ending to the story, which was always contained a moral lesson. He decided to use this time as an opportunity to try both.

Snowbird's life, as she had known it, was coming to an end but there would be a new beginning, which would be even better.

—◄►—

Kinoo began his story:

> *"Dear Child,*
>
> *Long time ago a group of our people went out on a hunt with the grand chief elder who had been the only one successful in previous hunts. He decided that on the next hunt he would take his only great-grandchild along with him.*
>
> *The grand chief elder killed many caribou and caught many fish. The child watched him proudly. The others caught nothing and were going to have to return to the people empty handed. But the grand chief elder had caught too much and could not carry it all himself. So, he asked the hunters to help him carry his good fortune.*

*The child helped carry some of the load too. The grand chief elder carried the biggest caribou to the camp. He soon found the load was too heavy.*

*When he arrived at his people's camp, the grand chief elder fell dead under the heavy load. The other people bowed down to the grand chief elder for sacrificing his life to feed his people. The grand chief elder had no family except the child. The rest of the band became the child's family and they made a promise to the Great Spirit to care for the child.*

*When the promise was made, a wren flew down from a tree and perched on the child's shoulder to protect the child. A feather dislodged from the wren and dropped to the child's feet. A Great Horned Owl and a Great Snowy White Owl flew over the body of the grand chief elder. Each bird dropped one of its feathers that landed at the child's feet beside the wren feather. The child now had three feathers.*

*The little people and the fairies whispered to the child that night. They told the child the feathers were a sign of protection and that great to know the future would come and there would be someone special that would leave the child's life. But in loved one's place would come something great as a result. A good woman would come into the child's life to take care of the child. The woman would be a wise woman like the Great Horned Owl that could see the future of this child and would make things possible for the child to do great things.*

*The child knew the grand chief elder had been taken away by the Great Snowy White Owl. The woman with the wren feathers would be a sign that she would protect the child. The child was to follow the woman.*

*This was the last prayer of the grand chief elder. The wren birds gathered around the child. All the people then wished the child good fortune to become wise too like the grand chief elder. She would go places beyond the grasslands, beyond the frozen lake, out into the world and do great things. The woman would always be there for the child for guidance. That is the story of the grand chief elder and the child hunter."*

Kinoo looked at Snowbird and smiled when he finished the story. Snowbird looked at the others—Maude, Bex and Shinski. She turned and replied to those sitting around her.

"I saw in my sleep at night the little people looking for lost souls in the hoodoos. I heard the fairies telling me I will travel beyond the grasslands. I think I am the child in your story, Kinoo," Snowbird said.

Bex, Maude and Shinski were silent but awed with the child's ability to associate the story with her situation. They knew she was an intelligent young lady at twelve years old.

Maude suddenly realized her cue and quickly spoke.

"Snowbird, you are that child and I am that woman, the mother, the *new* mother to give you guidance."

Maude stood up and took off the necklace, Bex had returned to her recently, and placed it around the child's neck. Maude pulled the wren feather from her earring and interwove it into the necklace. She had kept that wren feather for fifty years waiting to complete the journey with her dear murdered friend. Now the journey to find her friend had ended. She had made things right with her friend's soul. Maude's journey had ended quite differently than she had imagined. But her present life ended and yet a new one began simultaneously by adopting the child.

"I once had a friend whom I dearly loved. I found her and helped her return to the Great Spirit. Today I see more coming together of family and friends. This necklace is for you. It will keep you safe. It is a bond of our friendship," Maude said to Snowbird.

"Snowbird, I hope you will accept me, with the gift of this necklace, as one who will stand by you, protect you and help you in this world. I hope you will accept me as your new mother. With this necklace, I hope the two of us can become one bonded in love of family. Snowbird, I am your new mother, your *Nikâwiy*, if it is okay with you. I hope it is. The grand chief elder wishes great things for you as do I."

Maude felt the Great Spirit had guided her in her words that moment. Kinoo had felt the presence of the Great Spirit and the fairies helping him with his storytelling—giving him the exact words to say and the rightful ending. Shinski, Bex and Peter were stunned as they listened. Snowbird paid attention to Kinoo's every expression. Peter dabbed his eyes with his clean pressed handkerchief and joined in the group hug.

# 54

## Under Obi's Wing

$S$nowbird was overwhelmed being back with her family and beginning a different life with a new mother. Kinoo and Shinski wanted to go back to the rental house. Snowbird asked to stay with Obi. The group walked back to Obi's room to visit once more that day. Obi was resting quietly and the nurse said the group should not wake him.

"May I sit with him?" Snowbird asked.

"Sure, but it is not advisable for everyone to stay. Maybe just two of you?" the nurse pointed to Snowbird and Maude.

Kinoo and Shinski opted to wait in the cafeteria for a while to allow Snowbird and Maude the chance to visit with Obi.

"Peter do you have someone who could pick us up in a couple hours? The nurse wants to meet with me about Obi's tests results."

"Sure, I'll swing by to get you in a couple hours," Peter said.

Bex met with Obi's doctor in a private room.

"Ms. Hargrove, I have an update on Mr. Sakawa's condition. He displays all the symptoms of bile duct cancer in the most advanced IVB stages. That cancer is normally untreatable because it is usually not detected until it is too late. Additionally he tests positive for blood cancer, lymphatic cancer and even lung cancer. We are just trying to keep him comfortable but he does not have much time. I would say he might have a week. He might pass away today."

Bex swallowed hard and looked away. Obi had lived a hundred years. *So many years*, Bex thought, *how nice it has been for this man to see his great-granddaughter returned to him as his dying wish!*

"What do you suggest we do for him, doctor?" Bex asked.

"Well, the flight was hard on him. I understand his great-granddaughter has just come back into his life. Even though it's a happy occasion for him, it is a stressful time. He is in pain now. So in order to provide medication for him, he will have to remain here. His status has been approved and he can stay right where he is. Frankly, Ms. Hargrove, I don't expect him to live another day."

"Okay, I'd like to be the one to tell the family."

Peter had already gone. He had been advised of this probability. Bex walked to the cafeteria to get Kinoo and Shinski. The three walked to Obi's room. They stood in the doorway and watched Maude, Snowbird and Obi whispering and hugging each other—both women leaning over the hospital bed from both sides. It took Bex's breath away. She remained silent at the door not wanting to intrude on such a precious, private moment.

Snowbird began speaking. She was reveling in their loving embrace.

Kinoo walked over to the bedside and kissed Obi's forehead.

Snowbird hugged Kinoo. Then she spoke.

"Obi, I understand the Great Spirit is calling you," Snowbird said with her hand on his. "I know that. You will go to Him soon and complete your full circle. If you would like me to go with Ms. Maude, I will. She seems to be a good person and the fairies told me this in my dreams. Kinoo told a good story about a grand elder, a woman and a child who had gone on a hunt. I understand Maude is like us. She knows our customs. She is wise like you and Kinoo. She has black hair and braids like me. She will teach me the ways of being a woman and the ways of the *white man*. You taught me ways of our people and I am grateful. If you want me to go with her, I will. If you want me to go to the United States, I will do that too. I know you are sick. I love you. I want to be with you as long as the Great Spirit will allow you to be with me. My prayer has always been *for you to be with me until you are ready to go and I am ready to fly.*"

"Good, child. I'm proud of you. You have a grand opportunity with Maude. Go with her to the United States. You will go to a good school there. She will take care of you. Kinoo might go with you someday, too. But Kinoo is old like me. We belong to these lands, to these waters, to this sky. We are loyal to the Great Spirit above us."

Obi coughed which brought up a great mass of blood. He was feeling no pain but Snowbird knew this was not right. She was quiet. Her heart swelled with love, sadness and she bit her lip to keep strong for her great-grandfather.

"Obi, the little people and the fairies visited me almost every night while I was at the school. They told me they were watching over *me* for you."

"They told me they were watching over *you* for me. That we would come full circle together before you would rise up to be with the Great Spirit. I am here now. Thank you great-grandfather for being my good teacher, my best friend, and the wisest man I know."

Snowbird kissed the grand chief elder on the forehead.

Bex walked over and put her arms around Snowbird and Maude. Bex looked at Obi and smiled.

"All of us will take care of your great-granddaughter, sir. She is a special child. She will make a difference in this world. We will help her. I promise. We promise," Bex replied holding back tears.

Shinski stood back away from Obi's bedside for the family's sake, clinching her teeth and firmly gripping the back of the chair to hold back her tears.

Obi smiled looking up at his family and friends.

"I have lived one hundred times the twelve months and I have seen the beauty of dancing lights in the sky with all its many colors. I have watched the little people ride the bellies of the coyotes searching the hoodoos for our lost people; I have heard their cries and their howling. I have been blessed to have good people around me and those to love. The fairies have visited me in the between-times and have told me my fate. I have talked with the Great Spirit and He has promised to guide me back to Him. *I'm ready to go and you are ready to fly*, dear Snowbird. There is nothing more I can teach you," Obi spoke softly.

"My child, you will perform the next shaking tent ceremony guiding my spirit to the sky. I saw this in my sleep last night. I will not shake the tent again. When I go, the Great Snowy White Owl will bring good into your life. It's time for Snowbird to fly. Watch for the Great Snowy White Owl."

Obi smiled at Snowbird as he gently squeezed her hand.

"You will take my medicine bag. I give it to you this day. I will not be in this world much longer."

"Kinoo, you are witness to this. Please give Snowbird my medicine bag, the red pouch inside and my shaking tent. These are my worldly treasures and what my father passed to me. They are under my bed in my house and the tent is hidden in the bush."

"Snowbird, Kinoo will tell you the stories of the two bundles, the two souls and how we prayed for their union in the last shaking tent ceremony."

"Snowbird, when you perform the ceremony, you must start by thanking the Great Spirit for what was completed in last ceremony. Much progress and truth has come to pass since then. We have completed the soul of the poor fish—that of a poor child from the school yard and have reunited Kinoo with his lost daughter. You have come home! We have many things for which we are thankful. You must lift this up to the Great Spirit in thanks inside the shaking tent."

Obi was silent for a moment.

"Snowbird, now you must listen. I am sick because there is an evil giant among our people putting evil into this world. They put the evil into the water, into the land, into the air and our people have eaten this evil. So, in the next ceremony, you must ask the Great Spirit for guidance how to stop this evil."

Bex had been listening to Obi's last words. She thought about the class-action lawsuit Peter's firm was developing for all the people affected by the oil sands projects and all the toxic chemicals being dumped into the water source. She remembered the toxic chemical list on the toxicology report in Obi's file and on the list Dan had given her. She would ask God to guide her too with her legal representation.

Obi coughed again and laid his head back on his pillow. Snowbird put her head on Obi's chest and held his hand listening to every beat of his heart. Obi had been her lifeline for so many years while she had lain at his feet listening to every word, every story, every song, every heartfelt lesson watching Obi dance around his den in his moccasins teaching her the customs and dances of their people. Snowbird recalled how her heart had had a strong beat and how she had been confident when she had won the scholarship. She thought about how many of her people had come to Obi over the years asking him for guidance. She thought about the secret he had kept for almost a lifetime about the Grey Nuns who had beaten him.

Snowbird did not budge. Her family supported her in these last moments and allowed her to stay with Obi and lay her head on her great-grandfather's chest to glean all energy and last bits of love and hope she could.

A bluish light seem to exhale from Obi's mouth as he softly groaned one last time. The family saw the light rise up from Obi, swirl, then enter Snowbird's nostrils as she lay there with her eyes closed breathing quietly.

Snowbird drew back, surprised, as a shimmering blueish glow hovered in the room. Sunrays streamed through the window cutting through the magical haze.

A tiny wren bird flew by the window. As small as it was, it had caught Kinoo's attention and he nodded acknowledging its protective presence.

The family listened as Snowbird whispered, "My dear Obi, I hear your heart beating on your drum. I promise to take your words, your spirit with me, to protect the Earth and watch over our people. I promise to teach people how pollution is killing Earth and causing cancer." Snowbird kissed her great-grandfather's forehead. Snowbird stood up, opened her palm flat, made a circle in the air, closed her fist and pounded her chest softly. "Your last heartbeat is the one that begins my new life. The Great Spirit now has your soul."

# 55
## New Beginning

Obi's death had been witnessed by the people who cared for him the most. It was a moment of wondrous magic; it was surreal, a moment of truth for them. The Great Spirit had aligned the planets for something pretty spectacular to occur. The Great Spirit had opened doors for this family, especially for Snowbird.

Quickly the doctors had taken over attending to Obi. The family had been guided to another room. The representatives assigned to Obi and his family, responded with care and concern. The Wisdom Council was notified.

There was nothing else the family could do. They hugged each other and wept. It had been a wonderful good bye to Obi. Maude, Kinoo and Snowbird wanted to have time with each other and to share these moments with Bex and Shinski.

The representative, assigned to Obi, arranged for the group to be driven back to the rental house. The group thanked him and went inside the house.

Bex knew there would be a ceremony for Obi planned by the Wisdom Council. There would be Snowbird's shaking tent ceremony and she would have to inquire about other customs.

Bex made sure everyone was settled. Snowbird wanted to sleep in the recliner in the living room in the rental house because it reminded her of Obi.

Bex slipped off to the bedroom, she shared with Shinski, for some privacy while she called Peter. She knew he would be expecting this update. Peter asked Bex to give his condolences to the family.

Then Bex called Dan Jenkins in Chicago.

"Dan, Obi passed away," Bex began.

"Bex, I'm so sorry. I know you've grown quite fond of those

people up there. Is there anything I can do for you?"

"No, I just wanted to call you and hear your voice," Bex replied softly and paused.

"Bex, I wish I could be there to give you a hug. I'm so sorry. What are your plans, now?"

"Well, I have a few extra things to take care of in lieu of this new circumstance. We'll be attending Greg Randolph's memorial service and Obi's ceremony. Then I guess I'll be coming home."

"Okay, miss you. Take care. Call me if you need me."

"Thanks, Dan. I miss you too," Bex said and paused.

There was a silence like both expected the other to finish.

"Dan, I'll call when I get more information."

*Silence*

Dan broke the silence.

"Well, take care, sweetheart. I know it's been rough for you these last few weeks. Only you could have managed all this. You've always been a trooper, able to leap tall buildings in a single bound. You're truly a super woman, Bex. I just want you to know that!"

"Thank you Dan. You've always been there for me and I want you to know how much that has meant to me. See you soon."

Bex did not wait for another silence between the two, she ended the call. But she was realizing how much she cared for Dan.

＊

Obi's cancers were rare for the area and for the population count. Obi's name jumped to the top of the class-action lawsuit being prepared by Peter's firm. His death and health reports would be influential in the law firm's upcoming class action suit. That victim list was growing.

The Canadian government was taking a hard look at the oil sands situation. Those investors were being questioned constantly concerning their environmental safety practices.

N-GerDon Corporation, the largest investor, was splashed across the headlines week after week with allegations of being the largest company with numerous environmental infractions and citations of pollution and holding-pond leakage of toxic chemicals into the water source. Many of the companies began to appear in court addressing these issues. The fight was continuing as Peter had envisioned. Bex could see that to sue N-GerDon Corporation, for Obi's cancer, would be just like her one little pig farmer being the sole cause of killing half a billion fish in the Chicago waters. But it was 2017 and it was time to get into this fight to a bigger playing field with more players. There was strength in numbers and deep pockets to pay for damages.

But the punch in the gut or the silver lining, whichever way one wanted to perceive it, was when the price of oil began dropping and dropping fast. The oil sands projects were no longer a viable business; it was no longer as lucrative as it had once been. The investors were beginning to trend toward pulling out of these investment ventures.

Investors had said all along the Alberta Oil Sands Project would be efficient and lucrative—behind the scenes, this was a different situation. The investors never told the public there was no place to dump the residual, toxic-chemical waste. Investors never told the public the efficiency cost of this type energy was determined by subtracting the cost of toxic waste disposal from the companies' bottom-line profits and putting that line item elsewhere. Investors never told the public if you factor in that cost, the cost of this type energy, it would become the most expensive energy in the world to produce.

Investors never told the public upfront that only 3% of the bitumen could be mined in the oil sands project. That the other 97% of the bitumen in the earth was too deep to ever mine. The investors promised to return the land to its original state per numerous treaties' directives, dating back from 1867 through the late 1990s. Those treaties were changed *every* year from 1867 through the early 1920s. But these treaties also mandated the reclamation of the damaged lands. Investors knew that the reclamation would be financially prohibitive—probably impossible even if some felt it might be financially feasible.

All along, the investors' plans were to get in, dig fast to get as much bitumen/oil cakes processed as quickly as they could and get out, with most companies leaving the land just as they left it—not like they had found it. They left the land unusable for the most part. Few companies have left—they are still there extracting resources for the last forty-fifty years and counting. The days of this type energy venture is limited due to the shift in barrel prices and financial feasibility to continue without the needed profit. Few companies are apt to reclaim the land, as promised, certainly now, even more-so, in light of such reduced profits. Oil sands investors located in other parts of the world found there was no way around the inevitable residual toxic wastes from this process that was polluting the environment— just another sad commentary on how business seeks monetary gain, no matter the costs.

But Bex figured it was a matter of time. After all it had taken 150 years for Canada to admit to the abusive horrors of the residential schools' fiascos. Whether it would take another hundred years for Canada's oil sands investors to understand their blunder and for others around the world to see their folly, it would take the time it would take. Society would have to deal with it when that time came as another travesty. The class action lawsuit in such an environmental case might well exceed an amount unheard of in history—similar to what had happened in the IRSSA fallout.

—◦—

Greg Randolph's memorial service was held in Fort McMurray as planned. The crowd was small but attended by some high-level N-GerDon corporate executives, some of their employees and a handful of friends and *family*. His funeral was noteworthy, covered by all the local newspapers and electronic media streams recognized as an up-and-coming employee struck down in his prime. Shinski and Bex would be flying back to the U.S. soon. Surely this nightmare would be over soon!

# 56
### The Grand Centurion
—◦—

Peter arranged for the group to accompany Obi's body the following morning flying out from Fort McMurray in route to Fort Chipewyan. He had contacted the Wisdom Council who would meet them upon arrival.

N-GerDon Corporation had agreed to fly the family to the U.S. in one of their company jets as soon as they desired to leave the country. It was the least they could do since Bex and Shinski were stranded in Canada. They had a few more loose ends to manage before leaving.

Upon arrival in Fort Chipewyan, the North B&B had arranged for one of their assistants to pick up the group dropping them off at their desired destinations. Kinoo resumed his old job, the community taxi driver, and began to shuttle his new family wherever they needed to go. N-GerDon Corporation had negotiated a one month extension for Shinski and Bex to stay at the B&B. That would give them sufficient time to finalize plans to move to Chicago, which they had decided would be the home for the new family.

Kinoo drove Snowbird and Maude to Snowbird's deceased parent's house. Kinoo drove to his home. In the following days, there was a memorial service—a First Nations customary ceremony held for Obi prepared by their community people. The First Nations people take care of their own dead. They make all the arrangements, including transporting the body, and they utilize green burial techniques.

Kinoo, Maude and Snowbird washed Obi's body and dressed him in his shaking tent ceremonial dress and tightly bound him with leather, fur straps and placed him in an oak casket. They set up a teepee for his body and it was never left alone as they prepared for the Feast of the Dead. Many of the community members congregated to sing the songs of their people and perform sacred dances. The family attended as well as Shinski and Bex. The Wisdom Council promised to watch over the body while the Kiyasew family prepared to leave Canada.

The next day, in a private ceremony with Obi's people, his body was buried. Obi had wanted to be pushed out to sea, burned and given back to the Great Spirit in their green belief but the Ice Road had not melted. He was buried in the crowded cemetery in the little hamlet. He had given his life for his people and he was given back to the Great Spirit. It was a wondrous circle completing a lifetime of service to his community and then being lifted up to the Great Spirit.

After the burial, Snowbird was anxious about the upcoming shaking tent ceremony which she had promised Obi she would perform. Kinoo asked the Wisdom Council and the Circle of Elders if the Americans could attend the ceremony to honor Obi. This was a sacred ceremony, a closed ceremony for their people, but the Wisdom Council allowed it.

Bex and Shinski bought warm clothes from the Hudson Bay Trading Post that would be acceptable in the early morning hours since that time of day could still be quite chilly. Kinoo and Maude dressed in ceremonial attire remembering the ways of her people and enjoying this time with each other. This would probably be the last time they would ever be in Fort Chipewyan and maybe never return to Canada.

Snowbird wore the Indian chief costume the community had helped make for her performance in the Calgary student competition.

*I must wear the wren feather and the necklace with the hoodoo stone and the bone of the caribou to honor Obi. I will wear the necklace of friendship my new mother has given me.*

Kinoo and Snowbird shared what the ceremony would entail. Bex, Shinski and Maude did not know what to expect. The group met during the wee hours the next day just before the sun came up and made great homage to their dear friend,

Obi, in that last shaking tent ceremony. It would be one Snowbird would never forget. She would be the one to crawl inside the tent and pray to the Great Spirit.

Snowbird was flawless in her delivery. She had seen the shaking tent ceremony many times and had heard Obi's chanting. She had been taught well and had been a good student of Obi's lessons. She wailed in a high pitch asking the Great Spirit to hear her prayers.

1k

The Shaking Tent, graphic by Anne Michael

Bex, Maude and Shinski sat beside Kinoo in complete silence around the fire. The elders passed the smudge pot and Bex, Maude, Shinski and Kinoo put their finger into the pot emulating the other elders. They wiped their foreheads with their finger as they passed the smudge pot to the next person. The elders hummed. The fire burned. They all waited for Snowbird's signal.

Inside the tent, Snowbird carefully opened the medicine bag. She said a prayer for Obi as she opened it. She pulled out Obi's journal which she had never seen and opened it. She read a few pages and vowed to keep it sacred, to read it later and whispered a prayer of forgiveness on behalf of the abusive nuns. She pulled out the red bag which held the feathers wrapped in leather folds. She opened the flaps and stared at the beautiful feathers. She remembered the meaning of each as she picked them up and laid them aside. She whispered their meaning as she touched them, reverently.

Then a great wave of strength filled her body and the small flame of the tiny campfire inside the shaking tent turned blue. Little smoke curls rose up through the hole in the top of the tent.

The elders saw the blue smoke coming from the tent. Snowbird began to sing. Then she prayed loudly to the Great Spirit. She heard the elders join in with her song. They repeated her prayer and ended with a loud shrill-like whooping. Snowbird carefully picked up each feather and held it high then put each one down.

Then she grabbed both sides of the tent placing her hands tightly around the smooth, curved, tree branches laced together with leather straps. She shook the wooden cage so that it began rocking side to side as she thrust her body left to right.

Bex and Shinski looked up startled. They heard their friend chanting loud prayers and shouting, some angry cries, some cries of relief, louder then softer, quietly praying. Then the tent stopped rocking.

There was silence. The sun was beginning to peak out of the sky; the elders and the three women could no longer see Snowbird's silhouette through the animal skins wrapped around the tent frame. The fire inside the tent no longer revealed her shadow. The sun was rising; the sun had come up! It was a new day. Obi was gone. But his memory would live forever.

Snowbird climbed out of the tent totally exhausted. She was carrying the medicine bag. Blue smoke tailings from the tiny campfire, inside the tent, streamed from the hole in the top. Snowbird walked over to the elders. A bluish glow emanated from her as she moved toward them. She nodded to the three women staring at her in amazement. Snowbird knelt down and whispered a prayer of thanks for the circle of supportive elders, and their reverence to Obi. She was grateful of their acceptance of her ceremonial rights and their approval to include her friends in the ceremony. The elders quietly disbanded just after snuffing out the fire with their moccasins. They walked over to the shaking tent, picked it up and began taking it to its residing place deep in the bush.

"Kinoo, what are they doing with my shaking tent?" Snowbird asked. "Obi said it was mine. He said his father had given it to him and on his dying bed he gave it to me."

"My child, it is yours. You may do with it as you wish."

"I want to take it to Chicago with me," Snowbird said turning to Maude to ask if that was possible.

Maude turned to Bex.

"Well, if it will fit in the plane, I think we can take it with us," Bex replied.

"Snowbird, when we get to Chicago, I want to tell you the story of your great-grandmother, Princess Natawee. You'll find her an interesting woman who once had a teepee erected in the front yard of her mansion," Maude replied.

---

Kinoo had taken a leave of absence from his little job as the B&B taxi driver and decided to travel with Bex, Maude, Snowbird and Shinski to Chicago. Kinoo had not wanted to leave, but did not want to lose his daughter again—now he was Snowbird's grandfather. He had grown quite fond of Bex and

Shinski, too. In just a few weeks, he had a whole new family.

Bex called Dan. She was hopeful he could rent a large, fifteen-person van to pick them up the day after tomorrow at the Chicago airport.

"Need I ask why rent such a large vehicle, Bex?" Dan asked.

"Well, we sort of need it to transport everyone with all we are bringing home. There are quite a few people with me and one shaking tent," Bex explained.

"What is a shaking tent?" Dan asked.

"It is a complicated story. It looks like a very large bamboo chair, the kind you hang on the rafters of a large porch with a long chain. Except there isn't a chain, you don't hang it and you don't relax in it. You crawl inside and shake it. It's amazing; you'll have to see it. Snowbird wanted to bring it." "Snowbird is coming with you?"

"Yes. Snowbird, Maude, Kinoo, Shinski, all of our luggage and then some! And the shaking tent! I am bringing an entire family with me. They are now U.S. citizens and Kinoo wanted to come because Maude is his daughter. I'm not sure if I ever mentioned Kinoo and I don't think you've ever met Maude."

"It's a long story, Dan. I could update you but my cell phone would die in the sacrifice. It's been a busy month!"

Bex paused.

"Wow," Dan exclaimed. "I guess so. I thought you were on a sabbatical trying to decide what to do with the rest of your life in some peaceful B&B in remote Canada where you certainly couldn't get into any trouble. I knew something was up when you called asking for a hug over the phone and when you started asking if I was up for a class action lawsuit, which would extend across the border. So, am I off the hook on the class action lawsuit?"

"Not a chance, that one's coming down the *pike*, so to speak," Bex laughed.

"You know the Keystone Pipeline and the Oil Sands Project I've been mentioning? Well, Kander Law Firm is working on that lawsuit with a billionaire in the States. They have some work to do yet, but Obi is on the list so that means we are in the mix for a legal battle down the road—if you're game."

"I guess I'd better be trying to find a fifteen-person cargo van. When does your entourage arrive? What airline?"

"Well, we'll be arriving on a private N-GerDon jet. It'll pick us up in Fort Chipewyan and fly directly to Chicago O'Hara," Bex replied.

"What?" Dan asked totally surprised. "Didn't you just sue them and now they're flying all of you home to Chicago?"

"Yes, one last gesture from a company who is still mourning the loss of one of their best employees."

—◁▮▷—

It was quite a homecoming when the group began to disembark the airsteps of N-GerDon's company jet onto the tarmac at O'Hara with their luggage and the shaking tent being packed onto a baggage cart by a handler.

Bex was looking quite professional in the only Armani suit she had taken on the trip. Maude was looking chic in a sort of a 60s, hippy-type attire with fur boots, fringed ties, mid-calf skirt, wearing her new beaver-pelt jacket and feathers hanging from her ears.

Kinoo, almost a hundred years old, came limping down the airsteps holding one side of the railing with both hands. He had never flown before and glad to be on the ground again! His shoulder length gray hair was flowing behind him in the breeze; he wore a blue jacket revealing its red-plaid lining as the wind caught its flaps.

Shinski was quite the spectacle wearing high heels and her Canadian Lynx fur coat she wore on special occasions. Snowbird was wearing white jeans, a white parker with a big fur-lined hood, moccasins, and was striking with her contrasting long, jet-black braided hair. Snowbird had already run down the airsteps. She had caught up to the baggage handler and was walking beside her special cargo—*the shaking tent.*

Bex looked up toward the rows of windows at each terminal gate. She couldn't see anybody's face, but she was sure people were staring down at this crazy bunch wondering about this corporate jet with the words, *N-GerDon Corporation—Fort McMurray, Canada,* painted across its side, and the wild crew that had just disembarked its wings!

It was quite a sight for Dan when he spotted the plane and the infamous shaking tent—bigger than the size of a refrigerator. He twisted his mouth trying to figure if the rear doors of the van would accommodate the structure.

As soon as Bex came through the tunnel, he waved. He laughed at her little family in tow.

*I've got about five seconds to figure out where to hide,* he laughed staring at the oncoming group wondering what people were thinking.

"Bex, welcome home," Dan called out, grabbing her and giving her a huge bear hug. He gave her a big kiss, which embarrassed Bex but delighted Shinski! Bex lost her balance but quickly regained her composure and began to introduce everyone. She smiled back at Dan and winked at Shinski.

Shinski laughed.

"I'm her high-school friend, Shinski."

"Yes, you are," Dan laughed and shook her hand.

Dan quickly ushered the group to an area where customs officials would deliver the completed paperwork.

One caveat of private jets is that going through customs is non-negotiable. The good news is that the custom officials come to you! The officials had boarded the plane before they disembarked, asked questions and helped the group fill out their paper work. Getting the shaking tent through customs was a bit hairy since the structure was made out of Canadian timber which is not allowed to be transported across the border in the manner it was. An immigrant officer made the determination to honor its passage after hearing the explanations what it was, that it was inherited and part of a spiritual, cultural belief system. So the shaking tent was now a U.S. citizen too! Thank God the group didn't have to wait in line for someone to go through their bags and put a description on this special cargo.

An attendant expedited their passage and they were all waiting out at the curb loading the cargo into the van—trying to leave a space large enough in the rear to handle the tent. Some of the luggage was set inside the hollow of the tent's enclosure and some in the laps of the passengers. The seats were lowered in the back and it all seemed to fit.

"Good call, Bex," Dan commented when he jumped into the driver's seat. "It took every last inch of this big baby!"

"Wow," Snowbird laughed. "My tent is as big as this vehicle it seems."

Dan drove Maude, Kinoo, Snowbird *and* the shaking tent to Bex's Bungalow which Maude was renting. He helped unload what was staying there, including the tent, and then drove Bex and Shinski to Bex's apartment across the street from the cancer center.

Bex had offered Shinski a room in her apartment for as long as she wanted until she figured out what she might want to do with the rest of her life.

Within a few days, Maude had re-opened her café for business and Snowbird was enrolled in a public school in Chicago. It was 2017; the U.S. school system was quite modern and much different than the remote schools in Fort Chipewyan, which lagged in technology and supplies.

In the afternoons after school, Maude began to teach Snowbird how to run the little café. Maude was emotional that next afternoon when Snowbird had called her—*mother*! She said it again in the Cree language—*Nikâwiy*. Both were proud of their native tongue.

Snowbird enjoyed learning all about the café since this was how Maude—her new mother had been introduced to the United States. Snowbird was even wearing the wren feathers. She was following in her mother's footsteps even inheriting the café someday. Maude had promised this.

Kinoo spent his time watching the new flat screen television in the café, pushing the buttons on the juke box, staring at the shaking tent equaled in sized to the juke box sitting alongside. Kinoo sat with Maude on the barstools. They talked for hours about each other's lives and Snowbird's life growing up in Fort Chipewyan—as much as Kinoo could remember. Kinoo was a treasure trove of information since he had lived in Fort Chipewyan all his life. Catching up on fifty years would take them a while. The photo of Princess Natawee was rehung near the café front entrance.

Princess Natawee was Maude's great-grandmother and now Snowbird's great, great-grandmother. Maude was making plans to visit the old mansion just outside Chicago where this princess had once lived, *if it was still there.* Kinoo told tales of his father, Moose Jaw, the little boy sitting on Natawee's lap in the photo.

In Bex's apartment across from the cancer center, she and Shinski spent hours talking about what they wanted to do with their lives. Both were in limbo. Shinski had been thrilled when Bex began to date Dan. *She knew that union was destined.*

"You are well on your way to becoming the last one in our high school class to marry. Dan is a good catch, Bex. Don't screw it up!"

Dan began trying to talk Maude into serving Starbucks in her café or turning her corner café into a Starbucks franchise. Course he wanted a piece of the action too! Maude and Snowbird joked about making him a partner; but when they said he had to make the coffee and work in the café, everyone laughed trying to imagine Dan wearing an apron behind a counter.

# 57

## Home Sweet Home

—✦—

Shinski was beginning to come to grips with Greg's death and to compartmentalize her issues. She was grateful Bex had offered her a room in her apartment for an extended stay. She had had time to understand that accidents happen in this world and that life isn't fair. The accident wasn't her fault; time will heal her grief and she needed to pull herself up by her bootstraps and try to get her life back together.

"Bex, you know something," Shinski said one night when Bex arrived home late after a date with Dan.

"What's that, Shinski?"

"I never said this to anyone, Bex. When I married Greg, I saw him all the time. Then when he started traveling with his company, I never saw him. I was married; yet for a long time I hardly ever saw my husband. You grow apart when you don't see someone. I feel more connected to you, Kinoo, Maude and Snowbird than I ever did with my husband. I feel guilty about that. But, I've found a family and I'm happy."

Bex hugged her neck.

"Shinski, you are like family. Sometimes you get my goat, but I love you and would do anything for you, you know that. I think your compassionate side is breaking wide open, my friend. You're becoming a softy—a little teddy bear!" Bex said.

"You know, Bex, when you move after living in a place all your life, you feel like you've undergone a divorce. Then you live briefly in that place, don't make any friends and that is hard! Then you don't want to make friends in that place because you know you are leaving soon. You don't want that second emotional divorce so you don't make the effort. I was so unhappy in Canada. It just wasn't a good life for me. Greg said we would be moving around quite a bit during our stay in

Canada. I'm a people person and I didn't have any friends in Canada. Shopping for stuff was my endorphins. I like shopping; I can take that stuff with me when I move. You can't take friends with you!"

——

Shinski had spent her time, since arriving back in the States, sticking close to home—Bex's apartment. She loved having her own Starbucks, even if it was across the street on the second floor. But she was beginning to feel the need for transportation, to branch out—getting a little antsy not being able to go when she wanted to go, or shop. She was feeling much better emotionally and wanted to spread her wings a little. There didn't seem to be any of her type *anything* where Bex lived— even if it was still in Chicago.

Bex and Shinski spent the next couple days shopping for a car for Shinski; they found one and bought it. Bex drove off in her car headed back to the cancer center to interview more people. Shinski drove in the other direction ready to sightsee alone a bit or just drive enjoying her new-found freedom!

*I guess she won't be home for dinner,* Bex laughed, as she watched her friend drive off.

Shinski cruised down Michigan Avenue smiling as if she were back in high school. She thought about Bex and wished the two of them were out gallivanting around Chicago again. She circled back around making a left turn here and a right turn there, dodging one way streets, then headed out from the city. She thought she might try to find an old boutique she used to frequent. Chicago was not like it used to be. In fact, it had been quite a while since she had driven a car at all realizing Greg had always been the one to drive.

*When was the last time I drove in Chicago*, she thought as she headed away from the big city not believing how it had changed. *Where did all these people come from? Bex would be proud of me. I made it out of the city by myself!*

Shinski smiled. She drove around the north side then meandered through some of the suburbs. She thought she knew the Big Windy City after all these years but felt she was seeing Chicago for the first time—from a whole new perspective.

Shinski came upon a little street in a community where the houses in the little town had white picket fences. She stopped in front of one that looked like a southern plantation. She pulled into a small parking lot, to the side of the old mansion, and parked.

She walked inside and could see the home had been converted into a real estate firm, a café, a hair salon, a tiny clothing boutique and a postal service.

*Cute place! I'll have lunch and get my nails done!*

After enjoying her lunch, buying a little blouse and matching blazer in the boutique, Shinski walked through the mansion into a little hair salon on the first floor as a walk-in customer. They took her right away.

It had been a long time since she had seen the inside of a decent salon. The ladies were delightful; they were exactly what she'd expected of such a quaint little town—gossipy and full of interesting stories. Shinski was beginning to feel right at home.

She soon had a head full of foil strips, hair dye; and a salon attendant was busy manicuring her nails. Shinski's mouth dropped open. She had looked up on the wall. Near the stairway leading up to the real estate agent's office on the second floor she had seen a framed family photo, which she immediately recognized as that same photo hanging in Maude's café. She asked one of the salon owners to bring it to her.

"I don't believe this. Ladies, this is Princess Natawee."

"Well, of course it is. This is where she lived long ago. Everyone from around here knows that."

"You don't understand. I mean I know this lady. I mean, I know her great-grandchild, Maude. I know this woman. I mean I know who she is. Oh, just please get my purse over there. I need my cell phone. I have to call someone right away."

Shinski called Bex.

"Bex, you won't believe where I am this minute."

"Hope you didn't get a speeding ticket or that you're calling me from jail!"

"No. Seriously! I'm sitting in Princess Natawee's mansion having my hair done."

"What?"

"I'm serious."

"Where?"

"Well, I'm not sure exactly. When we parted, I drove all over the place. I moseyed through suburbs and came to this darling place. It's a house with boutiques, a hair salon, little café and I decided to get my nails and hair done."

Bex was used to this routine; she googled the old mansion while she listened to Shinski carrying on. She located it and was astounded. She thought she would have eventually found it herself if it existed. And it did! And here was Shinski getting her hair done on the first floor!

*Just meant to be! Like all the unbelievable events of the past few months,* Bex figured.

"Shinski, get a brochure or something, a name and find out who owns the place, if you can."

"Sure thing, amazing, I was just…"

Bex had already ended the call.

Shinski began drilling the salon owner about the property.

"The owner said the house had been for sale a long time when our co-op finally rented it from him and turned it into an office and salon space with a café and postal service. But he still owns it. The owner is elderly now. I know he *was* looking for someone to buy him out. His son has a real estate office just upstairs. He would certainly know," the stylist said.

Shinski walked upstairs and had a chat with the son.

That night when Bex and Shinski were alone in her apartment, Shinski said she was ready to do something big.

"Like what?"

"Well, I'm ready to buy a house!"

# 58

## Princess Natawee's Mansion

—◁▐▷—

Within a month, the cash settlements from the lawsuits came in for everyone. Bex thought back on the last two months and how they had been fraught with tension, exhaustion and determination.

Bex decided to meet with each of her clients and discuss their settlement and what to do with the award money and insurance policy payouts. She met with Shinski first. She had received Shinski's settlements and had compiled them on her behalf and planned a time to finalize everything. The package contained the wrongful death settlement, the life insurance payouts, Greg's last N-GerDon paycheck, an expense account check, Greg's yearly bonus check and stock options with a name transfer form for the surviving spouse. Shinski was looking at a value of well over $95 million dollars. Bex was astounded. Shinski had been thrilled. She and Shinski had set up trust funds, special accounts—money market, added her name to the current stocks and bonds, made bank transfers to settle name changes and so forth. Shinski said she wanted to earmark some money for charity work. Bex helped set aside a portion of her settlement until Shinski could decide what she wanted to do.

Actually Shinski had been hard at work behind the scenes the last month. She was working daily on two huge projects she wanted to keep as a surprise for her new little group of friends she now considered family. She knew exactly what she wanted to do with a big portion of her money. She had contacted Dan and the two of them had been extremely busy over the last several weeks buying a house.

Bex put Shinski's documents aside having fulfilled her duty to help Shinski place her wealth. Bex planned to finalize

Snowbird's settlement that next morning. Maude, Kinoo and Snowbird met Bex at her apartment and their settlements were discussed in front of the whole group so everyone would understand the details.

"Snowbird, you are a minor child. Your mother is your guardian and will be in charge of you and your affairs until you are of legal age—eighteen. I'm going to talk with your mother now while you listen. But what I am saying to her is for you. We are setting up money in trust funds in your name."

Bex was trying to dumb down the phraseology so a twelve year old could understand.

"Snowbird, you are a smart, thoughtful and responsible young woman. You will be able to go to the college of your choice and will not want for anything. But your mother will have the right to advise you and control your money for your benefit. I will be your advisor. You will not be able to withdraw any money without our consent and not until you are age eighteen. We will be protecting your money so you will have it when you are as old as we are or as old as Obi was!"

"Maude, on behalf of your daughter, you will be responsible for the trust funds we set up in her name. I'll advise you. The settlement for the wrongful death of her parents was awarded $15 million total. Snowbird received IRRSA money as beneficiary of her parents, grandparents and Obi. That totals $107,000. She receives life insurance payouts on each deceased parent totaling an additional $100,000. Also, she has a $2500 student scholarship in a trust fund and there are two N-GerDon final company paychecks for each parent totaling $8000.

Bex went to work immediately setting up a trust fund for Snowbird with executor, Maude Weidner, under the advising counsel, Bexley Hargrove.

"So Snowbird, you will have a total amount in your name as a nest egg for her future—a value of approximately $15,217,500. That would certainly buy you a college education, my dear."

Snowbird smiled rolling her head side to side and lifting her eyebrows not comprehending that amount of money.

"I'll be able to help a lot of people," she commented with a sideways grin.

Snowbird went over to the window seat in Bex's apartment and stared across the street at the beautiful grounds of the cancer center while Kinoo and Maude completed their settlement discussions.

Bex opened the final two reports. One was for Maude, the other for Kinoo.

"Maude, your check is for $16,000. It is a combination of the initial IRRSA, $10,000 and the two years you attended the Holy Angels Residential School which was $6,000. Your check is a combined, $16,000. If you would like, we can discuss the additional mental anguish of your friend's situation and apply for individual circumstances under several other categories of the IRSSA."

"No, I have completed that journey and my friend is at peace. I am at peace too. It is up to the Great Spirit now what to do with the actions of those nuns."

Maude, that concludes your settlement except that you have listed Snowbird as your beneficiary for your estate, which includes the café, right?"

"Yes, we went over my will yesterday and that is what I want—for Snowbird to have my café and anything else I have."

"Okay, we have you all set! The check for $16,000 is made out to you and me, I have signed it and all you have to do is put it in your checking account. So, here is your check."

"Kinoo, your check is for $55,000. It is for your initial year spent in the school—$10,000. And then for 16 years after that—$45,000. Your check is for a total of $55,000. We have set up a special account for you in a trust-fund for part of the money and an account for you to pull from monthly for your living expenses. Maude and I will help you with your tax liability on anything. And you've listed Maude, your daughter, as your beneficiary. Personal injury money is not taxable."

Bex thumbed through some documents to check the names.

"I was just checking to make sure we put the name *Maude* on the documents and not *Merinda*. We have to be consistent."

"No, she is Maude now," Kinoo said and smiled.

"Well, I think we're all through. If there are additional questions, Maude, you know where I am. With me as your advisor, you won't have any problems. I've done this a hundred times. Dan is good with this too."

Maude and Kinoo thanked Bex for everything. Snowbird hugged her neck and the three left for Maude's café.

—||—

Bex thought about Maude's restitution being only $16,000 for what she had been through and the fact that she was the one who adopted Snowbird and now has an aged parent living with her—Kinoo. How unfair for her to have received the smallest monetary award when it seemed to Bex, she had suffered the most.

But Maude had said she had made her pilgrimage to Canada, had finished what she had set out to do and was in good spirits with everything now. There would be no more fears of abuse, nuns, murders or graves. It had all been taken care of in her ability to bury her friend and to have IRRSA acknowledge the abuse and wrongdoing.

That agreement was one big umbrella package to absolve Canada's wrongdoing and the Apologies (in the appendix of this novel) given by several denominations was their fail-swoop attempt to absolve them of any wrongdoings, it appeared—*even murder.*

So for now, that was that. It is what it is. Bex had felt the agreement was just *hush money.* That is what $1.9 billion dollars bought the government of Canada. And what did the religious factions do monetarily? *She had not seen they had done anything directly compensating for their wrongdoing other than read their written apologies in public (*Appendix*).*

Bex felt so bad for Maude. She was probably the one who mentally suffered the most anguish over the fifty years having seen her schoolmate friend abused and seen the nuns stuff her body in that hole. She had run away to escape it, never saw her parents again and had to grow up in a different country with people who spoke a different language. And now she had adopted a teenage child, whom she didn't even know until a month ago. *What a giving person. Seemed hardly fair she only received $16,000,* Bex thought.

Bex was alone with the pile of papers on her desk. She had no job, yet her desk was full of documents and the upcoming lawsuit compilations.

Bex sat back staring at the last envelope. It was addressed to her from the Kander Law Firm. She opened it; there was a check and two letters. Bex waited to view the check amount. She read the letter accompanying the check. It was on company letterhead, so it was an official announcement of some sort. Bex read the letter thanking her for her compassion and emotional stake in the case and her contribution to the lawsuit with a compensation check enclosed. Peter Zacki had inserted a little handwritten note inside the envelope. It stated he could use another partner if she ever wanted to live in Fort McMurray, or if there were ever cross-border cases they could share; *he was up to the task if she was,* he had written. He asked Bex to give his love to Snowbird and that he wished everyone the best.

Bex put the letter down and wiped tears from her eyes.

Bex opened the check. It was her 2% contribution to the case, as she agreed. The check was for $1.6 million dollars. It had been the most gut-wrenching four weeks she had ever spent in her life.

Bex called Dan. No answer on his cell.

*What had he been up to these past several weeks?* Bex wondered, not being able to reach him as readily as she had in the past. Well, he was supposed to meet her at Starbucks on Friday—they would catch up then.

Bex pushed her seat back and was thinking about going to bed early. She managed to make it as far as the couch. She took a nap!

---

Shinski had had plans for her money. She had confided in Dan what her intentions were and told him she wanted to surprise Bex and Snowbird. They met at the Starbucks in the cancer center to talk.

"Well, what are you looking to do, Shinski?"

"I want to buy a house like I told Bex. So she knows that. What she doesn't know is that I want to buy Princess Natawee's mansion, which is located a bit outside of the city, northwest of Chicago. I've already talked with Maude and she is ecstatic. I have been thinking about this ever since I saw it. I've been thinking about Snowbird ever since I saw her hugging Obi. It tore my heart out to see that kind of love and respect. To see that child dressed up as a little Indian chief wanting to show Obi she had won the scholarship; to see her in the costume her people had made for her and how she wanted to help Obi preserve their people's heritage—I can't think of a better way to honor that type love and loyalty than to buy Princess Natawee's house for the family. That way Kinoo, Maude and Snowbird can live there in their ancestor's old family house."

Dan was stunned. "Shinski, I think that is one of the most generous, incredibly creative, amazing gifts anyone could ever do for them. It's genius. It's beyond words. Count me in. Whatever you need me to do. And I love the fact Bex doesn't know. What fun!"

"So since Maude has agreed…"

"Dan, I just need you to meet us at the real estate office. I've already set up everything. We just have to sign papers. I have even set up the banker who is familiar with the real estate and knows it could be commercial real estate but it is still zoned multi-use in that area. It can be a mixed-use facility or reverted back to a residence. So we are ready to go if you can meet us there. Well, can you meet us at 3 p.m.—today!"

"Today? Boy you work fast! Okay, it's about 9 a.m. now, so I'll be there at 3 p.m. if you give me the address."

Shinski jotted down the address and hugged Dan goodbye. She immediately took the elevator to the top floor of the cancer center to attend another meeting.

"Well, good afternoon, Mrs. Randolph. We have a place for you at the table beside me. We were finishing up some of the details we discussed yesterday. Please join us and we can just continue on with our meeting since your plans were the next topic for discussion. Please be seated. We are extremely excited. Here are the architectural plans you requested. And here is the area spacing in that wing for the name of the tower. Once you give us the name and what you want in that area, we'll get right on those plans."

"Thank you. I wanted to finalize some issues today so I can surprise the family with this news on Friday. They do not know anything about this yet!"

"This is amazing what you're doing, Mrs. Randolph. It'll take a couple years to complete the wing, but it will be exciting to watch its progress. It always is."

—◁▮▷—

That next afternoon Maude, Shinski and Dan met the realtor. The meeting did not take long.

"Well, Mrs. Randolph, you've bought a house," the realtor said and stood to shake Shinski's hand.

He then turned to Ms. Maude Weidner and handed her the deed, which was in her name.

"Well, ladies, I'd like to congratulate the two of you in a job well done. The house was meant to be in the family," the realtor commented.

Dan smiled and the threesome stepped aside to discuss the

rest of the week's plans.

"Shinski, I know you have another place you have to be. So Maude, how about you and I make a run for the courthouse to record the deed, finish up those details and talk a bit about when you might want to move in. Maybe you can remodel the home and turn part of it into business. You don't have to decide now. You have a place to live at the moment and so does Bex," Dan said.

The three parted ways to complete certain tasks before meeting again Friday at the cancer center's Starbucks.

Shinski ran to her car; she had a very important business meeting, the second one in two days. She was very excited. She ran to the elevator in the cancer center and tapped her feet impatiently for the elevator to reach her destination. She quickly exited on the top floor and walked into a crowded board room of members waiting for her arrival.

"Mrs. Randolph, you've had a busy week. Thank you for attending this evening's planning board meeting."

"Everyone, please welcome Mrs. Randolph again tonight— she is our major benefactor in the new in-patient tower at the cancer center."

The board of directors applauded her presence and the chairwoman began her presentation.

"As you know, the center is breaking ground in three months on a new in-patient tower. The cost is roughly budgeted for $1.5 billion dollars. Our major benefactor is here today to present a philanthropic gift. Mrs. Randolph, would you like to say a few words?"

Shinski stood up and gave the grandest speech of her life. She swayed the board members unanimously with her graciousness and her compassion eloquently delivered the story of Obigon Sakawa and the Great Snowy White Owl with its grandeur wing span, the meaning behind the owl and the cancers detected in Obi at one hundred years old. She told the story of the First Nation's people, the story of how Obi's family had perished except Snowbird, the great-grandchild who is now in the states. Shinski described the scholarship the child had won on the subject of respecting Mother Earth and that it was all about reminding others to protect the environment so that it would provide for the people in a clean, healthy way. She explained the thinking of respecting all living things and preserving heritage, family love—to honor loved ones and those who have gone before us. She won them over.

Shinski walked out of the meeting feeling like a million dollars or as she corrected herself, feeling several million dollars lighter! She was thrilled. She had named the wing and the board had approved it!

—⚡—

The next evening, Friday night would be exciting for everyone. Shinski, Dan and Maude had set up the evening to look as if just a few of them were meeting for a little Friday night get-together at Starbucks on the second floor of the cancer center—sort of an impromptu thing!

Dan had asked Bex to meet him there at 5:30 p.m. Maude had told Kinoo and Snowbird they were driving over to have dinner with Bex, Dan and Shinski and that they were meeting at Starbucks beforehand. Shinski was driving separately—*loving her new wheels.*

So everyone knew the meeting place. Shinski, Maude and Dan would take it from there once everyone arrived.

Everyone trickled in, hugged each other and sat down. Maude was all smiles.

"Maude, what's up with you? You're grinning ear to ear like you just swallowed a canary," Bex said.

"Swallowed a canary? What does that mean?" Maude replied.

"Just an expression," Dan laughed.

"Okay, what gives with everyone showing up here all smiles and no conversation?"

"We have some big news." Maude said.

"Shinski, do you want to do the honors?"

"Well, I can start it, I guess. Okay. Bex, you know the other day when I told you I wanted to buy a house? Well…"

"You bought a house, Shinski! Congratulations," Bex yelled out.

"Well, hold on. Yes, I bought a house," Shinski replied but was interrupted when Maude jumped up to finish the sentence.

"…for us, Ms. Hargrove. For Snowbird, Kinoo and me!" Maude cried out.

"…and guess where?" Shinski blurted out with a big smile.

"Oh. Let me do the honors, everyone. Please," Dan yelled out wanting to get in on the fun.

But he was too late; nobody could keep from shouting out the surprise in a total syncopated answer among the group.

"The Princess Natawee Mansion," one called out while another blurted halfway through that answer with, "The house where Princess Natawee lived," interrupted by "Princess Natawee's House," which together the shouting was totally confusing. With all that yelling Bex just looked confused. She could not make out any of the comments.

"What?" Bex cried out understanding she was the only one who didn't know!

Maude stood up and slowly answered, "Mrs. Randolph just bought Princess Natawee's mansion for us and we are going to live there as a family—Snowbird, Kinoo and I."

Bex was totally, undeniably and unforgettably dumbfounded.

"I don't believe it, I don't believe it. Really? No way!"

"Yes indeed."

Bex turned to Shinski amazed at how fast she had worked.

"You pulled this off, without my help? I'm stunned, Shinski. Not that you couldn't do it. I am just floored that you did it all by yourself!"

Shinski was smiling from ear to ear with a new haircut and flashing a set of French manicured nails.

"Well, I did have a wee bit of help. I signed the paperwork

Dan laid out before me," Shinski admitted.

"Dan?" Bex cried out looking at him, "You kept this from me all this time?"

"It was hard but we wanted it to be a surprise. Shinski really wanted to do this for Maude and Snowbird and just did it. She was amazingly competent at all this," Dan replied, feeling quite proud of Shinski.

Bex turned to Shinski. "You said you were thinking about a house. I thought it was for you!"

"I know, I thought it was funny. So I let you think that. I was thinking about the mansion ever since the first day I found it by chance and had my hair and nails done there. It was the best day of shopping I've had since Greg bought that Canadian Lynx for me a couple years ago."

"Well, I'm proud of you."

"And I also have a special announcement for you, Snowbird," Shinski continued.

"I am the major philanthropic benefactor in a new in-patient tower to be built right here at the cancer center that breaks ground in three months. And it will be named after your great-grandfather. This is the first time I've done something really special and game changing for someone else. I want to help you and I want to help others who become victims of cancer."

Shinski welled up with her own announcement as she stood there, swaying side to side, like a little high-school girl.

"Shinski," Bex cried out. "I'm totally flabbergasted. What has gotten in to you? You are changing before my eyes. You're not the same person. You've always been the little socialite that was incapable of doing anything on your own. I've always loved you like a sister and thought you needed someone to guide you in life and take care of you. You've always loved your furs and high heels. I'm so proud of you!"

Bex was astounded. She and the group stood and clapped for *Super Shinski*. Then they cheered for Bex. They hugged Snowbird, Kinoo and Maude and bowed to *Sir Dan*!

"I can do things, you know. Shopping is my hobby and I'm

good at shopping. These are just the two largest ticket items I've ever bought, that's for sure," she said laughing.

Shinski's expression turned serious.

"None of this would have been possible without you, Bex. You held us together, fought for us and struggled to make things right. You did so much for us, Bex. There could have been so many victims in this and you turned it all around so that we are all turned out winners."

"And you keep trying to make a difference in people's lives!" everyone shouted.

"Remember what I told you the first day I met you about your name, Bex, that it means *to go great heights and equally great depths*. This you have done for us," Maude replied.

Bex blushed. She hugged her friends unable to speak.

There was hardly anyone in the café at that hour so the Starbucks waiter yelled out their order, "Five venti lattes for Bex."

Everyone laughed. A blue flash shot across the room as Bex laughed.

"Dan, is that your cell phone catching a reflection?"

"No. I don't think so," Dan said pulling his cell phone from his pocket and checking to see if it was even turned on.

Another bluish light seemed to hover, flicker, and then disappear leaving a twinkling of silver dust lingering in the air, reflecting the light from somewhere.

For a moment everyone was stunned. Then Shinski commented that it had to be the sun reflecting off the plate glass windows from windshields of a cars passing by on the street below. But it was getting late and the sun was going down on the other side of the building.

Snowbird's mind turned immediately to the fairies when she saw the flickering. It was similar to the fairies' blueish light and she wondered if the fairies were nearby, following her to Chicago, wanting to join them in the celebration. She had dreamed of them the previous night. They had whispered to her that Obi was okay now with the Great Spirit and he would be watching over her in the future.

Snowbird picked up her venti latte and held it high in the air. The others did the same and touched each other's paper cup in salute.

"Obi, this is your dream. This center will be your legacy. This will be a way of truth and much healing from the Great Spirit. This place will make other hearts and souls come full circle again and again and again with love, faith and hope. You taught me so much. For this I am grateful and will always love and respect your memory!" Snowbird said.

"To Obi!" Maude replied.

"To Obi!" The others raised their lattes in respect.

Snowbird was now thirteen years old, *just thirteen*. She was a teenager. But her words were spoken with a maturity well beyond her years having been taught and guided by Obi and the Great Spirit to be a leader. She often thought she could hear the whooping and shouts of the little people calling the names of her ancestors or searching for other lost ones. She thought she could hear them from afar.

—◄│►—

That Starbucks celebration was a night nobody would forget. The family of six would be lifelong friends.

Well, maybe it was a family of *seven*. The shaking tent took up as much space as if it were another family member. Maude placed the shaking tent in their new mansion. She had sold the café in South Chicago and had opened a café in the mansion. For now, she was living with Kinoo and Snowbird on the $2^{nd}$ floor. No plans yet on what to do with the mansion—she had time!

—◄│►—

Six years later on the anniversary of Obi's passing, a cheer filled the halls of the new Obigon Sakawa Tower at Cancer Center of the Americas in Chicago, Illinois, USA. A large life-size Great Snowy White Owl was carved with full wing span and placed above a good sized bronzed plaque engraved with these words:

*"SIGHT BEYOND ILLUSION"*
*The Great White Snowy Owl*
*"The Obigon Sakawa Cancer Tower"*
Conscience of Mankind Guides All Respect and Honor

*In Appreciation to*
*Mrs. Amanda Shinski Randolph: Randolph Foundation*
*Sole Benefactor of the Obigon Sakawa Cancer Tower*
*Cancer Center of the Americas, Chicago, Illinois, USA.*

"All this—to Obi's legacy!" Bex cried out to the friends and family who had come to the celebration that day.

"Here! Here!"

Snowbird had clapped wildly when they unveiled the Great Snowy White Owl. She was an eighteen-year old young junior in college at the University of St. Francis in Joliet, Illinois. She had skipped a year based on her college entrance exams and submitting a letter explaining her personal experiences to the Dean of the School. She had declared her major, even as an undergraduate, in nuclear medicine and expressed her desire to work at the cancer center in Chicago, in the Obigon Sakawa Cancer Tower, under her great-grandfather's protective watch —*under Obi's Wing.*

Snowbird reached up and secured the wren feather behind her earlobe and whispered, "Obi, you are gone, but you are not forgotten."

Snowbird spread her arms out wide and positioned her body the same angle as the Great Snowy White Owl carving hanging on the wall and whispered,

"Kihtwám ka-wápamitináwáw, Obi!"

*Until we meet again.*

**THE END**

# APPENDIX

## INSPIRATION FOR THE STORY

1. The original inspiration for the story was a photograph taken by Anne Michael, the author, some forty years ago, November 1979. The photo depicted a double-mouthed, deformed fish pulled from the waters off the Sauk Creek Bridge in Port Washington, Wisconsin.

2. Significant events in Lake Norman, NC, where thousands of fish went belly up, were reported by the *Charlotte Observer, Denver Weekly and the Lincoln Time-News* over several years. The only explanation was a general comment about the heat, the power plant and non-native fish. Residents were extremely concerned and vacationers noticed! It is still a concern.

3. Further research regarding fish dying, en masse, uncovered a story regarding half a billion fish going belly up in Chicago in 2016 allegedly caused by pig manure being dumped into the waterways.

4. Researching deformed fish in the U.S. waterways led to a story about an elderly wife of a First Nations man who died of bile duct cancer, rare for the area and population count.

5. These stories led to a side issue regarding the taking of the First Nations land by the Canadian government for about a hundred years while continuously polluting their protected land and water, which poisoned and killed wildlife.

6. Finally, the above research led to the taking of the First Nations children with purpose of forced assimilation into the European culture. This discovery opened the flood gates to stories leading up to the largest class action lawsuit ever awarded in Canada and a major embarrassment of quite a number of major world religions caught in a scandal of child abuse and murder that skirted the edge of sheer insanity and total lack of humanity on the part of the Canadian Government, the Vatican and numerous other significant religious denomination. The First Nations people became engulfed in a lawsuit: First Nations People in Canada vs Canada: TRC and IRSSA.

7. Pulling in the cultural genocide lawsuit, made it necessary to include the facts concerning the environmental genocide, which the story alludes to being the next largest class action lawsuit against Canada with the plaintiffs, again, being the First Nations people. The story ends with the story's main characters working on the next class

action lawsuit. The author alludes to that lawsuit being encouraged in the real world. While writing the book, oil pipelines were being laid throughout Canada and the U.S. directing the construction through protected lands, burial grounds, unfit terrain, and greatly affecting the culture of some people and destroying the environment.

For all the reasons cited, the author felt a need to write the book, to educate and alert readers to travesties that could have been avoided—alerting readers to travesties—or *covered up*.

The author's photo of a deformed fish—November 1979:

Three belly-up fish articles:

www.denverncweekly.com                    Aug.5-11, 2011  page 11

## News

# Hundreds of fish found dead in Lake Norman

by **Will Bryant** and **Lauren Dunn**
news@denverncweekly.com

HUNTERSVILLE – More than 350 striped bass were found dead this week in Lake Norman near the McGuire Nuclear Station, Duke Energy reported.

The incident is the summer's first major fish kill since nearly 7,000 fish were found dead in the lake last summer.

While some have been quick to point the finger of blame at Duke Energy, company spokeswoman Hailey Wilson said the deaths occurred naturally.

"This is actually a completely natural phenomenon caused by a depletion of oxygen in the lake," Wilson said. "This is happening in lakes all over the Southeast."

The extremely high temperatures have pushed oxygen levels to deeper depths in the lake, trapping some fish at the cool bottom. Many of them can't survive at those levels.

Wilson pointed to other lakes in the area seeing similar incidents.

In Apex, Lake Jordan has also experienced fish kills but on a more severe scale. Lake Jordan has no power plant on its water that can be blamed for the unusual occurrence.

"The last few days it's been pretty bad," said Annie Howell, spokeswoman at Lake Jordan. Howell estimates that nearly 1,000 fish have died as a result of the warm water temperatures in recent weeks.

This is the fourth major fish kill in Lake Norman since 2004.

Along with last summer's 7,000 striped bass, 300 were reported dead in 2009 and another 3,000 floated to the surface in 2004.

However some in the fishing community maintain Lake Norman's fish kill problem can be traced back to McGuire Nuclear Station.

"It's passed off as a natural occurrence, but it is a natural occurrence to a point," said Capt. Gus Gustafson, a charter boat captain with years of experience on the lake. Gustafson believes the hot temperatures are being exasperated by discharge from the plant, what he called "thermal pollution."

And the problem has the potential to harm the area's economy as the lake and fishing draw hundreds of people each year, he said.

"We don't want people thinking the fish in our lakes are dead, because they're not," Gustafson said. "It will continue to have a negative effect on our tourism." ❑

Denver Weekly News, Denver, North Carolina

Lincoln Times-News, Lincolnton, N.C., Wednesday, August 11, 2010, pg 8-A NEWS

## Thousands of fish die in Lake Norman

CHARLOTTE (AP) --
Thousands of fish have died in North Carolina's largest manmade lake.

The *Charlotte Observer* reports Wednesday that 7,000 striped bass have been found floating on Lake Norman since July.

It is the third time in seven years the game fish have died en masse in the lake. About 300 stripers died last summer, while 3,000 died in 2004.

Fish biologists suspect the summer heat, a power plant cooled by lake water and non-native fish dumped into the lake by fishermen more than a decade ago.

The state stocks the lake with 162,500 inch-long bass yearly.

Striper guide, Gus Gustafson says about 16,000 normally grow to catchable size each year, so the fish kill represents half a year's harvest. He believes even more dead fish sank to the bottom, uncounted.

# Thousands of fish die in Lake Norman

CHARLOTTE (AP) --Thousands of fish have died in North Carolina's largest manmade lake.

The *Charlotte Observer* reports Wednesday that 7,000 striped bass have been found floating on Lake Norman since July.

It is the third time in seven years the game fish have died en masse in the lake. About 300 stripers died last summer, while 3,000 died in 2004.

Fish biologists suspects the summer heat, a power plant cooled by lake water and non-native fish dumped into the lake by fishermen more than a decade ago.

The state stocks the lake with 162,500 inch-long bass yearly.

Striper guide, Gus Gustaafson, says about 16,000 normally grow to catchable size each year, so the fish kill represents half a year's harvest. He believes even more dead fish sank to the bottom, uncounted.

Pig farmer article of approximately half billion fish belly up--
Summary by Anne Michael. Inspiration from Chicago Tribune article:
www.chicagotribune.com/investigations/ct-pig-farms-pollution-met-20160802-story.html
by David Jackson and Gary Marx--Chicago Tribune/Aug 05, 2016 at 4:57 AM, "Spills of
pig waste kills hundreds of thousands of fish in Illinois--Chicago Tribune."

In the Chicago Tribune article cited above, "pig farming is a huge business
in Illinois, with about $1.5 billion worth of pigs sold in 2012...Several pig
operations in the Illinois area pumped swine waste either unknowingly from
leaky pipes or intentionally into water sources... water black and (reeking) of
manure and dead fish...many farmers not admitting wrongdoing...killing massive numbers of fish."

The EPA, DNR, and the attorney general's office was the source for the
Chicago Tribune's discovery that "pollution incidents from hog confinements
killed at least 492,000 fish from 2005-2014...Pig waste impaired 67 miles of
the state's rivers, creeks, and waterways over that time...Fish kills do provide a
gauge of the environmental impact of the modern pig-raising facilities that
helped make Illinois the fourth-largest pork producer in the U.S."

While privacy laws prohibit revealing the companies who are the culprits of
this pollution, the Chicago Tribune was able to find out the name of companies
responsible "through copies of checks submitted to reimburse the state for re-
stocking fish." The article lists some of those influential producers
allegedly responsible, what officials are doing to combat the problem and several ongoing lawsuits regarding the pollution and its devastating results on the
environment. The article suggests there are many culprits, the details of the
major polluters are discussed in the article. The fact remains that there are
more than a few polluters in this fourth-largest pork producing state polluting
waterways and being fined by the government. It is always difficult to determine the damages from the pollutier. Visual fish kills, fish floating on the surface certainly grabs one's attention. A count of approximately half billion fish
floating on top of the water over a few years is concerning. Pig manure, en
masse, can be broken down into the same chemicals analysis reported to
be hazardous waste, like oil refinery waste pools discussed in this historical
novel, *Shaking Tent,* by Anne Michael.

## QUOTATIONS AND LESSONS LEARNED:
## PROTECTION OF MOTHER EARTH

1. "Sooner or later, we will have to recognize that Earth has rights, too, to live without pollution. What mankind must know is that human beings cannot live without Mother Earth, but the planet can live without humans." *Evo Morales*

2. "Plans to protect air and water, wilderness and wildlife are in fact plans to protect man." *Stewart Udall*

3. "Treat Earth well. It was not given to you by your parents; it was loaned to you by your children. We do not inherit the world from our ancestors; we borrow it from our children." *Native American proverb*

4. "We are all caretakers of the World! The world is mostly water and every living thing is mostly made up of water. Water is essential to life. Without water, we perish as a people; without water, all living things perish. We have not taken care of our water! And we are all caretakers of each other! 'If we don't teach our children and grandchildren *(to respect all nature and each other,)* what kind of world is it going to become? What kind of world are we going to leave for our children? I ask what kind of children are we going to leave to our world?" *Drift Pile First Nation, Fred Campiou- Cree Elder*

## PROTECTION OF EACH OTHER

5. "Our children are the rock on which our future will be built, our greatest asset as a nation. They will be the leaders of our country, the creators of our national wealth, those who care for and protect our people." *Nelson Mandela*

6. "Lord, I ask you to protect my kids: physically, emotionally, spiritually, mentally and in every way." *Psalm 46:1 The Bible*

7. "If we don't stand up for children, then we don't stand for much." *Marion Eldemon*

8. "Reality is harsh. It can be cruel and ugly. Yet no matter how much we grieve over our environment and our circumstances, nothing will change. What is important is not to be defeated, to forge ahead bravely. If we do this, a path will open before us." *Daisaku Ikeda*

## LESSONS LEARNED

9. **1ˢᵗ Lesson**: **Mother Earth-Treaty 8**: There were promises in the forms of Treaties between the Government of Canada created in 1867 and the First Nation's people that if the white man used the land that belonged to these indigenous people, they could still use the land in perpetuity for hunting, fishing and farming. And written in the numbered treaties, the First Nations people understood the white man would return the land to its original form when they finished using it. That was the overall understanding when the Treaty was signed in 1899. Instead it has been a slow industrial genocide. *(https://www.pinterest.com/bsambiance/native-indian/)*

10. **Treaty 8** "...was an agreement signed on June 21, 1899, between Queen Victoria and various First Nations of the Lesser Slave Lake area. The Treaty was signed just south of present-day Grouard, Alberta... is one of eleven made between the Government of Canada and First Nations. The Government of Canada had between 1871 and 1877 signed Treaties 1 to 7. Treaties 1 to 7 covered the southern portions of what was the Northwest Territories. The elements of Treaty 8 included provisions to maintain livelihood for the native populations in this massive region, such as entitlements to land, ongoing financial support, annual shipments of hunting supplies, and hunting rights on ceded lands, unless those ceded lands were used for forestry, mining, settlement or other purposes... This treaty still governs the region today, but much has changed in terms of its landscape and use. The original signatories of the treaty could not have predicted the energy resources under the soil and how they would change the promises of the treaty...As forests are clear cut and wetlands destroyed, the ability of the aboriginals in the area to live their traditional way of life has been diminished. The construction of roadways has opened areas to overfishing and hunting, further degrading the way of life promised in Treaty 8. In addition, sections of northeastern Alberta have been adversely affected by the pollution of air and water by oil sand extraction which has decreased the quality and value of fish and animals hunted by the local Indigenous People."
*(https://en.wikipedia.org/wiki/Treaty_8#/media/File:David_Laird_explaining_Treaty_8_Fort_Vermilion_1899_-_NA-949-34.jpg)*

TRC

(https://society6.com/product/new-world-isis_print#s6-105773p4a1v45)

11. "**The Oil Sands Project**…should not be considered a trade off since the project has become an issue with great concern over the impact on the environment and the lives of many indigenous groups. The treaty promised the continuation of the ability to hunt, trap and fish and that has been severely affected and the people are fearful of toxins in the water and in the fish and game caught. The situation has been described as 'slow industrial genocide' against the residents in the area. The treaty was meant to preserve the lands so the First Nations people would have a means of support. As it turns out, the fear is that all means of survival have been greatly reduced and they have had to turn to employment with the very entity that is destroying their land."

(http://www.academia.edu/3834427/A_slow_industrial_genocide_tar_sands_and_the_indigenous_people_of_northern_Alberta)

## 12. **Oil Sands of Alberta-**

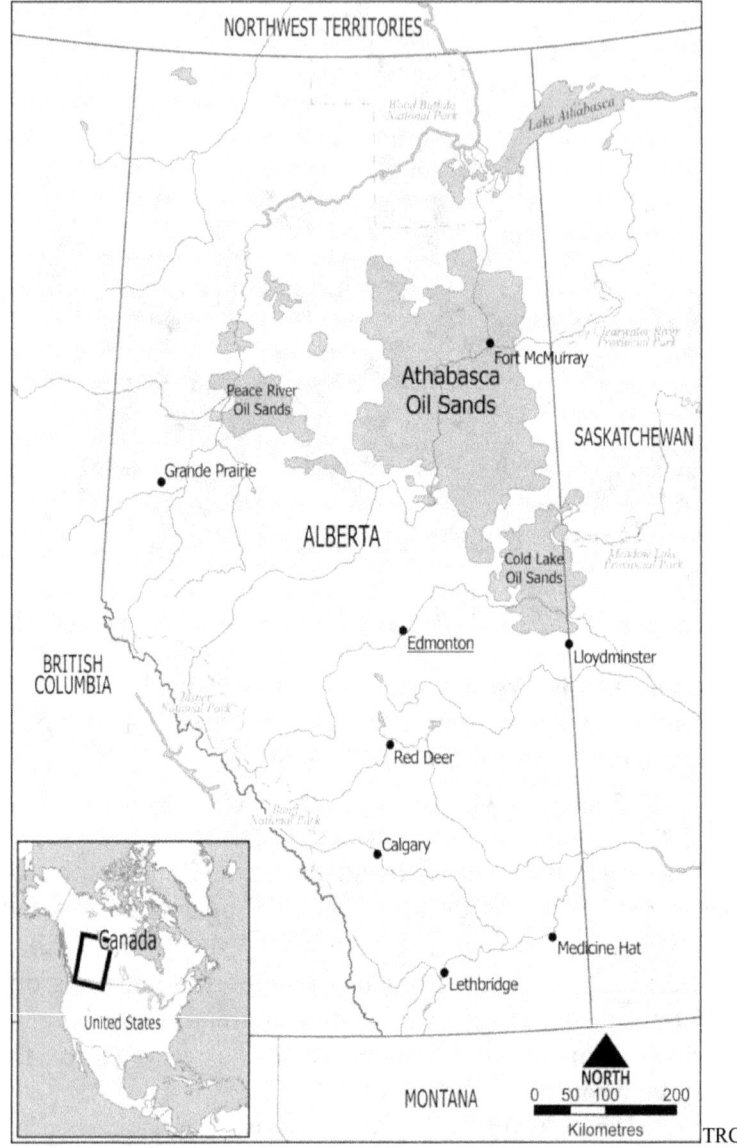

(https://upload.wikimedia.org/wikipedia/commons/7/7a/Athabasca_Oil_Sands_map.png)

## 13. **Mining in the Oil Sands-**

(http://www.the guardian.com/environment/gallery
/2015/aug/03/canadas-tar-sands=landscape-from-the-air-in-picture)

(http://www.businessinsider.com/photos-destructive-canada-oil-sands-
2012-10/#rrying-the-chunks-of-oil-sand-14)
Photos by Robert Johnson

(http://www.businessinsider.com/photos-destructive-canada-oil-sands-2012-10/#rrying-the-chunks-of-oil-sand-14) photos by Robert Johnson

Oil sands near Fort McMurray, Alta.
(Photo by Jeff Macintosh/ Canadian Calgary Herald 10.09.2104)
(http://www.calgaryherald.com/business/cms/binary/10089868.jpg?Size= sw620x65_)

(http://www.cbc.ca/news/business/total-s-joslyn-oilsands-project-on-
hold-) Oil sands near Fort McMurray, Alta.
(Photo by Jeff McIntosh/ Canadian Press)

(tailing_pond.jpg.) Photo by Jeff Macintosh
(https://www.thestar.com/news/canada/2014/11/27/oilsands_study_confir
ms_link_between_tailings_ponds_and_air_pollution.html)

14. **2<sup>nd</sup> Lesson: Protection of Humankind1876 Indian Act,
Treaty 6**—Promises were made in the forms of a formal written agreement between the Canadian government and the churches to force the children of the First Nation to learn the ways of the *white man*. When the *white man* took the indigenous children away from their families threatening parental incarceration if they did not consent, the families had no choice but to let their people go. They were told it would be in their best interest. They were told the children would come back to help their people and they would be able to fit into society and find good jobs. Instead it has been a 'cultural genocide' that has affected the First Nations' People generation after generation and has contributed to the low socio-economic status, the depression, the substance abuse, domestic violence, disease and early deaths of hundreds upon hundreds of people.

## 15. Residential Indian Schools in Canada

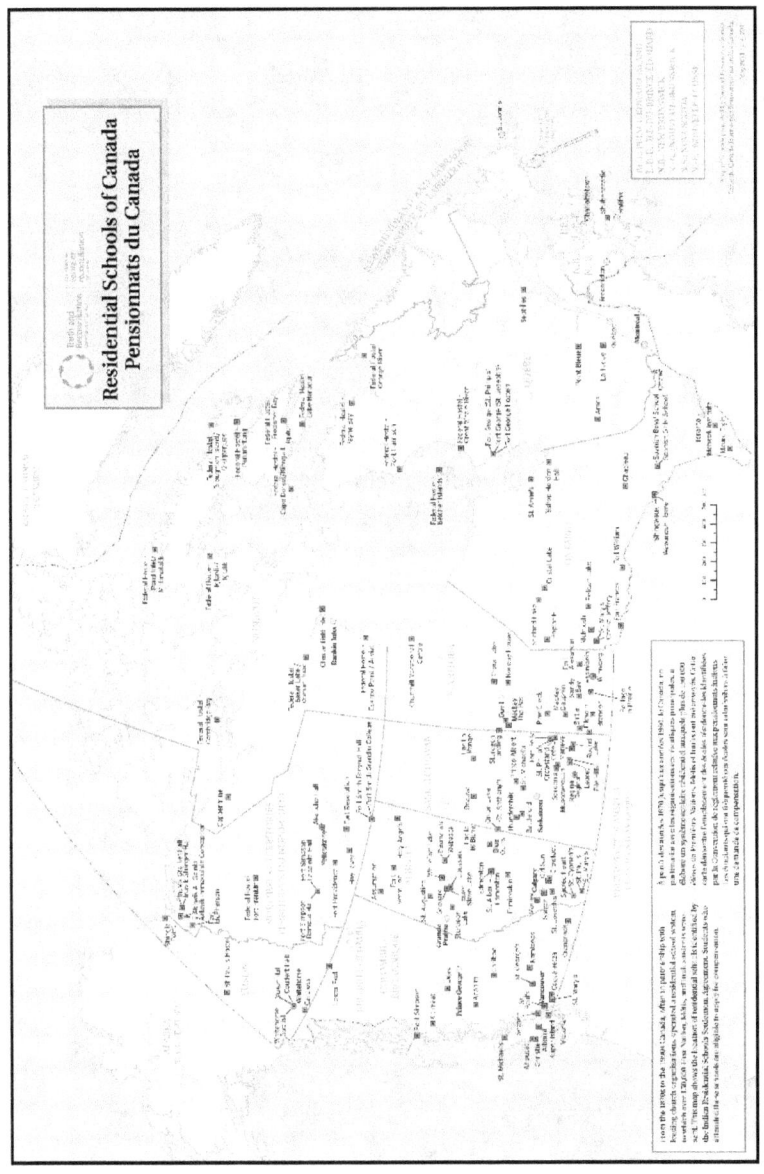

TRC
(https://www.google.com/search?Q=residential+schools+of+canada+map
&rlz=1C1LENP_enus561us567&espv=2&biw=1281&bih=627&tbm=isc
h&tbo=u&source=univ&sa=X&ved=0ahukewis8o6f6dboahxhpiykhxw-
angqsaqigw#imgrc= dbswdlijtzcfqm%3A)

TRC

(http://www.thecanadianencyclopedia.ca/en/article/residential-schools/)
Roman Catholic Indian boarding school, church and mission, Fort
Chipewyan, Alberta, circa. 1930 Library and Archives Canada, PA-
102543.

TRC

(TRC Report-IMAGE COURTESY OF © SENATE OF CANADA)

16. **Two Mass Graves-** found at site of residential schools

TRC

(https://s-media-cache-ak0.pinimg.com
/564x/08/c5/2f/08c52f0fa396e1aaa389ea9b743ff6ee.jpg)
A mass grave of children's skeletal remains at a residential
school.

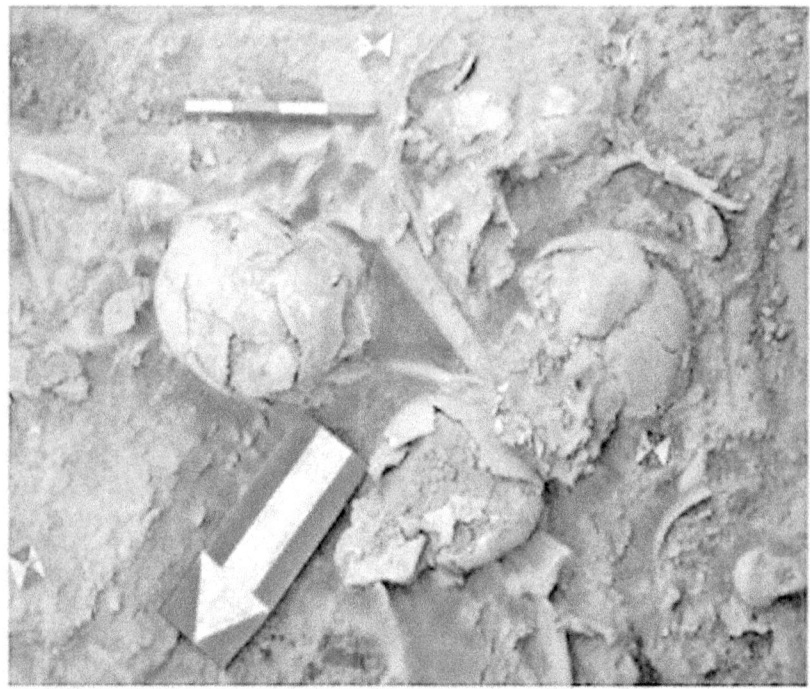

Mass Grave Identified near former Catholic Indian Residential School, Alberta

50,000 children died in Indian residential schools...the Catholic, Anglican and United churches responsible have been legally, but not morally absolved... noone has been brought to trial for these killings...the torture and abduction of children by clergy continues... (TRC Report).

http://revealingtruthinnovascotia.blogspot.com/2011/07/mass-graves-of-residential-school.html

17. **They Came for the Children** and took them to residential schools to assimilate them into the *White Man's ways.*

TRC

2039_T&Teng_web[1] (1) They Came for the Children (Historical Document) Canada, Aboriginal Peoples and Residential Schools, TRC Report.

TRC

2039_T&Teng_web[1] (1) They Came for the Children (Historical Document)
Canada, Aboriginal Peoples and Residential Schools, TRC Report.

# THE APOLOGIES

## CULTURAL GENOCIDE APOLOGIES

### I. GOVERNMENT of CANADA

"To the approximately 80,000 living former students, and all family members and communities, the Government of Canada now recognizes that it was wrong to forcibly remove children from their homes and we apologize for having done this. We now recognize that it was wrong to separate children from rich and vibrant cultures and traditions that it created a void in many lives and communities, and we apologize for having done this. We now recognize that, in separating children from their families, we undermined the ability of many to adequately parent their own children and sowed the seeds for generations to follow, and we apologize for having done this. We now recognize that, far too often, these institutions gave rise to abuse or neglect and were inadequately controlled, and we apologize for failing to protect you. Not only did you suffer these abuses as children, but as you became parents, you were powerless to protect your own children from suffering the same experience, and for this we are sorry.

The burden of this experience has been on your shoulders for far too long. The burden is properly ours as a Government, and as a country. There is no place in Canada for the attitudes that inspired the Indian Residential Schools system to ever prevail again. You have been working on recovering from this experience for a long time and in a very real sense, we are now joining you on this journey. The Government of Canada sincerely apologizes and asks the forgiveness of the Aboriginal People of this country for failing them so profoundly— On behalf of the Government of Canada: The Right Honourable Stephen Harper, Prime Minister of Canada, June 11, 2008. — (http://www.aadnc-aandc.gc.ca/eng/11—1---15644/1100100015649)

### 2. ROYAL CANADIAN MOUNTED POLICE-

"The Apology of The Royal Canadian Mounted Police (RCMP) with respect to the Indian Residential School legacy, May 2004 Giuliano Zaccardelli, Commissioner Royal Canadian Mounted Police Many Aboriginal people have found the courage to step outside of that legacy of this terrible chapter in Canadian history to share their stories. You heard one of those stories today. To those of you who suffered tragedies at residential schools we are very sorry for your experience. Healing has begun in many communities as you heard today, a testament that is a testament to the strength and tenacity of Aboriginal people and Aboriginal communities. Canadians can never forget what happened and they never should. The RCMP is optimistic that we can all work together to learn from this residential school system experience and ensure that it never happens again. The RCMP is committed to working with Aboriginal people to continue the healing process. Your communities deserve better choices and better chances. Knowing the past, we must all turn to the future and build a brighter future for all our children. We, I, as Commissioner of the RCMP, I am truly sorry for what role we played in the residential school system and the abuse that took place in that system." (See TRC Commission Report for additional reading of all other apologies)

## II. RELIGION- DENOMINATIONAL APOLOGIES
## 1. ANGLICAN CHURCH- APOLOGY

"TRC-Apology of the Anglican Church of Canada A message from the Primate, Archbishop Michael Peers, to the National Native Convocation, Minaki, Ontario, August 6, 1993 My Brothers and Sisters: Together here with you I have listened as you have told your stories of the residential schools. I have heard the voices that have spoken of pain and hurt experienced in the schools, and of the scars which endure to this day. I have felt shame and humiliation as I have heard of suffering inflicted by my people, and as I think of the part our church played in that suffering. I am deeply conscious of the sacredness of the stories that you have told and I hold in the highest honour those who have told them. I have heard with admiration the stories of people and communities who have worked at healing, and I am aware of how much healing is needed. I also know that I am in need of healing, and my own people are in need of healing, and our church is in need of healing. Without that healing, we will continue the same attitudes that have done such damage in the past. I also know that healing takes a long time, both for people and for communities. I also know that it is God who heals, and that God can begin to heal when we open ourselves, our wounds, our failures and our shame to God. I want to take one step along that path here and now. I accept and I confess before God and you, our failures in the residential schools. We failed you. We failed ourselves. We failed God. I am sorry, more than I can say, that we were part of a system which took you and your children from home and family. I am sorry, more than I can say, that we tried to remake you in our image, taking from you your language and the signs of your identity. I am sorry, more than I can say, that in our schools so many were abused physically, sexually, culturally and emotionally. On behalf of the Anglican Church of Canada, I present our apology. I do this at the desire of those in the Church like the National Executive Council, who know some of your stories and have asked me to apologize. Appendix 4 • 381 I do this in the name of many who do not know these stories. And I do this even though there are those in the church who cannot accept the fact that these things were done in our name. As soon as I am home, I shall tell all the bishops what I have said, and ask them to co-operate with me and with the National Executive Council in helping this healing at the local level. Some bishops have already begun this work. I know how often you have heard words which have been empty because they have not been accompanied by actions. I pledge to you my best efforts, and the efforts of our church at the national level, to walk with you along the path of God's healing. The work of the Residential Schools Working Group, the video, the commitment and the effort of the Special Assistants to the Primate for this work, the grants available for healing conferences, are some signs of that pledge, and we shall work for others. This is Friday, the day of Jesus' suffering and death. It is the anniversary of the first atomic bomb at Hiroshima, one of the most terrible injuries ever inflicted by one people on another. But even atomic bombs and Good Friday are not the last word. God raised Jesus from the dead as a sign that life and wholeness are the everlasting and unquenchable purpose of God. Thank you for listening to me."

## 2. PRESBYTERIAN CHURCH APOLOGY

"Statements of The Presbyterian Church in Canada The Confession of The Presbyterian Church in Canada as adopted by the General Assembly, June 9, 1994 The Holy Spirit, speaking in and through Scripture, calls The Presbyterian Church in Canada to confession. This confession is our response to the word of God. We understand our mission and ministry in new ways in part because of the testimony of Aboriginal people. 1) We, the 120th General Assembly of The Presbyterian Church in Canada, seeking the guidance of the Spirit of God, and aware of our own sin and shortcomings, are called to speak to the Church we love. We do this, out of new understandings of our past not out of any sense of being superior to those who have gone before us, nor out of any sense that we would have done things differently in the same context. It is with humility and in great sorrow that we come before God and our Aboriginal brothers and sisters with our confession. 2) We acknowledge that the stated policy of the Government of Canada was to assimilate Aboriginal people to the dominant culture, and that The Presbyterian Church in Canada co-operated in this policy. We acknowledge 382 • Truth & Reconciliation Commission that the roots of the harm we have done are found in the attitudes and values of western European colonialism, and the assumption that what was not yet molded in our image was to be discovered and exploited. As part of that policy we, with other churches, encouraged the government to ban some important spiritual practices through which Aboriginal people experienced the presence of the creator God. For the Church's complicity in this policy we ask forgiveness. We recognize that there were many members of the Presbyterian Church in Canada who, in good faith, gave unstintingly of themselves in love and compassion for their Aboriginal brothers and sisters. We acknowledge their devotion and commend them for their work. We recognize that there were some who, with prophetic insight, were aware of the damage that was being done and protested, but their efforts were thwarted. We acknowledge their insight. For the times we did not support them adequately nor hear their cries for justice, we ask forgiveness. We confess that the Presbyterian Church in Canada presumed to know better than Aboriginal people what was needed for life the Church said of our Aboriginal brothers and sisters, "If they could be like us, if they could think like us, talk like us, worship like us, sing like us, and work like us, they would know God and therefore would have life abundant." In our cultural arrogance we have been blind to the ways in which our own understanding of the Gospel has been culturally conditioned, and because of our insensitivity to Aboriginal cultures, we have demanded more of the Aboriginal people than the Gospel requires, and have thus misrepresented Jesus Christ who loves all people with compassionate, suffering love that all may come to God through him. For the Church's presumption we ask forgiveness. 5) We confess that, with the encouragement and assistance of the Government of Canada, the Presbyterian Church in Canada agreed to take the children of Aboriginal people from their own homes and place them in residential schools. In these schools, children were deprived of their traditional ways, which were replaced with Euro-Canadian customs that were helpful in the process of assimilation. To carry out this process, the Presbyterian Church in Canada used disciplinary practices which were foreign to Aboriginal people, and open to exploitation in physical and psychological punishment beyond any Christian maxim of care and discipline. In a setting of obedience and acquiescence there was opportunity for sexual abuse, and some were so abused. The effect of all this, for Aboriginal people, was the loss of cultural identity and the loss of a secure sense of self. For the Church's insensitivity we ask forgiveness. Appendix 4 • 383 6) We regret that there are those whose lives have been deeply scarred by the effects of the mission and ministry of The Presbyterian Church in Canada. For our Church we ask forgiveness of God. It is our prayer that God, who is merciful, will guide us in compassionate ways toward helping them to heal. 7) We ask, also, for forgiveness from Aboriginal people. What we have heard, we acknowledge. It is our hope that those whom we have wronged with a hurt too deep for telling will accept what we have to say. With God's guidance our Church will seek opportunities to walk with Aboriginal people to find healing and wholeness together as God's people. Statement on Aboriginal Spiritual Practices, The Presbyterian Church in Canada, 2015 First Nations, Inuit and Métis people, before any encounter with Christianity, found meaning, spiritual benefit, and the presence of the Creator through life-giving Indigenous spiritual practices that have deeply rooted traditions. Through the churches' participation in the residential school system, The Presbyterian Church in Canada contributed to the banning of those traditions. The Presbyterian Church in Canada presumed to know better and in our cultural arrogance tried to suppress practices whose value we were then incapable of perceiving. We acknowledge in a spirit of repentance our role in failing to recognize and respect these spiritual traditions and practices. The church believes that faith and devotion, reverence for life, truth and goodness coexist both in and outside of our own Christian experience. As part of the churches' commitment to a journey of truth and reconciliation, The Presbyterian Church in Canada has learned that many facets of Aboriginal traditional spiritualties bring life and oneness with creation. Accepting this has sometimes been a challenge for The Presbyterian Church in Canada. We are now aware that there is a wide variety of Aboriginal spiritual practices and we acknowledge that it is for our church to continue in humility to learn the deep significance of these practices and to respect them and the Aboriginal elder who are the keepers of their traditional sacred truths. Some of our congregations have been blessed with experiencing various traditional Aboriginal practices when Aboriginal elder, Aboriginal members of our church and Indigenous people visited our congregations as guests, and graciously shared some of these practices and the traditions that give rise to them. These practices are received as gifts and serve to enrich our congregations. Ceremonies and traditions such as smudging, the circle/medicine wheel, drum songs 384 • Truth & Reconciliation Commission and drumming, and Indigenous wisdom teachings have been some of the practices our church has experienced as gifts from Aboriginal brothers and sisters. We acknowledge and respect both Aboriginal members of the Presbyterian Church in Canada who wish to bring traditional practices into their congregations and those Aboriginal members who are not comfortable or willing to do so. The church must be a community where all are valued and respected. It is not for the Presbyterian Church in Canada to validate or invalidate Aboriginal spiritualties and practices. Our church, however, is deeply respectful of these traditions. We acknowledge them as important spiritual practices through which Aboriginal people experience the presence of the creator God. In this spirit the Presbyterian Church in Canada is committed to walking with Aboriginal people in seeking shared truth that will lead to restoring right relations."

## 3. ROMAN CATHOLIC APOLOGY

"Statements from Roman Catholic orders of men and women religious who worked in residential schools. An Apology to the First Nations of Canada by the Oblate Conference of Canada Reverend Doug Crosby, Oblates of Mary Immaculate, President of the Oblate Conference of Canada on behalf of the 1200 Missionary Oblates of Mary Immaculate living and ministering in Canada, July 24, 1991. The Missionary Oblates of Mary Immaculate in Canada wish, after one hundred and fifty years of being with and ministering to the Native people of Canada, to offer an apology for certain aspects of that presence and ministry. A number of historical circumstances make this moment in history most opportune for this. First, there is a symbolic reason. Next year, 1992, marks the five hundredth anniversary of the arrival of Europeans on the shores of America. As large scale celebrations are being prepared to mark this occasion, the Oblates of Canada wish, through this apology, to show solidarity with many Native people in Canada whose history has been adversely affected by this event. Anthropological and sociological insights of the late 20th century have shown how deep, unchallenged, and damaging was the naïve cultural, ethnic, linguistic, and religious superiority complex of Christian Europe when its people met and interrelated with the Aboriginal people of North America. As well, recent criticisms of Indian residential schools and the exposure of instances of physical and sexual abuse within these schools call for such an apology. Given this history, Native people and other groups alike are realizing that a certain healing needs to take place before a new and more truly cooperative phase of history Appendix 4 • 385 can occur. This healing cannot however happen until some very complex, long-standing, and deep historical issues have been addressed. It is in this context, and with a renewed pledge to be in solidarity with Native people in a common struggle for justice that we, the Oblates of Canada, offer this apology: We apologize for the part we played in the cultural, ethnic, linguistic, and religious imperialism that was part of the mentality with which the people of Europe first met the Aboriginal people and which consistently has lurked behind the way the Native people of Canada have been treated by civil governments and by the churches. We were, naively, part of this mentality and were, in fact, often a key player in its implementation. We recognize that this mentality has, from the beginning, and ever since, continually threatened the cultural, linguistic, and religious traditions of the Native people. We recognize that many of the problems that beset Native communities today— high unemployment, alcoholism, family breakdown, domestic violence, spiraling suicide rates, lack of healthy self-esteem—are not so much the result of personal failure as they are the result of centuries of systemic imperialism. Any people stripped of its traditions as well as of its pride falls victim to precisely these social ills. For the part that we played, however inadvertent and naïve that participation might have been, in the setting up and maintaining of a system that stripped others of not only their lands but also of their cultural, linguistic, and religious traditions we sincerely apologize. Beyond this regret for having been part of a system which, because of its historical privilege and assumed superiority did great damage to the Native people of Canada, we wish to apologize more specifically for the following: In sympathy with recent criticisms of Native Residential Schools, we wish to apologize for the part we played in the setting up and the maintaining of those schools. We apologize for the existence of the schools themselves, recognizing that the biggest abuse was not what happened in the schools, but that the schools themselves happened—that the primal bond inherent within families was violated as a matter of policy, that children were usurped from their natural communities, and that, implicitly and explicitly, these schools operated out of the premise that European languages, traditions, and religious practices were superior to Native languages, traditions, and religious practices. The residential schools were an attempt to assimilate Aboriginal people and we played an important role in the unfolding of this design. For this we sincerely apologize. We wish to apologize in a very particular way for the instances of physical and sexual abuse that occurred in those schools. We reiterate that the bigger issue of abuse was the existence of the schools themselves but we wish to publicly acknowledge that there were instances of individual physical and sexual abuse. Far from attempting to defend or rationalize these cases of abuse in any way, we wish to state publicly that we acknowledge that they were inexcusable, intolerable, and a betrayal of trust in one of 386 • Truth & Reconciliation Commission its most serious forms. We deeply, and very specifically, apologize to every victim of such abuse and we seek help in searching for means to bring about healing. Finally, we wish to apologize as well for our past dismissal of many of the riches of Native religious tradition. We broke some of your peace pipes and we considered some of your sacred practices as pagan and superstitious. This, too, had its origins in the colonial mentality, our European superiority complex which was grounded in a particular view of history. We apologize for this blindness and disrespect. One qualification is, however, in order. As we publicly acknowledge all certain blindness in our past, we wish, too, to publicly point to some of the salient reasons for this. We do this, not as a way of subtly excusing ourselves or of rationalizing in any way so as to denigrate this apology, but as a way of more fully exposing the reasons for our past blindness and, especially, as a way of honouring, despite their mistakes, those many men and women, Native and white alike, who gave their lives and their very blood in a dedication that was most sincere and heroic. Hindsight makes for 20-20 vision and judging the past from the insights of the present is an exact and often cruel science. When Christopher Columbus set sail for the Americas, with the blessing of the Christian Church, Western civilization lacked the insights it needed to appreciate what Columbus met upon the shores of America. The cultural, linguistic, and ethical traditions of Europe were caught up in the naïve belief that they were inherently superior to those found in other parts of the world. Without excusing this superiority complex, it is necessary to name it. Sincerity alone does not set people above their place in history. Thousands of persons operated out of this mentality and gave their lives in dedication to an ideal that, while sincere in its intent, was, at one point, naively linked to a certain cultural, religious, linguistic, and ethnic superiority complex. These men and women sincerely believed that their vocations and actions were serving both God and the best interests of the Native people to whom they were ministering. History has, partially, rendered a cruel judgment on their e orts, showing how, despite much sincerity and genuine dedication, their actions were sometimes naïve and disrespectful in that they violated the sacred and cherished traditions of others. Hence, even as we apologize for some of the effects of their actions, we want at the same time to arm their sincerity, the goodness of their intent, and the goodness, in many cases, of their actions. Recognizing that within every sincere apology there is implicit the promise of conversion to a new way of acting, we, the Oblates of Canada, wish to pledge ourselves to a renewed relationship with Native people which, while very much in line with the sincerity and intent of our past relationship, seeks to move beyond past mistakes to a new level of respect and mutuality. Hence . . . We renew the commitment we made 150 years ago to work with and for Native people. In the spirit of our founder, Blessed Eugene De Mazenod, and the many dedicated missionaries who have served in Native communities during these 150 years, we Appendix 4 • 387 again pledge to Native people our service. We ask help in more judiciously discerning what forms that service might take today. More specifically, we pledge ourselves to the following: •We want to support an effective process of disclosure vis-à-vis Residential Schools. We offer to collaborate in any way we can so that the full story of the Indian Residential Schools may be written, that their positive and negative features may be recognized, and that an effective healing process might take place. • We want to proclaim as inviolable the natural rights of Indian families, parents and children, so that never again will Indian communities and Indian parents see their children forcibly removed from them by other authorities. • We want to denounce imperialism in all its forms and, concomitantly, pledge ourselves to work with Native people in their efforts to recover their lands, their languages, their sacred traditions, and their rightful pride. • We want, as Oblates, to meet with Native people and together help forge a template for a renewed covenant of solidarity. Despite past mistakes and many present tensions, the Oblates have felt all along as if the Native people and we belonged to the same family. As members of the same family it is imperative that we come again to that deep trust and solidarity that constitutes family. We recognize that the road beyond past hurt may be long and steep but we pledge ourselves anew to journey with Native people on that road. An Apology to the First Nations of Canada by the Missionary Oblates of Canada Ken Forster, Oblates of Mary Immaculate, Provincial of the Oblates of Mary Immaculate, Lacombe Canada, March 29th 2014 In 1991, on the eve of the 500th anniversary of the colonization of the Americas, the Missionary Oblates of Mary Immaculate made a public apology to the Native People of Canada. Today in the context of this final National Truth and Reconciliation event, the Oblates of Lacombe Province would like to renew this apology and pledge once more our desire to journey in solidarity and mutual respect with all the First People of Canada. Through the first centuries of contact, the relationship of non-native to First Nations People was deeply wounded by the settlers' attitude of cultural and religious superiority and the imposition of colonial power. For the last many decades the Indian Residential Schools have come to epitomize the harm of that colonial relationship. The good that came out of the Schools came at an unbearable cost to the First Nations. The primal bond inherent within families was 388 • Truth & Reconciliation Commission violated as a matter of policy, as children were separated from their natural communities. These schools operated out of the premise that European languages, traditions, and religious practices were superior to those of First Nations and as such contributed to the domination of aboriginal culture, language and the integrity of the family itself. We missionaries played a significant role in the implementation of this awed policy. For this we sincerely apologize. The residential environment made children very vulnerable. We wish to apologize for failing to protect the children in our care, and for the times when we placed the reputation of the institution above the well-being of the students. The significant number of incidents of abuse has shocked society and the church. These acts are inexcusable, intolerable, and a profound betrayal of trust. We deeply, and very specifically, apologize to every victim of such abuse. As missionaries, with a desire to serve, we commit ourselves to that deeper service Jesus Christ modeled for all Christians when he washed the feet of his disciples. Our hope for the journey forward is that we may serve not from a place of 'above' or 'below', but from a place of friendship, of equality, and of respect. As a gesture of reconciliation, we, Missionaries Oblates of Mary Immaculate, would like to place a copy of these words along with the Apology of 1991 into your care. Statement on behalf of Congregations of Women Religious involved in the Indian Residential

Schools of Canada Sister Marie Zarowny, Sisters of Saint Ann, at the General House of Oblates of Mary Immaculate, Rome, April 30, 2009. E statement was delivered by Marie Zarowny, on behalf of the Congregations of Women Religious involved in the Indian Residential Schools of Canada, to a delegation of Aboriginal leaders, residential school Survivors, and Roman Catholic officials in Rome on April 30, 2009. Father Guillermo Steckling and Members of the Oblate General Council, thank you for welcoming us to your home and for providing me with this opportunity to say a few words. National Chief Phil Fontaine, Elder, Chiefs and Representatives of Canada's First Nations, Inuit and Métis, especially those of you who are former residents of the schools; Archbishop Pettipas and other representatives of the Catholic Entities; Ambassador Anne Leahy; other distinguished guests. As I begin, I want to say, as I did earlier today, what an honour it has been for me to have shared the profound experiences of these last few days with you. I will carry this experience with me for as long as I live and will speak of its various meanings, some already spoken today and others yet to be discovered as we continue to contemplate and ponder its significance."

## 4. CONGREGATIONS OF WOMEN RELIGIOUS APOLOGY

"Appendix 4 • 389 As we draw to a close the formal part of these days together, it is a privilege for me to speak on behalf of the Congregations of Women Religious that provided, over a long period of time, hundreds of their members to teach and care for children in the Residential Schools. Some of these institutions, especially in the far north were started to care for orphans when almost all the adults of entire villages died as a result of various flu epidemics. We were invited to help the children, at least, survive. In these instances and in the schools themselves in other parts of the country, we were motivated by a sincere desire to further the education, health and Christian formation of the Aboriginal people in such a way that they would be able to achieve their rightful place in an evolving Canadian society. We wanted them to grow into personal fullness, to be proud of themselves and of their giftedness and to be able to live with a sense of innate dignity. For many students, however, this was far from their experience. How could our good intentions have had such tragic consequences! We were products of the times in which we lived, with the teaching methods, cultural misunderstandings, social attitudes and theology of those times. As well, some of our members suffered from emotional problems that they took out on the children. We now know that the residential school system itself, initiated by the federal government and in which we participated, was racist and discriminatory, bringing about a form of cultural oppression and personal shame that has had a lasting effect not only on those who attended the schools but also on subsequent generations. We carry immense sorrow for having contributed to this tragedy, a sorrow that is not momentary but that stays within our hearts. We also now know that many children in our care suffered unspeakable abuse and mistreatment. Some Sisters have been accused of actual abuse; many others have been accused of not protecting those in their care. We are deeply grieved by all these revelations. Good intentions and genuine love on the part of many of our Sisters for the children in our care were not enough and in fact were often not experienced as such. At the same time, many of our members formed lasting friendships with the children in their care; we have all been enriched by these relationships and are grateful for them. Our priorities in working on the settlement agreement were that suffering be acknowledged, justice be done through adequate compensation and that there be a way for us as women religious to both contribute to and to enter into a process of healing and reconciliation with you. Throughout the last 150 years or so, our involvement in the schools has not been our only ministry with First Nations. We have served as pastoral workers and counselors on reserves and other First Nations communities: teaching, providing health care, visiting families, helping with religious education, supporting those in leadership of various kinds, and participating in community events. Although our numbers 390 • Truth & Reconciliation Commission are small now and we have withdrawn from several communities, to the extent we are able and at your invitation, we commit ourselves to continue to live and serve in your midst. Institutionally we commit ourselves to use what influence we have to continue to support your efforts to achieve justice within Canada, including adequate housing, education, health care, healing programs and land rights. We also commit ourselves to enhance our efforts to foster awareness and understanding between Aboriginal and non-Aboriginal Canadians and to diminish in some way persistent attitudes of racism and superiority. Personally, I commit myself, to the extent I am able, to assist the continuing process of creating a new future in Canada and the Church, one in which all people are appreciated and live with dignity and mutual respect. And now a more personal word to National Chief, Phil Fontaine: You have been a brother to us, Phil, working with us each step of the way to first help us understand the depths of hurt experienced by you and your people and then to walk with us to new understandings. This has not been an easy journey for you or for us but we have travelled it together. As a result our bonds with you and your people have deepened. You have also consistently expressed the desire of many of your people that we continue to be in relationship with you, and you have helped that to happen. We thank you for all the ways you have assisted in this process and we pray our Creator's abundant blessing upon you. In closing, I return to an earlier comment. Each of our involvements, whether educational, political, spiritual or other, has resulted in deep and lasting friendships between our Sisters and many First Nations people. We treasure these friendships and look forward to them deepening in the years to come."

## 5. JESUITS APOLOGY

"Statement of Reconciliation, The Jesuits in English Canada Delivered by Father Winston Rye, S.J., at the Truth and Reconciliation Commission of Canada's Québec National Event, Montreal, April 25, 2013 Let me begin today by first acknowledging all Survivors of the Residential Schools and their families, the Elder present, the Commissioners, Church and community leaders and members of the wider communities. We thank you sincerely for the invitation to share in this important event. The Jesuits in English Canada want to take this special occasion to honour the Survivors. It has taken great courage, strength and generosity for you to come forward and to share your story with all of us here, a story of loss, grief, hardship, but also of resistance and healing. Appendix 4 • 391 We also greet the children and grandchildren of the Survivors, who suffered in turn from their parent's trauma in the Residential Schools and learned from their character and bravery. We come today to pay tribute to the individuals who attended the Spanish Residential School; both boys and girls. We recognize and embrace the students who attended the St. Peter Claver Residential School for Boys, St. Charles Garnier Collegiate and St. Joseph's School for Girls, some of whom are with us today in the audience. This gathering is a symbol of hope and a reminder to all of us that such abuse must never happen again. I stand here on behalf of the Jesuits to say that we are truly, deep within our hearts, sorry for what we did to injure individuals, families and communities by participating in the Canadian Residential School system. When the Jesuits first met with First Nations people 400 years ago, we recognized the greatness of your traditional spiritual beliefs. That openness was lost in the 20th Century. The legacy of the Residential Schools is a terrible cloud on our legacy of friendship. Today, we are relearning how to trust each other in a deeper understanding of our own faith through the lessons that your Elders have taught us. It has been a struggle for the Jesuits to recognize that we became an active part of a system aimed at the assimilation of your traditional culture. It was not until it was much too late that we realized the harm that we had done. The Jesuits are proud to still count many of our former students as friends and colleagues. We are grateful for the forgiveness and understanding that you have extended to us over the years. We humbly thank you for sticking with us and continuing to welcome us in your homes and communities. We come to celebrate the achievements of our students. We recognize that what they achieved as professionals, athletes and community leaders was not because of our efforts at the school—but through their own strength of character and love of knowledge. We also come to acknowledge the students who were brave enough to confront us about our role in the Residential School system some thirty years ago. We treated you as dissenters and malcontents rather than listening to what you had to tell us. Through litigation and lawsuits, we learned about harsh conditions, poor food, brutal punishment and horrible incidents of sexual molestation. You turned to the courts because the Jesuits turned away from you. As educators, we have been shocked by stories of bullying, inadequate clothing, strapping and beatings for minor offences. Our school harbored individuals who molested or abused students. Bed wetters were tormented by older students and staff alike. The food was not fit for the needs of growing boys and girls. 392 • Truth & Reconciliation Commission Children who were much too young were taken from the love of their families and placed under the guidance of men and women who had little training and less compassion. Most of all, we have heard stories of the inherent unfairness of the system. Students were given the strap for things that they did not do. Bullies were rewarded and victims punished. Abuse was not disclosed because there was no one who would hear a student's cry for help. We are still struggling with how it could possibly have happened. We realize that the abuse might have been uncovered and punished many years ago, if there had been someone that the students could turn to. We failed in putting the needs and interests of the Jesuit priests and brothers ahead of the welfare of our students. We vow that this will never be "the way things are" ever again. Amongst the heartache, we have delighted in stories about how students outwitted their teachers and kept their spirit alive through practical jokes and ingenuity. Our students understood their instructors and their human frailties so much better than their teachers understood them. They fought against the unfairness of the system with humor and good nature. We have heard of brave students who were resourceful enough to set out for their home communities. We are ashamed of the harsh punishments that they received when they were brought back by the authorities. We offer a sincere prayer of thankfulness that no young lives were lost at our school because students ran away. We have learned from these harsh lessons and have become stronger from your example. To the students who have defended us and taken our part, we are truly grateful. We will strive to prove ourselves worthy of the respect and love that you have shown your teachers. We are deeply grateful to the communities that have continued to welcome us as pastors and as friends in the years since the Spanish Residential Schools closed. We are humbled by your love and forgiveness. We have never had to beg for reconciliation; you have offered it to us freely for so many years by your example. We ask for your forgiveness for any role that our school may have played in sowing distrust and division between Catholic and Protestant families. It is not enough to decry the narrow mindedness of the times. By teaching intolerance in our schools, we sowed division where it had never existed. Many of you have asked when the reconciliation between the churches will occur. We desire and pray that it is happening today as we move together in healing with our friends in the Ecumenical Working Group. Finally, we have learned of the terrible inequality that continues to exist between the educational opportunities for white students and students from First Nations in Canada. Young people are still being transported to white communities, to obtain an Appendix 4 • 393 education in an environment that is foreign to them. This is exactly what happened in the past and we seem to be reliving it again. We share Shannen Koostachin's dream that in our lifetime we will see equal opportunities for education in the home community of every Canadian. We will do everything in our power and influence to ensure that this comes to pass and the injustices of the past are not perpetuated. You had the courage to stand up and speak out about the past. You can help us all to open our minds and our hearts to understand and to stop the destruction now and not have to go through this all over again. Today we stand before you to pledge our support in the rebuilding of your language and culture. We cannot undo the things that are done, but we can take positive and meaningful steps to rebuild. We have opened our Archives so that the whole picture of the Residential Schools can be seen. We will unlock the doors to the ancient books that preserved the languages of the First Nations and make copies available to people in their own communities. These precious resources will never again be the exclusive property of white scholars and academics. We thank the Commissioners for challenging us to undertake this journey of self-examination and reflection with them. We will work hand in hand with our students past and present to bring all these things to pass. May the Creator God who sees all and knows what is truly in our hearts bring us together. May the Blessed Kateri Tekakwitha guide us that we can learn from each other, for she is a model for us all. May we come once again to call each other 'friend.'"

## 6. MENNONITE AND BRETHREN APOLOGY

"Statement of Anabaptist Church Leaders Presented to the Truth and Reconciliation Commission of Canada at the Alberta National Event, Edmonton, March 2014 Signed by Tim Dyck, General Secretary, Andreangelical Mennonite Conference, Douglas P. Sider Jr., Canadian Director, Brethren in Christ Canada, Willard Metzger, Executive Director, Mennonite Church Canada, Willy Reimer, Executive Director, Canadian Conference of Mennonite Brethren Churches, and Donald Peters, Executive Director, Mennonite Central Committee Canada. We are leaders of a group of Canadian Christian churches known as Anabaptist denominations. Our delegation includes Mennonite Church Canada, the Angelical Mennonite Conference, the Canadian Conference of Mennonite Brethren Churches, the Brethren in Christ Church of Canada, and Mennonite Central Committee 394 • Truth & Reconciliation Commission Canada. Many people from our churches have come to the Truth and Reconciliation Commission events, including this one, to volunteer, to listen, to learn. We acknowledge that we are all treaty people and that we are meeting on Treaty 6 territory, on land that is part of an historic agreement between First Nations people and newcomers, an agreement involving mutuality and respect. Throughout the period of the Truth and Reconciliation Commission events across the country, we have watched and listened with respect, as residential school survivors have told stories with graciousness and courage, sharing experiences of the Residential School Legacy from its beginning. We are humbled to witness this Truth and Reconciliation Commission event. As we have listened to your stories, we've added our tears to the countless tears that you have shed. We acknowledge that there was, and is, much hurt and much suffering. We have learned much and we have much to learn. We heard the wise words of Justice Sinclair encouraging us to acknowledge that all of us, in one way or another, have been affected by the Residential School experience. We recognize that being part of a dominant culture, our attitudes and perspectives made the Residential School experience possible and that these attitudes and perspectives became entrenched in our relationships and in our culture. We regret our part in the assimilation practice that took away language use and cultural practice, separating child from parent, parent from child, and Indigenous people from their culture. We regret that, at times, the Christian faith was used, wrongly, as an instrument of power, not as an invitation to see how God was already at work before we came. We regret that some leaders within the Church abused their power and those under their authority. We acknowledge the paternalism and racism of the past. As leaders of Mennonite and Brethren in Christ church communities, we acknowledge that we have work to do in addressing paternalism and racism both within our communities and in the broader public. We repent of our denominational encounters with Indigenous people that at times may have been motivated more by cultural biases than by the unconditional love of Jesus Christ. We repent of our failure to advocate for marginalized Indigenous people as our faith would instruct us to. We are aware that we have a long path to walk. We hope to build relationships with First Nations communities so that we can continue this learning journey and walk this path together. We are followers of Jesus Christ, the great reconciler. We are aware that words without actions are not only ineffective but may also be harmful. We commit ourselves to take your challenges to us very seriously. We will seek to model the reconciling life and work of Jesus in seeking reconciliation with you. We will encourage our Appendix 4 • 395 churches to reach out in practical and loving ways, including dialogue and expressions of hospitality. We commit ourselves to walk with you, listening and learning together as we journey to a healthier and more just tomorrow."

## II. APOLOGY: RECONCILIATION AND RESTITUTION-FOR CULTURAL GENOCIDE -STILL RESOLVING

"...Since the last Canadian Residential Indian School closed in 1996, former students have pressed for recognition and restitution, resulting in the *Indian Residential Schools Settlement Agreement in 2007* (IRSSA), an agreement between the federal government and the churches that operated the residential school." This was created in addition to a formal apology by Prime Minister Stephen Harper, June 11, 2008 in a speech saying, 'wrong has caused great harm, and has no place in our country.'

In total, an "estimated 150,000 First Nation, Inuit, and Métis children attended residential schools...the largest class action settlement in Canadian history to date, the IRSSA, September 10, 2007, recognized the damage inflicted by those schools, and established a multi-billion-dollar fund ($1.9 billion) to help an estimated 80-90,000 former students in their recovery," (TRC). The IRSSA, which came into effect in September 2007, has five main components:

1-The Truth and Reconciliation Commission (TRC)
2-Commemoration (plans arising out of the TRC)
3-Health and Healing Services (AHF)..."
4-The Common Experience Payment (CEP)
5-Independent Assessment Process (IAP)

The apology to these people for the abuse of their children, summarized in horrific detail in the five-volume report, is based on over 6500 witness-accountings TRC (*Truth and Reconciliation Commission Report*) 2009.

(1) Under the TRC, some $60 million was set aside for a five year commission that would "provide opportunities for individuals, families, and communities to share their experiences."

(2) To respect the people's culture ignored and demeaned, the Settlement Agreement established a fund of more than $20 million for "commemorative projects."

(3) In 1998 the federal government issued a Statement of Reconciliation that acknowledged the abuses suffered by former students, and established the multi-million-dollar ($125 million) Aboriginal Healing Foundation (AHF).

(4) Under the IRSSA, the CEP paid former students $10,000 for the first year attending such residential schools and then $3,000 for each

subsequent year in residence. Supposedly by the end of 2012, some 98 per cent had received payment.

(5) Under the IRSSA, the IAP was established to assess sexual abuse and serious physical and psychological abuse. The IAP has paid out-of-court settlements totaling over $1.7 billion toward the $1.9 billion and will continue hearing complaints until around 2017.

The government is currently finishing its first stage of reconciliation after more than a century of abuse. The TRC research reporting offices closed December 18, 2015. It took approximately eight years to complete the commission report. Since then, the stages of the reconciliation have continued as these people try to find closure and resolution to a lifetime of suffering for themselves and a realization of a future generational demise of their heritage, their health and welfare.

This I.R.S.S.A. Agreement is intended to close a hundred year Canadian disgrace. However, practices such as these have been in place worldwide in similar fashion for years even before the Canadian implemented what they had observed elsewhere, such as in New France, French colonies on continental North America initially the area along the shores of the St. Lawrence River, Newfoundland, Acadia (Nova scotia) expanding into the Great Lakes region and parts of the Appalachia West (as it was known back then). Similar suits and reconciliations are ongoing worldwide."

## III. APOLOGY: ENVIRONMENTAL GENOCIDE- RECONCILIATION AND RESTITUTION- UNRESOLVED

But the taking did not end with forcing the Indigenous children into schools where good intentions to assimilate them into the Euro-Canadian culture abysmally failed. At the same time, the taking of the lands in certain treaties dating back to the 1880s, is considered by many First Nations people to have been a manipulation of these people by the government. And as the years passed many more agreements have been signed, some revisited, and lands set aside for these people's use. However, more often since these and other lands have been placed in use for endeavors that have breached a large portion of the previous agreements. And for the destruction of these lands little has been done to appease the First Nations people and the contested, destructive activities continue to deeply affect these people. Influential figureheads around the world have weighed in on this travesty, but the problem continues. Rare cancers are affecting these people supposedly caused from the toxins resulting in the oil sands projects. There have been few apologies, at best, for this toxic assault to humans and this environmental genocide.

## I. WORLD LEADERS: VATICAN-POPE:

"A Pastoral Letter on The Integrity of Creation and the Athabasca Oil Sands to The Faithful of the diocese of St. Paul on The Occasion of the Jubilee Year in Honor of St. Paul by †Luc Bouchard Bishop of St. Paul in Alberta, Canada, January 25th, 2009: *The Integrity of Creation and the Athabasca Oil Sands:*(The Letter excerpt)…"

"Faced with the widespread destruction of the environment, people everywhere are coming to understand that we cannot continue to use the goods of Earth as we have in the past. . . A new ecological awareness is beginning to emerge- the ecological crisis is a moral issue."
—Pope John Paul II, Jan. 1, 1990, Peace with God the Creator, Peace with all of Creation (par. #'s 1 & 15).

"Alongside the ecology of nature there exists what can be called a 'human' ecology, which in turn demands a 'social' ecology. All this means that humanity, if it truly desires peace, must be increasingly conscious of the links between natural ecology, or respect for nature, and human ecology. Experience shows the disregard for the environment always harms human coexistence and vice versa."
—Pope Benedict XVI— Jan. 1, 2007, The Human Person, the Heart of Peace (par. #8).

"Earth will not continue to offer its harvest, except with faithful stewardship. We cannot say we love the land and then take steps to destroy it for use by future generations."
—Pope John Paul II— September 17, 1987.

"…The world has enough for everyone's need, but not enough for everyone's greed."
—Mahatma Gandhi—Leader of India toward independence for thirty years.

"John Paul II today delivered the most sweeping papal apology ever (during a public mass of pardons), repenting for the errors of his church over the last 2,000 years…to underline the apology's religious significance, seven cardinals and bishops stood before the pope and cited some of the key Catholic lapses, past and present, including religious intolerance and injustice toward Jews, women, indigenous people, immigrants, the poor and the unborn."
—Pope John Paul II— March 12, 2002.
https://www.theguardian.com/world/2000/mar/13/catholicism.religion

"…There is no peace without justice, no justice without forgiveness."
— Pope John Paul II on World Day for Peace, 2002—

There has not been a cohesive effort to compensate these Indigenous people for continuing to take the land for major operatives who gain grossly and exorbitantly. The lands have provided two hundred billion dollars thus far to Alberta—a double-edged position since in order to obtain those profits approximately one fifth of Alberta's land surface is subject to total destruction without acceptable reclamation to return the land to what it once was—beautiful. Problems and fears concerning the toxins released, puts the environment at risk which in turn puts the health of humans at risk, and is continually being contested.


## 2. CELEBRITIES-MOVIE STARS AND BILLIONAIRES:

"The environment is in us, not outside of us. The trees are our lungs, the rivers our bloodstream. We are all interconnected, and what you do to the environment ultimately you do to yourself."

—Ian Somerhalder—American actor, TV drama series- Vampire Diaries 2009.

Excerpts from the April 2014 article, *Billionaire in Ft Chip, What was Tom Steyer Doing in This Isolated Canadian Town?* by Emily Atkin, a staff writer @newrepublic, covering science and the environment, Formerly@thinkprogress-

["Tom Steyer, a California billionaire, involved with many ventures, and a board member of the Center for American Progress visited Fort Chipewyan in 2014, a remote community in northern Alberta and spoke in great depth with a business partner and long-time friend, Ted White. He was there on business to see the tar sands himself, the heart of the Keystone XL Pipeline project for which he opposed. He was there to talk with the leaders of the community who claim the tar sands are polluting and killing their people and the environment. Seyer clearly understood the lay of the land and where the waters run and that traditional means of survival has been destroyed and the residents are being sickened with cancer thought to be the result of the tar sand projects and their pollution. He was certain of that after the trip.

Steyer told the people he was putting his money where his mouth is assisting the "funding of ACFN's legal defense to determine exactly what could be done." But his primary purpose in coming was to pledge $100 million dollars in the lawmaking process opposing the pipeline's construction. Steyer also visited the tar sands which he named the "tar sands loop," focusing on the operation by "Syncrude Canada Ltd. and the tailings ponds which hold the toxic wastes. His conclusions after that visit were that, "pollution regulations in Canada were likely too lax," that "the people in Fort Chip are very formidable facing that pollution," that the "greenhouse gas emissions were not the only consideration in whether to condone tar sands extraction," advising that the Obama administration needed to re-evaluate before approving the pipeline. Steyer alluded to the answer not being "solved by calculators and money" but "dedication to a value system" appearing to mean a value system first of the "heart and soul" and then the reverence to protecting the environment.

But that was when Obama was in office. Now with Trump at the helm, his mantra is reining in of the EPA. So slashing their workforce and budget might prove to be even more detrimental to a cause that has been feuding for some forty years ever since the power companies were first built and ever since the Key stone XL Pipeline was just a thought. The tar sands projects has been well underway for some 40 years with many worldwide entities involved in investments planned out some forty plus years into the future. Much of the tar sands extraction is quick and dirty and the companies take the money for the manufactured oil and get out. But in getting out, much of the harm to Earth's surface is just left in ruins and mile-deep holes that spread out for miles that were supposed to be put back to its original state per the Original Treaties signed by the Indians and the Canadian governments. Over the years without expert, expensive, legal representation, the Canadian government, and world-wide companies that have left the internal disagreement up to the Canadian government have continued to do business with the government no matter the issues internally with the First Nation's People. The People have made agreements without solid representation and have been abused legally. And the saga continues throughout Canada wherever the pipelines are being proposed. The ventures put water, air, land, health of the people at risk."]

(https://thinkprogress.org/what-was-tom-steyer-doing-in-this-isolated-canadian-town-5913a2ae071#.hpba2h3qa_ .

## WHAT IS LIFE WORTH?
Approximately $1.7 billion dollars (of the $1.9 billion financial obligation of Canada) has been paid as of the date of this publication to the survivors of those schools. More than 200 schools and about 150,000 students came through those schools. It is reported that abuse was normal in the school as witnessed by some 6500 students from that system. More victims are surfacing. These survivors have had a lifetime of extreme reprehensible, emotional suffering.

According the U.S., the VHL or *value of a human life* is $8.7 million. That value is based on how much it cost to feed, cloth, educate and reasonably care medically for a human being over the course of a lifetime per the actuary tables. That differs around the world with socio-economic conditions.

## WHAT IS OUR WORLD WORTH?
Some environmentalists suggest $54 million PER YEAR, yes, per year.

"In an ambitious bid to put a price tag on Mother Nature, a group of conservation-minded ecologists and economists has estimated that it would cost $33 trillion per year to replace the Earth's "ecosystem services": environmental resources such as fresh water and soil, and processes such as climate regulation and crop pollination. The authors of the study, which appears in *Nature*, say societies must overhaul their policies to avoid facing a bill of this magnitude...Lead author Robert Costanza, an ecologist who directs the Institute for Ecological Economics at the University of Maryland, and a dozen colleagues from Brazil, the Netherlands, Sweden, and the United States first agreed on a list of 17 categories of goods and services provided by nature, including processes such as nitrogen fixation and resources such as crop varieties. They then partitioned Earth's surface into 16 "biomes," or environmental types, such as oceans, estuaries, and tropical forests, and judged which services each biome provides...they sifted through scores of published studies for estimates of the value per hectare of each service in each biome...such as a 1981 study estimated that for each hectare of U.S. wetlands destroyed, the lost ability to soak up floodwaters increased annual flood damages by $3300 to $11,000. The group then tallied the lowest and highest estimates for each item, and concluded that all of the items put together were worth $16 trillion to $54 trillion **PER YEAR**, for an average of $33 trillion. In comparison, the U.S. gross domestic product in 1996 was about $6.9 trillion...In a similar study in press at the journal *BioScience*, Pimentel and co-authors pin the yearly benefits from the global ecosystem at just $3 trillion...Stanford University economist Lawrence Goulder, '... to the fact that ecosystem services are absolutely essential for human life... there's no price we could pay that would be enough' to replace them."

http://www.sciencemag.org/news/1997/05/how-much-world-worth

Five oceans are fed by the waters downstream of the Alberta Oil Sands Project. The project is a $1.4 trillion dollar bonanza. Some reports state Alberta receives about 70% of that; others say it is about $200 billion. There are quite a few other investors who gain.

In our haste to find alternative energy sources, we might just find ourselves delving into enterprises for greed alone. Haste makes waste. And too much toxic waste will take us all down to a point of no return. Trump is trying to get rid of or drastically downsize the environmental protections agency (EPA) and that is when our waste will "**E**ventually **P**ollute **A**ll."

# NOTE TO THE READER
## HISTORICAL & CURRENT BACKGROUND
Indian Act, Numerous Treaties and Agreements
Between the *Savage* and the
*Civilized Euro-Canadian Culture*

**1800s-** In the late 1800s, North American original inhabitants, (the indigenous, the First Nations Aboriginal people), executed legally-binding promises in the forms of numbered treaties with the Canadian government. These were sealed with handshakes, peace pipes and included detailed map drawings of ownership—legal documents. (http://www.thecanadianencyclopedia.ca/en/article/numbered-treaties/).

Canadian government Indian Agents often issued engraved coins depicting a white man and a native chief shaking hands to ratify the agreements.

(Library and Archives Canada/C144184) TRC
Firstpeopleofcanada.com/fp_treaties_two_views.html

TRC

During this period, another law was enacted upon these people (*forced*). It was the *Indian Act* whereby both the Canadian government and major religious denominations devised a program to assimilate the indigenous children into the *white man's* ways. These children were mandated to attend a certain school, one of 200 residential homes built across Canada for this purpose. The white man referred to these people as *"uneducated savages, stupid."* The families of these children were devastated with this Indian Act. Many of their children were taken, even kidnapped from their homes as early as birth, to these schools some thousands of miles from the homes—many never seen again.

Teaching the culture of the people ceased immediately. Thus began the period where the First Nations people began to die out as a culture, as a group. The whitewashing began; that was the law at the time. And the practice continued over the next hundred years.

And if that were not bad enough, another group of legal documents were being ratified affecting these First Nations people. These were the land-use agreements—Treaties #6, #7, and #8 signed in the late 1800s.

Skipping over to the late 1900s, the Canadian government now wanted to revisit those very same land-use agreements. Specifically, Canada now wanted to alter the agreements regarding them and develop that "protected land described in the Agreement" for profitable alternative energy endeavors; mainly the controversial projects surrounding the Canadian pipeline oil projects and the projects mining sticky asphalt, bitumen in the Athabasca Oil Sands of Alberta, Canada— resource extraction. In taking the land for this purpose, the projects created toxic waste disposal issues as an end-product after extreme earth excavation mining for this oil venture. The extensive separation process resulted in useful fuel oil. But the toxic waste was dumped into tailing ponds and this and the defilement of the land in major site excavations flew in the face of keeping the environment clean, safe and protected in perpetuity for these peoples' livelihood.

It is a very complicated issue. The controversy is that promises and treaties have been broken by the Canadian government. And now other worldwide powers have appeared on the scene as new investors in the Canadian venture and staked out their claims buying or renting the lands from Canada. These outside investors contend their mining contracts are with Canada and not the First Nations people. And that if the government is in the wrong, they are the ones liable—not them. Canada seems to contend, *inevitability, whatever land is left on Earth will be eventually developed no matter whether old treaties say to protect lands in perpetuity or not.*

**1980s**—Meanwhile over the last decades, the investor-pool has continued to grow worldwide. The United States, Russia, Yugoslavia, Japan, many other countries in Europe, and all the other major oil companies around the world have all joined in the race to make quick money in the oil pits. First Nations people continue aggressively and furiously to contest this as environmental genocide and a breach of contract.

This story is also about the cultural genocide. The Canadian embarrassment of taking and abusing the youth of the First Nations children to assimilate them into the English culture, even the killing of such children placing them in mass graves is laid at the feet of their government, even Buckingham Palace, the Vatican, and other major religious denominations. This revelation, finally coming to light after a century, deeply anguishes and outrages the First Nations people. Witnesses to the abuse are continuing to surface. In a country "known for kindness and being a beacon of light to the rest of the world," this story shakes Canada to its core.

These two genocides plague the First Nations people in an ongoing conflict expanding decades. While taking the lands was vile enough hundreds of years ago, and the defilement horrific, the fear is the lands can never be reclaimed to its original state and provide as it once did. And even attempting that awesome task appears to be financially impossible, not feasible for Canada or its outside investors. Some have tried.

Huge craters exists now dug to some 250 feet, void of life, an intentional, necessary defilement to get at the bitumen—an eyesore for some 54,000 square miles. And now it has been determined the bulk of the bitumen is too deep for mining. The three oil sands projects scattered in the northern part of the Province of Alberta, if condensed, would represent an area about the size of Ohio, USA and represent about one fifth the size of Alberta. When the cost of a barrel of oil is high, the oil sands projects are profitable. When the cost of oil is low, as it has been for some time, hovering around $30-$40 per barrel, many outside investors are now pulling out of the Canadian Alberta Oil Sands Project all together. This abandonment has further darkened the future for these Indigenous people and Alberta. Left are the tailing ponds, the excavated earth, the black holes, the loss of tens of thousands of acres of trees and once beautiful wilderness. One example by Syncore, an investor in the oil sands of Alberta, to reclaim Earth's defiled land after its exploitation, was started in 1968. That area is still not returned to its original condition which so far has taken almost fifty years (2017 at the time of this writing).

A disturbing fact is that only three percent of the bitumen can be mined. The remaining ninety seven percent is too deep. So is the venture worth it?

2017—Addressing these issues seems to result in a prevailing attitude the First Nations people must learn to fit into modern society. They must change their ways and attitudes, that there should be a mutual effort and sacrifice made to benefit all mankind's ever growing need for energy. And as for trying to keep these lands protected for the First Nations people, the comments are that there is too much profit to be made in mining these lands for some ancient agreements to stand in the way.

Interesting cultural beliefs play a large part in the story. Twilight fairies whisper to the First Nations People in the in-between-times at night, imprinting advice and warnings as the fairies lightly brush the human cheeks with a Swisher feather. These people believe feathers symbolize character and state-of-mind. The wren bird is readily available, and is seen as constant protection of these indigenous people. The wren feather is sacred protection; the swisher feather is a sign of gaining insight to make the right decisions. —Adaptation of First Nations beliefs—

The little people riding coyote bellies at night into the hoodoo mounds, across the prairie grasses, is a belief that spirits of ancestors roam each night looking for lost souls. When the souls are found, it is believed they assist in completing the sacred circle giving rise up to be with the Great Spirit. —Adaptation of the First Nations beliefs—

Woven into a compelling tale that unravels in gripping horror, this story is inspired by historical events of social and environmental importance. One event dating back to the mid-1880s and the other event dating back some forty years: the two travesties continue to plague Canada and its indigenous people. The story involves a journey that crisscrosses North American borders—Canada and the United States—grappling with issues of exploitation. One issue is a hardened venture to produce alternative energy and the other with the kidnapping of First Nations children to assimilate them into Euro-Canadian culture.

These exploitations have created such sad destruction: of life, culture, environment and even murder—all laid at the steps of certain groups: Canada, whose monarch ruler is ultimately Buckingham Palace, the Roman Catholic Church, whose utmost authority and instruction comes from the Vatican, and a group of other religious denominations, each standing as individual institutions, whose guilt must be considered through mere association albeit perhaps at arm's distance in this regard.

The responsibility for the environmental destruction can be laid at the steps of the Government of Canada, it appears, since its leaders stated that all land will inevitably be developed no matter if an agreement has been made to the contrary (regarding the contested Alberta Oil Sands Project by the First Nations people). This story invokes careful consideration to whether agreements, contracts and laws can stand the test of time. Or whether they can be just ignored and discarded as ancient, resulting in obscene injustice for the victim. These victims are the First Nations people who live according to what is stated in contract and have little to no recourse if the more powerful partner (Canada) decides to simply ignore or manipulate its treaties continuously and proceed as if the prior agreements never existed because they are continuously changing the rules for their benefit.

In this novel, the author weaves the characters in a struggle to find truth—two chief elders, a United States legal immigrant, a former environmental lawyer, and two First Nations Indigenous children discover frightening aspects of their pasts ultimately resulting in hopeful reunification of family.

Under the watchful eyes of the soul searchers, the hoodoo people, assisted by outsiders, are allowed to enter the realm of the First Nations' spiritual beliefs. Lost souls complete their sacred circles. The dead speak up in mysterious ways shedding light on the truth.

This story is based on the accountings of 6500 witnesses (Canadian document, 2009 TRC: the Truth and Reconciliation Commission) revealing horrendous truths of abuse in schools purposed to assimilate the Indigenous children. Their photographs and their testimony are recorded for posterity. That record is available in the public domain and *"usable in any manner without copyright infringement."*

The story is also based on true events of the controversial *wrest of the tar sands* to separate the prized bitumen from the Athabasca oil sands in the production of usable oil. The resulting harm of this process is a continual leaching of toxins into the earth and involuntary ingestion of these cancer-causing toxins is at the heart of the controversy. The toxins are destroying the environment and causing cancer among the people. The employment of these people, with the Oil Sands companies, is a constant emotional struggle: a survival necessity, but equally, an emotional travesty.

# BIBLIOGRAPHY

1. https://archive.org/stream/adictionarycree00watkgoog/adictionarycree00 watkgoog_djvu.txt.
2. http://www.native-languages.org/cree.htm.
3. https://thinkprogress.org/what-was-tom-steyer-doing-in-this-isolated-canadian-town-5913a2ae071#.hpba2h3qa.
4. https://oil-sands-of-alberta.wikispaces.com.
5. https://society6.com/product/new-world-isis_print#s6-105773p4a1v45.
6. https://en.wikipedia.org/wiki/Treaty_8#/media/File:David_Laird_explaini ng_Treaty_8_Fort_Vermilion_1899_-_NA-949-34.jpg.
7. https://www.google.com/search?Q=oil+sands+project+map&rlz=1C1LE NP_enus561us567&espv=2&biw=1111&bih=627&tbm=isch&tbo=u&so urce=univ&sa=X&ved=0ahukewjlv53o5dboahxg6sykhw5mbo4qsqihg#i mgrc=rqgfndqwrlgpvm%3A.
8. http://www.crhnet.ca/sites/default/files/library/Scanlon.pdf.
9. http://www.legalline.ca/legal-answers/your-legal-obligations-when-in-an-autmobile-accident/.
10. http://www.ibc.ca/on/auto/crisis-management/crash/.
11. Insurance Bureau of Canada Edmonton, AL 1-780-423-2212.
12. Royal Canadian Mounted Police AL Canada.
13. www.rcmp-grc.gc.ca/detach/en/find/AB.
14. http://itcc.org/mass-graves-of-children-in-canada-documented-evidence/(Prince Charles).
15. https://oil sandstruth.org/.
16. https://www.aadnc-aandc.gc.ca/eng/1100100015644/1100100015649.
17. https://www.pinterest.com/bsambiance/native-indian/.
18. http://www.academia.edu/3834427/A_slow_industrial_genocide_tar_san ds_and_the_indigenous_people_of_northern_Alberta.
19. firstpeopleofcanada.com/fp_treaties/fp_treaties_two_views.html.
20. http://www.businessinsider.com/photos-destruction-canada-oil-sands-2012-10/#rring-the-chunks-of-oil-sand-14.
21. http://www.cbc.ca/news/business/total-s-joslyn-oilsands-project-on-hold-1.2658660.
22. http://vandocument.com/wp-content/uploads/2013/09/sized_Willard_Be_a_Good_Girl.jpg.
23. https://www.google.com/search?Q=healing+art+for+survivors+of+reside ntial+schools+Canada&rlz=1C1LENP_enus561us567&espv=2&biw=13 66&bih=609&tbm=isch&tbo=u&source=univ&sa=X&ved=0ahukewjnjvi 439boahw10h4khfpsbvyqsaqigw#imgdii=qw-huotmdpphwm%3A%Bqw-huotmdpphwm%3a3bihb_ydmxamfpzm%3A&imgrc=qw-huotmdpphwm%3A.
24. http://www.trc.ca/websites/trcinstitution/index.php?P=890.
25. http://www.myrobust.com/websites/trcinstitution/File/Reports/Survivors_Speak_English_Web.pdf.
26. http://222.myrobust.com/websites/trcinstitution/File/Reports/Executive_S ummary_English_Web.pdf.

27. http://www.myrobust.com/websites/trcinstitution/File/Reports/Principles_EnglishWeb.pdf.
28. http://www.robust.com/websites/trcinstitution/File/Reports/Volume_1_History_Part_1_English_Web.pdf.
29. http://www.robust.com/websites/trcinstitution/File/Reports/Volume_1_History_Part_2_English_Web.pdf.
30. http://www.myrobust.com/websites/trcinstitution/File/Reports/Volume_2_Inuit_and_Northern_English_Web.pdf.
31. http://www.myrobust.com/websites/trcinstitution/File/Reports/Volume_3_Metis_English_Web.pdf.
32. http://www.myrobust.com/websites/trcinstitution/File/Reports/Volume_4_Missing_Children_English_Web.pdf.
33. http://www.myrobust.com/websites/trcinstitution/File/Reports/Volume_5_Legacy_English_Web.pdf.
34. http://www.trc.ca/websites/trcinstitution/File/2015/Honouring_the_Truth_Reconciling_for_the_Future_July_23_2015.pdf.
35. http://www.trc.ca/websites/trcinstitution/File/2015/Findings/Principles%20of%20Truth%20and%20Reconciliation.pdf.
36. http://www.trc.ca/websites/trcinstitution/File/2015/Findings/Survivors_Speak_2015_05_30_web_o.pdf.
37. http://www.trc.ca/websites/trcinstitution/File/2015/Findings/Calls_to_Action_English2.pdf.
38. http://www.dailykos.com/story/2013/4/14/1200994/-Native-schools-and-stolen-generations-U-S-and-Canada.
39. http://oil sandstruth.org/tar-sands-101.
40. http://oil sandstruth.org/.
41. https://ourworld.unu.edu/en/canadas-oil-sands.
42. https://en.wikipedia.org/wiki/Truth_and_Reconciliation_Commission_(Canada) and its References:

42.1 Residential School Settlement.
42.2 "Honouring the Truth, Reconciling for the Future - Summary of the Final Report of the Truth and Reconciliation Commission of Canada" (PDF). The Truth and Reconciliation Commission of Canada. May 31, 2015. Retrieved February 19, 2017.
42.3 Connie Walker (December 10, 2015). "Connie Walker and the firsthand legacy of residential schools". CBC Radio. Retrieved July 30, 2016. It's taken years to voice and acknowledge the damage caused by residential schools through the Truth and Reconciliation Commission.
42.4 Mark Kennedy, "At least 4,000 Aboriginal children died in residential schools, commission finds", Ottawa Citizen, Canada.com, January 3, 2014, accessed October 18, 2015.
42.5 "Indian, church leaders launch multi-city tour to highlight commission". CBC. March 2, 2008. Retrieved, June 11, 2011.
42.6 "Statement of apology to former students of Indian Residential Schools". Aboriginal Affairs and Northern Development Canada. Ottawa, Ontario, Canada: Government of Canada. June 11, 2008.

Retrieved June 17, 2015.

**42.7** "Truth and Reconciliation Commission", Oxford English Dictionary. Retrieved October 26, 2016.

**42.8** "Reconciliation", Oxford English Dictionary. Retrieved October 26, 2016.

**42.9** Garneau, David (2012). "Imaginary Spaces of Conciliation and Reconciliation" (PDF). West Coast Line, 46 (2), Retrieved February 19, 2017.

**42.10** "What We Have Learned: Principles of Truth and Reconciliation" (PDF). What We Have Learned: Principles of Truth and Reconciliation The Truth and Reconciliation Commission of Canada. 2015. Retrieved February 18, 2017.

**42.11** Amagoalik, John (2012). "Reconciliation or Conciliation? An Inuit Perspective" InDegagné, Mike- Dewar, Jonathan- Lowry, Glen. "Speaking my truth": reflections on reconciliation & residential school (PDF) (Scholastic Edition/First Printing. Ed.). Aboriginal Healing Foundation, ISBN 9780988127425. Retrieved February 19, 2017.

**42.12** Rice, Brian; Snyder, Anna (2012). "Reconciliation in the Context of a Settler Society: Healing the Legacy of Colonialism in Canada". InDegagné, Mike; Dewar, Jonathan; Lowry, Glen. "Speaking my truth": reflections on reconciliation & residential school (PDF) (Scholastic Edition/First Printing. Ed.). Aboriginal Healing Foundation, ISBN 9780988127425. Retrieved February 18, 2017.

**42.13** Durham, Jimmie, and Jean Fisher. "The Ground Has Been Covered." art forum (Summer, 1988): Print (p. 3).

**42.14** Yuxweluptun, Lawrence Paul, Tania Willard, and Karen Duffek. Lawrence Paul Yuxweluptun: Unceded Territories. Vancouver: Figure I, 2016. Print. (p.7).

**42.15** Tuck, Eve; Yang, K. Wayne (September 8, 2012). "Decolonization is not a metaphor". Decolonization: Indigeneity, Education & Society. 1 (1), ISSN 1929-8692.

**42.16** Judge at head of residential school investigation resigns, CBC, October 18, 2008, Archived from the original on November 3, 2012, retrieved October 20, 2008.

**42.17** New commissioners for native reconciliation, CBC, June 10, 2009, retrieved June 16, 2009.

**42.18** Coulthard, Glen Sean (2014). Red skin, white masks: rejecting the colonial politics of recognition. University of Minnesota Press, ISBN 9780816679652.

**42.19** Querengesser, Tim (December 2013). "Glen Coulthard & the Three Rs", Northern Public Affairs, 2 (2): 59–61, Retrieved February 19, 2017.

**42.20** Rubenstein, Hymie; Rodney, Clifton (June 22, 2015). "Truth and Reconciliation report tells a 'skewed and partial story' of residential schools". National Post, Post Media, Retrieved June 29, 2015.

**42.21** Kennedy, Mark (January 3, 2014). "At least 4,000 Aboriginal children died in residential schools, commission finds". Canada.com. Retrieved January 9, 2014.

**42.22** "Huge number of records to land on Truth and Reconciliation Commission's doorstep," CBC. April 23, 2014.

**42.23** Black, Conrad (June 6, 2015). "Canada's treatment of aboriginals was shameful, but it was not genocide". National Post. Post Media. Retrieved June 29, 2015.

**42.24** Black, Conrad (June 6, 2015). "Canada's treatment of aboriginals was shameful, but it was not genocide". National Post. Post Media. Retrieved June 29, 2015.

**42.25** Rubenstein, Hymie; Rodney, Clifton (June 4, 2015). "Debunking the half-truths and exaggerations in the Truth and Reconciliation report". National Post. Post Media. Retrieved June 29, 2015.

**42.26** Laenui, Pōkā. "Federalism and the Rights of Indigenous People: A Hawaiian Perspective." (2007): n. Page. Web. <https://www.scribd.com/document/144346438/Federalism-and-the-Rights-of-Indigenous-P-1>. (p. 5).

**42.27** Schwartz, Daniel (June 2, 2015). "Truth and Reconciliation Commission: By the numbers". CBC. CBC. Retrieved March 28, 2017.

**42.28** Truth and Reconciliation Commission of Canada: Calls to Action (PDF) (Report). Truth and Reconciliation Commission of Canada, 2012. Retrieved June 14, 2015.

**42.29** TRC, NRA, INAC – Resolution Sector – IRS Historical Files Collection – Ottawa, file 6-21-1, volume 2 (Ctrl #27-6), H. M. Jones to Deputy Minister, December 13, 1956. [NCA-001989-0001].

**42.30** Canada, Statistics Canada, Aboriginal People in Canada, 19.

**42.31** United Nations, Convention on the Rights of the Child, Concluding observations, 12–13.

**42.32** Moseley and Nicolas, Atlas of the World's Languages, 117.

**42.33** https://en.wikipedia.org/wiki/Everett_mckinley_Dirksen_United_States_Courthouse.

43. http://oilsandstruth.org/contact.

44. https://archive.org/details/TheGreyNunsInTheFarNorth.

45. http://www.care2.com/causes/why-we-need-to-stop-illinois-from-turning-into-a-pigsty.html.

46. http://www.huffingtonpost.ca/2012/03/27/alberta-oil-sands-royalties-ceri_n_1382640.html.

47. https://www.youtube.com/watch?v=3M-tio1l2Hc (Shaking Tent).

48. https://www.pinterest.se/pin/66146688250617049/ (Residential school).

49. https://en.wikipedia.org/wiki/Treaty_6.

50. https://www.aadnc-aandc.gc.ca/eng/1100100028706/1100100028708.

51. http://www.thecanadianencyclopedia.ca/en/article/treaty-8/.

52. buffett.northwestern.edu/documents/working-papers/Energy_10-005_Urquhart.pdf.

53. https://www.ncbi.nlm.nih.gov/pmc/articles/PMC2679626/.

54.https://books.google.com/books?id=pAbHrpAj3CcC&pg=PA185&lpg=PA185&dq=bile+duct+cancer+example+of+high+levels+of+arsenic&source=bl&ots=RFSpDuPinm&sig=fA-KoQ9shcdsEdzIxZIXOVd-lsg&hl=en&sa=X&ved=0ahUKEwiV6KS9rqXVAhWM8CYKHa9iA9oQ6A

EIQDAD#v=onepage&q=bile%20duct%20cancer%20example%20of%20high%20levels%20of%20arsenic&f=false (Cancer Epidemiology: Principles and Methods: World Health Organization).

**55.** http://www.cancer.net/cancer-types/bile-duct-cancer/view-all.

**56.** http://healthcare.utah.edu/huntsmancancerinstitute/cancer-information/cancer-types-and-topics/bile-duct-cancer.php.

**57.** https://www.youtube.com/watch?v=tvvSyVOVJw0 (sound of a Snowy Owl).

**58.** https://en.wikipedia.org/wiki/Snowy_owl.

**59.** http://www.greenpeace.org/canada/Global/canada/.../Boreal Forest_FS_Footnote_rev_4.pdf

**60.** http://www.residentialschoolsettlement.ca/settlement.html

# REFERENCES

**1.** Fictional characters and illustrations, 1a through 1k (main characters and illustrations) used in the book created by Anne Michael.
**2.** Fictional use of the dilapidated interior of the Birtle Indian Residential Home in Manitoba Canada as an image to fictionally depict the interior of Holy Angels Indian Residential Home is Fort Chipewyan, Alberta Canada. Photographer unknown. (https://www.pinterest.com/pin/341992165436075529/).
**3.** Fictional use of ice road incident depicting melting ice and truck event in story. (http://www.google.com/search?Q=truck+sinks+in+the+ice+rod+of+alberta+canada&rlz=1C1LENP_enus561us567&espv=2&biw=1003&bih=418&tbm=isch&tbo=u&source=univ&sa=X&ved=0ahukewjgxqgsrndoahwtdsykhsw2c30qsaqija&dpr=1.25#imgdii=gkoho5bowanp5m%3A%3bgkoho5bowanp5m%3A%3By3SBDfcZTivySM%3A&imgrc=gkoho5bowanp5m%3A).
**4.** Fictional use of a winter image of Fort Chipewyan in Alberta Canada depicting cold remote region with vast flat terrain beside Lake Athabasca. Photographer Bill Frymire. (http://www.billfrymire.com/blog/spirit-eagle-completed/).
**5.** https://thumbs.dreamstime.com/z/drumheller-hoodoos-trail-alberta-49093017.jpg. (https://www.flickr.com/photos/jeffreysullivan/24665836215/in/photostream/).
**6.** Coyote in the Grasslands- artwork by author, artist, Anne Michael.
**7.** Coyote and Great-grandfather Obigon in story, artwork and imagery by author, artist, Anne Michael.
**8.** Fictional use depicting a road in Fort Chipewyan. Photo by Frank Kuin. (http://frankkuin.com/en/2014/06/19/fight-over-alberta-oil-sands-development/)
**9.** Fictional use of photo depicting Obigon's house in story fashioned after the photo The Old Hunt House- Calgary (Glenbow Museum photo archives). (http://www.cbc.ca/news/canada/calgary/hunt-house-oldest-history-calgary-1.3393826).
**10.** Fictional character, Princess Natawee, fashioned after story of princess and fur trader. (http://montanawomenshistory.org/brokers-of-the-frontier-indigenous-women-and-the-fur-trade/Brokers of the Frontier: Indigenous Women and the Fur Trade).
**11.** Maps created by Anne Michael.
**12.** Saddledome in Calgary. https://www.google.com/search?q=calgary+saddledome&sa=X&rlz=1C1LENP_enUS561US567&espv=2&biw=1053&bih=736&tbm=isch&tbo=u&source=univ&ved=0ahUKEwjpibPEz4LPAhUBRSYKHceyBD4QsAQIMA&dpr=0.9#imgrc=RQ4M0zQf1DGo8M%3A.
**13.** Port Washington, Wisconsin, circa 1979, photos by Anne Michael.
**14.** Genealogy charts fictional, artwork by author, artist, Anne Michael.
**15.** Images in the Appendix with the notation of "TRC" are copyright free and referenced in the Bibliography.
**16.** Oil Sands of Alberta photos referenced with website image and credit within the book. Photos by Jeff Macintosh and Robert Johnson.

## AFTERWARD
## July 4th, 2017

There is no kinder act than to help the poor, hungry and homeless. This we do as Christians, civilized worlds, independent free nations for the sake of charity, humanity and love for thy neighbor.

Two children's home organizations, in particular, have enlightened me over the last twenty years as to their purpose, their successes and their ongoing drive to help children and families at risk be productive in their world:

One such organization is Thompson's Children's Home. It used to be called Thompson's Orphanage and is run by the Episcopal Diocese. I have met some very happy students living there under the care of concerned, supportive, cottage mothers and likewise have worked with devoted administrators and have walked their inviting campus on Saint Peter's Lane in Charlotte, NC.

Recognizing another school with which I have had the honor to be associated is the Crossnore's Schools Home for Children on DAR Drive in Crossnore, NC which was started in 1909 by the Sloops couple. It was an honor to support the efforts of the wonderful folks at this home over the years through an organization, the North Carolina Daughters of the American Revolution who have given their time and donations to that worthy cause.

Former students of these homes scattered across North Carolina have shared how grateful and happy they were to have been offered a place to live, be educated, given food and be loved in a family environment.

In my Sunday school class, the week of July 4th, 2017, one of my classmates, Tim, shared a personal story growing up in such a home in South Carolina. He described his experience as being shown kindness, supportive of education, served substantive food and enjoying the four hundred acres of the school grounds and always meeting an encouraging staff who knew how to discipline sternly but in a kind manner.

Tim shared stories of love shown to children at the Baptist Connie Maxwell Children's Home in Greenwood, SC started in 1872 with several locations across South Carolina.

For the most part, the children who attend these schools have come from broken homes or from poor families who could not care for them financially. They found acceptance and love in those homes. Many stayed in the home for normally eight years. The age of children accepted to these schools ranged from three to about twelve.

There is a world of difference in being accepted and loved in these type homes and in the Canadian Residential Indian homes where over the past 150 years, the children *"Indians"* (as the indigenous peoples were called back then and through much of the 1900s) were taken, forced to attend the schools, stripped of their culture, beaten or killed, their names changed, shipped thousands of miles from their family to other schools across Canada. The purpose was to assimilate them into the Euro-Canadian culture. The children were forbidden to make family contact and then turned out into the world after a mandatory residence to fend for themselves. Many today think the Indigenous children, who were forced to leave the school at a certain age because they had maxed out of the schools, became the unfortunate forerunners of what we know today as the human trafficking problem of Canada and ultimately the human trafficking problem in North America and internationally.

This problem did not solely derive from Canada. The Indigenous peoples in the United States, in the Northwestern and Midwestern states also experienced the type assimilation. Many children attending those schools were also abused and upon leaving those homes at graduation were also caught up in this travesty.

The main difference between the Residential Indian Schools and most other children's homes is that for 150 years these homes in Canada (and elsewhere) have operated under a distinct determination to *kill the Indian* in the child. And if they could not, other more definite measures were taken. Today, 6500 witnesses have come forth to tell their story and the story of those they loved and some of their classmates buried in mass graves.

For all those children, young and old who have never been told they are loved? You are loved!

We cannot forget the equivalent manifestation of taking the children and destroying their culture with taking their lands and destroying their environment.

Where does it stop? Harmful toxins are still polluting the waters (allegedly causing terminal cancers in humans, killing living things and ruining the environment). This water runs downstream of the Alberta Oil Sands Project byway of the Tricontinental Divide through Canada, into the Great Lakes, into the Mississippi, into the Gulf of Mexico; then across Canada to the Pacific Ocean on one side, the Atlantic Ocean on the other and north into the Arctic Ocean.

Pollution into those waters flows downstream in three ways to five major oceans of the Earth and through several major inland waterways across many sacred burial grounds!

There is a tipping point to this continued abuse. We have reached it. The First Nations generations carry the burden of the forced assimilation. The people of the world carry the burden of the environmental pollution. Our actions have caused it—millions of deaths are because of our actions.

A beautiful song was written in the mid-1800s and still beloved today. It sums up this novel—giving thanks for all things:

For the Beauty of the Earth
TEXT: Folliott S. Pierpoint, 1835–1917
MUSIC: Conrad Kocher, 1786–1872

1.  For the beauty of the earth,
For the beauty of the skies,
For the love which from our birth
Over and around us lies,
Lord of all, to thee we raise
This our hymn of grateful praise.

2.  For the beauty of each hour
Of the day and of the night,
Hill and vale, and tree and flow'r,
Sun and moon, and stars of light,
Lord of all, to thee we raise
This our hymn of grateful praise.

3.  For the joy of human love,
Brother, sister, parent, child,
Friends on Earth, and friends above,
For all gentle thoughts and mild,
Lord of all, to thee we raise,
This our hymn of grateful praise.

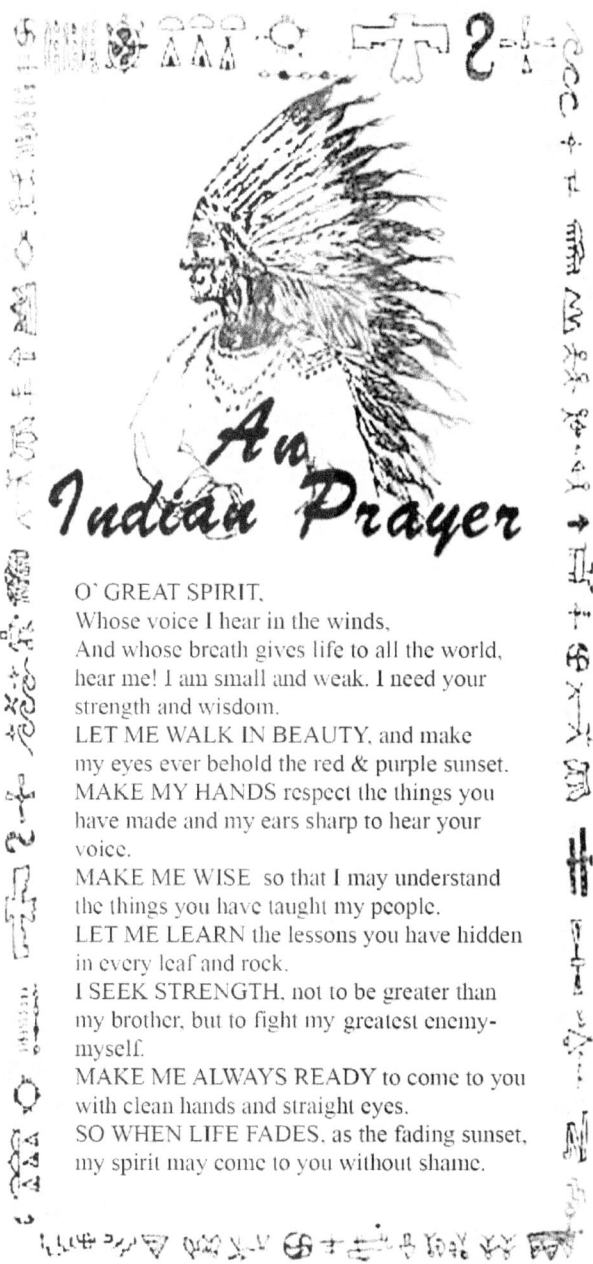

**An Indian Prayer**

O' GREAT SPIRIT,
Whose voice I hear in the winds,
And whose breath gives life to all the world,
hear me! I am small and weak. I need your
strength and wisdom.
LET ME WALK IN BEAUTY, and make
my eyes ever behold the red & purple sunset.
MAKE MY HANDS respect the things you
have made and my ears sharp to hear your
voice.
MAKE ME WISE so that I may understand
the things you have taught my people.
LET ME LEARN the lessons you have hidden
in every leaf and rock.
I SEEK STRENGTH, not to be greater than
my brother, but to fight my greatest enemy-
myself.
MAKE ME ALWAYS READY to come to you
with clean hands and straight eyes.
SO WHEN LIFE FADES, as the fading sunset,
my spirit may come to you without shame.

Author unknown

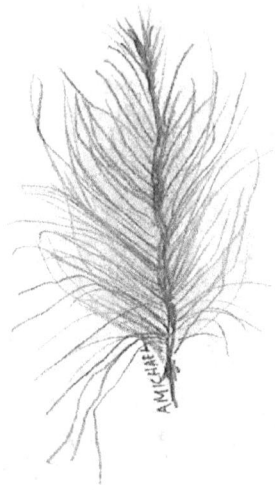

"May the road rise up to meet you.
May the wind be always at your back.
May the sun shine warm upon your face;
The rains fall soft upon your fields
And until we meet again,
May God hold you
In the palm of His hand."

*An old Irish blessing*

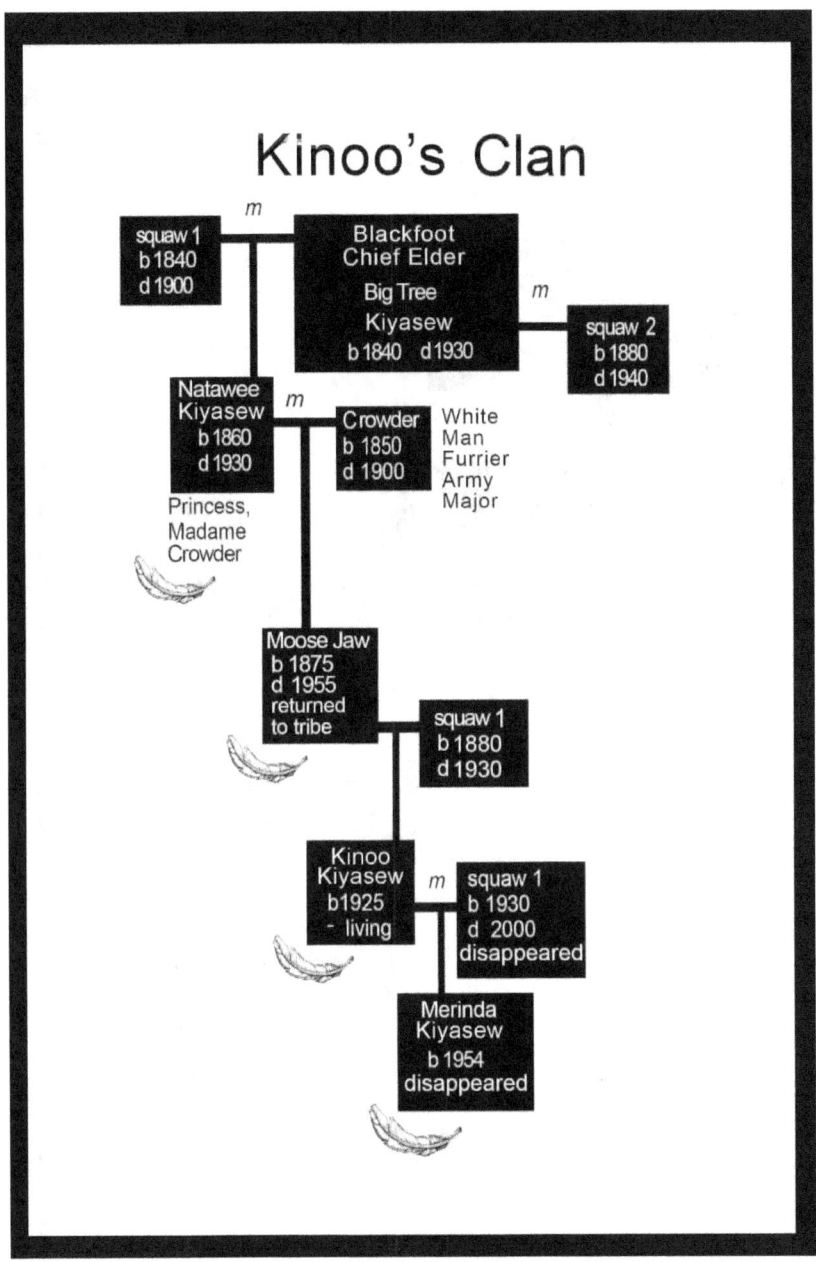

# Kinoo's Clan

Fictitious Genealogy of Kinoo Kiyasew
From the Blackfoot Chief Elder Clan of Big Tree Kiyasew
Created by Anne Michael

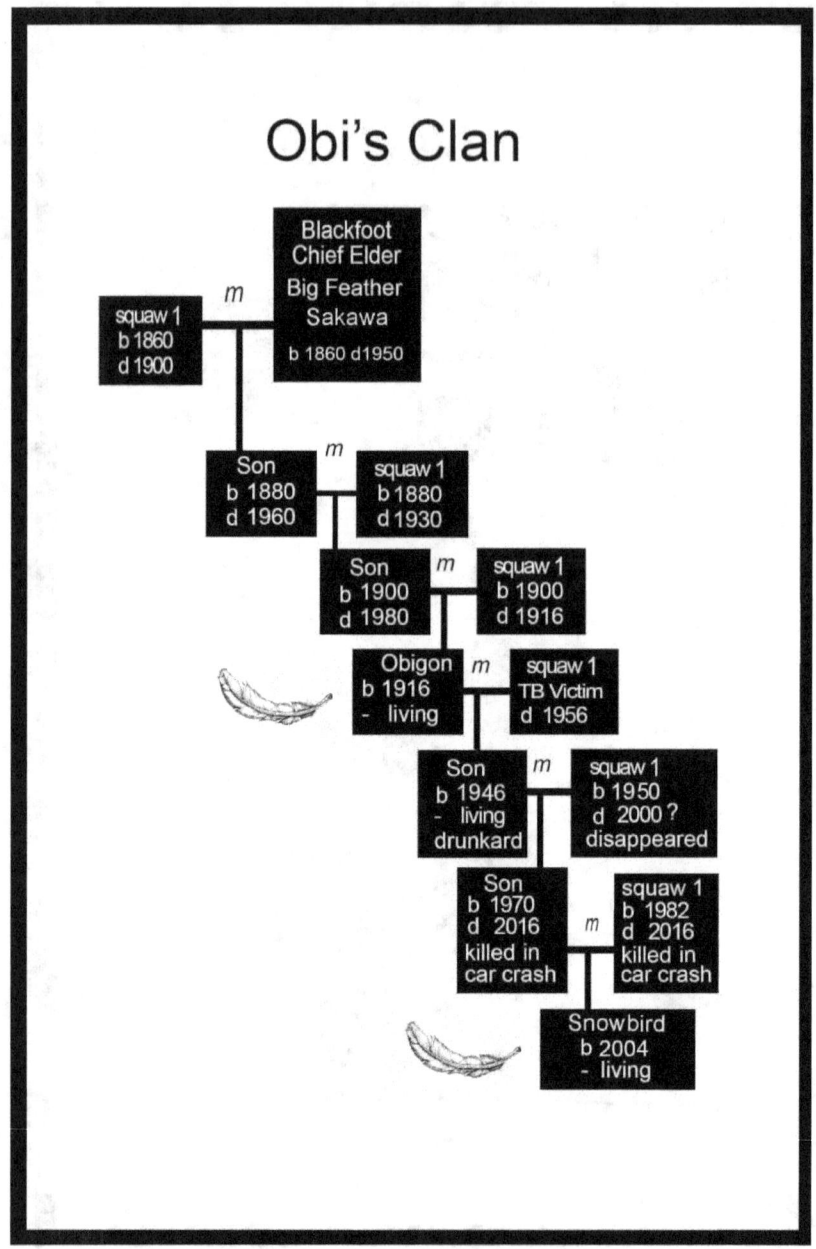

# Obi's Clan

**Blackfoot Chief Elder Big Feather Sakawa** b 1860 d1950

*m*

**squaw 1** b 1860 d 1900

**Son** b 1880 d 1960

*m*

**squaw 1** b 1880 d 1930

**Son** b 1900 d 1980

*m*

**squaw 1** b 1900 d 1916

**Obigon** b 1916 - living

*m*

**squaw 1** TB Victim d 1956

**Son** b 1946 - living drunkard

*m*

**squaw 1** b 1950 d 2000 ? disappeared

**Son** b 1970 d 2016 killed in car crash

*m*

**squaw 1** b 1982 d 2016 killed in car crash

**Snowbird** b 2004 - living

Fictitious Genealogy of Obigon Sakawa
From the Blackfoot Chief Elder Clan of Big Feather Sakawa
Created by Anne Michael

Many thanks to friends, family and pertinent individuals focused on similar concerns that shared their insight in the development of this book: to Beth Michael, for your thoughts, your editing skills and your encouragement, to my son who has challenged me with his thoughts and goals about life, education and the world, to the Lincolnton Writers Club: Kay, Allyson, Kelly and Carol. To Faye and Henry Fogle—neighbors for all their patience and late night discussions, to the New Horizons Group at the Denver United Methodist Church who constantly seek ways to improve our community's health and well-being of its residents, to Tim—who experienced most of his childhood growing up in the Connie Maxwell residential schools, to the Westport Community Association and its residents for staunch support in the environmental issues, to Jim Klein, the Cove Keepers and the Lincoln County Board of Commissioners for their constant support during various service years between 2001-2014, to the National Coalition Against Domestic Violence and to Karen Parker Thompson— Safe Alliance of Charlotte who continues to be drawn into my life sharing concerns for women and children issues, to all teachers especially Sue Johnson Little—my sixth grade teacher, who tries to make a difference in the world one child at a time for about fifty years, to the Rotary Club of Denver for their time and effort directed toward community and world health reform, to my mother and father, Bonnie and George Michael who have supported the need for solid education, exemplified parental role modeling and instilled in each of their children a belief system of fairness and doing for the common good harkening to Alexander the Great who said, *"Remember upon the conduct of each, depends the fate of all."*

# The Author

Anne Michael is a native of Charlotte NC—retired since 2000 to the Lake Norman area of NC. She has been an active advocate for the protection of women-and-children-at-risk lobbying in Washington DC for VAWA (Violence Against Women Act), working with Safe Alliance of Charlotte NC, battered women's shelters, the National Coalition Against Domestic Violence NC and USA, interviewed with Michael Bolton—the Emmy-award singer and her personal experience highlighted in a special documentary program aired August, 2003 on Lifetime Television and captured in a memoir, *Me Too-The Cover Up*. She continues to write and speak on issues involving culture and environment.

She has been an advocate for environmental protection working with county officials fighting for the health and safety of the water—especially active in three circumstances over a span of ten years when erosion concerns threatened her community's greatest asset: Lake Norman. Anne pitched in spearheading the concerns of 800 Westport Community residents. This group's constant pressure on the county resulted in the implementation of a County Sediment and Erosion Control Ordinance.

In Anne's historical novel, based on true events, the heroine mirrors the Erin Brockovich/Sherlock Holmes-type efforts to search out the truth. Through an emotional heartache, a budding love story and family loyalty, the emotional grit and tenacity of her characters succeed in winning victory for the victims at hand but there remains an ongoing concern for mankind regarding culture and environment.

To Brandon and Emily,
Your life is just beginning!

www.ingramcontent.com/pod-product-compliance
Lightning Source LLC
Chambersburg PA
CBHW071632260626
47170CB00001B/73